The Betrayal

The Betrayal

Marina Martindale

Good Oak Press, LLC

Good Oak Press, LLC
P.O. Box 51244
Denton, TX 76206-1244
www.goodoakpress.com

Editor: Cynthia Roedig
Proofreader: Gloria Gray
Cover Design: Good Oak Press, LLC
Cover Illustration: Wes Lowe
Typesetting: Good Oak Press, LLC

Printed in the United States of America

This book is a work of fiction. The characters, corporations, and small businesses depicted in this story are fictitious. Any and all real locations have been used fictitiously and without any intent to describe any real individuals who may be affiliated with those locations. Any resemblance to any actual persons, living or dead, is purely coincidental.

Acknowledgements

Special thanks to the team who helped me create *The Betrayal*. To my good friend and beta reader, Geneva Jarrett. Many thanks also to Rob Resetar, John Einweck and Roscoe Freund for sharing your experiences as professional musicians. Thanks again to my friend and editor, Cynthia Roedig, for another outstanding job. Once again, some of your comments had me rolling on the floor. And finally, a big thank you to Wes Lowe for another outstanding cover illustration. Once again, it was a pleasure working with you.

To Kristen

❧ONE❧

EMILY ST. CLAIRE reached for another tissue to dab the sweat off her forehead and grab her water bottle, but the once-cold liquid had turned lukewarm. She took a few swallows and glanced at the clock on the waiting room wall. It was only eleven-fifteen. The air conditioning had stopped working at nine forty-five. Ninety minutes of down time and the office was sweltering. She heard Dr. Lerner's voice coming from the hallway. He was performing a root canal and having to apologize to his patient for the added discomfort of the heat.

The front door opened as she gulped down the last of her water. Andrea, who worked a few doors down, stepped inside and walked up to the counter in front of Emily's desk. Her makeup was beaded and creased, and wisps of her red hair had stuck to the sweat on the side of her face. "It feels even hotter in here than it does in our office," she said.

"Must be one of Murphy's Laws," said Emily. "The air conditioning will always conk out on the hottest day of the summer."

"Any word on when they'll get it fixed?"

Emily shrugged her shoulders. "Your guess is as good as mine. I tried calling the property manager again about twenty minutes ago, but I'm still getting a busy signal. I'm sure by now they're aware of the problem."

"Yeah, I kept getting busy signals too, which means they must really know. Meantime Dr. Hapner had me reschedule all our afternoon patients. Turns out two of them are really sick, so they're on their way right now. Then, once we're done, we're closing up shop and calling it a day. I love the idea of having an afternoon off, but why does it have to be on a day when it's over a hundred and ten degrees outside?"

"It's the price we pay for living in Phoenix. At least we don't get snowed in during the winter."

"Yeah, but a good, old-fashioned ice storm would sure feel nice right about now, and I'll bet you're glad now that you got your new haircut."

Emily ran her fingers through her short, blonde hair. It felt strange to no longer have her long locks. "It's lower maintenance all right, but Jesse wasn't too thrilled with it."

"That figures. So have you told him yet?"

"No, not yet."

"Well, keep me posted. I'm anxious to hear how he reacts. Meantime, I have to get back to work. I just wanted to stick my head in the door to see how you're doing. Hopefully, we'll all be back to normal by tomorrow morning."

"I'm sure we will be."

"Are we still on for lunch Friday?"

"You bet. See you, Andrea."

Andrea took her leave while Emily called the property manager once again. This time her call went through. After punching a few buttons, she got a live person on the line. A repairman was on the way, but the air conditioning would not be back online until much later in the day. She heard footsteps as she hung up. Dr. Lerner had finished with his patient. His normally crisp, white shirt was wrinkled and soaked with sweat.

"Any word on the air conditioning?" he asked.

"I'm afraid it won't be back on until the end of the day. Meantime your eleven-thirty has already rescheduled for next Tuesday. Your next patient is due right after lunch."

Dr. Lerner frowned. "And if it's this hot now, it'll be unbearable by this afternoon. Go ahead and take care of Mrs. Baxter. After that, I want you to call everyone who was supposed to come in this afternoon and have them reschedule. We're taking the rest of the day off. Hopefully, we'll all be back to normal by tomorrow morning."

"I'm sure we will be. Thanks, doctor."

He nodded and walked away. Fifteen minutes later Emily stepped out into the blazing midday sun and smiled to herself as she walked across the parking lot. She wanted to stop at the grocery store on the way home so she could prepare a surprise dinner for Jesse. Hopping into her car, she fired up the engine, and turned the air conditioning on high. After a few hot moments, the air began to feel deliciously cool. Another smile broke out across her face as she drove off. Tonight's dinner would be the perfect opportunity for her to tell Jesse the time had come for him to keep his end of their bargain.

She soon turned into the grocery store entrance and hunted for a parking space. Once inside the store, she grabbed a cart headed down the aisles. Tonight, she would prepare Jesse's favorite dish; her famous chicken divan. She picked out her ingredients and tossed in a bouquet of fresh flowers before heading to the checkout lane.

Ten minutes later she pulled into her driveway and frowned. Annette's white Honda Civic was parked in front of the house. Jesse's assistant usually didn't come on Wednesdays, so something unexpected must have come up. Emily sighed as she pressed the button to open the garage door. Shutting down the engine, she quickly grabbed the grocery bags and hurried out of the hot garage. The air conditioning felt heavenly as she stepped inside the house and went straight to the kitchen.

"Hi guys. I'm home."

There was no response. The house seemed unusually quiet. Emily set the bags on the counter and went down the hallway. Jesse had converted one of the downstairs bedrooms into his office. She tapped on the door and smiled as she slowly pushed it open.

"Hey guys. The air conditioning went out and I'm—"

Her smile suddenly faded. The room was empty. The lights were out, and Jesse's computer was shutdown. She was getting a funny feeling, but quickly brushed it off. Perhaps Jesse and Annette were out by the pool. She went to the living room and opened the sliding glass door.

"Jesse! Annette!"

Again, there was no answer. The backyard was eerily quiet and there was no one by the pool. Emily closed the door and headed toward the staircase. The upper floor contained the master suite and a rarely used guest bedroom. Jesse would be leaving for Houston on Friday to facilitate a seminar. Perhaps he and Annette had gone upstairs to decide what he should pack. Emily took a deep breath and started up the stairs. Upon reaching landing, she heard muffled voices behind the bedroom door. Jesse must have had the TV on. She hurried up the remaining flight and stepped inside.

❧TWO❧

THE BEDROOM LIGHTS were out and the blinds had been pulled. Emily gazed into the dimly lit room, for the moment unable to comprehend the scene she saw before her. A naked Jesse was kneeling on top of their unmade bed; his back turned toward the door. His head was bent down, out of Emily's view. A pair of feminine legs straddled his shoulders. She heard a woman crying out in ecstasy. As it reached a crescendo, Emily heard her own high-pitched scream.

Jesse's head instantly shot up and the legs on either side of him began kicking. The startled woman sat up and leaned toward her side, her head peering around Jesse's body.

"What the hell is going on in here?" shouted Emily.

Annette's expression went from shock to anger as she brushed a strand of frazzled hair away from her face. "Get out of here!"

"Like hell! This is my house, bitch! You get out!"

Annette yanked on the sheet, desperately trying to cover herself as Emily marched up to the bed.

"I said get the hell out of my house, bitch!"

Jesse shielded Annette with his body as he grabbed Emily's wrists. "Emily! Stop!"

Emily screamed in his face and he tightened his grip. As she struggled to free herself, Jesse looked at Annette.

"Get dressed and get out. Now!"

Annette scrambled off the bed and quickly gathered up her clothes. She raced to the bathroom, slamming and locking the door behind her as Emily shrieked incoherently. Jesse yanked on her wrists.

"Emily! Calm down."

"Go to hell!" She spat into his face, but Jesse kept his grip.

"Emily, she's leaving. Let her go."

Moments later a hastily dressed Annette flung the bathroom door open and tore out of the room. Her footsteps thumped loudly as she raced down the stairs. The front door slammed an instant later. Jesse held onto Emily's wrists as they heard an engine fire up and the sound of squealing tires. He slowly released her once the car sped away.

Emily's arms fell limply to her side and she stood in a dazed silence. Jesse wiped the spittle off the side of his face with the back of his hand before hopping off the bed and picking up his up briefs.

"So how long has this been going on?" Emily's voice sounded mechanical.

"Not long." Jesse hurried into the bathroom, turning on the water and leaving the door ajar. He returned a moment later, wearing the briefs.

"And how long is not long?"

"A few weeks." Jesse took a seat on the edge of the bed; his eyes focused on the floor. "I know this sounds like a tired old adage, but she's really not that important to me."

"Really?"

He looked up at her. "Emily, I swear, on everything that is holy, that I never intended to hurt you, and I never intended to cheat on you."

"Did you now?"

"For what it's worth, I've been careful. I used condoms, you know, just in case."

"And that's supposed to somehow make me feel better? We're married Jesse, and you've just broken our vows. It's grounds for divorce."

"I know, and there's no excuse for what I've done. It's only happened few times, not that I expect you to take it as an excuse either. Nor will I insult your intelligence by telling you some lame story about her seducing me. It just happened. We're both equally at fault."

"What about Gary?" asked Emily.

"He doesn't know, although I'm sure he'll find out soon enough." He paused for a moment. "Annette's been complaining about the fact that she and Gary have been living together for three years now, but he's still telling her he's not ready for marriage. Maybe it was a revenge sort of thing."

"So that's her excuse. What was your reason?"

"I don't know." Once again, Jesse stared down at the floor. "I guess I had a seven-year itch. Or maybe an eight-year itch. I know it's no excuse, because there is no excuse, but please believe me when I tell you I still love you as much as the day I married you." He paused once again. "I know I've been I've been taking you for granted, and I guess I allowed myself to get bored." He looked into her eyes. "I know how bad this looks, but Emily, please believe me when I tell you I don't want to lose you. I'm willing to see a marriage counselor, or do couples therapy, or whatever it takes to earn your trust again."

"I see. So, what about Annette?"

"I'll fire her. Right now. I promise, I'll never see her again."

Emily started to laugh, but it was a strange, cackling laugh. "She's my cousin, Jesse. You'll still see her at all the family get-togethers, although from here on out I'll have to restrain myself from poisoning her." She cackled again.

"You wanna know something funny? The air conditioning broke down at the office today, so we took the afternoon off. I'd planned on fixing us a nice romantic dinner, because I was going to tell you something. I've decided to go back to school to finish up my degree, so I've applied to ASU. I've even applied for a scholarship."

"I'm glad, Emily. You've sacrificed a lot to help me out. You really have. I owe everything I have to you, and now it's your turn."

"Damn straight." She walked up to the closet and slid the door open, reaching inside to pull a large suitcase down from the top shelf.

"What are you doing?" asked Jesse.

Emily flung the suitcase down on top of the bed, nearly knocking Jesse over. "While I certainly mean no disrespect to our local university, my first choice always has been the University of Southern California, so I've just decided that's where I'll be going." She opened a dresser drawer and started dropping her undergarments into the suitcase.

"Emily, please. You're not thinking clearly right now. Let's go downstairs. I'll pour us a couple of stiff drinks, and we'll sit down and have a long talk."

"I'm fine, Jesse." Her voice sounded oddly calm as she opened another drawer and gathered up her nightgowns. "However, you may want to run down to the kitchen, whenever you get the chance. I stopped at the grocery store on my way home and I left the bags on top of the counter. There's some fresh chicken in one of them and you probably don't want it to spoil."

He watched as she took some of her blouses and t-shirts out of the closet, carefully folding them and placing them into the suitcase, along with a few other garments and a couple pairs of shoes. Once the bag was stuffed, she zipped it shut and yanked it off the bed. It hit the floor with a loud thud. She stepped into the bathroom, returning a moment later with her toothbrush, make-up bag and a hairbrush. She unzipped the front pocket and stuffed everything inside.

"Well, I guess this is all I can take with me, for now. You're still going to Houston on Friday, right?"

"Look, Emily, I—"

"No problem, Jesse. I'll come over on Saturday and pick up the rest of my personal belongings. We'll let our lawyers decide who gets rest."

She raised the telescopic handle and pulled the bag out the door. It made loud thumping sounds as she dragged it down the stairs. To her relief, Jesse didn't follow her. She quickly grabbed her purse and stepped into the garage where she struggled to lift the heavy bag into the trunk. Once inside, she slammed down the lid and slipped behind the wheel. Jesse stared down from the bedroom window as she backed her car out, but Emily refused to acknowledge him. She quickly put the car in gear and drove away.

❧THREE❧

EMILY GLANCED AT the dashboard clock while she waited for traffic light to change. It was nearly one o'clock. In the hour since she left Dr. Lerner's office, her entire world had collapsed around her, and she wasn't sure where to go next. Should she look for a hotel room? Or would she be better off staying with her father? He never been fond of Jesse, but he wasn't one to say I told you so either. The light turned green. Without hesitating, she pointed her car toward her father's house. Ten minutes later she pulled into the driveway.

The house looked quiet. Her father didn't get off work until five o'clock, and Susan worked until seven, assuming today wasn't her day off. With any luck, Emily would have the place to herself for a few hours. She still had the house key her parents had given her when she was a teenager. Hopefully, Susan hadn't changed the locks. She slowly put her key in the lock. It turned. As she stepped into the foyer, Lurch gave her an enthusiastic greeting. Lurch was part sheepdog, part collie, and part something else, although no one knew exactly what, but whatever he lacked in pedigree, he more than made up for in love and affection. He put his big paws on Emily's chest, and she wrapped her arms around him.

"I know, buddy. It's good to see you too."

She gave the dog a pat on the head and stepped into the kitchen. To her relief, Susan was nowhere to be found. She fixed herself a glass of ice water and stepped into the family room. A number of family photos stood on top of the mantle. Emily picked one up and gave it a closer look. It had been taken at the University of Arizona, shortly after the commencement ceremony had ended.

Jesse stood in his cap and gown, his face beaming as he held up his diploma. Emily stood at his side, her face glowing as she showed off her engagement ring.

"I think we can safely throw this one away now."

Emily took the photo from the frame and ripped it in half, taking the pieces back to the kitchen and dropping them into the wastebasket beneath the sink. She refilled her water glass and took it down the hallway to her old room. Her old posters had been taken down years ago and replaced with other artwork, but it still had the furniture she grew up with. A framed photo sat on the nightstand. It had been taken shortly after the family had moved into the house. A fourteen-year-old Emily sat next to her mother on a chaise lounge by the pool. She picked it up and caressed the glass over her mother's face with her finger.

"I miss you, Mom. Every day, and most especially today."

She set the photo down and plopped down on top of the bed. Lurch came up and joined her. She wrapped her arms around him and burst into tears.

* * *

"Emily?"

She slowly opened her eyes. "Hey, Dad." She blinked a few times. "Sorry, I must have dozed off. What time is it anyway?"

"Almost five-thirty." Roger had a concerned look on his face. "Obviously something's not right, so why are you here?"

Emily sighed as she fought back the tears. "The air conditioning went out at Dr. Lerner's office this morning, so we all left early. When I got home, I found Jesse and Annette, upstairs, in our bedroom, having sex."

"What?" The shock resonated in Roger's voice.

"They're having an affair, Dad. Jesse admitted it's been going on for some time now, so I packed a bag and left." She started choking up. "I didn't know what else to do. I hope you and Susan won't mind if I stay here, at least for a few days."

He gave her long, lingering hug. "Emily, you're still my baby girl. Of course, you can stay here."

The tears came once again. Her father held her until calmed down.

"What about Susan? I don't want to crowd in."

"Susan is in Boston. Her sister had to have surgery a few days ago, so she's looking after her."

Emily felt her body relax. Her relationship with her father's girlfriend had always been tense. "I see. Well, hopefully, I can find a more permanent place to stay before she returns."

"Don't worry about it, Emmy." Roger's face turned sad. "I guess there must be something in the air, because lately things haven't been going so well with Susan and me either."

"Oh, no. Please don't tell me this has something to do with me. I know she and I have had our differences, but I never wanted to get between you and her."

"Don't worry. It has nothing to do with you, or your brother for that matter. I know the two of you never had the best relationship, but I appreciate the fact that you at least tried to get along with her. She tried too, but you two were like oil and water. You just didn't mix. I've also come to realize that she and I aren't as compatible as I once thought. She'll always be special to me, but her being away for the past few days has given me a chance to think things through, and I've decided the time has come for us to go our separate ways."

"I see. Have you told her this?"

"We discussed it, and we both finally admitted that neither one of us has been happy for some time now. I think deep down, she's just as relieved as I am. She'll start looking for a new place once she returns, and she'll be staying with her son until then. She won't be coming back here, except to get her things. Maybe while you're here, you can help me pack them up."

"I'd be happy to, Dad."

He gave her hand a squeeze. "So, kiddo, it looks like you and me are in the same boat."

"I guess so, and I'm sorry."

Roger gave her a reassuring look. "I'll be fine, Emmy. There're still plenty of other eligible women out there, so I'm not worried, but regardless of what happens, please know that your mother has been and always will be the love of my life. No other woman will ever take her place."

"I know, but I don't expect you spend the rest of your life alone either."

"Good to know." He patted her hand. "So, what about you? I take it you'll be getting a divorce."

"I don't see any other option. He cheated on me. He broke our wedding vows. How can I ever trust him again?"

"You can't, so you're doing the only thing you can do. You're still young, Emily. You'll find someone else."

"I'm twenty-eight years old, Dad."

He gave her a grin. "Trust me, that's nothing. Your life is just beginning, so you have plenty of time. The next one will be someone much more worthy of you."

"It's okay. You can say it. You never liked Jesse."

"It was never a matter of my liking him or not," said Roger. "I simply didn't think the two of you were a good match. He's a hard worker, I'll give him that, but he's never been supportive of you. You've been blessed with a special gift which very few people have, and you were well on the way to becoming a concert pianist until Jesse came along. It was always your life's dream, but somehow you let Jesse convince you to give it up."

Emily started to say something, but her father cut her off.

"I know. It was only supposed to be a temporary arrangement, and you were supposed to finish your degree once he established himself. But that was eight years ago, Emily, and while he's been busy making a name for himself you've been stuck in a dead-end job. Every time I asked you when you planned on going back to school you said you didn't know, because Jesse kept saying he wasn't ready for you to quit your job. I also offered, many times, to move your piano to your house, but again, Jesse kept saying no. He always said he was going to buy you a new one, but he still hasn't gotten around to it." Roger looked her in the eye. "This isn't about him still needing your income, because he no longer needs it. He's now making more than twice the money you are. The reason he doesn't want you to go back to your music is because he doesn't want you upstaging him."

"I really don't know the reason, but I've finally decided to take matters into my own hands. I've applied to ASU and I've applied for some scholarships as well. I'd planned on making him a special dinner tonight so I could tell him. Instead, I ended up announcing it while I was packing my bag. I also told him that under the circumstances, I've changed my mind. I want to go to USC instead."

Roger's face lit up and he gave Emily a big smile. "Well now, that's the best news I've heard in a long, long time."

"So would it be okay if I borrowed your computer later on this evening? I'd like to get started on my application tonight."

"Of course." Roger's expression turned serious once again. "So, what about Annette?"

"What about her?"

"She's still your cousin."

"A biological accident. As far as I'm concerned, we're no longer related. Now I understand why Mom and Aunt Heather were never that close."

"Speaking of whom, you need to call your grandmother and have a talk with her, the sooner the better. You need to get to her before Heather and Annette do. Otherwise, they'll twist things around and make you out to be the bad guy."

"I know, Dad. I'll call her soon, but could you do me a favor first?"

"What's that?"

She reached into her purse and handed him her keys. "My suitcase is in my trunk, but it's a little too heavy for me to lift out. Would you mind getting it for me?"

"I'd be happy to. Meantime it's getting late. Would you like to go out and grab a bite to eat? Maybe we can celebrate you're going back to school."

"Not tonight, thanks. I'm really not that hungry. We'll take a rain check, if you don't mind. We'll go out and celebrate once I get accepted to USC."

"Sounds like a plan. Susan made a couple of casseroles before she left, so I'll go pop one in the oven." He stopped in the doorway before stepping out. "And Emily, welcome home."

❦FOUR❧

JESSE WASN'T USED to the anger, frustration and utter helplessness he felt as he watched Emily's car drive away. His immediate concern was damage control. He had spent years cultivating his image as the man who helped people take control of their lives. Now his own life had taken an abrupt turn in the wrong direction. Word of his infidelity would be damaging enough. Having his wife's first cousin as his mistress could create a potentially career-ending scandal. He stepped away from the window, grabbed his cell phone, and placed a call to Annette, pacing around the room as he waited for her to pick up. She answered on the third ring.

"Are you all right?"

"Are you freaking kidding me?" Her voice shrilled in his ear. "Hell no, I'm not all right. What the hell was she doing barging in like that?"

"I don't know. I never got the chance to ask, but this is her house. Or at least it was." He took a deep breath. "You and I need to talk, face to face. First thing tomorrow morning."

"Hey, you'd better not be trying to pin the blame on me." The anger resonated in Annette's voice. "It's not like I put a loaded gun to your head."

Jesse immediately sniped back at her. "No, but you could have kept your legs crossed." He stopped and took another deep breath. He had to remain calm. "Sorry, Annette. There's really no sense in either one of us playing the blame game. We're both equally at fault, and I've already told her we're both equally at fault."

"Look, Jesse I—"

"Just go home to Gary, okay? Try to stay calm and act like nothing's wrong. If he says anything, just tell him you're upset because we had an unexpected cancelation and I took it out on you. I'll see you tomorrow morning, my office, nine o'clock."

"What about Emily?"

"She packed a bag and left. I have a hunch she went to her father's house. We'll finish this conversation tomorrow." He disconnected the call and headed off to the shower.

* * *

The doorbell rang at precisely nine o'clock the following morning. A nervous looking Annette waited on the other side. She was wearing his favorite dress. Jesse wondered if it was perhaps out of spite. He led her into the dining room and asked her to take a seat at the table.

"Would you like some coffee?" he asked.

"I'm fine. Thanks."

He noted the stress in her voice as he sat down across from her and placed an envelope on the table. "I think we both know what happens next. I'm going to have to let you go. I really don't have much choice."

"Please don't tell me you're going to try to get her back."

"Yes, as a matter-of-fact, I am," he said, firmly. "In spite of everything, I still love her."

Annette winced at his words. "So, what about me?"

"Don't worry, I'm still looking out for you. Not only am I giving you two weeks' severance pay, I'm also referring you to another job. Under the circumstances, I think I'm being more than fair."

"I wasn't talking about the job. I was talking about us."

He looked her in the eye. "There is no us, Annette, and there never was." Jesse cleared his throat and pushed the envelope across the table toward her. "I'm referring you to a colleague of mine. Her name is Gloria Fontaine. She's a life coach and speaker who mostly works with women's groups. Her expertise is on balancing marriage, family, and career, that sort of thing."

"I see."

"Her assistant is expecting. She's due in a few weeks, and she won't be coming back once the baby's born. So yesterday afternoon, after I got off the phone with you, I called Gloria. I told her you and your cousin were having serious issues over an unrelated family matter, and that it might be best for all concerned if you left. Gloria understood and I gave you a glowing recommendation, so she would like to talk to you. I also found out she'd be paying you more than what I've been paying you. Gloria does a lot of traveling, and she likes to take her assistant with her."

"Which would be a nice, convenient arrangement for a mistress you want to get rid of, wouldn't it, Jesse?"

He bristled. "Fine. Have it your way. I thought I was doing you a favor."

"Sorry." Annette dropped the envelope into her purse. "Okay, you've had your say. Now it's my turn."

"There isn't anything else to say, Annette, other than it's over."

"Not so fast." She gave him a sultry smile. "Yeah, we got caught, but now that it's out in the open, it's really for the best for everyone involved. You need to let Emily go. She wants to be a concert pianist. It's what she's always wanted, but you've held her back for far too long, so let her go follow her dream. Then, once you're divorced, you can marry me."

Jesse rolled his eyes. "Let's be realistic, okay? I've told you, many times, that I don't love you, and we both agreed this would be a fun little diversion and nothing more. Once it was over, it was over. You'd stay with Gary, I'd stay with Emily, and we would never speak of it again. There was never any expectation of a long-term commitment."

"Yeah, but that was then. Admit it, Jesse. You've grown tired of Emily. It's not your fault and it's not her fault. It's not anyone's fault. It's just one of those things that happened, so you came to me because I meet your needs. I'm younger, I'm prettier and I'm sexier, and I'm the one who gets your heart pumping." She locked her eyes onto his as she stood from her chair and slowly unbuttoned her dress.

"Knock it off, Annette."

Annette licked her lips and slowly pulled the dress open, revealing she was wearing nothing underneath. She placed Jesse's hand on her breast and helped him give it a squeeze.

"So, where were we before Emily came in and so rudely interrupted us? Oh wait, I remember." She pulled him up from his chair and led him by the hand to the living room. Tossing her dress aside, she laid down on the rug in front of the fireplace. Jesse shook his head and smiled in spite of himself as he unbuttoned his shirt. Once they had finished, Annette sat up and gave him a knowing look.

"All right, Jesse. I'll go talk to Gloria and you can try talking to Emily, even though it won't do you any good. Just remember, I have no intention of giving you up. In the meantime, I need to use your shower." She gave him a grin as she picked up her dress and ran upstairs.

∽FIVE∾

EMILY HELD HER breath as she unlocked the door to Dr. Lerner's office. To her relief, the air conditioning was working. She booted up her computer and stepped into the break room to brew a fresh pot of coffee, bringing a cup to her desk as Cathy, the hygienist, arrived.

"Morning, Cathy."

"Morning." Cathy looked at Emily more closely. "No offense, but you look like hell. Are you okay?"

"I didn't sleep very well last night."

"Sorry to hear it. So, what happened?"

Emily fought back the tears. "It's Jesse. When I got home yesterday afternoon, I caught him in the act with my cousin. They're having an affair."

"What?"

A tear ran down Emily's cheek. "My husband is having an affair. With my cousin."

"Oh my god. Emily, I'm so sorry." Cathy paused for a moment, unsure of what to say next. "Look, if you want to take the day off it's okay. Dr. Lerner and I will manage."

"I appreciate the offer, but what would I do? Spend the day staring at the four walls and feeling sorry for myself? I'm better off staying busy. Besides, I didn't get the chance to finish filing all the insurance claims that needed to be done yesterday."

"Well, alright, if you're sure, but if you decide you want to leave early, it's okay. Just let Dr. Lerner or me know."

"Thanks, Cathy. I'll be fine."

Their first patient walked into the waiting room. Emily tried to focus on her work, but the ugly scene from the day before kept replaying in her mind. The last morning patient arrived at eleven-forty. Once Cathy took her down the hallway, Emily stepped out. Drs. Hapner and Lawrence's pediatric office was two doors down. Entering the office, she noticed a small boy with his mother in the waiting room. Andrea looked up with her usual smile when Emily approached her desk.

"What's up?" Andrea's smiled faded as she looked at her friend more closely. "Are you okay?"

Emily kept her voice low. "Not really. You want to run out and grab a sandwich as soon as you're done here? I really need to Talk to someone."

"I'm brown-bagging it today. Why don't you run across the street to the minimart and get something? We can either talk here, or I can come over to your office."

"I prefer my office. We'll have more privacy."

Andrea tilted her head toward the young boy and his mother. "No problem. I'll be there as soon as we're done here."

Thirty minutes later Emily led Andrea into the empty break room. Dr. Lerner was eating out, as usual, while Cathy was busy running errands. Emily popped a small carton of soup into the microwave and poured herself a cup of coffee, offering some to Andrea.

"No thanks. I brought a soda." Andrea unzipped her lunch bag as Emily took her soup from the microwave and sat down. "So, tell me what happened."

"We closed up shop early yesterday, just like you did, but when I got home, Annette was there."

"She's Jesse's assistant, right?"

"She is, but she only works part-time, and she's never there on Wednesdays. I went inside the house, but they weren't in Jesse's office." Emily stopped and took a deep breath. "They were upstairs, in our bedroom, and I caught 'em in the act."

"The act?" An astonished look came over Andrea's face. "Holy crap! Emily, I don't know what to say, other than I'm totally shocked. Jesse St. Claire, of all people, cheating on his wife? It's the last thing I would have ever expected, and what's Annette's problem? She's your cousin for crying out loud."

"I'm afraid it's a family feud that's been passed down to the next generation."

"What do you mean?"

"My mother and Annette's mother were sisters, but they were never close. I blame my grandmother for that. My mother was the older sister and she had a very good soul. Aunt Heather, on the other hand, was more rambunctious, and apparently my grandmother held my mother over my aunt's head as the perfect daughter, or so the family stories go. Of course, my aunt resented being treated like a second-class citizen, and who can blame her? Problem was, she took it out of my mother, when my mother had nothing to do with it. It was all Grandma's doing."

"I see."

"Then, to make matters worse, Aunt Heather's husband, Carlo, turned out to be a womanizer who only married her for her money. Not only did he cheat on her, he left her, and their two daughters, once my aunt's trust fund was depleted. In the meantime, my father was a faithful husband and a good provider, so Aunt Heather's resentment of my mother grew even more. Fast-forward a few years. Jesse and I are married. His speaking career starts taking off, and he needs an assistant."

"So why didn't he give you the job?" asked Andrea.

"He still needed me to pay the mortgage and keep the lights on, or so he said. Then one day Grandma calls. She says Annette is trying to work her way through college and she insists that Jesse hire her as his assistant, so he agrees. For a time there I'd really hoped she and I would have a better relationship than what our mothers had, but she's turned out to be a lost cause. Aunt Heather may have been jealous of my mother, but she knew where the boundaries were, and she knew not to cross them. Annette, on the other hand, is a schemer, just like her father was."

Andrea shook her head in disbelief. "I'm so sorry, Emily. I knew you weren't particularly close to your aunt, but you've never told me much about her, until now, and I had no idea your cousin was that kind of person. So, what do you plan on doing?"

"I'm afraid I'll have to divorce Jesse." Emily chocked back the tears. "I don't think I really have much of a choice."

"I'm so sorry, Emily. I don't know what else to say."

"I'm afraid there isn't much you can say. Jesse cheated on me and he betrayed me. There's nothing anyone can do."

"At least you have your music."

"I haven't touched a piano for over a year. My baby grand is still at my dad's house, so I finally bought an electric keyboard and I tried to turn one of the downstairs bedrooms into a music room, but it was next to Jesse's office. Whenever I played, he complained about it being a distraction. The only time I was able to play was when he was on the road."

Andrea thought it over. "You know, Emily, maybe this happened for a reason. Jesse was holding you back."

"Yeah, my dad thinks so too, but it still hurts, you know. In spite of everything, I still love Jesse. I married him for life."

"I know you did, and I know it hurts. I've been through a divorce myself. We all think we're getting married for life, but sometimes things happen, and it doesn't work out. Emily, you still have your whole life ahead of you, and it's going to get better. I promise."

Emily's soup was getting cold. She picked up her spoon and swirled it around the carton. "So, Andrea, I was wondering if you have any plans for this coming Saturday."

"I'm not sure. Why?"

"Jesse will be in Houston, and while he's away I'm having a little moving party. I need to get the rest of my clothes, as well as empty out my music room. I went online last night and rented a small storage unit. I don't have anything really heavy, just a small, antique desk, along with a couple of bookcases. I just need someone to help me load the stuff, and I need to find a pickup truck. I sent Megan an email this morning. She said she could help for a couple of hours, but it'll go faster with an extra pair of hands, and I'd love it if you could bring Randy's truck. We'll have to get an early start, before it gets too hot. Then, once we're done, I'm treating everyone to breakfast."

"What about your dad?"

"He'd already made plans to take a fishing trip with a few of his buddies, so it'll just be us girls."

"I think I can probably help, and I'll see what I can do about a truck." Andrea glanced at her watch. "I have to get back to work pretty soon. I still have some catching up to do."

"You and me both. Thanks, Andrea. I owe you one."

* * *

Emily arrived home before her father. After another enthusiastic greeting from Lurch, she took her phone from her purse. Her father was right. She needed to talk to her grandmother and putting it off any longer would be unwise. She looked up the number and hoped for the best as she pushed the call button. Her grandmother answered after the second ring.

"Hi, Grandma." Emily tried to sound normal.

"Emily?"

"Yeah, Grandma, it's me. I just thought I'd call and say hi."

"Well, hi Emily. I just got home from playing golf with Aunt Lily, Aunt Darlene and Aunt Polly. I was about to run to the shower and change my clothes. We'll all be meeting at the country club at six-thirty for cocktails and dinner."

Barbara Leary was a well-to-do widow who lived in her Flagstaff condominium during the summer months. She spent most of her time at the country club playing golf and bridge with her friends, who she always referred to as aunts whenever she mentioned them to any of her family. It was a habit Emily found extremely annoying.

"Grandma, do you have a minute? I really need to talk to you about something."

"Of course. What's up?"

"It's about Jesse and me. We've split up. We've decided to go our separate ways."

"What?" Barbara's voice sounded stern. "So, what's your reason? Why are you doing this?"

"I caught him cheating on me."

"I see." Barbara paused for a moment. "Look, Emily, I can understand you being upset, but a divorce is such a drastic step. Have you thought about marriage counseling?"

"Grandma, he cheated on me. How can I ever trust him again?"

"I know, but I don't think you should divorce him without at least giving marriage counseling a try. Besides, what would all my friends think?"

"I don't care what anyone thinks. He broke our vows."

"Emily, you need to calm down. Men are men. They all tend to stray—"

"Dad didn't."

"Your father was the exception." There was a no-nonsense tone in her grandmother's voice. "Your grandfather, however, went astray a couple of times, but I didn't divorce him. We had an image to maintain, so I bit my tongue and let him get it out of his system. His indiscretions never lasted long, and afterwards he always came home to me. Despite everything, he was still A good husband and a good provider."

"Times have changed, Grandma, and Jesse's never been much of a provider. I'm the one who had to give up my dream and pay the bills while he built his speaking career. Remember? And this is how he thanks me. Not only is he cheating on me, Annette is the other woman."

Barbara's tone turned angry. "Now you just hold on a minute. I don't ever want to hear you talk that way about your cousin, Emily Louise. Annette isn't having an affair with your husband and you know it. She's worked very hard to help him get where he is, and he's been very pleased with everything she's done for him. I think you're just jealous because they've taken a liking to one another, but they're just good friends. She has no desire for your husband, and she never has."

"So when was the last time you spoke to her?"

"Just a few days ago," said Barbara, "and I asked her about Gary. She told me they were happy and doing well. Jesse's name never came up during the conversation, not even once. As I said before, she isn't having an affair with your husband. You've obviously misunderstood something."

"I hate to say it, Grandma, but you're wrong. Annette is indeed having an affair with my husband. I came home from work early yesterday and I caught them in the act. They were upstairs, in my bedroom. They were both naked and they were having sex, so what was there for me to misunderstand? I saw it all, with my own eyes."

There was a moment of stunned silence on the other end of the line. "You'd better not be lying about this, Emily."

"What reason would I have to lie about something like this?" Emily's voice was shaking. "I'm living a nightmare. Not only is my husband cheating on me, the other woman is my own flesh and blood. The reason why I called you is because I wanted you to hear about it from me."

"Look, Emily, I need to get ready to meet my friends, but I'll call you later, and when I do, you and I are going to have a long, serious talk."

"About what?"

"About this. I don't want you doing anything to create a scandal."

"I'm not the one creating a scandal. That would be your other granddaughter's doing, not mine. Maybe you should go have a long, serious talk with her instead of me. I didn't do anything wrong. I just wanted you to know that I'm divorcing Jesse."

Emily disconnected the call before her grandmother could respond and quickly powered down her phone. Lurch cocked his head as he watched her.

"Remind me, Lurch, not to return any of her messages until she's more reasonable. And Mom, if you can hear me, please, tell me how you managed to put up with her for all those years."

Emily dropped the phone back into her purse and wandered into the living room. It stood in front of the window, patiently waiting for her. She stroked the smooth ebony curves. It had a sweet, delicious smell all its own. Emily sat down on the bench, her foot resting on one of the pedals as she slowly lifted the lid. The keys were genuine ivory, off white with a slight yellowish undertone. As she gently touched them a smile broke out across her face. The vintage Steinway baby grand was in perfect tune. She stroked more of the keys and a familiar melody began to emerge, Beethoven's *Moonlight Sonata*. The tempo was a bit rusty, the tune somewhat hesitantly played, but each note nonetheless touched her very core. Music never came from Emily. It came through her. Music was her soul, connecting itself to the Divine. She savored each note until she reached the two final chords. Afterwards she sat quietly, finally feeling at peace.

❧SIX❧

EMILY SMILED AS she looked through the peephole. Megan Connors stood on the other side. Emily greeted her friend with a warm embrace and invited her to the kitchen for coffee. Megan, too, had been shocked to learn of Jesse's infidelity. Andrea arrived a short time later and Emily introduced her two friends to one another.

"Now, if you two ladies will wait here for just a moment, I have something for you. Be right back."

She dashed out of the kitchen, returning a moment later with a vase of long-stemmed red roses. Her friends ogled as she set it on the table.

"I'll bet I know who sent those," said Andrea.

"And you'd be right," said Emily. "I admit my first thought was to dump them in the trash, but then I remembered my two best-buddies were coming over today, so they may as well take them home and enjoy them. There's a dozen, so you each get six, but you'll have to decide among yourselves who gets the vase."

"Well, hopefully I'm still one of your best buddies," said Andrea. "I'm afraid I wasn't able to borrow Randy's truck after all. However, I did manage to find someone else at the last minute, who was more than happy to lend a helping hand. He should be here any second."

"Sounds intriguing," said Megan. The doorbell rang before Andrea could respond.

"Must be our mystery man." Emily stepped away to answer. A handsome, middle-aged man, with salt and pepper hair, stood on the other side.

"Dr. Hapner. What a pleasant surprise. So what brings you here?"

He nodded toward the street and gave her a warm smile. "I heard you were in need of a pickup truck so I came to offer my services, and you can call me Sean. I'm off the clock today."

"Okay, Sean. Everyone else is in the kitchen. Why don't you come grab a cup of coffee, and we'll get going. Megan has to be at work by ten, and we need to get this done before it gets too hot."

* * *

The knot in Emily's stomach grew tighter as she pulled into the driveway and pressed the remote. The garage door slowly rolled up, revealing Jesse's silver Lexus sedan parked inside. Her heart sank. Annette must have taken him to the airport. She took a deep breath and pulled into her old spot, taking her empty suitcase from the trunk, along with several flat boxes and a few rolls of packing tape. The others helped her carry everything inside.

"What a beautiful home," said Andrea.

"Yes, it was." Emily led them down the hallway and opened the first door on her right. Inside stood a small, antique desk and chair. Her computer sat on top of the desk, with an electric keyboard set up on the opposite wall. Andrea walked up to a pair of bookcases full of trophies.

"Wow. Look at that," she said.

"Those are all from her piano competitions," said Megan. "She started doing them when she was in the fourth grade."

"Third," said Emily.

Megan shrugged and smiled. "Okay, I stand corrected. It was the third grade, but it was also before I met her. She was still competing, and still winning trophies in high school, when I finally did meet her. I even went to some of her competitions."

While Megan was talking, Emily grabbed the tape and started putting boxes together. "Uh-oh. I forgot the packing paper. If you'll excuse me, I'll be right back."

"Need help?" asked Sean.

"Sure." They stepped out, returning a moment later with the packing paper and remaining flat boxes. Emily instructed them on how to pack the trophies before she grabbed her suitcase and headed upstairs. Her body tensed up as she opened the bedroom door. Inside, the bed was freshly made, and she spotted a small, hand-written note left on top of her pillow.

I know what I did was wrong. I've fired Annette and I'll be looking for a new assistant as soon as I return. Please, don't leave me. I still love you, and I'll do whatever it takes to win you back.

Emily started to crumple the paper, but then thought better of it. She dropped it back on the pillow and packed up the rest of her clothes as quickly as she could. Before long the bag was filled. Zipping it shut, she jumped at the unexpected sound of a man calling her name.

"Whoops. Sorry, Emily. I didn't mean to startle you."

"It's okay, Sean. I guess I'm a little on edge today."

"Perfectly understandable. Do you want me to take the suitcase downstairs for you?"

"Please do. It's probably a little too heavy for me to carry. I just need to grab a box for the other things I have left, and then I'll be done up here." A wave of sadness came over her as she looked around what had been her bedroom for more than three years. Once she left, she doubted she would ever see it again.

"Are you alright?" asked Sean.

Emily tried to shrug it off. "I'm fine. Let's take that bag downstairs."

Forty-five minutes later everything was packed and loaded, but Emily's sadness grew as they drove away from the house. The sun was turning hot when they arrived at the ministorage. They quickly unloaded and headed to a nearby diner for breakfast, but Emily remained subdued over the meal. Andrea and Megan said their goodbyes once the check was paid. Each reminded her to call them if she needed anything. After they left Sean turned his attention to Emily.

"Are you sure you're okay?"

"I'm fine, Sean. I'm just, you know, feeling a little blue, that's all."

He reached over and touched her hand. "I understand. What you're feeling is perfectly normal. So, do you have any other pressing business to get to?"

"No, not really. What about you?"

"Me neither. So, why don't we order another cup of coffee?"

"Thanks. I'd like that."

He flagged down their waitress. Once their cups were refilled the conversation took a more serious tone.

"I really am sorry this happened to you. If it's any consolation to you, I went through a similar thing, about a year ago."

"Really?"

He nodded as he sipped his coffee.

"Well, now that you've brought it up," said Emily, "I seem to recall Andrea once mentioning something about you going through a divorce, but she really didn't elaborate."

"Because I kept all the gory details to myself." His face turned sad as he set his cup down. "It's not easy being a doctor's wife. Unlike other professions, we take our work home with us as people have medical emergencies at all hours of the day and night. Even with my partner and I taking turns being on call, it still put a tremendous strain on my marriage. It was all the years of dinner plans being cancelled at the last minute because someone sprained their ankle on the soccer field. It was missing too many of my son's basketball games because someone else's child fell seriously ill, and it was all the Thanksgiving dinners I had to miss because someone popped up with appendicitis." His phone rang. He quickly checked the caller ID and sent the call to voice mail.

"See what I mean? But least this time it wasn't my answering service. So, as I was saying, as the years went by it took its toll, and it got harder and harder for Chris to cope. So one day she finally told me she'd had enough, and I was served a few days later. We sold the house, divided up the property, and agreed to joint custody of Andrew. He turned eighteen last March and he'll leave for college in a few weeks. Thankfully, he's our only child, so we won't have to worry about custody and visitation anymore."

"I'm sorry it happened, Sean."

"It's okay. The point I'm making is that I've walked in your shoes. So if you need a friend, I'm here. Call me, anytime, if you ever need to talk."

"Thanks. I may take you up on your offer."

"Please do. In the meantime, what are your plans? Your future plans?"

"I'm going back to college. Once was the day I wanted to become a concert pianist, so I've applied to USC."

"Good for you. So when do you start?"

"With any luck, about a year from now."

"In that case," said Sean, "I'll keep my fingers crossed. In the meantime, I know people, and I'll keep my eyes and ears open. If I hear of any place where you can play, you know, private parties, wedding receptions, that sort of thing, I'll let you know."

"I appreciate the thought, I really do, but at the moment I'm afraid I'm out of practice. Jesse discouraged me from playing."

"Well, Jesse's gone, and you need to get yourself back in the game, the sooner the better, especially if you have any aspirations of going to USC. A few gigs would probably look good on your resume." He took one of his cards from his pocket and jotted a phone number on the back. "Here's my private cell number. Call me, anytime, if you need to talk."

❧SEVEN☙

BEING A PUBLIC figure had its drawbacks. High on the list was the potential for stalkers, so Jesse had a home surveillance camera installed above the front door. Activated by a motion detector, it alerted him by text and email whenever it was triggered. Most of the time it was the mailman, or a delivery driver, or the cleaning lady. The rest of the time it was Emily or Annette, and he deleted the footage once he determined it wasn't a potential threat.

He checked his messages when he returned to his hotel room. Two alerts waited in his inbox. The first was footage of Emily, along with Megan, Andrea and a man he had never seen before. The second piece of footage came about an hour later. This time they were loading a few boxes, along with Emily's desk and chair, into the back a pickup truck and driving away. While not unexpected, it would, nonetheless, have to be addressed once he got home. He was still determined to do whatever it took to keep his marriage and career intact.

The following afternoon he stepped out of the shuttle van and handed the driver a generous tip. He felt somewhat relieved as he unlocked the front door. At least Emily had turned the security alarm back on when she left. He quickly entered his code and disarmed it. Heading upstairs, he found his note resting on top of the bed. A second note had been placed next to it. Emily would be mailing him her house key on Monday. That was it. There was no good-bye, nor was there a go to hell either. It simply meant that the marriage was over, and he had no one but himself to blame.

"Oh, knock it off, Jesse," he said out loud. "You wanted a taste of the forbidden fruit and you got caught. So now you're going to take the advice you keep giving everyone else. Stop playing the blame game and take control of your life."

He unpacked his bag. As expected, Emily's side of the closet was now completely empty. Once he finished, he grabbed his phone and sat down on the bed, taking a deep breath and hoping for the best as he waited for her to pick up. Her greeting was hardly warm.

"So what do you want, Jesse?"

"I just got back from Houston, and I wanted to know if you're okay."

"I'm fine," she said with a hint of sarcasm. "Thank you for asking."

"Emily, I'm not looking for a fight, okay? I just wanted to let you know that I've fired Annette. It's over between us, once and for all, and my next assistant will either be man, or a mature woman. I've learned my lesson. It'll never happen again."

"Whatever, Jesse. I no longer care. Neither one of us can go back and undo what's happened, so it's time to move on. I'm divorcing you, and that's final. After that, I'm moving to California."

"What about us? I want you back. I'll do whatever it takes, even if it means selling the house and moving to California myself."

"You can move to Timbuktu for all I care. It's over, Jesse. Now just so you know, I only took the stuff that belongs to me and was never community property. The desk and chair belonged to my mother, and I won all those trophies long before I met you. You have no use for my keyboard, you don't need my computer, and you don't need any of my clothes, unless you've been cross-dressing behind my back."

"I'm not a cross-dresser," he said bluntly.

"Of course not. You were just having sex with my cousin."

"Not anymore. Look, Emily, can we please—"

"We're done, Jesse." Emily's voice was firm. "My attorney will be in touch. In the meantime, I would appreciate it, very much, it you'd stop calling me."

"Wait! Emily, please—" He heard the silence on the other end of the line and slammed his phone down in anger. "Fine! Have it your way, bitch, but don't expect to have an easy time of it, because I'll fight you tooth and nail every step of the way."

His phone suddenly rang. He quickly grabbed it, hoping it was Emily, but it someone else.

"What is it now, Annette?"

"Whoa! You don't need to be such a grump. I was just wondering if you got home okay."

"I did. Thank you for asking. Sorry for coming off like a jerk."

"Understood. So what's got you all huffy?"

"Your cousin. Who else?"

"Look Jesse, it's like I told you before, you need to let her go so she can follow her dreams. I'm the one you really want."

"In my bed, yes. As my wife, no."

She started laughing. "Well now, we'll just have to see about that, won't we? The reason I'm calling is because Gary's out having a few beers with his buddies while I'm sitting here all by myself, feeling lonely and blue. How 'bout you?"

"Yeah, I could use a little company too, but only for about an hour or so, if you know what I mean." He stepped into the bathroom, taking out the box of condoms he'd hidden underneath the sink. "So why don't you come on over for a little while? And wear your little blue dress, with nothing on underneath. That really turned me on when you wore it the other day."

"You got it. I'm on my way."

❧EIGHT❧

THE UNIVERSITY contacted Emily after they received her application. She would need to schedule a weekend in Los Angeles the following February for an audition. Fortunately, it was several months away, giving her plenty of time to prepare. In the meantime, her father insisted she stay with him. He wanted her to save as much money as she could, so he only asked for a nominal amount for her room and board. Her life soon fell into a predictable routine, going to work, coming home, and spending the evening playing her piano. She also decided to postpone filing for her divorce until after she was accepted. Her immediate concern was her music, and she didn't want any unpleasant distractions getting in the way of her once in a lifetime opportunity. Jesse certainly wasn't going anywhere, and, at least for the moment, he wasn't calling her.

She was finally feeling like herself again as she unlocked Dr. Lerner's door and went straight to the break room to brew a fresh pot of coffee. The calendar may have said mid-September, but it would still be over one hundred degrees that afternoon, a typical late summer day for Phoenix. She filled her mug and was walking back to her desk as Dr. Hapner stepped into the waiting room. She greeted him with a smile.

"Morning, Sean."

"Morning, Emily. Have you got a moment?"

"Sure. What's up?"

"I found you a gig."

She raised her brows. "Really?"

"Hey, I meant it when I said I know people. One of my patient's mothers is an artist. She's having a show in a few weeks at a gallery in Scottsdale, so I asked her if she'd be interested in having a pianist at her opening. She thought it was a great idea, so she'll be calling you." He handed her a business card. "I wrote her name and number on the back, and I gave her Dr. Lerner's number too, if that's okay."

Emily grinned from ear to ear. "Of course it's okay. I mean, why wouldn't it be? Like you said, a few gigs would look good on my resume." She stepped around the counter to give him a hug and a quick kiss on the cheek. "Thank you for thinking of me. It means a lot."

"You're welcome, and please, let me know if this works out. If it does, I'd like to take you to dinner to celebrate."

Cathy walked in the door before she could reply. Dr. Hapner quickly excused himself while Emily returned to her desk. She checked her email during her mid-morning break. The reply to one of her messages wasn't what she had hoped for. She closed the app and went back to work. Andrea arrived at noon and Emily brought her to the break room.

"You seem a little preoccupied, so what's up?" asked Andrea.

"I'm afraid Mr. Scrooge has arrived early to ruin my Christmas."

"Say what?"

Emily opened her lunch bag. "Last spring, before everything went to hell, I decided to surprise Jesse with a Caribbean cruise. It was supposed to be right after the New Year, while everyone else was still recovering from the holidays. I put down a deposit in May, but in the weeks following the calamity, I'd forgotten all about it. That is until last week, when I got an email reminding me that the remaining balance was due."

"So why don't you cancel it?"

"I tried, but apparently, I can't. I just got an email a little while ago from the cruise line. They said it's non-refundable, and being a newbie, I didn't even think to get travel insurance. So now I'm stuck."

"Well maybe it's not such a bad thing after all. You could still go, and it'd be a nice little break before your big audition."

"You know, I hadn't thought of that," said Emily. "So, would you like to come with me? It'll only be for a week, and I've reserved a nice cabin with a balcony."

"It sounds wonderful, but I get horrible motion sickness. It's all I can do to ride in a car from Phoenix to Tucson, so I'm afraid I'll have to pass." A big smile came over her face as she thought it over. "Why don't you take my boss with you? He's overdue for a vacation, and he'd probably pick up the tab as well."

"We're just friends, Andrea. It's strictly platonic between him and me, and right now I'm still legally married to Jesse. If all goes according to plan, I'll be moving to California in less than a year. Now isn't the time for me to get involved in a new romance."

"Says who? They say the first one after a big break up is never a keeper, and he's been living like a monk ever since Chris left. A little fling would probably do both of you a world of good. Then, when the time comes for you to leave town, you can end things on a good note."

Emily gave Andrea a strong look and shook her head. Andrea laughed and shrugged it off.

"But then again, it's a trip to the Caribbean. If all else fails, maybe your dad or your grandmother could go with you."

"Dad, maybe. Grandma, definitely not. She's still in denial over Annette being Jesse's mistress. She says I'm jealous and made the whole thing up."

"You've got to be kidding me. So what's up with her?"

"I think Grandma is finally feeling remorseful about favoring my mother over Aunt Heather for all those years, and now that Grandpa's gone, she's been pretty much left on her own. Aunt Heather isn't that close to her, which is perfectly understandable. So Grandma's way of making up for it is to favor Aunt Heather's two daughters over Nick and me."

"Wouldn't it be easier if she just apologized to your aunt?" asked Andrea

"You'd think, but you don't know my grandmother. Barbara Leary never apologizes. Not to anyone. Ever. And don't confuse her with the facts. She's right and you're wrong, regardless of whatever the facts may be. According to her, admitting you made a mistake is a sign of weakness, and any sign of weakness would destroy her perfect image, don't you know?"

"So let me guess the rest. One granddaughter sleeping with the other granddaughter's husband would ruin her perfect image, so rather than deal with reality, she'll just call the wronged granddaughter, who also happens to not be her favorite granddaughter, a liar. Right?"

"That pretty much sums it up, although she hasn't called me a liar, at least not yet. She's just saying I misunderstood something."

"You caught Jesse in the act with your cousin. What could you have possibly misunderstood?"

"Exactly, which is what I told her, word for word, but she refuses to accept it. So, until she changes her attitude, I'm not speaking to her."

"Well, I'm sorry to see you go through this," said Andrea, "but I think you're doing the right thing by backing away from the old girl, at least for now. Hopefully, she'll wake up one of these days."

"I hope so too."

"I wouldn't worry too much about that cruise, Emily. I'm sure you'll find someone to go with you, and when you do, go have yourself some fun. You certainly deserve it."

❧NINE❧

THE MID-OCTOBER weather had gone from blazing hot to comfortably warm. Emily left work a half-hour early, the butterflies roiling in her stomach as drove to her first performance in several years. Once she arrived, she grabbed her keyboard and a blonde woman in a blue dress greeted her as she stepped inside the gallery.

"You must be the musician."

"Yes, I am. I'm Emily St. Claire."

She extended her hand. "Of course. Nice to meet you, Emily, and welcome to Hanson Sisters Fine Art. I'm Gillian Palmer, one of the gallery owners. If you'll follow me, I'll show you where to set up."

"Thanks. I'll also need to use the ladies' room so I can change."

Gillian pointed out a door off to the side as she led Emily into a smaller gallery. They walked toward the center of the room where she pointed out an electrical outlet on the floor.

"We'd like for you to set up here. If you need anything, please let me, or one of the staff know."

Emily looked around the room. The walls were covered with brightly colored paintings of abstract patterns of flowers and leaves. The Mozart and Bach sonatas she planned on playing would set the perfect mood.

"I will. Thank you, Ms. Palmer."

"You're welcome, and please, call me Gillian." She motioned toward the refreshment table. "And please, feel free to help yourself to a soft drink, or a snack, when you take your break."

A man walked up to Gillian and the two quickly stepped away. Emily set up her keyboard and hurried off to change. The black slacks and beige sweater she brought gave her a simple, but elegant, look. By the time she finished touching up her hair and makeup the first few patrons had arrived.

Emily took a deep breath and tried to shake off her anxiety as she sat down at her bench. After saying a silent prayer, she began playing. To her relief, the music flowed through her, as it always had, and before long she noticed a few patrons watching her. One man in particular caught her eye. He appeared to be in his mid-thirties, with sandy-colored hair and a warm smile. He kept walking back and forth between the paintings and the piano. She finished her set and glanced down at her watch. She had been playing for nearly forty-five minutes. It was time for a short break. As she stepped away from her keyboard, she made a sharp turn and nearly collided with the sandy-haired man.

"I'm so sorry," she said apologetically.

"No, my bad." He gave her a warm smile. "You play very well, by the way."

"Thank you."

"Are you done for the night? Or will you be playing some more?"

"I'll be back. I'm just taking a break."

"Of course." He extended his hand. "The name's Kyle Madden, by the way."

She smiled in return. "Emily St. Claire. Nice to meet you, Kyle." They shook hands and casually strolled up to the bar.

"So, Emily, what do you do when you're not playing the piano?"

"Nothing nearly so glamorous, I'm afraid. I'm an office manager for a dentist. How 'bout you?"

"I'm a homicide detective with the Phoenix Police Department, but don't worry, I'm not on duty tonight."

"Really? I never would have guessed. So what brings you here?"

He pointed across the room. "The lady standing over there, talking to those two other people."

"The blonde? In the blue dress?"

"That's her. Her name is Gillian Palmer."

"Yes, I know. We've already met."

"Have you now?" He flashed her another smile. "Then she probably told you she and her sister own the gallery."

"Something like that. So how do you know her?

"Awhile back I worked a case involving her ex-husband, and I stopped by one day to interview some of the staff. Afterwards I somehow ended up on the email list, but you know, I honestly do enjoy coming to the openings and seeing what's new, assuming I can get the night off. So, what about you?"

"One of my friends knows the artist. He suggested I come play for her opening."

Another woman walked up them, giving Emily a strong look as she grabbed Kyle by the arm. "Come with me. I want to show you something."

She quickly whisked him away, making it obvious to Emily that she didn't want her talking to Kyle. Emily stepped up to the bar and asked for a glass of iced tea. Taking a few sips, she heard a familiar voice behind her.

"There you are. I just got here, and I've been looking for you. So how's it going?"

She turned and greeted him with a warm hug. "Actually, Sean, it's been going quite well. I admit I felt a little nervous at first. It's been a long time since I've played in pubic, but I quickly got back into it."

"Sorry to miss your first set. I had to stop by the hospital to check on a patient, and it took longer than I expected."

"No worries. I'll be here for about another hour or so."

"Sounds good. You know, I've never heard you play before, so I'm really looking forward to it. By the way, have you had dinner yet?"

"Not yet. I didn't have time."

"Me neither, and I seem to recall telling you I'd take you out to celebrate. There're some really good restaurants in the neighborhood, so I'll buy you dinner when you're done."

"Thanks, I'd like that. Meantime, I'd better get back to work."

She returned to her bench and started her next set, looking around the room as she played. Kyle was still watching her, but this time from a distance. He and the woman soon left, and as the door closed behind them, Emily suddenly felt disappointed. She glanced around the room and noticed the crowd had started to wane. By seven forty-five, most had left. Sean gave her a congratulatory hug once she finished her last sonata.

"Well done, Emily. I enjoyed listening to you. Very much."

"Thanks. I had fun playing here."

"Do you need help packing up?"

"I'm good, as long as you don't mind helping me haul it out to my car."

"It would be my pleasure, ma'am."

Gillian soon appeared, presenting Emily with an envelope and asking her if she would be interested in playing for other openings. Emily's face was beaming when she left. She followed Sean to a nearby restaurant, and once they were seated, he ordered their wine, raising his glass as soon as it arrived.

"Here's to the first of many new gigs for you." They bumped their glasses together and took a sip. "You know, Emily, it's been wonderful watching you grow and blossom over these past few weeks. It's never easy when a marriage ends, especially under circumstances like yours, but you've handled yourself with grace and dignity. You have a great life ahead of you, and I know you're going to go far."

"Thanks, and you're right. It hasn't been easy, as you can imagine. Friends like you, and Andrea, and Megan, not to mention my dad, have made it all possible. I don't know what I would have done if I hadn't had all of you to lean on."

"That's what we're here for."

Their waiter arrived and they turned their attention to their menus, making small talk once they placed their orders. Their salads soon arrived, and the conversation turned more serious.

"So, Emily, have you decided what's next?"

"I'm trying to get into the University of Southern California."

"I know you are, and I have no doubt whatsoever that you'll make it, but it's still almost a year away. What are your plans in the meantime?"

"I don't know" she said with a shrug. "I haven't really thought that much about it. Right now, I'm just taking things one day at a time."

"I understand. More than you know." He paused for a moment. "I guess what I'm asking is if there's anyone new on the horizon?"

Kyle's face flashed across her mind, but she quickly brushed it off. "I'm afraid there isn't. Right now, I simply don't have the time."

"I understand, but you're too young, too beautiful and too vibrant to be all alone in the world. Yes, I know you have your piano, and yes, I understand it's very important to you, but every once in a while, you need to make some time for you." He picked up his wineglass. "You know, we're both in the same boat. We both thought we had partners for life, but then life threw us a curve ball and proved us wrong. It's been a hard blow for both of us."

"I know what you mean. I keep wondering what I did wrong. Why did my husband lose interest in me? Obviously, I failed to meet his needs, but how? Wasn't I good enough for him?"

Sean reached across the table and squeezed her hand. "No, you didn't fail him. He just wasn't the right man for you." He stopped and cleared his throat. "I'm not looking for anything serious right now, and neither are you, but we're both on our own, we both enjoy each other's company, and I find you incredibly attractive. I'd like to be more than a friend to you, if you'll have me."

"So what are you saying, Sean?"

"What I'm saying is we've both been badly hurt by the people we loved and trusted the most, and we both need a chance to heal and rebuild our self-esteem. I'd like for us to take things to the next level, but I'm not ready for anything permanent yet, and neither are you. What I'm looking for is a much-needed rebound relationship with a special friend, and I'm hoping you could be that friend. Then, when the time comes, and we're ready to move on, we can both walk away feeling grateful to the other, and we'll always have a special place in our hearts for one another."

"I see." She took a sip of her wine. "You are aware that technically, I'm still married."

"But you are getting a divorce?"

"Yes, I am. However, Jesse has made it clear that he'll contest it, so I'm waiting until I get accepted to USC before I file. I don't want any distractions."

"He can contest it all he wants, but the court will still grant the divorce."

"I know, but at the moment I simply don't have the time to be forcibly dragged into marriage counseling. We've separated. I don't wear my wedding rings anymore. As far as I'm concerned, my marriage is over."

He gave her a mischievous grin. "I see. So, are you still living with your father?"

"I am."

"And would he have any objections?"

"I'm sure he would."

Their waiter stopped by to get their salad plates. Their entrees arrived a short time later. Once again, they made small talk over their meal. As soon as they finished, Sean looked her in the eye.

"I meant what I said before. I'd like to take our relationship to the next level and invite you to my place for a nightcap. My son went off to college, so it's just me, on my own. You're under no obligation, of course, and you're free to go if you should change your mind later on. There'll be no hard feelings."

Emily held his gaze for a moment. She knew she wasn't ready for a serious relationship, but Andrea's words about the how first one after a divorce was never a keeper echoed through her mind. Sean had been a good friend, and she knew he meant it when he said there would be no hard feelings if she changed her mind.

"I'd love to have a nightcap, but I'm not making any promises, okay?"

<h1 style="text-align:center">❧ TEN ❧</h1>

EMILY FOLLOWED Sean to back to his place. The small house was simply furnished with a slightly lived-in look. He offered her a seat on the sofa, along with another glass of wine. After pouring her a glass he poured a glass for himself and sat down next to her.

"So, Emily, how are you feeling?"

"I'm fine. I've had a wonderful evening. Tonight, I overcame a major obstacle."

He gently brushed a small strand of hair away from her eyes. "Really? How intriguing."

"Yes," she nervously said. "It's been a long, long time since I've played in front of an audience. I didn't know what to expect. What if they didn't like me?"

"You need to give yourself more credit. You're an accomplished musician. I was impressed at just how good you really are. You need to let go of your inhibitions and learn to trust yourself."

He wrapped his arms around her and kissed her. It was a long, passionate kiss. He ran his fingers over her lips and kissed her again. Afterwards he gave her a smile while his fingers gently stroked her forearm.

"Are you okay with this?"

Emily suddenly felt confused. "I'm not sure. I care about you, Sean. I care about you a lot, but I—"

"It's okay. Like I said before, this is a rebound relationship for both of us. There'll be no strings attached. We're simply going to have fun and enjoy one another's company." He kissed her again, his hand slowly and carefully working its way down to her breast. He softly caressed her nipple. "It's been a long time since a man has truly appreciated you, hasn't it?"

"Yes. Yes, it has, but—"

He put his finger on her lips. "I know. You're still hurting over what Jesse did to you, but I want you to know that you're still a desirable woman, and you need to feel desired again."

Sean kissed her again and gently massaged her breast. Emily knew she should resist, but Sean was right. Jesse had done more than betray her trust. His actions had left her doubting herself as a woman, and she wanted to feel desirable again. She moaned softly. Taking his cue, Sean lifted up her sweater and unhooked her bra. His tongue swirled around her nipple. She moaned louder and arched her back. "I think we're ready," he said.

He took her by the hand and led her to a room at the end of the hallway. Emily nervously kicked off her shoes as he pulled the bed covers down. He kissed her passionately once again, pulling off her sweater and bra. As they fell to the floor, he gazed at her and smiled.

"Just as I thought. You're incredibly desirable." He kissed and sucked her breasts. She let out a soft moan and began rubbing his shoulders and back. He unzipped her trousers, giving her another smile as they dropped to the floor.

"I'll be right back," he said. "Don't go anywhere."

Emily nodded and smiled in return, trying to conceal her nervousness as Sean stepped away. He returned a moment later in his briefs, carrying a tube of lubricant and several foil packets. Setting them on the nightstand, he gave her a smile and a wink. "In my line of work, I get plenty of free samples. So, what's your favorite color?"

"What?"

Sean laughed. "What's your favorite color? I have several for you to pick and choose from."

"Really?" She laughed nervously. "I'm not sure. Purple, I guess."

"Then purple it is." He set one of the packets aside and kissed her again, caressing her back and shoulders as he gently sat her down on the edge of the bed. She looked up into his eyes and he gave her a reassuring look.

"You look nervous, but it's okay. I won't hurt you; I promise." He took her by the shoulders and slowly eased her down across the bed. He waited for her to get comfortably settled before removing her panties. Tossing them aside, he reached down and lifted her feet off the floor, gently placing her heels on the edge of the bed. Emily took a deep breath, once again feeling vulnerable. She closed her eyes and listened to the sound of her pounding heart as she felt his hand gently brush her outer thigh. His stroke was as light as a feather.

"Emily, you're more beautiful than I could have possibly imagined."

Her eyes remained closed and she continued to lie quietly. She heard him tear the packet open. A moment later he knelt down in front of her. She pulled her legs in close, her knees clamped tightly together.

"You don't need to be so shy with me. I'm a doctor. I see plenty of naked bodies in my line of work. I won't hurt you, I promise, so please, just lie back and relax."

She took a deep breath as he slowly pulled her knees apart and softly stroked her inner thighs.

"There you go. That's better, and by the way, each and every inch of you is a sight to behold." He slipped a finger inside her, probing deep as he pushed down on her belly with his other hand. Her body tensed up as he felt his way around.

"It's okay. I simply must play doctor for a moment. I see you have all of your equipment, and as long as I'm in here, I may as well check this too."

He pushed on something deep inside. Her body jerked as she gasped with pleasure.

"Well now," he said with a flirtatious tone. "I see that's working just fine. So, what about this?" He pressed his thumb into her sweet spot. She let out a soft groan as he began working both places at the same time while he pressed down on her with his other hand. She moaned with pleasure.

"That's it. I want you to forget about all your troubles and just enjoy yourself. Did you know that back in the Victorian days, doctors used to do this sort of thing to their female patients? It's how they treated them for hysteria. Now, I'd be happy to explain all the health benefits sexual pleasure has on your body, but somehow I think you'd prefer it if I just let you experience it for yourself."

Her moans grew louder and more intense as her body began to writhe with pleasure.

"That's it. I want you to let yourself go. Don't think about anything. Just let the doctor make you feel good." His thumb and fingers kept working. Her pleasure grew. She let out another loud groan.

"There you go. That's right. Don't hold back, you sexy thing, you. Just close your eyes and concentrate on how good this feels."

The sweet sensation burned in her body. The more it intensified the harder he worked her. She felt herself squeezing down on his fingers as they pushed even deeper inside. Her moans grew louder and more intense. Unable to hold back any longer, she screamed in unbridled ecstasy as her body writhed. She felt as if she'd taken flight. As she slowly came back down, she felt his arms reach underneath her to reposition her on the bed and turn her on her side. She felt his now naked body cuddle next to hers as he kissed her on the cheek and rubbed her thigh.

"There you go. That felt good, didn't it? I'll let you rest for a little while, and then I'm going to make love to you."

She nodded in return, still lost in the afterglow. He kissed and caressed her breasts as he waited for her to get her second wind. Once she caught her breath, he placed her hand on him, showing her what he liked. She, too, had a gentle touch. Now it was his turn to immerse himself in pleasure as he stroked her again. When he finally rolled on top of her and entered her, she wrapped her legs around him and held him tight until he reached his release. It felt good to once again hold a blissfully exhausted man in her arms, and for a brief moment she imagined he was Kyle. Her thoughts rattled her. Why was she so drawn to a man she had hardly met and who, in all likelihood, would never see again?

"Are you alright?" asked Sean

"Yes. Yes, I'm fine." It was her turn to give him a reassuring smile. "It's just feels so different being with another man."

"I understand. I want you to know that you're an amazing woman, and I'd love nothing more than to make love to you for the rest of the night. However, it's getting late, and I don't want your father to worry."

"I know." Emily reluctantly got out of bed. Sean stepped away while she dressed, returning a short time later in his bathrobe. When she was ready to leave, he walked her to her car and gave her a passionate goodnight kiss.

"Drive careful and send me a text to let me know you got home alright."

"I will."

"I also meant what I said. You're an amazing woman, and I really would like to see you again."

"I'd like that too, Sean."

He kissed her one last time before she started up her car and drove away.

* * *

Emily found her father anxiously waiting when she arrived home. "Hey, Dad, what's up?"

"Where the hell have you been? It's nearly midnight. I was getting worried."

"Sorry, Dad." She set her keyboard down in the entryway and stepped into the kitchen. Her father was right behind her as she opened the refrigerator and poured herself a glass of juice.

"Sean Hapner came to the opening, but he didn't get there until late. Once I finished, he invited me out to dinner. Afterwards we started talking, and we lost track of the time. I'm sorry if I upset you."

"So what was so fascinating?" he sternly asked.

"I'm sorry?"

"What did you two talk about that was so interesting?"

"Life after divorce."

"Really?" Roger's voice remained stern. "You need to be careful, Emily. You're still a married woman. Don't give Jesse any ammunition he can use against you."

"We're just friends, Dad."

She took her glass into the family room and sat down on the sofa. Roger followed her, taking his seat on his recliner. Emily steered the conversation to a safer topic, and a dreamy look came over her face.

"Dad, do you think there's such a thing as love at first sight?"

"I suppose. I knew your mother was someone special when I first met her, but I wouldn't call it love at first sight. That came later. Why do you ask?"

"I met the most interesting man tonight at the opening. He kept watching me while I played. There was something about him. It's hard for me to explain."

"I see," said Roger. "So, did he come over and introduce himself?"

"Sort of. When I got up to take my break I turned around and literally walked into him. That's when he introduced himself. His name was Kyle. He said he was an off-duty police detective."

"Really? So why he didn't take you out to dinner, instead of Sean?"

Emily suddenly looked sad. "Turned out he had someone with him. I don't know if she was just a casual date, or someone he's seriously involved with, but she sure swooped down on him in a hurry as soon as she saw him talking to me. And that, as they say, was that, but even so, I can't seem to get him off my mind for some reason. Strange, isn't it? How you can be so strongly drawn to someone you've hardly met and don't even know."

"I'd say you're barking up the wrong tree, Emmy. He has a girlfriend, or maybe a wife. Either way, he's unavailable and you're in an emotionally vulnerable state yourself. That said, let's be careful with Dr. Hapner until you're completely divorced, and speaking of which, have you found a lawyer yet?"

"Not yet, and we've been over this before. Jesse has made it abundantly clear that he intends to contest the divorce, which means he'll probably ask the court to order me to go to some sort of marriage counseling. That for me would be a complete waste of time, and right now I need to focus all my energy on my music. I don't want him thwarting my chance to get into USC."

"I understand, but legally he's still your husband, so you need to watch yourself. So the next time you're going to be out this late, you either call me or send me a text. I'm still your father, you know."

Emily got up from the sofa and kissed him on the cheek. "I know you are, Dad. I love you, and again I'm sorry I upset you. Goodnight. I'm going to bed."

❧ELEVEN❧

JESSE CLOSED THE folder and pushed it across his desk. "That's all for now, Yolanda."

"Very well." She picked up the folder and dropped her pen into her purse. "I'll start working on it first thing tomorrow morning, and unless something unexpected comes up, I'll see you next week. Same day and time?"

"Yep, same day and time. I'll walk you to the door."

Yolanda Lopez was Jesse's new assistant, and so far, he had been pleased with her work. A fifty-something mother of five, she was anything but sexy with her stocky build and graying hair, but what Yolanda lacked in looks she more than made up for with her job skills. She had many years of experience as an administrative assistant and was much more organized and detail oriented than Annette.

After seeing Yolanda out, Jesse went upstairs to pack. He was scheduled to fly to Cincinnati the following morning to present a keynote address for a business conference. His phone beeped as he stepped into the bedroom, and a frown came over his face. Annette had sent him a text message.

"Would you like to fly before your flight?"

In the three months since Emily had left, Annette had gone from sexy to stifling. Convinced she would soon become the next Mrs. Jesse St. Claire; she had become much too vocal about her emotional needs. At the same time, however, Jesse was hesitant to end the affair. He still had his own needs, for which Annette was all too willing to oblige. He sent her a short reply to let her know he was expecting her. She arrived an hour later, and he mumbled a less than enthusiastic greeting as he opened the door.

"Well hello to you too. Aren't you happy to see me?"

"Sorry, Annette. I'm a bit rushed today. I only have time for a quickie, and then you'll have to go. So, don't just stand there. Go upstairs and get undressed. I'll be up in a few minutes."

She shot him a hard look. "What's gotten into you today?"

"Nothing. I just told you I'm very busy and we're wasting time. You need to go upstairs and get yourself ready."

She continued to glare at him. "So what am I? A call girl? Someone you can barely squeeze into your busy schedule?"

"Yeah, something like that. You keep thinking I'll divorce Emily and marry you, and I keep telling you it won't happen. If marriage really is your goal, then maybe you should dump Gary, and me while you're at it, so you can start fresh."

"I get it." Annette's voice remained huffy. "Either you've called Emily, or she's called you, or she finally got around to having you served."

"None of the above, sweetie. You're a blast in bed, I'll give you that, but it's all there is between us. Lots of great, hot sex, but nothing more." He reached over and pinched her nipple. "So? What are you waiting for? Go get into bed. I'll be up in a couple of minutes."

"Typical," she said in disgust. "You men are all alike. Sure, you want to have your fun, but then, when things start getting serious, you all start in with your 'I don't want to make a commitment' crap."

Jesse pointed toward the staircase. "That way. I'll be up in a few minutes."

He stepped into the bedroom a short time later. Annette was curled up on top of the bed, wearing a lacy black negligee. She greeted him with a smile as he quickly undressed. He stepped into the bathroom to get a condom before climbing on top of the bed and pulling her nightgown up to her waist.

"Well, aren't you going to kiss me?" she asked.

Jesse shook his head. "Not today. I already told you. I'm on a tight schedule and I just don't have the time."

Annette started to protest, but Jesse reached down and began massaging her. She leaned back and closed her eyes as she softly moaned. A minute later he applied the condom and quickly relieved himself. Once he was finished, he hopped off the bed and gathered up his clothes.

"That's it, sweetheart," he said. "We're all done here. Time for you to get dressed and go."

Annette sat up and shot him an angry look. "What about me? I wasn't finished yet."

"Then maybe you should hold that thought for Gary. He'll be off work in another couple hours. That'll give you plenty of time to get home, wash up and put some clean panties on."

Annette's face flushed with anger. "You arrogant, egotistical, son of a bitch. Is that all I am to you? Just a sex toy?"

"Bingo! You finally got it." Jesse turned and started toward the bathroom.

"You son of a—"

He spun around and quickly cut her off. "The thrill is gone, Annette. Sure, we had some laughs in the beginning, but I told you from the very start it would be a fling and nothing more. I also meant it when I said I'm getting Emily back. So, if you'll excuse me, I need to go clean up."

Annette tried a different tactic. "Oh c'mon, Jesse. Who do you think you're fooling? If you really wanted Emily back you wouldn't be doing the deed with me, which means you're hardly being fair to her."

Jesse froze for a moment in the bathroom doorway. As he slowly turned to face her, his eyes turned into icy cold slits.

"Don't you dare go there. You, of all people, have no business trying to be noble where Emily is concerned. She's your cousin, and you betrayed her."

Annette returned his angry look. "You're the one who came on to me. Remember?"

"Yes, I did. As I recall, it happened right after you threw yourself at me."

"Now you wait just a—"

"We're wasting time, Annette, and I haven't got all day. I'm taking a quick shower and you had better be gone when I get out."

She jumped off the bed and started getting dressed. "Okay, fine. I'm leaving, but don't worry, I'll be back."

"We'll have to see about that."

"And what does that mean?"

"It means you need to go home to Gary. Poor bastard."

"What?"

Jesse gave her another cold, hard look. "He still doesn't have a clue, does he? He has no idea that all this time you've been screwing another man behind his back."

The color faded from her face. "What the hell has gotten into you?"

"I already told you. I'm tired of you thinking I'm going to fall in love with you, because I won't. I keep telling you that, over and over again, but for some reason you can't get it through that thick skull of yours. It's never going to happen. Not now. Not ever. Not only do I not love you, I can't trust you. You've never felt so much as a shred of guilt over Gary, so who's to say you wouldn't cheat on me someday?"

"I would never cheat on you, Jesse. You know that." Annette smoothed out the wrinkles on her blouse as she spoke. "And I honestly never meant to hurt Gary either. I've simply fallen out of love with him. I fell out of love with him the moment I met you. I'm only staying with Gary until you tell me you're ready for me to move in with you. I know it may sound cruel, but I really don't have a choice. I can't afford to get my own place."

"So you say." Jesse stepped into the bathroom, reappearing a moment later in his bathrobe. "You're never moving in here, Annette, because I don't love you. I never have, and I never will. I'm still in love your cousin, and I intend to get her back."

Annette was becoming desperate. "Oh c'mon, Jesse. You know you don't really mean that. You wouldn't have cheated on her if you still loved her."

"Yes, I do mean it. I'll admit I took her for granted for a long time, and, in a moment of weakness, I made a terrible mistake. One I'll regret for the rest of my life. Go home, Annette. Go home to Gary."

"You want to talk about regrets? Fine! We'll talk about regrets." Her voice turned into an ear-piercing shrill. "You dump me, and I'll make damn sure you'll have something to regret. I'll tell the whole world how the great Jesse St. Claire, the man with all the answers, cheated on his wife. With her cousin."

Jesse calmly folded his arms across his chest. "Go ahead. Do whatever you want. I'll tell the world I fired you because you're incompetent, and you're just a disgruntled ex-employee trying to stir up trouble. You'll also need to figure out a way to explain it to Gary while you're at it, because once you go public about our affair, he'll toss your sorry butt out the door."

She stuffed her negligee in her bag. "Don't think for one moment that this is over, Jesse."

He opened bedroom door. "It's time for you to go."

"Fine. I'll see you when you get back. Maybe by then you'll be yourself."

"Don't count on it," said Jesse, firmly. "It's taken me awhile, but I now finally realize you're more trouble than you're worth." He walked her to the front door. She gave him a parting smile as she stepped across the threshold.

"I'm sorry you're in such a bad mood today. Have a good trip and I'll call you Sunday."

"No, I don't want you calling me anymore. In fact, I'm blocking your number. This has gone on far too long, and it's time to call it quits. You need to go home to Gary and stay there. It's over. We're done."

Her smile turned into a glare. "Don't go there, Jesse, or you'll regret it. I guarantee it."

"Have a good life, Annette." He slammed the door in her face and ran upstairs to shower.

๛TWELVE๛

EMILY SCANNED THE room and quickly spotted the familiar head of long dark hair. She looked at the hostess. "I see her. She's right over there, thanks." Emily walked up to the booth by the corner window. Megan looked up and greeted her with a smile.

"There you are. I didn't realize their Sunday brunches had gotten so popular. I'm glad I got here a few minutes early. I figured I'd better grab a table while I could."

"No problem." Emily sat down across the table from Megan.

"So, how have you been, stranger? Long time, no see. You look great, by the way. Much better than you did the day we helped you move your stuff out of Jesse's house."

"I am doing better, thanks."

"I'm glad. So how was your Halloween? Did you do anything special?"

"Nah," said Emily. "I just hung out at home with Dad, and we took turns handing out candy to the trick-or-treaters. It's always fun seeing the kids in their costumes."

"They're cute alright. So how was your gig at Hanson Sisters?"

"Nerve wracking, at least at first. It's been ages since I've played to a room full of people. But once I got started, I quickly fell back into it. The women who own the place were impressed. They'd like to have me back for other events."

"I'm so proud of you, Emmy. You're bouncing back."

"Thanks. You know, I met the most interesting man while I was there."

"Really." Megan looked intrigued. "So, tell me more. I want details. Lots of details."

"He was about thirty something, fairly tall, with light brown hair and blue eyes. He was good looking too. He said he was a police detective who worked a case awhile back involving one of the gallery owners; something about an ex-husband, but he really didn't have much chance to elaborate because it turned out he didn't come alone. His girlfriend suddenly materialized out of nowhere and whisked him away in a hurry. Still, I keep seeing his face in the back of my mind. Weird, huh?"

"Well, maybe not," said Megan. "It could be a sign that you're getting over Jesse, which would be a good thing. Then you mentioned something about Dr. Hapner."

"Yeah. We've started seeing one another, if you know what I mean. We've both agreed it won't be anything long-term. It's just a rebound thing for both of us. His wife left him about a year or so ago." Emily's face turned slightly pink. "He's really something. Being a doctor, he knows how and where to please a woman. He wants to help me learn more about my sexuality, and so far, he's been quite a teacher."

"I see." Megan's face turned a little pink as well. "Just be careful, okay? You're still married you know, and you don't want Jesse to find out."

"You and my dad both."

"Have you had him served yet?"

"Not yet. It's been such a long time since I've played the piano seriously and I'm busy getting myself back into it. Meantime Jesse doesn't want a divorce, and I simply don't have the time to be forcibly dragged into marriage counseling."

Their waitress stopped by to take their drink orders. Once she left, Megan turned her attention back to Emily.

"I know you have your heart set on going to USC, but have you considered all the other baggage that goes with it?"

"Such as?"

"The cost of living in California is incredibly high, and the university isn't in the best part of town, so you'd be commuting a fair distance to boot, and the traffic is awful. There are other schools out there just as good, if not better. The other day I was telling my aunt about you, and she said The University of North Texas has one of the best music schools in the country. It's about forty miles or so from Dallas, so the cost of living there would be cheaper, and you wouldn't have all the headaches that go along with living in LA."

"I've heard of it," said Emily.

"No doubt you have. I'm just saying it wouldn't hurt to apply at some other places too. We're talking about the rest of your life, you know, and there's no guarantee you'll be accepted at USC. You really should have a back-up plan in place."

Their waitress delivered their drinks and they headed to the buffet, returning with overflowing plates. As they sat back down Emily changed the subject.

"So, how busy is a hair salon right after New Year's Eve?"

"Certainly not as busy as it is during the holidays or just before Valentine's Day. Why do you ask?"

"Well, before everything turned sour with Jesse, I'd signed us up for a Caribbean cruise. It was supposed to be a surprise, to make up for our not having much of a honeymoon. Anyway, I tried to cancel it, but it turns out I can't, and being a novice traveler, I didn't think to buy travel insurance. So, I've decided to make Jesse's loss your gain and invite you to come along with me. You keep saying you're overdue for a vacation, and you've also told me you're like an independent contractor, so that means you can take some time off, right?"

"Wow. Let me think about it for a moment." Megan's face quickly lit up. "You're right. I am overdue for a vacation, and you and I could have a lot of fun. I'll see what I can do."

❧ THIRTEEN ❧

BY MID-NOVEMBER Jesse was feeling more like himself. Emily still hadn't served him, and he wondered if the time had come to reach out to her. As he put on his tie, he realized that for the first time in months, he felt hopeful for the future. He grabbed his briefcase and headed off to meet a prospective client for dinner at a swanky Scottsdale restaurant. As expected, the meeting went well. The man seated across the table from him was making some last-minute notes on his tablet.

"So does this proposal work for you?" asked Jesse.

"Absolutely."

"And are we in agreement on my fee?"

"We are indeed. Congratulations, Mr. St. Claire. We have a deal."

"Thank you, Mr. Stuart. I'll have Yolanda email your contract, along with the other paperwork, first thing tomorrow morning."

They rose from their table and shook hands. As Jesse watched the other man walk away, something unexpected caught his eye. Emily was seated at a table on the other side of the room. Jesse quickly looked away and sat back down. So far, she hadn't noticed him. She seemed much more interested in her dining companion. The man seated across from her looked familiar, but Jesse couldn't place him, so he grabbed his tablet and tried to concentrate on his email to Yolanda. A server soon stopped by to pick up his check and refill his coffee. After he left Jesse continued to watch Emily. He winced when he saw the man reach over to touch her hand as he talked. Finally, Jesse hit the send button and dropped his tablet back into his briefcase. He remained at his table and sipped his coffee while he tried to act casual, although it was hard for him not to stare.

Emily and her companion soon got up to leave. The man helped her with her coat and leaned down to kiss her once she got it on. Jesse's heart sank while another part of him felt very angry. Emily and her companion turned and started toward Jesse's table. He quickly pushed his napkin to the floor, taking his time to pick it up as they walked by. Once they were gone, Jesse hastily put on his coat and followed them to the parking lot. Their car was parked a few spaces away from his, but they were much too involved with each other to notice as he unlocked his door and slipped behind the wheel. His stomach twisted as he watched them kiss again. This time the man brushed his hand across Emily's backside and Jesse hoped against hope that they weren't sleeping together. As they got into their car, Jesse fired up his engine and followed them out of the parking lot, being careful to keep a discreet distance.

Ten minutes later they pulled into the driveway at a small house. Jesse pulled over across the street and watched as their car entered the garage. As the door rolled back down, he noticed Emily's car was parked in the driveway. A few windows lit up inside the house. Five minutes later the lights turned off, one by one, and the house went completely dark. Jesse felt as if he had been kicked in the gut. Now he fully understood how Emily must have felt the day she walked in on him and Annette. He remained in his car in stunned disbelief.

* * *

Emily writhed and moaned with pleasure as Sean caressed her. He entered her and she wrapped her legs tightly around him, thrusting her body against his as she climaxed. Now it was his turn. She held onto him, feeling his body tighten and then slowly relax. They kissed and held each other in the afterglow, and she soon dozed in his arms. She came to a few minutes later and glanced at the clock on the nightstand. It was nearly ten o'clock. She tried to sit up, but a pair of hands reached up and pulled her back down.

"So, where do you think you're going?" Sean softly brushed his lips along the top of her ear, and she felt a tingle go down her body.

"It's getting late. I don't want my dad to worry."

"Then you'll have to send him a text. Tell him you'll be home in another couple hours."

"Another couple of hours?"

He ran his hand down her middle. "That was the main course. Now I want dessert."

"Sean Hapner, who would have ever guessed that underneath that white coat was such a virile man? You're turning me into a nymphomaniac. You know that, don't you?"

He gave her a knowing grin. "Of course I do, and I'm doing it on purpose. They don't call me the doctor of love for nothing. I know how to cure a broken heart, and yours is definitely on the mend." He stroked her and kissed the side of her neck as she moaned once again. "That's my girl. You send Daddy a text message while I go draw us a nice, warm bubble bath. I'm going to wash every inch of you, and then I'm going to eat you for dessert." He licked his lips. "Umm, yummy."

* * *

It was nearly eleven-thirty when Sean finally walked Emily out to her car. He opened the door for her, kissing her again as he fondled her breast. She laughed as she playfully pushed his hand away. He waited as she got inside. Once she was settled in her seat, he bent down to kiss her goodnight.

"You must be freezing in that bathrobe," she said.

"But I'm still hot for you."

"I know, but it's late, and we both have to go to work tomorrow"

"I know, dammit." He closed her door and she rolled the window down. He leaned inside and kissed her one last time.

"Goodnight, Emily. Drive safe."

"Will do. Goodnight."

She waited in the driveway while he walked to the front door and turned back to wave good-bye. She looked in the rearview mirror after he went inside, reaching into her purse for her hairbrush. Her hair was growing long again, and she needed to smooth it out before she got home. She was about start the car when she heard footsteps. Looking around, she thought Sean had come back out, but it wasn't him. This man wore a coat and tie, and he was coming up from behind. Her heart skipped a beat as he came closer. Her hands were shaking as she tried to start the car, but she wasn't quick enough. She let out a gasp as he bent down and peered in the driver's side window.

"Hi, Emily. Remember me? I'm the guy you're still married to."

<h1 style="text-align:center">🙂FOURTEEN🙂</h1>

EMILY'S HEART pounded in her chest. She tried to speak, but the words wouldn't come. Jesse looked more hurt than angry. Emily looked down to avoid his eyes, but Jesse's voice was calm and quiet.

"Get in on the passenger's side. I'm driving."

"Wh-what?"

"This way. Come with me."

Her body was shaking too hard for her to move. Jesse opened the driver's side door and unfastened Emily's seatbelt. He gently pulled her out of the car and walked her to the passenger side, guiding her into the seat and buckling the seatbelt. Emily was still shaking as he closed the door. He quickly hopped in the driver's side and fired up the engine. Emily started getting her bearings back as they drove away.

"What the hell are you doing here?" she asked.

"I had to meet a client tonight at The Saddleback."

Emily muttered an explicative under her breath.

"What was that?" asked Jesse.

Emily remained silent.

"I see," said Jesse. "So, as I was saying, I had a meeting tonight at The Saddleback, and I saw you having dinner with Romeo. So, who is he?"

"None of your damn business."

"Interesting choice of names, but okay, I'll buy it. So, have long have you two been sleeping together?"

"That's also none of your damn business." Emily's voice had an acidic tone. "Where are you taking me, Jesse?"

"Home."

"To my father's house?"

"Nope. I'm taking you to our house, and once we get there, you and I are going to have a long, serious talk."

She started to say something but thought better of it and reached for her phone instead.

"What are you doing?"

"I'm sending my father a text message, and I'm really tempted to tell him you've kidnapped me. However, you've seriously pissed me off, so I've decided I'm going to have it out with you, once and for all. Therefore, I'm letting him know that I'm running later than expected, and to please not wait up for me." Emily seethed in silent anger for the rest of the drive. Jesse flipped down the visor when he turned into the driveway.

"I see you still have your garage remote."

"Yeah, I forgot to send it back to you. Sorry for the inconvenience. Why don't you go ahead and take it?"

"We'll see. You just might change your mind." Jesse drove the car into the garage. Once inside, he opened the passenger door and escorted Emily to the kitchen.

"Would you like some coffee?"

"No thanks."

"Well, I'm going to brew a fresh pot. We have a lot to talk about, so please feel free to help yourself later on if you change your mind. Go take a seat in the living room. I'll be there in a minute."

Emily stepped into the living room, not sure if she should stay or bolt and run. At least Jesse didn't seem angry. He soon joined her and set his mug down on the coffee table. He appeared to be calm and collected.

"Please, take a seat. Make yourself comfortable."

"I see you've rearranged some of the furniture."

"Yes, I have, and I'll explain the reason why in a little while, but first we some other business to discuss."

Emily took her seat on the sofa as Jesse sat down on the opposite end.

"So, as I've already told you, I had to meet some prospective clients tonight at The Saddleback. I had no way of knowing you'd be there as well. In fact, I didn't even see you until the meeting broke up. So, after my client left, I decided to stay behind. You didn't see me, but I sure got a good look at him. I assumed the two of you were just friends, or at least I hoped it was all you were.

Then, when you left, I followed you out to the parking lot. That's when I realized he was your lover, not a friend."

Emily's eyes blazed with anger. "You son of a bitch! You followed us back to his place, didn't you?"

Jesse's voice remained calm. "Yes, I did, but I kept my distance. I parked across the street and waited for you to come back out. You were in there for several hours, and when you finally came out, I noticed he was wearing his bathrobe. You were having sex with him, weren't you?"

"Like you have room to talk."

"Which is precisely the point. I don't have room to talk, but I do want you to know something. It wasn't until that moment that I fully understood all the pain I've put you through, because I got to experience it first-hand myself." A tear ran down from the corner of his eye as his voice trembled. "It's been one hell of a lesson to learn, and I can't say I didn't have it coming." He took a deep breath as he struggled to compose himself.

"So, I can now do one of two things. I can get angry with you, and believe me, I was pretty damn angry once I realized what was happening. Or I can do the other thing and forgive you. We're still married. I'm still your husband, and tonight you spent over two hours in another man's bed. While you were there, I had plenty of time to think things through, and I kept reaching same inescapable conclusion. Who the hell am I to condemn you?" He reached over and squeezed her hand. "So, I forgive you. Under the circumstances, it's the only thing I can do. I just wanted you to know."

Emily's eyes welled up with tears and she didn't know how to respond. As she softly wept, Jesse squeezed her hand again.

"So, now that I've forgiven you, I'm asking you, as your husband, who is he? I have a right to know. I also want to know how long you've been seeing one another?"

"His name is Sean. Sean Hapner."

"Hapner?" Jesse's eyebrows furrowed as the realization slowly dawned on him. "You mean, Dr. Hapner? Andrea's boss? The pediatrician, two doors down from Dr. Lerner?"

Emily nodded her head in reply.

"I thought he was married."

"He was," said Emily, "but not anymore. He and his wife split up. About a year ago."

"I see. So, how long have the two of you been seeing one another?"

"Not long. Only for a few weeks."

"Is it serious?" he asked.

"No, not really. It's just a post-divorce fling for both of us."

"Except we're not divorced. I've never been served, and so far as I know, you've never even filed for a legal separation."

Emily's defenses came back up. "Don't get the wrong idea, Jesse. This has nothing to do with me still wanting us to be together. I'm going back to school to complete my degree. I've applied to two different universities, but thanks to you, I've spent years not touching a piano. I have a lot of catching up to do, so right now I can't be distracted by a divorce."

"So you say, but do you want to know something? There are plenty of other people out there going through divorces. Over the years I've met quite a few of them at my workshops, and even though they're dealing with some really heavy-duty issues, they're still able to do their jobs and take care of their families. Some even manage to work and go to school while they're going through their divorces. So let's be honest with one another, shall we? You're a highly skilled pianist, even if you are out of practice, and you would still be able to play, even after you had me served. So please, stop lying to me, and stop lying to yourself. The reason why you haven't gotten around to filing is because you don't want to."

Emily remained defensive. "No. That's not it at all. You cheated on me, Jesse."

"I know I did, and I just caught you cheating on me."

"But this—"

"I know where you're going, but the fact that we now live under different roofs doesn't make what you've done any less wrong than what I've done. We've both cheated on each other, and we're both equally guilty. Right now, the only one difference between us is that I've forgiven you, but so far, you're unwilling to forgive me."

"All right, Jesse. Now that you've brought it up, how is Annette these days? Is she still as tasty as she was before?"

He took another deep breath. "You two are definitely related, but for the moment I'm letting it slide. To answer your question, I wouldn't know. She's out of the picture. Permanently."

"Really?" Emily remained unconvinced.

"I'm going to be completely honest with you. She came to see me the day after you left. I told her that under the circumstances, I would have to find another assistant. She seemed to be okay with it. I even referred her to another job. However—"

"You had sex with her again, didn't you?"

He looked her in the eye. "As a matter of fact, I did. And the reason why was because I was extremely angry with you. I did the deed with her for the very same reason you've been doing the deed with Dr. Hapner. Revenge." He paused for a moment to gather his thoughts.

"I'm still trying to come to grips with why I ever allowed myself to become involved with her in the first place. It wasn't because I'd fallen out of love with you. I still love you. I always have. I think it happened because I'd been taking you for granted for so long that I allowed the romance to die. You were like a comfortable old shoe, and then your cousin came along. She reminded me of you, in a lot of ways. She kept whining and complaining about Gary, and she kept asking me if I thought she was sexy and pretty. Then one day one thing led to another, and, in a moment of weakness, I succumbed. Not only had I been taking you for granted, I'd been doubting myself as well. I guess I wanted to prove to myself that I was still desired by the opposite sex. I'm not trying to make excuses for what I did. In fact, I'm going to man up and admit that what I did was wrong. Very wrong. It has been and will always be the biggest mistake, and the deepest regret, of my life."

"You said she's out of the picture, for good. So what happened?"

"She somehow convinced herself that I would marry her once we divorced. I kept telling her it would never happen, but she just wouldn't listen. Then one day she told me she'd go public with our affair if I dumped her."

"Annette has always lived in her own little dream world," said Emily. "When she was little, she was notorious for throwing temper tantrums whenever she didn't get her way. So, what did you do after that?"

"I called her bluff. I told her if she went public, I'd simply say I fired her for being incompetent. I also asked her how she planned on explaining it to Gary. She stormed off after that, and I'm happy to say she's not been seen or heard from since. She can rot in hell as far as I'm concerned, and, just so you know, since that time I've been on my own as well." His eyes welled up.

"I want you back, Emily. I even rearranged the furniture to make room for your baby grand. It'll go right there." He pointed out an empty spot across the room. "Yes, I admit I kept you from your music, and I did it on purpose. That too was wrong for me to do. I did it because deep down, I was afraid that if you became successful you might wake up one morning and decide you didn't need me anymore. If it had happened, I would have been lost without you, but it still happened anyway, and for that I have only myself to blame." Tears rolled down his face. He tried to brush them away. "Sorry."

Emily's voice softened. "I wouldn't have left you."

"What?"

"I said I wouldn't have left you, Jesse. What reason would I have had to do that? Yes, I probably would have had to do some traveling, just like you do, so we wouldn't have had as much time together as we had before, but we would have managed somehow. And while I was on the road, I wouldn't have cared about any other men who were out there. There was only one man I ever wanted to be with, and that man was you." She too felt tears coming on. "But now it's too late, isn't it?"

"I don't know. Is it? It's entirely up to you to decide."

"What do you mean?"

"I've said I've forgiven you and I've told you I want you to come home, but you're still angry with me, and you're still harboring a lot of resentment toward me. So unless you're willing to let it go, it would be pointless for us to continue."

Unable to hold herself back, Emily burst into tears. "I don't know what to do anymore. I really don't."

Jesse moved next to her and wrapped his arms around her.

* * *

It was nearly three o'clock in the morning when Roger heard two cars pull into his driveway. He anxiously flung the front door open as he prayed it wasn't the police bringing bad news. To his relief, Emily and Jesse stood on the other side. Their eyes were red and swollen. It was obvious that both had been crying.

"What's going on here?"

"Can we come in, Dad? We need to discuss something with you."

"Of course." He led them to the family room, taking his seat on the recliner as they sat down on the sofa. "So, what's going on?"

"Earlier this evening, I found out about Emily and Dr. Hapner," said Jesse. "She admitted they've been having an affair for the past several weeks."

"What?" Roger gave his daughter a strong look while Emily stared down at the floor.

"It's true, Dad."

He turned to Jesse. "How did you find out about this? Have you been spying on her?"

"No, sir. It happened quite by accident. Earlier this evening I had a client meeting at The Saddleback. Emily just happened to be there, with Dr. Hapner, and when they left, I followed them back to his place. She's still my wife. I have a right to know if she's become involved with another man."

"So what did you do?"

"I parked across the street and waited," said Jesse. "When she finally came back out, I approached her."

"So where was Dr. Hapner?"

"I waited until he went back inside, which, as you can imagine, wasn't easy for me to do. He never knew I was there. That's when I approached Emily, and then I took her back to our house. Along the way she sent you a text message so you wouldn't worry. After we got there, we had that talk."

"And?"

Jesse and Emily looked at one another as he took her hand. "Under the circumstances, I can't condemn her for what she's done. I freely admit that I cheated on her before she cheated on me, so I've forgiven her. Despite everything that's happened, we still love one another, and we want to try to work things out, but we're both fully aware that we have a long and difficult road ahead of us."

"What about Annette?"

"She's gone. For good. I fired her the morning after Emily caught us, and since that time I've made it abundantly clear that I don't ever want to see her again. Emily tells me that Barbara has sided with Annette, which I'm sorry to hear, and she tells me that she and her grandmother are no longer speaking."

"No, they aren't, although I'm hoping they'll be able to work through it."

"It still remains to be seen, Dad," said Emily.

"In the meantime, she and I have our work cut out for us," said Jesse. "We're both guilty of adultery. We've both admitted to one another that what we did was wrong, and what we each did was done out of anger toward the other. We both understand that we need to learn better ways of dealing with our problems, so we've agreed to see a marriage counselor. I've also admitted that I've kept her from her music. It was wrong for me to do as well, so I now support her decision to go back to school." He squeezed her hand

and grinned. "She's still hoping for usc, but I'm pulling for North Texas." His expression turned serious again.

"We've also agreed that we're not ready for her to come home. I have a colleague who's a marriage and family counselor. I'll call him in a few hours and schedule the first available appointment. Then, once we're ready, she'll come home, and she'll bring the Steinway with her. We've also agreed that she'll quit her job. I don't want her working in such close proximately to Dr. Hapner. I'd like for her to leave immediately, but I understand her loyalty to Dr. Lerner, so I've agreed to let her give him two weeks' notice, which she'll be doing as soon as she arrives for work this morning. She's also agreed to tell Dr. Hapner it's over. In the meantime, I'd like for her to continue staying here with you, and I'll take care of her room and board."

Roger looked at Emily. "Are you sure this is what you want?"

"I still love Jesse, Dad, and I want to be able to trust him again. I have to at least give it a try."

Roger turned his attention back to Jesse. "It's not that I dislike you, son, but I'm going to be brutally honest with you. I've always had my doubts about you being the right man for my daughter, and despite everything you're telling me, I can't help but wonder if all you're doing is postponing the inevitable."

"I know you've had your doubts, and I know I've fallen short of your expectations. All I can tell you is we've turned a corner, and I promise to do better."

"Well then, I suppose time will tell. She's an adult, so I'm going to respect her wishes, and I sincerely hope it works out, for both your sakes. In the meantime, it's very late, and she needs her rest."

"I understand."

Jesse got up to leave and Emily walked him to the door. They hugged and kissed goodnight before Jesse stepped out. Emily closed the door behind him, but she still couldn't look her father in the eye.

"I thought you were only seeing Dr. Hapner as a friend." Roger's voice growled as he spoke. "I raised you better than this, Emily. You're still a married woman. So what the hell were you thinking?"

Emily stared at the ground. "I'm not sure, Dad."

"Well then, I guess you should consider yourself lucky. If I'd caught my wife with another man, I would have freaking killed her, regardless of the circumstances."

✨FIFTEEN✨

ANDREA HAD BARELY sat down at her desk when Emily came rushing through the door.

"Emily? Are you alright? You look awful."

"I only got a couple hours' sleep last night. Is your boss in?"

"Dr. Hapner?"

"Yes."

"He should be in his office. He tries to get as much of the paperwork done as he can before he starts seeing patients."

"Thanks."

"Emily, wait—"

Andrea was too late. Emily had already started down the hallway toward Sean's office. His door was open, so she tapped on the doorframe and stepped inside.

"Emily? What are you doing here?" He looked at her more closely. "Are you alright?"

"Yes and no. We need to talk."

He pointed to one of the chairs in front of his desk. "Please, have a seat, but first, would you mind closing the door?"

She quickly shut the door and took her seat. "Jesse found out about us."

Sean looked shocked. "How? Did you tell him?"

"Of course not."

"Then what happened?"

"Apparently he had a client meeting last night at The Saddleback."

"Oh my god. Did he see us?"

"Yes, he saw us," said Emily, "and then he followed us back to your place."

"I noticed a car was behind us, but I thought it was a neighbor."

"No, it wasn't a neighbor. It was Jesse. He saw us go into the house. Then he waited until I came back out."

Sean looked puzzled. "But I walked you out to your car myself. There wasn't anyone out there, at least who I could see. You were fine."

"He waited until you went back inside. That's when he approached me."

"Emily, I'm so sorry. I didn't hear a sound. If I had, you know I would have come running. He didn't hurt you, did he?"

"No, he didn't. I'm fine, but he was shocked, of course. Then he said he wanted to talk, so we went to his place. We've decided to work things out."

"Really?" Sean sounded skeptical. "So, what about Annette?"

"She's gone. He said he'd fired her, and I remember my grandmother mentioning something about it right before she and I stopped speaking." Emily looked him in the eye. "This means I can't see you anymore, Sean, and I'm sure you can understand why. I'm also giving Dr. Lerner my notice."

"I understand."

"But before I go, I want you to know that you've been a true friend, with or without the benefits, and you really did help me through a very dark time in my life." She stood from her chair and extended her hand. "So my wish for you is that the next one will be a keeper. For what it's worth, I think you'd be a great catch."

A sad look came over his face as they shook hands. "I understand, and I know we'd both agreed there'd be no strings attached, but lately a part of me had been thinking that maybe once your divorce went through, we could have some sort of a future together, but I guess it wasn't meant to be."

"No, I'm afraid it wasn't."

"You'll always be special to me, Mrs. St. Claire. You've helped me through a rough time in my life as well."

He walked her to the door and kissed her on the cheek before he opened it. "Thank you for everything, Emily. I'll sincerely miss you, and I wish you the very best."

"You too, Sean." She gave him a quick nod and hurried away.

* * *

Emily found Dr. Lerner in his private office. He glanced up from his paperwork as she stopped at the doorway.

"Good morning, Emily." He studied her more closely. "Are you alright? You look a little pale."

"I didn't sleep very well last night."

"I see. So what was keeping you up?"

"Jesse and I accidentally ran into one another last night, and we ended up talking until the wee hours of the morning. He realizes he made a huge mistake, so we've decided to work things out."

Dr. Lerner looked surprised. "But weren't you were making plans to go to school out of state?"

"I am, and Jesse will go with me when the time comes. In the meantime, we've both agreed that I need to concentrate fulltime on my music, so I'm giving you my two-week notice, effective today."

"I see." Dr. Lerner's expression turned sad. "Well, we're certainly going to miss you."

"And I'll miss you and Cathy as well. You've been a terrific boss to work for. I'll get in touch with the agency this morning and let them know you'll be needing a new office manager."

"Please do. I'd appreciate it."

A huge sense of relief came over Emily as she returned to her desk. Jesse called a short time later to let her know they would see the marriage counselor the following Monday. Andrea arrived at lunchtime and followed Emily into the breakroom, but she looked concerned as they took their seats.

"What on earth is going on with you today? Dr. Hapner has been acting depressed ever since you flew out the door. Did you two have an argument?"

"No. Jesse found out about us."

Andrea looked shocked. "Oh my god. Are you okay?"

"Yes, I'm fine. We're all good."

"I see. So, what happened?"

Cathy stepped into the room and Emily didn't want to say too much. "Short story long, we've decided to work things out."

"And I wish you the best of luck on that." Cathy sat down to join them. "Dr. Lerner says you'll be leaving in two weeks. We're going to miss you."

"And I'll miss you too. It's been great working with you."

Cathy gave Emily a warm smile. "Thanks. It's been great working with you as well. Just try to think about us every once in a while, once you're rich and famous concert pianist. Okay?"

↱SIXTEEN↰

JESSE TOOK EMILY to dinner on Saturday night, calling it a date night. They had their first session with the marriage counselor following Monday. Both had issues to resolve, but each was willing to compromise with the other. Jesse kissed Emily goodbye when he walked her to her car, and he accepted her invitation to join her and her father for Thanksgiving dinner the following Thursday. It would be a more subdued celebration than previous years. Afterwards he stayed and helped with the cleanup.

Emily's final day with Dr. Lerner came the following Friday. He and Cathy treated her to lunch at an upscale restaurant, and they invited Andrea to come along. Over the meal, Andrea mentioned her boss was doing well, but Emily changed the subject before Andrea could elaborate. Afterwards both women hugged each other goodbye and promised to keep in touch.

Jesse and Emily continued their sessions with the marriage counselor. Jesse thought they were making progress. He still loved Emily and he was willing to do whatever it took to win her back. Emily, however, continued to harbor some doubts. Jesse's infidelity had completely blindsided her, and rebuilding her trust would be difficult. She still thought of Kyle from time to time, and her lingering attraction to him troubled her.

As Christmas approached, the marriage counselor suggested they spend the holiday together. Roger had already made plans to spend Christmas in Minneapolis with Nick and his family, so Jesse invited her to San Diego for a beachside holiday. Emily hesitated at first, only accepting his invitation after assuring her they would stay in separate rooms.

Jesse picked Emily up early Christmas Eve morning, and after few hours' drive they arrived at the Hotel del Coronado. Emily loved the beautiful Queen Anne architecture. The hotel's famous, red-roofed turrets were decked out with glittering holiday lights, and she was even more amazed once they stepped inside the lobby. Dark oak panels covered the walls. The wood-beamed ceiling was two stories high, and the elegant chandelier had a sparkle all its own. Topping off the scene was a big, beautifully decorated Christmas tree.

"It's quite a place, isn't it?" said Jesse.

"It certainly is, and it's not that I don't appreciate it, but can we afford it?"

Jesse smiled and squeezed her hand. "Don't worry, my dear. Rank has its privileges. I know people, and I was able to get us a special rate."

"You've been here before, haven't you?"

"A few times, but only for business. I've worked a few conferences here and it was a place I always wanted to bring you." He gave her a kiss. "Merry Christmas, Emily. I want you enjoy a few days of pampering. With everything I've put you through, you certainly deserve it."

Once they checked in, Jesse led Emily to the historic elevator. Stepping off on their floor, he walked her to her room. It, too, was beautifully furnished. Jesse waited with her until her bags arrived. Afterwards he tipped the bellman and kissed her on the cheek before going next door to his room to change. Ten minutes later they headed off to the beach. They stopped to admire the ice rink that had been set up on the sand and they held hands as they strolled along the shore. Emily watched the waves as they crashed into the sand. It felt as if they were washing away the long nightmare she had been living. Suddenly, she felt a cold shiver running down her spine.

"Are you alright?" Jesse sounded concerned.

"I'm fine. I just felt a little chill for a moment, but I'm okay now."

"You know, it is getting a little cool out here." Jesse wrapped his arm around her shoulder and kissed her cheek once again. "It's also time to head back in and get ready for dinner. Did I mention this place has restaurants that are out of this world?"

* * *

Emily heard a knock at her door as she put on her earrings. Jesse waited on the other side. Once again, he greeted her with a kiss.

"You brought your little black dress."

"Indeed, I did. As I recall, it was your favorite."

"And it still is."

As he stepped into the room her phone started ringing. She reached into her purse and frowned as she checked the caller ID.

"Who is it?" asked Jesse.

"My grandmother. Somehow it figures. I haven't heard from her in weeks, and now, here she is. Her sense of timing is impeccable. She's always had a knack for raining on people's parades, and I'm really tempted to let it go to voice mail."

"Don't." Jesse's voice sounded firm. "Otherwise, she'll keep calling back, every half hour, until you answer. Besides, it's Christmas Eve, and you and I are on our way back to where we belong. It's time to let it go and wish her a Merry Christmas."

Emily shook her head as she accepted the call. "Hi Grandma. Merry Christmas."

"I just got off the phone with your brother." Her grandmother's voice had its usual demanding undertone. "I know your father is in Minneapolis and you're at home alone, so why don't you come over here?"

"Where are you, Grandma?"

"I'm at your Aunt Heather's house. I'm with her, and your cousin."

"Which one?"

"Tonya. Gary and Annette have other plans tonight, but I'll be seeing them tomorrow. Meantime, I'm very concerned about the fact that it's Christmas Eve, and you'd rather be home by yourself instead of reaching out to your family."

"Actually, Grandma, I already had an invite from Eddie and Gwen. You know, my other cousins. On Dad's side of the family."

"Oh."

Emily heard the distinct sound of disapproval in her grandmother's voice. "Besides," she said, "this year none of you invited me to any of your holiday celebrations."

"So, I'm inviting you. Now." As usual, her grandmother's invitation sounded more like a command.

"Sorry, Grandma, but I won't be able to make it. At the moment I'm in California, with Jesse."

"With Jesse?" Barbara sounded stunned.

"Yes, Grandma, I'm with Jesse. He's still my husband, and we're trying to work things out."

"Well, hallelujah. It's about time you came to your senses. I've been telling you for months now that this was nothing more than a misunderstanding that's been blown way out of proportion. It's about time you stopped telling all your vicious lies about your cousin. You know, he fired her because of you, and she's—"

Jesse could hear Barbara's end of the conversation through Emily's phone. "May I?" he asked, under his breath. Emily gladly handed him her phone.

"Merry Christmas, Mrs. Leary." Jesse tried to sound upbeat.

"Well, Jesse. Merry Christmas to you too." There was a phony sweetness in Barbara's voice.

"Thank you." His voice took on a serious tone. "I'd like to take a moment to set the record straight, if I may, once and for all. There was never any misunderstanding about anything on Emily's part, and everything she's told you is the truth. I fully admit that last summer I had an inappropriate relationship with your other granddaughter, and Annette was a willing participant in that relationship. It was a huge mistake on my part, and Emily did indeed catch us in the act. It damn near cost me my marriage, and I've taken full responsibility for my wrongdoings. I don't know what Annette may have told you, but my decision to fire her was mine and mine alone, and I'd think by now my reason should be pretty clear. At the time I let her go, Emily and I weren't speaking to one another, so please, quit blaming her for something she didn't do. And by the way, I also referred Annette to another job, with better pay I might add, but for whatever reason, she wasn't hired."

For the moment Barbara was speechless. Jesse went on.

"I want Annette out of my life, Mrs. Leary. Emily wants her out of her life as well, and I'm sure you can understand the reason why. I'm sorry it's come to this, and I'll always regret my part in creating a rift in your family, but I'm afraid it's the way things will have to be from now on. Emily and I will be here in California for the holidays, and then she and Megan will be leaving for their cruise right after the first of the year. We're hoping she'll be ready to move back home once she returns, and then maybe we can have you over for dinner. In the meantime, we'd like to wish you, and your daughter, and Tonya, a very Merry Christmas, and we look forward to seeing you sometime in the New Year."

He disconnected the call and handed the phone back to Emily. "Hopefully that'll shut the old battleax up for a while. So are you okay?"

"I'm fine," she said, "and I hope you finally got through to her, because she sure wouldn't listen to me."

"I think she may have gotten the message. At least for now." He smiled and gave her a reassuring hug. "But even if she didn't, it's not your fault. I know she's your grandmother, but it's a toxic relationship. You have every right to live your life in peace and to not have to put up with her abuse. In the meantime, you're sure you're okay?"

"I'm fine, Jesse."

He looked into her eyes and kissed her. "In that case, I guess we'd better get going. I made dinner reservations for seven o'clock, but hold that thought, okay?"

She gave him a nervous smile and they headed out.

* * *

Emily stifled a yawn as she unlocked her door. "You were right. That restaurant was out of this world. I haven't had a meal that good in a long, long time, but it's been a long day and I'm beat. So if you don't mind, I'm going to take a nice, long bubble bath, and then I'm going to bed. Goodnight, Jesse."

"Goodnight, Emily, and Merry Christmas."

She looked into his eyes and smiled. "Merry Christmas, Jesse and thank you again for bringing me here. This place really is magical."

He wrapped his arms around her and kissed her passionately. She welcomed his embrace. When the kiss was over, she stood breathless.

"I think that's enough for now." Her voice sounded nervous. "Good night. I'll see you in the morning."

"Good night, Emily. I'll see you bright and early. Tomorrow's Christmas. We have presents to unwrap." He gave her a quick peck on the lips and headed back to his room. Once inside, he grabbed the remote and turned on the television set. He spent some time channel surfing, but was unable to focus, so stripped down to his shorts and climbed into bed. Unable to make himself comfortable, he looked at the clock on the nightstand. It was a few minutes past ten. He tried channel surfing again, and once again, nothing grabbed his attention. He looked back at the clock. A mere five minutes had passed. Tossing the remote aside, he hopped off the bed and reached for his phone and paced around the room as he waited for Emily to pick up

"You okay?"

"I'm fine, Jesse. I was just about to step into the bathtub."

"The hotel is haunted, you know. I just wanted to make sure you're okay."

"Don't worry. There's no ghost in here. Remember me asking the bellman about it when he delivered our luggage? This isn't Kate Morgan's room, and neither is yours."

"I know. I was just making sure." He started making ghostly sounds, smiling at the sound of her laughter.

"Stop that," she said with a giggle.

"I'm not doing anything. I told you, this place is haunted."

"Yeah, by you." The laughter remained in her voice. "I'm fine, Jesse. Good night. My bathwater awaits, and I don't want it getting cold."

"No worries. I can come over and help you keep it warm. After all, we need to conserve water, and what better way to do it then by taking a bath together."

After an awkward moment of silence Emily took a more serious tone. "Actually, I really am tired. It's been a long day and I need to get some rest. I'll see you in the morning. Bright and early."

He realized he had pushed her a little too hard, so he tried to conceal his disappointment. "Well, now that you mention it, I'm kind of tired myself. So I'll see you tomorrow morning, my room, and we'll open our presents."

"Sounds like a plan. Good night, Jesse."

"Goodnight, Emily."

* * *

Emily stepped up to Jesse's doorway as the room-service waiter came out. Entering the room, she wished him a Merry Christmas as she took her seat at the foot of his unmade bed and set her shopping bag down next to her feet. Jesse handed her a cup of coffee and gave her a quick kiss.

"I see you still have your favorite green robe."

She glanced down and ran her hand along the fabric. "Yes, I do, and even though it's getting a little ratty, it's still very comfy. Hope you don't mind me wearing it."

"Not at all. It's Christmas morning, so please, relax and make yourself comfortable." He reached into his duffle bag, taking out a small, giftwrapped box before taking his seat next to her.

"Merry Christmas, Emily."

"Thank you." She carefully unwrapped the box. Inside was another small box, only this one was black velvet. Lifting the lid, she found a beautiful emerald ring in an ornate white gold setting. A small diamond was mounted on each side of the emerald.

"Jesse, I don't know what to say."

He wrapped his arm around her shoulder and kissed her on the cheek. "I wanted to get you something really special. Something to symbolize our getting back together. And since green is my favorite color, and emeralds are your birthstone, I thought this would be the perfect gift." He took the ring from the box and carefully placed it on her right ring finger. "Just as I thought. It's fits perfectly, and it looks fabulous on you."

The stones sparkled as Emily admired it. "It's beautiful, but I'm afraid my gift to you isn't nearly as elegant."

"It's alright, Emily. Just having you here with me is all the present I want." He took her into his arms and kissed her passionately as he ran his hands up and down her back. He felt her body tremble.

"Are you alright?"

She shook her head, as her eyes welled up with tears.

"It's okay, Emily."

A tear rolled down her cheek. He gently brushed it away as he spoke. "Don't be nervous. I'm not going to hurt you. Not ever again." He gave her a soft kiss, running his lips down her neck and shoulder before he reached down and untied her robe. She wore a simple white cotton nightgown underneath. He kissed her again, slipping his hand inside her gown, gently caressing her breast. He heard her softly moan.

"Are you ready?"

"I'm not sure."

He held her in his arms. "It's okay." He stroked her face, running his fingers through her hair and kissing her again. She started to relax. He kissed and stroked her all over, slowly and carefully pulling her nightgown down to her waist. She sighed in contentment as he kissed her breasts and gently eased her down on the bed. He pulled her nightgown off and gazed at her naked body. She returned his gaze with a frightened, vulnerable look.

"I love you, Emily." His voice choked with emotion as he spoke. "And I'm giving you my solemn vow, right here and now, that I will never, ever do anything to hurt you again."

He gently stroked her as he kissed her, this time with more passion as he worked his way down, hearing her soft moans as he stroked her. He stopped for a moment and quickly undressed. Her skin felt soft and warm as he lay back down next to her, kissing her breasts. She giggled as he kissed his way down the rest of her body and kissed his way back up again.

"You liked that, did you?"

"Yes," she said with a laugh. "Can you do it again? And take your time."

"As you wish, my lady."

He slowly kissed his way down a second time. She arched her back, moaning with pleasure at the warm sensation as she felt when he finally kissed her sweet spot. He continued to kiss and please her. Her pleasure grew until she finally let herself go, her body twisting and writhing in her ecstasy. As she began to relax, he slowly kissed his way back up, his tongue swirling around her nipples as she stroked his head.

"So, did my lady like that?"

"She sure did."

Now it was his turn. She began pleasing him and he closed his eyes, moaning in his pleasure. He soon entered her. She wrapped her legs around him as he sucked on her breast while his groans grew louder and more intense. He soon reached his release, and she held him tight. He came down and her body trembled again.

"Are you okay?" he asked.

"I don't know." She paused for a moment. "I'm still coming to grips with everything that's happened, and I wasn't sure if you'd ever want me back."

"Well of course I want you back." He gave her a reassuring squeeze as he kissed her and stroked the side of her face. "But I wasn't sure if you would take me back either." He held her close, resting his head on her chest.

"I still love you, Jesse. I always have. I'm just not sure if I'm ready to move back in with you."

"And I still love you too, so I want you to take your time. I want you to go on your cruise with Megan, just like you planned, and give yourself sometime to decide what you want. It's what we've both agreed on."

"I know, and hopefully I'll be ready to come home once I get back."

He brushed the side of her face. "I hope so too, but even if you're not, I'm patient. What matters is you'll come home someday, and once it happens, we'll be together for the rest of our lives."

❧SEVENTEEN❧

JESSE GLANCED AT the caller ID and smiled. "Hi Emmy. Do you miss me already?"

"You know I do."

"You must be getting ready to head for the airport."

"Megan's on her way to pick me up, but I have a problem."

"What's up?"

"I can't find my passport, and I've searched everyplace imaginable for it. Could I have left it in your safe?"

"It's entirely possible. I'm in my office, so if you'll hold on for a second, I'll take a look." He set the phone down and walked up to the small safe sitting in the corner. Sure enough, Emily's passport was inside. He picked up the phone and smiled again.

"It's right here. Now you have an excuse to stop by and tell me goodbye one more time."

"Okay, but Megan will be with me," said Emily with a laugh.

"I know, but I'm going to miss you like crazy while you're gone."

"Me too."

"You don't know how good it feels to hear you say that." He heard a doorbell ringing in the background, along with Lurch's barks. "Sounds like Megan has arrived."

"She has indeed. We'll be there shortly."

* * *

Megan turned her car into Jesse's driveway and parked in front of the garage. Emily quickly hopped out.

"Wait here. I'll only be a minute." She ran up to the front door and rang the bell. Jesse greeted her with a smile and handed over her passport as she stepped across the threshold.

"Here you go," he said. "Make sure you keep it in a safe place."

"I know, I know."

He wrapped his arms around her. "I know you're excited, and I know you'll have a good time, but just be careful, okay? Stay with your group when you do your off-ship excursions. The Caribbean is a beautiful place, but don't go wandering the back roads by yourselves."

"I know, Jesse. Don't worry, we'll be fine."

He gave her a kiss and walked her out Megan's car. "Have fun, be safe, and I love you."

"I love you too, Jesse."

He opened the car door, saying a quick hello to Megan as Emily sat down in the passenger seat. He closed the car door and waved goodbye. As the car slowly backed into the street, he turned and stepped back inside the house. Megan was about to drive away when an older man, walking a dog, stepped off the curb and approached them. Emily asked her to wait as she rolled her window down.

"Well, hello, Jorge. How have you been?"

"I've been good, Emily. How 'bout you? I haven't seen you in a long time. Not since the morning you moved your things out. Is everything okay now?"

"It couldn't be better." She introduced him to Megan, saying Jorge and his wife lived two doors down.

"Jesse and I have been working things out. My buddy and I are taking a short trip together, and then when I return, I'm moving back in."

He gave her a warm smile. "I'm glad, Emily. Marta and I have wondered about you, and we were hoping you were okay."

"I'm fine."

"Well then, you two ladies have a safe trip, and I'll see you when you get back."

"Thanks, Jorge. Please tell Marta hello for me."

"Will do."

They waved goodbye and Megan drove off.

* * *

Jesse was busy at his computer when the doorbell rang again. He glanced at the clock. Emily had been gone less than ten minutes. He rushed to the front door.

"Hi honey. What'd you forget this time?" His smile instantly faded once he realized who stood on the other side. "What the hell are you doing here?"

"Now is that any way to greet an old friend? You know, for a moment there I really thought you missed me. Not who you were expecting, huh?"

His tone turned hostile. "What do you want, Annette?"

"Why I've come to see you, of course. You and my grandmother must have had quite a conversation on Christmas Eve. I hear Emily's going on a cruise with Megan, and imagine my surprise when Grandma told me the two of you were working things out. With all of this going on, you and I need to have a long talk."

"There's nothing to discuss. I also told your grandmother, quite clearly in fact, that we both want you out of our lives, but before you go, I need to return something that belongs to you."

"What is it?"

"Your scarf. The orange one. The one you said was missing. The other day I found it in the back of the bedroom closet. I was going to mail it to you, but since you're here, I'll go get it for you, and then I want you to leave. Wait here. I'll be back in a minute."

He closed the front door but didn't think to lock it. A strange feeling came over him as he headed up the stairs. He turned around when he reached the top landing. Annette had come inside the house, and she was following him up the stairs. He blocked her path as she reached the top.

"I told you to wait outside." His voice was stern.

"I'm not leaving. Not until you and I have a talk."

"In that case, I'm calling the police." He started down the hallway toward the bedroom.

"Now is that anyway for you to treat the mother of your child?"

He spun around again. "What did you just say?"

"Congratulations, Jesse." A triumphant smile broke out across her face. "You're about to become a daddy."

"You're lying."

"No, I'm not." Annette reached inside her purse and took out a white plastic stick. "I did the test earlier this morning and it came out positive. Here, come and take a look for yourself."

Jesse scowled as he stood his ground and folded his arms across his chest. "Get that thing away from me. I don't need to see it because it's not my baby. Go home to Gary. He's the father."

"We split up."

"When?"

"A few weeks ago. I finally told him about us."

"Liar. I spoke to your grandmother on Christmas Eve, remember? She said she was at your mother's house, with her and your sister. She also said you and Gary weren't there because you had other plans, but she'd be seeing the two of you on Christmas day. Go home, Annette. Gary can help you decorate the nursery."

"It's not his baby. It's yours."

Jesse started laughing. "You stupid, pathetic little bitch. I guess Emily never told you, did she?"

"Told me what?"

"I couldn't father a child if I wanted to. Why do you think that after eight years of marriage, Emily and I still don't have any kids?"

"You're lying."

"No, I'm not, but as long as we're on the subject, I may as well tell you the whole story. My freshman year of college, I answered an ad in the student newspaper. The medical school needed sperm donors for some sort of study, so I was more than happy to volunteer my services. Then someone called me a few days later. There was a problem. My sperm count was extremely low, so I went back and they ran some tests. They poked and prodded and did all kinds of nasty little things to my manhood. Finally, they told me I had some sort of genetic defect. I'm shooting blanks. I can't produce enough sperm to father a child."

"And Emily knows this?"

"Of course she knows this. I told her about it before we got engaged, and she was okay with it. With her music, she wasn't sure if she wanted kids either."

Annette pondered his words and shook her head. "No, I'm not buying it. You're lying."

Jesse took a couple steps toward her, his eyes ablaze. "I have had enough of you, you lying little slut. This isn't my baby, so I'll get a court order for a paternity test."

Annette stepped backwards, losing her balance as she backed into the staircase. For a brief instant Jesse saw a look of panic on her face, but he wasn't close enough to grab her. She never had the chance to scream. Her body plunged backward, her head smashing into the rails as she crashed down on the landing.

"Annette!"

Jesse raced down the stairs, staring in horror once he reached the landing. Annette's body briefly jerked and twitched. Afterwards she lay completely still. Her eyes were open, but she had a blank stare. He waved his hand in front of them and snapped his fingers, but she didn't respond. He felt along the side of her neck for a pulse but couldn't find one. Her blank, unblinking stare remained as blood began oozing from her nose and the corner of her mouth. A small pool formed at the back of her skull while more blood seeped from her ears.

"No!"

Jesse knew he had to call for help. His hands shook violently as he reached into his pocket for his phone and punched the numbers in. An eternity seemed to pass before someone finally answered.

"Nine-one-one. What is your emergency?"

"There's been an accident." His voice shook, making it difficult for him to speak. "Someone just fell down the stairs. She hit her head when she fell and she's not moving. She's bleeding and I can't find her pulse."

"Calm down, sir. I'm dispatching the paramedics. Have you tried CPR?"

"No. I never got around to taking the training." He choked back a sob as he spoke. "Besides, I don't know if it would do any good. There's blood everywhere." The realization finally hit him. "Oh, god! She's dead, isn't she?"

"Please sir, try to stay calm. The paramedics are on their way. I'll stay on the line with you until they arrive."

"We were talking. Up on the top landing, but then she stepped backward and fell. I never touched her. One minute she was there. The next minute she wasn't. It all happened so fast. Oh, god, this can't be happening." He let out a few more choking sobs, desperately trying to pull himself back together while he gave the dispatcher his address. She remained on the line, telling him to stay calm. He soon heard distant sirens. They grew louder as they came closer.

"The paramedics have arrived, sir," said the dispatcher. "As soon as you let them in, I'll disconnect the call."

Jesse rushed down the lower flight of stairs and flung the front door open. Two paramedics hurried in as the dispatcher hung up. He led them to the landing, anxiously standing by as they examined Annette. One medic grabbed a defibrillator and tried to jump start her heart. After a few unsuccessful attempts the other medic shook his head.

"She's gone." He grabbed a clipboard and started writing while his partner radioed their dispatcher. More sirens could be heard, and two police officers entered the house. One immediately called for backup while the other took Jesse aside and started questioning him. Jesse's voice sounded flat as he tried to explain what happened.

"Her name is Annette Claiborne. She's my wife's cousin. I went to get a scarf she'd accidentally left here. We were talking at the top of the stairs when she somehow lost her balance and fell. It was an accident. I swear, on everything that is holy, that I never, ever touched her."

"I understand, sir. A detective is on his way. He'll want to speak to you as soon as he arrives. In the meantime, is your wife here?"

"No. She's on her way to the airport. She and her friend are on their way to Miami. They're going on a cruise."

"What airline is she flying?"

"American."

"What's the flight number?"

"I don't know."

"Can you find out for me?"

Jesse led him to his office, handing him a sheet of paper lying on top of his desk. "Here's a copy of her itinerary."

"Thank you, and would you mind taking a seat in here? The detective will be here shortly."

Jesse sat down at his desk and buried his face in his hands, desperately hoping it would somehow all go away. He overheard a hub of activity happening outside. People were coming and going. Someone was taking photos. One man announced that he was from the county medical examiner's office. Another voice mentioned something about notifying next of kin. He looked up when a man with graying hair and a business suit entered the room and presented a badge.

"Mr. St. Claire?"

"Yes?"

"I'm Beau Fowler. I'm a detective with the Phoenix Police Department and I'm in charge of this investigation. I need to ask you a few questions."

"Of course." Jesse pointed to the chair across his desk. The detective sat down and took out a small notebook.

"Okay, Mr. St. Claire, can you tell me what happened?"

"Her name is Annette Claiborne. She's my wife's first cousin, and for a time she was also my assistant."

"Is she still working for you?"

"No. I terminated her employment last July."

"May I ask why?"

Jesse shifted in his chair. "At the time I was romantically involved with Ms. Claiborne. Then my wife came home unexpectedly one day and caught us in the act. She immediately packed her bags and left. I fired Ms. Claiborne the following day."

"I see. So what happened after that?"

"You mean was I still seeing her? After I fired her?"

"Yes."

Jesse hesitated for a moment. "Yes. I continued to be, involved, with her for several more weeks."

"Are you still involved with her?"

Jesse looked the detective in the eye. "No, sir, I'm not."

"All right. So who finally ended the relationship?"

"I did."

"When was this?"

"This past September. It was sometime around the middle of the month, although I can't recall the exact day."

"Was that the last time you saw her? Until today?"

"Yes, sir, it was. Since that time my wife and I have been in the process of reconciling. We've both made it abundantly clear to the rest of the family that we wish no further contact with Annette."

The detective took more notes. "I see. So why was she here today?"

"I'm not sure. I certainly didn't invite her. I did, however, have a telephone conversation with Barbara Leary, my wife's grandmother, on Christmas Eve. I mentioned that Emily, that's my wife, and I were seeing a marriage counselor and were in the process of working things out, and that she'd be moving back in sometime after the first of the year. Barbara must have passed the information on to Annette."

"So where's your wife now?"

"At the airport. She's on her way to Miami. She's going on a cruise with one of her friends. I gave one of the other officers my copy of her itinerary."

"You said your wife would be moving back in soon, correct?"

"Yes. At least that's what we were hoping. She's been living with her father since last summer."

"Was she also by chance here today?"

"Yes, she was. She called me and said she couldn't find her passport. Turned out it was in my safe, so she stopped by to pick it up on her way to the airport."

"When was this?"

Jesse looked at his watch. "About an hour ago."

"Was Ms. Claiborne here when your wife was here?"

"No, she was not. Annette showed up about ten minutes after Emily left."

The detective stepped outside. Jesse heard him talking to someone, but he couldn't make out what they were saying. He returned a short time later.

"Another detective is on his way to the airport to question your wife."

Jesse was becoming exasperated. "Look, I've already told you that Emily wasn't here when this happened. She left about ten minutes before Annette showed up."

"I understand, but we still need to talk to her. She also needs to be informed of her cousin's death." Jesse cringed while the detective went over his notes. "We found a home pregnancy test strip next to Ms. Claiborne's body. Can you explain why it's there?"

"She told me she was pregnant, and that I'm the father."

"Are you?"

Jesse shook his head. "No sir, I'm not. I'm unable to father a child."

"I see. However, we'll still need to take a DNA sample from you so we can compare it to the fetus. Don't worry. It's just a swab on the inside of your mouth. We'll also need to take your shirt into evidence. We need to run some tests on it."

Jesse's heart skipped a beat. "Am I under arrest?"

"Not at this time. We're still trying to determine what happened."

"It was an accident. I swear, on everything that is holy, that I never laid a hand on her. I went upstairs to get a scarf she'd accidentally left here sometime last summer. I told her to wait outside, but she came inside the house, uninvited, and she followed me up the stairs. That's when she showed me the test strip, and we argued over my being the father of her unborn child. During that argument she somehow lost her balance and fell, but I swear, I never, ever touched her."

As Beau scribbled more notes on his pad Jesse finally realized he could be charged with manslaughter. He felt his stomach tighten, and he held his breath as a uniformed officer stepped into the room and approached the detective.

"Sir, there's a neighbor outside who you might want to talk to."

"I'll be right out."

The officer stepped away. Beau turned his attention back to Jesse.

"I'm going to step outside for a few minutes. While I'm away someone will be coming in to take that swab and take your shirt into evidence. I'll send someone upstairs to bring you another shirt."

"Will I be done then?"

"No, I'm afraid not. We're still gathering evidence, and no doubt I'll have more questions for you. In the meantime, you need to stay in this room and not go anywhere. We're going to be here for a while."

❧EIGHTEEN❧

EMILY AND MEGAN sipped their coffee as they watched other passengers coming and going while they waited for their flight to be called. A sandy-haired man, wearing a business suit, caught Emily's eye. He too was scanning the crowd, and as he looked her way, he stared back at her. Her heart skipped a beat once she realized who he was. An airport police officer stepped up to join him as Emily tapped Megan's forearm.

"Do you recall me telling you about the man I met last fall, when I did that gig at the art gallery?"

"Yeah, I think so."

Emily nodded toward him. "That's him, right over there, standing next to that other cop. I wonder what he's doing here."

"Are you alright? You look a little flushed."

Emily tried to shrug it off. "I'm fine. You know, I've thought about him a few times since that night. I was just curious."

"Well, you know what curiosity did to the cat, and now it looks like Mr. Policeman and his sidekick are heading our way."

The man quickly approached them. "Emily St. Claire?"

"Yes, I'm Emily."

His face lit up as he looked at her more closely. "I know you. We met a few months ago. You were playing the piano at Hanson Sisters Fine Art."

"Yes, that was me, and I remember you as well. You're Kyle Madden, and you're a police detective."

His demeanor changed as he presented her with his badge. "Yes, I am, and I'm afraid I'm here on official police business. I need to talk to you two ladies in private. If you'll please come with us."

"What's going on?" asked Megan.

"I'll explain in a minute. If you would please come with us."

"What about our flight?"

"I'll explain in a minute, Ms. Connors, if you'll kindly follow me."

Megan was becoming agitated. "How do you know my name?"

"It's okay, Megan," said Emily. "Let's go find out what's going on. Our flight won't be leaving for another forty-five minutes. The plane isn't even here yet."

As they followed him from the gate the airport officer led them through a side door into a restricted area. They walked down a hallway to a small, stark room with a table and chairs inside. Emily wondered if it was some sort of interrogation room. Kyle told to her to go inside and take a seat.

"If you'll please wait out here with the other officer, Ms. Connors, I'll be with you shortly."

"We haven't done anything wrong, so what's going on?"

"It's okay, Megan." Emily wanted to reassure Megan as much as herself. "There's probably been some sort of mix-up about something. Whatever it is, we'll get it straightened out."

Kyle followed her into the room and closed the door behind her. His expression turned sober as he sat down across the table from her and took out his pen and notepad.

"Mrs. St. Claire, I brought you here because I'm afraid I have some bad news. There's been an incident involving your husband and your cousin, Annette Claiborne, and I regret to inform you that your cousin has died."

Emily was stunned. "What?"

"It happened about an hour ago, at your residence."

"You mean my husband's residence."

Kyle looked puzzled. "Your husband's residence?"

"Yes. My husband and I separated this past summer. I'm currently living with my father."

"I see." Kyle stopped and cleared his throat. "Yes, it was your husband's residence. Were you by chance there today?"

"Yes, I was. I couldn't find my passport, so I called Jesse. Turned out it was still locked up in the safe, in Jesse's office. I'd forgotten to take it with me when I moved out. Anyway, Jesse works out of his home. He's a motivational speaker. You know, he does workshops and seminars, that sort of thing."

"Yes, I know. However, I'm trying to find out what happened. When did you go to your husband's residence?"

"Megan and I stopped by there on our way here."

"And what time was that?"

"I'm not exactly sure. It was sometime around nine o'clock, give or take a few minutes."

"All right. So what happened when you arrived?"

"Nothing out of the ordinary. I told Megan to wait in the car while I went to get it. Jesse met me at the front door and handed it to me, then he walked me back out to the car. He said goodbye and Megan and I left." She paused. "Is Jesse all right?"

"He's fine. He wasn't injured."

"So what happened?"

"I'm getting to that. Did you happen to see your cousin while you were there?"

"Annette?"

"Yes. Did you see Annette while you were there?"

Emily's demeanor instantly changed. "No, I most certainly did not see my cousin while I was there. Trust me, if I'd so much as seen her car parked somewhere down the street, I would have spoken up about it. So would you please tell me what's going on?"

"I take it you and your cousin did not have a good relationship."

"That, Detective Madden, is the understatement of the year." There was a hint of sarcasm in Emily's voice. "No, Annette and I do not have a good relationship. So, I'm asking you once again, would you please tell me what's going on?"

"All we know at this point is that your cousin showed up, apparently unannounced, at your husband's residence, sometime between nine and nine-fifteen this morning. Your husband says he went upstairs to retrieve something that apparently belonged to her. He said she followed him up the stairs, but then she somehow fell down the stairwell and suffered a fatal injury as a result. Right now, I'm afraid it's all I can tell you. The case is still under investigation."

"Oh my god, I have to go. Right now." She stood from her chair and grabbed her purse, along with her carry-on bag.

"I'm sorry, Mrs. St. Claire, but I'm afraid you can't leave just yet."

She gave him a strong look. "Oh yeah? Watch me."

She opened the door and the airport officer stepped forward, blocking her path. Kyle stepped forward and closed the door, motioning for her to return to her seat.

"You'll be free to go in a few minutes, I promise. I just have a couple more questions for you. I also need to let you know that your husband's home is still cordoned off. You won't be able to enter until after they've completed their investigation, and it may take several more hours."

"What about my husband? Can I at least call him?"

"I'm sorry, but at the moment he's still being questioned."

"Is he under arrest?"

"Not at this time."

"Will he be arrested?"

"I don't know." Kyle pointed to the chair. "But if you would please return to your seat, we can finish up our business here."

Emily grudgingly sat back down while Kyle went over his notes.

"So, you and your cousin did not have a close relationship. Why was that?"

"She was having an affair with my husband, and I caught them in the act."

Kyle raised his brow. "I see. So when was this?"

"Last summer. At the time Annette was Jesse's assistant. I packed my bags and moved out of the house the same day I caught them, then Jesse fired her the following day. Their other relationship ended a few weeks later. At least that's what Jesse tells me. Then, just before Thanksgiving, I agreed to go with him to see a marriage counselor, and we were in the process of reconciling. Megan and I had planned our cruise several months ago, and I was hoping to be ready to move back in with my husband when we returned." She stopped and thought it over for a moment. "Oh my god. Could Jesse still be involved with Annette? Could he have still been seeing her all this time? While he and I were trying to work things out?"

"I don't know, Emily. I'm afraid you'll have to take it up with your husband. All I can tell you right now is your cousin is dead, and we're trying to establish what happened. So, for now, let's not jump to any conclusions, okay?" Realizing she was fighting back tears, his voice took a softer, gentler tone. "Anyway, I think we're done here. I need to ask Ms. Connors a few questions, and while you're waiting, I'll have one of the officers bring you a glass of water."

"Thank you." She paused for a moment. "So what about our flight?"

"We've already alerted the airline, and they've pulled your luggage aside. If you'd like, I'll see if one of the airport officers can have an airline representative speak to you while I talk to Ms. Connors."

"Thank you, Kyle. I'd appreciate it."

"My pleasure, but before you go, is there anything else that you can think of that might shed some light on this case?"

"I don't know. I haven't seen or spoken to Annette since the day I caught her with Jesse. However, for reasons I can't explain, my grandmother took Annette's side over mine. She kept insisting that I'd misunderstood something, and she claimed I was spreading vicious lies about Annette. I caught her in bed with my husband. What was there for me to misunderstand?"

"I don't know, but I'm sorry it happened."

"Me too. My life's been a living nightmare ever since." She paused for a moment. "You know, I really thought we were working everything out and it was finally going to be okay. Jesse and I just got home from San Diego. We went there for Christmas, but while we were there my grandmother tried her best to spoil it for me."

"Did she? So, what did she do?"

"She called Christmas Eve night. I hadn't spoken to her for some time, so I tried to wish her a Merry Christmas, but then she started in about Annette. She really did seem surprised though when Jesse and I told her we've been trying to work things out. And knowing Grandma like I do, you can rest assured she would have passed the information along to Annette."

Kyle took more notes. "Perhaps she did, and just so you know, it may be necessary for us to interview her, as well as other family members, while we continue our investigation. I realize this is a difficult time for all of you, but we need to find out what happened. Hopefully, it'll turn out to be nothing more than tragic accident. Then you, and the rest of your family, can have some closure."

"Thank you, Kyle. So, are we done here?"

He handed her his card. "We are, at least, for now. However, we still may need to contact you again for more information." He paused for a moment. "And off the record, I'm truly sorry all this happened to you, and I'm sorry your trip got spoiled."

He opened the door and waited for her to step outside as he asked Megan to come in. She came out a few minutes later.

"Oh, Emily, I'm so sorry." She gave her friend a hug.

"Thanks, Megan, and I'm sorry your vacation got ruined. I spoke to someone from the airline while you were in there, and I was able to get a full refund for our flight. All we have to do is stop by the baggage claim and pick up our luggage."

"Sounds like a plan, and then I'm taking you home."

❧NINETEEN❧

BEAU PRESENTED his badge to the man waiting in the foyer. "I'm Detective Fowler."

"Jorge Mendoza. I live two doors down."

"Nice to meet you, Mr. Mendoza. So, what can I do for you?"

"Well, earlier this morning, while I was out walking my dog, I noticed Jesse walking Emily to a car parked in their driveway. He waited for her to get inside before he went back in the house. So I went up to the car right after it had backed out onto the street. I hadn't seen Emily for a long time. I just wanted to say hello and ask how she was doing."

"I see. So tell me, how was she acting? Did she seem nervous or upset about anything?"

Jorge shook his head. "No, not at all. She seemed happy, and she was genuinely happy to see me. She said she and Jesse have been trying to work things out and she hoped to be moving back in, real soon. We said goodbye and the car drove off."

"What kind of car was it?"

"A small, silver sedan, something like a Chevy or a Honda. I really wasn't paying much attention to the car. I was more interested in Emily. I haven't seen her in a long time."

"Did you happen to see her cousin, Annette Claiborne?"

"Is she the young lady with the shoulder-length reddish-brown hair?"

"Yes."

"I've never actually met her. I used to see her around here from time to time, but not lately. Emily once told me she was Jesse's assistant."

Beau took some notes. "I see. So did you happen to see her today?"

"Well, sort of. I was on my way back when I noticed her car was parked in the street, right in front of Jesse's house. It wasn't there before."

"Did you happen to see Ms. Claiborne?"

"No, she wasn't there. The car was empty when I walked past."

"When was this?"

"It was shortly after Emily left."

"I see." Beau handed him one of his cards. "Well, Mr. Mendoza, I'd like to thank you for stopping by. We'll contact you if we need to talk to you again."

"Of course."

As Jorge stepped out another man wearing a business suit came inside. Beau quickly approached to him.

"Lieutenant. What brings you here?"

"I was in the area on an unrelated matter when I heard the chatter on the radio, so I thought I'd stop by and have a look, and by the way, the media's found out as well. A news van just pulled up across the street. So, what's going on?"

Beau walked him to the staircase. "We have a deceased twenty-two-year-old female who was, at least for a time, the homeowner's mistress. She was also his wife's cousin."

The lieutenant raised his brow. "I see. Interesting. Very interesting, indeed. Do you happen to know who the homeowner is?"

"His name is Jesse St. Claire."

"And do you know who Jesse St. Claire is?"

"He said he's a motivational speaker."

"Who happens to be a well-known motivational speaker at that. I attended one of his seminars about a year ago. He's big on helping people take control of their lives, although it appears that his own life may be in need of control."

Beau chuckled. "Well, we all make mistakes."

"Indeed. Do you think he killed her?"

"At this point I'm not sure, although it's entirely possible. He claims it was an accident. He's been consistent with his story, and so far, we haven't uncovered anything to suggest otherwise. There's no sign of a struggle, and there's no indication of bruises or defense marks on either one of them. We did, however, find a home pregnancy test strip with a positive reading next to the body. He insists he's not the father, but we'll be doing a DNA test on the fetus."

"Of course."

"We know that he and his wife had separated as a result of his relationship with the deceased. He said they're in the process of reconciling, so there could be a possible motive. We'll know more once the autopsy is performed. Speaking of which, I have to be in court tomorrow to testify in the Rodriquez case."

"No problem. Madden can attend the autopsy."

Beau stood by as the lieutenant looked around. Annette's body remained on the landing. Purple blotches had broken out on her face and her skin was turning gray. The lieutenant asked a few questions of the other investigators before turning his attention back to his detective.

"You know, if we were to find anything to suggest foul play, it could really help the county attorney."

"I hear he plans to run for governor," said Beau.

"He may indeed, although he's keeping his cards close to the table. But should he decide to run, a conviction in a high-profile case would certainly give his campaign a boost. Then again, if it turns out to be an accident, something else is bound to come up." He turned to leave. "Keep me posted, Beau."

"Will do."

The lieutenant stepped out as someone else came in with a stretcher and a body bag. Beau stood by, deep in thought as he watched them take Annette away. He was long overdue for a promotion. That was undeniable. Now, at long last, it would be his turn. All he had to do was to get an arrest and conviction in a high-profile case. Not only would he get his promotion, he might even help elect the next governor of Arizona. It would be a win-win for everyone. Well, almost everyone. Life wasn't always fair, and sometimes people simply happened to be in the wrong place at the wrong time. He took a deep breath and headed back to Jesse's office.

* * *

Jesse was still seated behind his desk when Beau came back in, carefully closing the door behind him. "I see you've changed shirts," he said.

"That's right, detective, and I willingly surrendered the one I had on before. So tell me, do I need to call my lawyer?"

"Well, maybe, but before you make that call, there's something I'd like to discuss. Just you and me, off the record."

Jesse's radar immediately went up. "Really?" he asked.

"Now don't be so cynical, Jesse. I'm here to help you. I really am. You have a serious problem on your hands. You have a dead woman in your house, and she's not just any woman. She's your former mistress. She was also pregnant, and you may or may not have been the father."

"That's it. I'm calling my lawyer."

"Not so fast." Beau maintained eye contact with Jesse. "What if I were to tell you that I could make all of this go away?"

Jesse started getting a bad feeling. "Is this some sort of trick to get me to confess to something I didn't do?"

"No, not at all. Now please hear me out. I know it was an accident, just like you said it was. However, because of extenuating circumstances, you know, her being your ex-mistress and all, it'll have to go before a grand jury. Otherwise, people will start asking questions."

"I knew it! You're trying to set me up." Jesse stood from his chair and reached for his phone. "I've heard enough. I'm calling my lawyer."

Beau grabbed the phone. "It's not a trick, Jesse. It really isn't. You forget that grand jury proceedings are secret. I'll testify that there's no evidence whatsoever of any wrongdoing. It was a tragic accident, and it happened just the way you said it did. You even called nine-one-one and tried to get her help."

"Yes, I did, and I was pretty shook up when I made the call. You have it all on tape. I've told you everything that happened, and I've told you the truth. So, why do I have a feeling there's a catch?"

Beau looked him in the eye. "I wouldn't exactly call it a catch."

"All right. Then what is it?"

"I prefer to think of it as reciprocity."

"Reciprocity?" Jesse felt confused. "Reciprocity for what? I'm telling you the truth."

"So you say, Jesse. So you say."

"And what is that supposed to mean?"

"It means that right now I can go either way with this. I can tell them your story. It was a tragic accident." He bore his eyes into Jesse's. "Or, I can tell them that you admitted to killing her. You even admitted to destroying the evidence."

Jesse felt his hackles go up. "Look, I don't know what kind of sick, twisted game you're trying to play here, but it's not going to work. You want to arrest me? Go ahead. As soon as we get to the station, I calling my lawyer and he'll Have me out on bail before the day is over. In the meantime, you still can't prove I killed her, because I didn't. There's no evidence proving I did because none exists. Yes, she may have been my mistress at one time, but it's circumstantial, and the DNA tests will prove I'm not the father of her unborn child. I was simply trying to return her scarf, and while we were talking, she lost her balance and fell. I never laid a hand on her."

The detective flashed a sinister smile. "You don't get it, do you son? People can and do get convicted on circumstantial evidence, and it wouldn't take much to convince a jury you pushed her." He grabbed Jesse's jaw and squeezed it in his hand.

"You're such a pretty boy, aren't you? Do you have any idea of what would happen to a good-looking guy like you inside a jailhouse? Why you'd be fresh meat for a pack of hungry wolves. They'd jump on you the minute the guard locked the door to your holding cell, and trust me, by the time they finished with you, you'd be in serious need of medical attention. And it would happen before you ever saw a judge or posted bail, assuming you even got bail, but if that's the way you want it, I'm all too happy to oblige you." He released Jesse and reached for his handcuffs.

"Jesse Edward St. Claire, I'm placing you under arrest for the—"

"Alright! Alright! Stop with the handcuffs. So, what is it that you me to do?" Jesse regretted his words the moment he spoke them while Beau smiled and put his handcuffs away.

"It's a simple, really. I just need you to help me get a promotion."

"What?"

"You heard me. I've been busting my fanny for this department for almost thirty years now, and during that time I've been passed up for promotions time and time again. So now you're going to help me get one."

"I see. So, what exactly is it that I have to do?"

"It's no big deal, Jesse. It really isn't. All you have to do is follow my lead. You didn't kill Annette. Someone else did."

"Who?"

"You'll find out soon enough."

The realization finally dawned on him. "I get it. You need a conviction in a high-profile case so you can get your promotion."

"Bingo." Beau grinned from ear to ear.

"And don't get me wrong. It's not that I don't appreciate you keeping me out of jail, but if you wanted to convict someone for killing Annette, why wouldn't you pick me? I'd be the most likely suspect."

"Because I may need your services in the future. You see, my lieutenant and the county attorney have been friends since college, and the county attorney may be running for governor. If he does, we'll want you to help with his campaign, and if he wins, it could make for some even bigger opportunities for yours truly."

"I see."

"Good, and I'm happy to see that we've been able to reach a mutual understanding. So, from here on out, you'll do everything I tell you to do. Got it?"

"Yeah, I got it." As they shook hands Jesse realized he had just sold his soul.

"Alright, Jesse," said Beau. "You stay here. I'll be back in a little while. I need to talk to Detective Madden. He's also working your case, but he's to know nothing about this. Not a word. Not now. Not ever. I'll be back once I'm through talking to him, and then we'll go over what you can and cannot say to him." As he started to leave, he stopped in front of the door and looked back at Jesse.

"Oh, and one more thing. You don't breathe a word about this to anyone, and I mean anyone, not even your lawyer, regardless of what may or may not happen. Because if I go down, I'm taking you down with me."

❧TWENTY❧

AS MEGAN PULLED into the driveway the shock wore off and Emily became weepy.

"How could he do this to me? All this time I thought he'd learned his lesson and he was being faithful. How could he do this to me?"

"We don't know for sure if he did anything wrong," said Megan. "You said it yourself. You and Jesse told your grandmother you were getting back together, and you know she would have told Annette the first chance she got. Annette might have shown up just to make you believe something was still going on when there wasn't. Anyway, it doesn't matter now. She's dead. She can never hurt you again."

Emily took a tissue from her purse and dabbed her eyes. "Don't be too sure about that. If it turns out that she and Jesse really were still seeing one another it would be her way of getting back at me from the grave, and I'd leave him for good this time."

"I understand, but until we know for sure let's not jump to any conclusions, okay?"

"That's exactly what Kyle, I mean, Detective Madden said. He said they're still trying to determine what happened."

"Yes, they are. So let them finish their investigation, and let's wait for Jesse to call you. In the meantime, we'll take your bag inside and I'll help you unpack."

"I'm okay, Megan."

"No, you're not, and I don't think you should be alone right now. I also think you should call your dad."

"Later." Emily stepped out of the car and hastily grabbed her bag. Once inside the house, she parked her bag in the entryway and headed straight to the kitchen. Megan followed her and took a seat at the table.

"Would you like some of coffee, Megan?"

"No thanks. I'm good."

"Suit yourself." Emily reached into one of the cupboards and set a coffee can down on the counter.

"I know what you're thinking, Emily."

"No, you don't."

"Yes, I do." Megan's voice was firm. "You need to give him the benefit of the doubt."

Emily remained silent as she filled the coffee maker and switched it on. "We should be on our way to Miami by now, but we're not, because once again, my life gets turned upside down." She choked back another sob. Megan got up and hugged her.

"I know, and I'm sorry. Hopefully, it'll all be resolved soon. Then you go on another cruise, and maybe next time Jesse can go with you."

"We'll see." Emily brushed away a tear as she opened another cupboard and grabbed a coffee mug. "Meantime I have luggage to unpack." She poured herself some coffee, taking her mug with her as she fetched her bag and headed down the hallway to her room. Megan followed, this time sitting down on the bed and making small talk while Emily unpacked. Emily kept checking the time, but her phone never rang. Once she finished, she asked Megan to rejoin her in the kitchen, this time offering her a rum and Coke. Megan asked for a plain Coke instead, and Emily sighed loudly as she set their drinks on the table.

"And here I was, really looking forward to having one of these when our ship left port."

"I know you were, but don't worry, the Caribbean will still be there. As I said before, you and Jesse can go in a few weeks, after Annette's funeral, and after this mess is all cleared up."

"I'm not going to the funeral," said Emily. "Don't get me wrong. I'm sorry she's dead, but I honestly don't feel any sense of grief or loss. I did all that last summer, when I grieved over losing the Annette I thought I knew, not the Annette she really was."

"She was still your cousin. You should be there, if for no other reason than to support the rest of the family, and speaking of which, you still need to call your dad. Detective Madden mentioned he'd be notifying the rest of the family as soon as we left the airport. It'd be better if he heard about it from you, instead of on the news."

"Yeah, I suppose you're right." Emily stepped away to get her phone, but it started ringing as she came back in the kitchen. She shot Megan a look as she glanced at the caller ID. "Looks like I'm too late." She punched the call button and tried to sound upbeat. "Hey, Dad."

"Emily. Thank goodness you answered." Her father sounded anxious. "I just got out of a meeting and heard the news reports on the car radio. What the hell happened? And are you okay?"

"I'm not entirely sure. We were at the airport, waiting for our boarding call, when a police detective approached us. He said Annette was dead, that it was some sort of accident, and it happened at Jesse's house."

"What else did he tell you?"

"Not much. He said they're still questioning Jesse, and they're still trying to determine what happened."

"I see," said Roger. "When I left this morning I overhead you on the phone, saying something about your passport being in Jesse's safe."

"Yes, I'd forgotten it was still there. I had to have it in order to board the ship."

"I understand. So did you go over there to pick it up? Or did Jesse bring it to you?"

"Megan and I stopped by Jesse's house, on our way to the airport, but Annette wasn't there. Everything was fine when we left."

"You're absolutely certain Annette wasn't there?"

"I'm positive. She wasn't there. Trust me."

"Well, I'm grateful for that, and I'm on my way home."

"Dad, really, I'm fine."

"No, you're not, and I don't want you there alone. It's only a matter of time before the media shows up at the house, and I don't want you talking to them. I'm also wondering if we shouldn't speak to a lawyer."

Emily was stunned. "Why? I haven't done anything wrong. Annette wasn't there, at least not while I was there. She would have shown up after I left."

"I understand, but there's a very bad history between you and your cousin. I don't want anyone trying to use it against you."

"But I wasn't there when it happened. Megan was with me. She can vouch for me."

"I know you weren't there, and I hate having to say this, but I've never really trusted Jesse, and I especially don't trust him now. According to what I'm hearing on the news, he was there when happened, and if there were no other witnesses, then what's to stop him from trying to pin the blame on you?"

Emily's blood turned to ice. "Oh my god. Do you really think he would do something like that?"

"He cheated on you, Emily, and now he's facing a possible murder rap. Who knows what could happen next? I should be there in another five minutes or so. In the meantime, I want you to lock the doors and close the blinds. Don't open the door to anyone, and I mean anyone, unless it's the police, until I get there, okay?"

"Okay. I'll see you when you get here." Emily disconnected the call and turned to Megan. "My dad's on his way."

"I gathered that."

"He's worried that Jesse might try to point the finger at me."

Megan was aghast. "I hadn't thought of that, but he's right. Thank goodness I was with you. I'm a witness." She stopped for a moment. "And then there was that other guy. What was his name? You know, the neighbor."

"That's right." Emily's face lit up. "I forgot about Jorge stopping us so he could say hello. That makes him a witness too."

Emily stepped away to pull the blinds and check the doors. A few minutes later Lurch's ears perked up. His tail wagged as he headed to the side door, whimpering with excitement. Roger stepped inside, greeting his daughter with a long embrace.

"You okay?" he asked.

"I'm fine, Dad."

He greeted Megan before taking his seat at the table. "So, what happened? I want to know everything, and I mean everything, from the time you left here, to when the detective spotted you at the airport."

"There really isn't much to tell," said Emily. "Jesse handed me my passport, then he walked me to the car and kissed me goodbye. Then Megan and I went to the airport."

"Well, at least you have a witness." He nodded toward Megan as he spoke. "But are you absolutely certain Annette wasn't there? She could have been hiding in another room."

"I know her car. Trust me, if I'd seen it anywhere near the house, I would have said something."

"That's fine, but I'm not taking any chances. We've all heard horror stories of innocent people being wrongly accused and sometimes even convicted." He grabbed his phone and looked up a number, waiting for the connection to go through. A cheerful woman soon answered.

"Yes. Good morning, Brenda. Is Steve Hudson in his office?"

"May I ask who's calling?"

"My name is Roger Olmstead. Steve updated my will and family trust, about a year ago."

"He's here, but he's on another line. Would you like to leave a message?"

"Yes. Please have him call me right away. Tell him it's urgent." He gave her his number and disconnected the call as Emily tried to change the subject.

"Good heavens, will you look at the time? It's almost lunchtime. Megan, can I fix you anything?"

"I'm good." Megan reached for her purse. "And now that your dad's here, I think I should head on out."

"You know, Megan, the ship won't leave port until tomorrow afternoon. You could still go on the cruise without me. It's okay, really. Why don't you call the airline and see if you can catch a later flight?"

"It's okay. It wouldn't be much fun without you, and besides, you need me here as a witness. No doubt they're going to want to ask me more questions."

Emily walked her to the front door. "I'm so sorry, about everything."

"Hey, it wasn't your fault."

Megan stepped out and Emily went back to the kitchen to start preparing lunch. She had no sooner opened the refrigerator when she heard a knock at the front door.

"Megan must have forgotten something."

"No! Emily wait."

Roger was on her heels, but he wasn't fast enough. Emily opened the front door. A woman with long dark hair stood on the other side, but she wasn't Megan.

"Aunt Heather?"

"You! You did it! I know you're responsible for this!"

"Heather, calm down." Roger stepped between her and Emily. "I know you're distraught, and I'm terribly sorry for your loss. We both are, but Emily wasn't there. She had nothing to do with it."

"Of course you're sticking up for her, Roger, but I don't care if she was there or not. She hated Annette. She wanted her out of the way, so she put Jesse up to it." Heather focused her gaze on Emily; her eyes filled with hate. "This is all your doing. I don't care if it takes me the rest of my life, I'll to see to it that you rot in jail."

"Go home, Heather," said Roger. "I'll call you a cab. You shouldn't be driving right now."

"I can take care of myself, Roger, and you can bloody well kiss my ass. Enjoy what time you have with your daughter, because it won't last long. You're going to lose her, just like I lost mine. I guarantee it."

Heather stormed away while Roger gently guided a badly shaken Emily back inside.

"This is what I mean, Emily. This is why I want you to have a lawyer. What do you think she's going to tell the police?"

"I know."

She followed her father back into the family room, taking a seat on the sofa and trying to recompose herself. Roger's phone rang a short time later. Steve Hudson was returning his call.

"What can I do for you, Roger?"

"I'm calling about my daughter, Steve. This morning her cousin fell down a flight of stairs and died as a result of her injuries. It happened at my son-in-law's home."

"I see. So are you worried about a possible lawsuit?"

"This isn't a personal injury type of case. Have you been listening to the news?"

"No, I haven't. Why do you ask?"

"My son-in-law and my daughter's cousin had an affair last summer. In fact, my daughter caught them in the act."

"I see."

As Roger recounted the events to Steve they played back in Emily's mind. She desperately hoped she could still trust Jesse.

"Under the circumstances, I think you can appreciate why I'd like for her to have legal counsel. Her aunt, her cousin's mother, just showed up at my door and threatened her. She's accusing her of being a party to her cousin's death. Never mind the facts."

"I agree, Roger. It sounds like there are some extenuating circumstances, so it might be wise for her to retain an attorney until she's been officially cleared. However, I'm not a criminal lawyer, and our partner who practiced criminal law retired last year."

"I see."

"There is, however, someone who I can recommend. Frederick Carlton Lancaster. He's one of the top criminal defense attorneys in the state. He worked with one of our other attorneys on a case awhile back. His services won't come cheap, but in my opinion, there's no one better."

"The name rings a bell. I know I've heard it somewhere before."

"No doubt you have," said Steve. "He's been involved with a number of high-profile cases throughout the years. Hopefully you won't need him, but if it were my daughter, I'd get him on retainer before the end of business today."

"I agree."

"I'll transfer you to my secretary. She'll give you his information."

"Thank you, Steve."

"Anytime, and good luck."

* * *

"Okay Jesse, one more time, from the top."

Jesse took a deep breath and tried to swallow, but the big, dry lump in his throat wouldn't allow it. "I need a glass of water."

"In a minute," said Beau. "I just want to make sure you have your story straight."

"I've got it."

"Okay, then. Let's hear it one more time. From the top."

Jesse took another deep breath. Cold, nervous sweat covered his body as he went over his story once again. With each word he spoke, his hatred of himself grew.

"Okay," said Beau, "I think you have the facts, or, should I say, your representation of the facts, down pat, but you need to sound more sincere."

"Damn you."

Beau gave him a twisted smile. "Now that sounded sincere."

"My god." The reality of what he was about to do weighed heavily on him. "I just want this nightmare to be over."

"And it will be. This time tomorrow, you'll be sitting pretty."

"Yeah, but at what cost?"

"Stuff happens, Jesse. You of all people should understand that we can't always have everything we want in life, and sometimes we have to give up something we love for the greater good, which, in this case, means I move up the ranks while you stay out of jail."

Jesse leaned back into his chair and closed his eyes as he tried to ignore the growing wave of nausea brewing deep inside.

"Anyway, that ought to do it. For now." Beau stood from his chair and extended his hand. "I'm going to go file my report, and remember, you'll have to stay downstairs until we remove the crime scene tape. Better yet, you may want to stay in a hotel."

Jesse remained in his chair, refusing to acknowledge Beau as he stepped out. Once he heard the front door close, he turned toward the window and watched as Beau got into his car and drove away. One patrol car remained. A few minutes later the last officer stepped out and drove away while the growing army of news reporters remained. Jesse sighed as he closed the blinds. No doubt the press would have his home under siege for the next few days.

He reached into his desk drawer and took out a flash drive and quickly copied the day's security camera footage. At least the cops bought his story about the camera being offline. Download complete, he locked the flash drive in his safe and deleted the files from his computer. As he shut down the computer, the bile in his stomach came up his throat and he raced to the bathroom, barely reaching the commode in time.

❧TWENTY-ONE❧

EMILY GLANCED AT the dashboard clock as her father drove out of the parking lot. It was a few minutes past four. Seven hours had passed since Annette had taken her tumble down the stairs, and there was still no word from Jesse. The foreboding feeling in her heart grew stronger.

"Do you think they'll allow him his one phone call from jail?"

"What was that?" asked Roger.

"I was thinking about Jesse. He still hasn't contacted me. I'm starting to wonder if they've taken him into custody."

"I don't know, but if they have, it's because they have the evidence to prove some sort of wrongdoing on his part. I know he's your husband, and I know you want to think the best, but I'm afraid it's entirely possible that he killed Annette."

"It was an accident. It had to have been an accident."

"And I hope you're right, Emmy, I sincerely do, for both your sakes, but from what we know so far, it's not looking good. We need to be prepared, just in case the worst happens."

Emily stared out the window and remained silent for the rest of the ride home. As Roger turned the car onto their street, they saw several news vans parked around the house.

"Damn, I was afraid of that," he said. "Keep looking straight ahead. Don't acknowledge them, and don't speak to them. Remember, we have no comment."

"I know, Dad."

Emily held her breath as her father pulled into the driveway and pressed the remote. Two reporters approached their car as they waited for the garage door to open, but they didn't follow them inside. Both sighed in relief once the door rolled down behind them. Roger exited the car first, helping Emily out of the passenger seat and walking her inside the house.

"I really think you should go lie down for a while. You've had a rough day."

"I'm fine, really," said Emily. "I'd like to spend a little time with my piano. That always makes me feel better."

She headed off to the living room and started playing *Chopin's Polonaise No. 6.* As she played, she heard a knock at the door, along with her father talking to another man. She tried to ignore her seething anger at the intrusion. As she finished the final chord she looked up in surprise at who stood by watching her.

"Nice. Just like that night at Hanson Sisters. You're incredibly talented. No, you're gifted."

"Thank you, Kyle. However, something tells me you're not here to admire my music."

"No, I'm afraid not. I just need to go over a couple of the details with you. It won't take long, I promise."

"Of course."

He pulled out his notebook. "Can you give me your best guess as to the exact time you arrived at your husband's home this morning?"

She thought it over for a moment. "Megan's car radio was playing in the background. I'm positive they were doing a top of the hour newsbreak."

"Do you know the station?"

"I'm not sure. It's was one of those mix stations. You know, the ones that play current tunes with classic rock."

"I see, and what kind of car did your cousin drive?"

"A white Honda Civic. I don't know the exact model year, but it's at least five or six years old and it's well used. It has a number of dings and scratches, and there's a good-sized dent in the left rear bumper. It's a very distinct car. I'd recognize it anywhere."

"And you didn't see that particular vehicle parked in front of your house when you went to pick up your passport. Is that right?"

"No sir, I did not. It wasn't there. I would have noticed if it was."

Kyle made a couple of notations before closing his notebook and putting it back in his pocket. "Thank you, Mrs. St. Claire. That ought to do it."

"Am I being charged?"

He smiled and shook his head. "No. You weren't there at the time, and you have two witnesses to back you up."

"What about my husband?"

"So far as I know, he's still being questioned by the other detective. He's a very thorough investigator and he likes to take his time. Trust me, if there was any wrongdoing on your husband's part, he'll get to the bottom of it."

"But what if it really was an accident?"

"If it was, he'll let us know. I know this is a difficult time for you, but you're going to have to be patient and let us finish up the investigation. In the meantime, my shift is ending and I'm off the clock. Do you mind?" He stepped up to the piano to take a closer look. "This is a magnificent instrument."

"Thanks. It's nearly sixty years old. My grandmother was the original owner. She passed it on to my mother, who passed it on to me."

"I see, and I can see it's been well cared for."

"Do you play?"

"A little, but not as well as you. I took lessons when I was young, then I played keyboard with a rock band when I was in my teens and early twenties. Those gigs helped put me through college. I have a keyboard at home and still dabble with it occasionally, but with all the long hours I put in it's hard for me to keep up with it."

"I understand."

"Anyway, I need to head back to finish up my paperwork. Again, I'm sorry for your loss."

"Thank you, Kyle."

Roger walked him to the door, returning a moment later. "Well, that was certainly interesting," he said.

"Indeed. Do you remember that night last fall, when I played at Hanson Sisters?"

"How could I forget? It was the night you had dinner with Dr. Hapner and didn't come home until very late."

"I know, Dad, but do you remember me telling you about meeting an interesting man that night, and asking you if you believed in love at first sight?"

"Maybe. I'm not sure."

Emily smiled. "That was the man I was telling you about. Kyle. Detective Madden." Her smile quickly faded. "How odd that he should reappear now, and under such strange circumstances."

"Nothing odd about it. He's a cop, and he's investigating a case involving your husband."

Emily returned to her music as she anxiously waited for the phone to ring. She stopped an hour later to join her father when he turned on the television to watch the local news. As expected, all of the stations were covering Annette's death, with two reporters giving live updates from the front of their house.

"Hopefully they'll leave after the six o'clock broadcast," said Roger. "If it were up to me, I'd have them all arrested for trespassing."

"I hear you. Trouble is, they're all staying out on the sidewalk."

The front doorbell rang, followed by a loud knock.

"Except for that one." Roger's voice was firm. "You stay here. I'll get rid of whoever it is." As he stepped away, the banging on the door grew louder.

"Phoenix police! Open up!"

Emily followed her father to the door. Another man in a business suit presented a badge. Two uniformed officers stood behind him.

"I'm Detective Beau Fowler. I'm here to take Emily St. Claire in for questioning."

"I'm Emily, and I've already spoken to Detective Madden. Twice. So what's this about?"

Beau motioned to the two uniformed officers, who immediately surrounded Emily.

"Am I under arrest?"

"Emily, don't say anything—"

"I'm in charge here, sir." There was an icy tone in the detective's voice. "No, you're not under arrest at this time. However, I'm taking you in for questioning, and I suggest you remain cooperative."

"It's okay, Dad." Emily grabbed her sweater and her purse. "I'll call you as soon as I'm done, and you can come pick me up. I wasn't there and I didn't do anything wrong. It'll be fine." She put on her sweater and followed the officers outside.

ᕫTWENTY-TWOᕬ

EMILY KEPT TO herself as she rode to the police station. Once they arrived, she was ushered into a small, windowless room and told to take a seat at the small table set off to the side. Detective Fowler sat down across from her, shuffling through a small stack of papers as he spoke.

"All right, Mrs. St. Claire, so can you tell me why you came to your husband's home this morning?"

"To pick up my passport. I was supposed to leave on a cruise this morning, and I needed my passport. I thought I had it with me, but then I realized I didn't. When I couldn't find it, I called Jesse. Turned out it was in his safe."

"So what did you do then?"

"I told Megan, my friend, that we'd need to stop by on our way to the airport to pick it up."

"Did you?"

"Yes, I did, and then Megan and I left. Look, I already went through all of this earlier today with the other detective. Annette wasn't there. Everything was fine when I left. I didn't do anything wrong."

He bored his eyes into hers. "Really?"

Emily stood her ground. "Yes, really. My passport was in Jesse's safe. I stopped by to pick it up, and Jesse gave it to me. He walked me back out to Megan's car and kissed me goodbye. After that I left. End of story."

"Is it now?"

"And what is that supposed to mean?"

Beau leaned back into his chair and folded his arms across his chest. "It means, Mrs. St. Claire, that I'm hearing two entirely different accounts of what happened at your husband's home this morning, and I'm not sure who to believe." He paused for a moment and looked her up and down. "Is that the same cardigan sweater you had on this morning?"

"Yes, it is. Why do you ask?"

"Would you mind taking it off for me?"

"Why?"

He gave her a hard look. "Because I need to have some tests run on it. You can either hand it over willingly, or I can get a court order. The choice is up to you."

Emily slowly removed her sweater and handed it over to him. "Fine, have it your way, but you won't find whatever it is you're looking for because it isn't there."

Another officer entered the room, taking the sweater and placing it into an evidence bag. Once he left, Beau leaned back into his chair and gave her a skeptical look.

"As I was saying, your husband is telling a different story. Quite a different story indeed."

"I'm sorry, I don't understand."

"So you say, so let me fill you in. For starters, your cousin came over this morning to apologize."

"Really?"

"Indeed, but you never gave her a chance."

Emily became defensive. "What do you mean, I never gave her a chance? She wasn't there. I never saw her."

"She was there, Mrs. St. Claire. You came in, and Jesse gave you your passport, just like you said he did, but then he asked you if you'd mind waiting for a moment before you left. He said Annette was there, and the time had come for the two of you to mend fences and move on."

"That, sir, is a blatant lie." Her voice was stern. "Annette wasn't there. Look, if this is some sort of a trick to get me to confess to something I didn't do it won't work. I never saw Annette. She wasn't there."

"So you say, but according to your husband, Annette was there. She came to apologize, but as soon as Jesse told you she was there you flipped out. He said you ran up the stairs, thinking she was in the bedroom. He said Annette heard you, so she followed you up the stairs. She was trying to apologize to you, Mrs. St. Claire. She came because she wanted to make things right, but according to Jesse, you never gave her a chance."

Emily didn't know whether she should laugh or cry. "This is amazing. I've never heard any of this before. Annette wasn't there. I never saw her."

"She was there, Mrs. St. Claire. Your husband tells me you started shouting at her, but by the time he got to the staircase, Annette had already fallen. So, did you push her?"

"No, of course not. She wasn't there. I never saw her. None of this ever happened. Did Jesse actually tell you this?"

"Yes, Mrs. St. Claire, he did. In fact, I have his statement right here, if you'd like to look it over."

He pulled a sheet of paper from his stack and handed it over to her. Emily's hands trembled as she picked it up.

"He also tells me you were having an affair with a man named Sean Hapner."

"Yes, I was seeing Dr. Hapner, but only for a very short time. It was after Jesse and I had separated. So what does that have to do with anything?"

"What it tells me, Mrs. St. Claire, if you'll pardon the pun, is that you're hardly the saint you'd like people to think you are. According to Jesse, you were having an extra-marital affair long before he became involved with your cousin. And then, when you found out about Annette, you left him and tried to make yourself out to be the injured party when, in reality, your husband was the injured party long before you were. Even so, Jesse tried to make things right. He took you back, despite the fact that you'd cheated on him first. Then this morning your cousin showed up. According to Jesse, she wanted to clear the air with him before she approached you, but then you arrived, so Jesse decided to take the opportunity. He wanted you and your cousin to make things right before you left town, but instead you killed her, in a jealous rage."

Emily's voice was shaking. "None of this is true. Not one word, I swear, on everything that is holy, none of what you've just described ever happened. Look, I have a witness. Megan was there. Jesse walked me out to her car and kissed me goodbye, right in front of her."

"I know that, Mrs. St. Claire, and it wouldn't be the first time someone lied to protect a friend, would it?"

The door burst open. A silver-haired man in a business suit stepped into the room. "Don't answer that, Emily."

Beau tried to conceal his anger. "Frederick Carlton Lancaster. To what do I owe the pleasure?"

"I'm here on behalf of my client, Emily St. Claire. Is she being charged?"

"Not yet, but she will be soon."

Emily handed him her copy of Jesse's statement. "Jesse's lying. He's fabricating some far-flung story that I'm somehow responsible for Annette's death. It's all a lie. Annette wasn't there when I was there, and I have witnesses."

"Please, Emily, don't say anything more." He took the paper and began reading it over.

"Mr. St. Claire is a highly respected man in the community," said Beau, "which makes him a very credible witness."

Lancaster glared at the detective. "Who also had an extramarital affair with his wife's cousin. Now his former mistress is dead, under questionable circumstances, and without any eyewitnesses. Mrs. St. Claire on the other hand has two witnesses who say she left her husband's home this morning in good spirits and was hardly acting like a woman who'd just murdered her husband's mistress. You have nothing, detective, and my client has nothing further to say." He turned to Emily. "We're leaving."

He motioned for her to follow him. Beau gave her a hard look as she followed her attorney out the door. She shivered in the cool evening air once they stepped outside.

"I'll take you home."

"Thank you, Mr. Lancaster." Her voice was still shaking.

"You're welcome, and please, call me Freddie. Most of my clients do."

"Alright. Thank you, Freddie."

They walked up to a white Porsche. He opened the passenger door, waiting for her to take her seat before slipping behind the wheel and firing up the engine.

"So, what did you tell him?"

"Not much," said Emily. "I keep reiterating, over and over again, that Annette wasn't there and I never saw her. The other detective, Madden, already told me I didn't do anything wrong and I wouldn't be charged. So why is this detective doing this to me? And why did he take my sweater into evidence?"

"Apparently Jesse can be pretty convincing when he wants to be, so now the cops are looking for any piece of incriminating evidence they can find. He was also trying to pressure you into saying something he could use against you."

"I know. He even brought up a relationship I had after Jesse and I had separated. He said I cheated on Jesse first. That's a lie. Why are they even bringing it up?"

"To make you look bad, so the grand jury won't be as sympathetic to you." Freddie hit the accelerator and the Porsche peeled out of the parking lot. "From here on out, you don't talk to the police unless I'm there. If he, or any other officer, shows up at your door again you call me, immediately, and you tell them you won't talk without your attorney present. That's what you're paying me for, remember?"

"Good to know. So, in the meantime, what do I do?"

"You go on with your life, as best you can, and you let me do my job."

"And what about Jesse?"

"I'm afraid Jesse is now off limits. He's trying to frame you and he's not to be trusted."

"But we're still married. We still love each other, or at least, I thought we did. How could he do this to me?"

"You'd be amazed at what people will do when they suddenly find themselves facing the possibility of going to prison. Jesse is responsible for your cousin's death. Either he pushed her, or if it was an accident, he somehow caused it. Either way, he's trying to save himself by shifting the blame on you. I'm sorry to be the one who has to tell you this, but you need to give up any hopes of reconciliation and divorce him, the sooner the better, because if you don't, he'll be your undoing. I don't practice family law, but I can give you the names of several colleagues who do."

Emily wept silently for the remainder of the drive. Once they arrived at her father's house Freddie shielded her from the news reporters as he walked her to the front door. Stepping into the foyer, she collapsed into her father's arms.

"I'll send a statement to the media," said Freddie. "That should help keep them off your backs. In the meantime, keep your doors and windows closed and don't talk to them, under any circumstances."

"So what happened?" asked Roger.

"I think we'd all better sit down."

Roger led them into the living room. Once everyone had settled Freddie brought them up to date.

"Jesse has turned against her. He told the police Annette was there when Emily stopped by to pick up her passport, and that Emily pushed her cousin down the stairs."

"My god," said Roger, "my worst nightmare is about to come true."

"You did the right thing by contacting me."

"But there's no evidence," said Emily. "None exists, because I wasn't there when it happened. So how can they charge me when there's no evidence, and when I have witnesses?"

"I'm afraid it happens, more often than you think." Freddie looked her in the eye. "Most people believe our justice system is about finding the truth, but it doesn't always work out that way. All too often it's about going after whoever's the easiest to convict. Whether or not they actually did the crime is irrelevant."

"Does this mean I'm going to be charged?"

"Not if I have anything to say about it, but if the worst should happen, I'll be there to defend you, and trust me, I have plenty of reasonable doubt to present to a jury. It would be highly unlikely that you would ever be convicted."

"This is a nightmare. All I did was stop by to pick up my passport."

"Which has, unfortunately, put you in the wrong place at the wrong time." Freddie's tone turned compassionate. "I have a good track record. Over the years I've had many clients in far worse circumstances than yours who never faced charges, or, if they did, the case was either dropped, or they were acquitted. In the meantime, I want you to do what I've told you. Go about your daily business as best you can, but don't volunteer any information to anyone, and if the police should show up again, day or night, you call me, immediately. You've got my number."

He reached into his pocket for a business card and jotted some names on the back before handing it to her and turning his attention to Roger.

"I also told her she needs to divorce Jesse, as soon as possible, because he's now her enemy. I just gave her a list of several good attorneys she may wish to contact."

"Thanks, Freddie, I appreciate it. I'll also be calling Steve Hudson in the morning. He's the attorney who referred me to you, and I think there may be someone in his office who handles divorces as well."

"Then by all means follow up on it." Freddie turned his attention back to Emily, his tone once again compassionate. "I'm sorry this happened to you, but if I may speak candidly; any man who would have an extramarital affair with your cousin hardly has your best interests at heart, and I honestly think you deserve someone better. In the meantime, I'll be bringing in my own team of experts, and I'm going to do everything in my power to try to prove that Jesse is the one responsible for your cousin's death. Then, when this is all over and done with, you can move on with your life."

❧TWENTY-THREE❧

BEAU FOWLER ARRIVED at the station in the middle of the afternoon and found the usual stack of paperwork piled next to his computer. As he took his seat and began sorting through it, someone threw another folder on his desk.

"Madden? What's up?"

"I could ask the same." Kyle's voice resonated with anger. "What were you thinking dragging Emily St. Claire in here last night?"

"Her husband says she did it."

"Got proof?"

"I'm working on it," Beau said defiantly.

"You're wasting your time. I interviewed her extensively at the airport yesterday. She wasn't acting the least bit guilty, and both she and the Connors woman were consistent with their accounts of what happened. I also spoke to Jorge Mendoza earlier today. He stated that Annette Claiborne's car wasn't parked in front of the St. Claire house when Emily left, but he says it was there a short time later."

"He could be mistaken."

"Maybe, but I doubt it. Now, are you ready for the real bombshell?"

"Sure, Kyle. Lay it on me. What have you got?"

"I went to the autopsy this morning. Annette Claiborne wasn't pregnant."

"What?" asked a dumbfounded Beau.

"She wasn't pregnant. There was no fetus. The medical examiner said it appeared that she'd finished her menstrual period within the past few days."

"Could she have had a miscarriage?"

"No. After the autopsy I went to her residence and spoke to Gary Murkowski, her significant other. According to Murkowski, Annette has been on the pill the entire time they've been together, and they've been together for about three years. He even showed me her pills, and I took them into evidence. He says also said she's never been pregnant, at least not during the time he's known her."

Beau scratched his head in disbelief. "All right, so then where did the positive pregnancy test strip come from?"

"At this point, we don't know. However, there have been cases of pregnant women selling positive pregnancy test strips online, so I've taken Ms. Claiborne's laptop and smart phone into evidence. We'll have our guys go over them to see what she's been up to. Perhaps she was trying to blackmail Jesse in some way. If so, he'd have a motive for pushing her down those stairs."

Beau tried to conceal his simmering anger and frustration. "I'm not so sure about that, Kyle. Jesse claims he's unable to father a child. He's even given his consent to access his medical records, which I intend to do. So even if she were trying to blackmail him, it wouldn't have worked. Therefore, he would have had no reason to push her down the stairs. However, I did learn that Emily St. Claire had an extramarital affair herself with a man named Sean Hapner. Perhaps she's the one who's pregnant."

Kyle raised his brow. "But surely after eight years of marriage, she knows he can't father a child. So, assuming she is pregnant, she probably wouldn't want him knowing about it, and why would the test strip be in her cousin's possession? It doesn't make any sense."

"I'd love to bring her in for more questioning, but she's now retained the services of one Frederick Carlton Lancaster, and there's no way he'll allow her to talk. Guess I'll have to subpoena her medical records."

"It may not be necessary. Let's see what's on Ms. Claiborne's computer first, and just so you know, Beau, I've been doing my job for some time now, and I know an innocent person when I see one. Emily St. Claire is innocent. I'd stake my career on it. The only thing she's guilty of is marrying a schmuck who couldn't keep his fly zipped, and who, at the very least, may be guilty of manslaughter."

* * *

Beau had to figure out his next move, and he had to do it quickly. He needed to bring Benjamin Morris a winnable, high-profile case, but it was now apparent that Annette Claiborne had indeed come to Jesse's home in an attempt to blackmail him, just as Jesse had said. Kyle was right. It not only gave Jesse a possible motive for killing her, it would also make it much harder to convince a jury she had come over to apologize for her past transgressions. He took a deep breath as he approached Jesse's house, pushing past the reporters as he made his way to the front door. He rang the bell several times, following up with a loud, hard knock.

"Phoenix police. Open up!"

The door cautiously opened. "Oh, it's you." Jesse's greeting sounded less than enthusiastic.

"We need to talk." Beau pushed his way inside, firmly closing the door behind him.

"About what?" said Jesse. "I went along with your plans, and now I'm paying the price. Not only am I a prisoner in my own home, I just sacrificed my marriage and gave up the only woman I've ever truly loved."

"The only woman you ever truly loved? Really? Then why were you doing the horizontal mambo with her cousin? And speaking of the late Ms. Claiborne, we have a serious problem. The autopsy just revealed she wasn't pregnant."

Jesse raised his brow. "Well now, somehow that doesn't surprise me. Annette was nothing if not a lying little tramp, but even if she had been pregnant, the DNA tests still would have proven I wasn't the father. So, where's the problem?"

"The problem, Jesse, is it confirms that she came here to blackmail you, which gives you the perfect motive for murder."

"But I didn't kill her. My god, how many times do I have to tell you this? Yes, we argued, but I never touched her. She lost her balance and fell. It was an accident."

"I know that, Jesse. The problem is convincing the grand jury it was an accident. I'm trying to help you, I really am, but now we're going to have to come up with a viable explanation, and perhaps a new strategy."

Jesse was becoming flustered. "Look, why don't I just come clean? I'll tell them I got scared, and in a moment of weakness, I lied, but now I'm coming forward and telling the truth. Yes, I realize it'll damage my career, and I'll probably have to pay a hefty fine along with it, but at least my conscience will be clear, and I'll be able to live with myself again. And, if I'm lucky, I may even get my wife back."

"No, Jesse, that won't work. I already told you if I go down, you're going down with me."

"I'm not going to implicate you. I'll simply tell them I got scared. In the meantime, you still can't prove I killed her, because I didn't. Yes, I realize I'm in for a rough ride, but I'm pretty sure I'll be vindicated in the end. It was an accident. You can't prove it was murder, because it wasn't, and then, when it's all over and done with, I'll pack up and go someplace else and start over. At least by then I'll be able to put it all behind me."

"You still don't have a clue, do you? So please, allow me to refresh your memory. I don't care if it was an accident or not, I'll still say you pushed her down those stairs, and once I do good luck convincing a jury of your innocence. If you want to remain a free man, you'll do as I say. What we have to do now is come up with a good explanation for why she had the test strip if she wasn't pregnant."

"Alright, alright." Jesse stopped to think for a moment. "Maybe it was a false positive. After all, those things can't be one hundred percent accurate, can they?"

"Nope. Won't work. According to the autopsy, she'd just finished her period, and her boyfriend says she's been on the pill for years. Madden even took her pills into evidence."

Jesse thought it over again. "Well, since we've already stated that she came over to apologize, I suppose I could say that she told me she and Gary were having a baby. She even showed me the test strip so I'd believe her, and yes, I believed her. Hell, I even congratulated her. Of course, I had no idea she was lying, and I'm just as shocked as the rest of you. Gee, I can only speculate, but my best guess would be that she made up the story to invoke sympathy from Emily and me, you know, being as she and I had once had an affair and all."

Beau mulled it over. "Well, I suppose it could be as good of an explanation as any other, and you were emotionally distraught when I questioned you yesterday. Be sure to keep your story straight, because sooner or later you'll be questioned by Madden."

"I understand. So, what about Emily? Are you still going to charge her?"

"I'm trying. The problem is she's now retained Frederick Carlton Lancaster."

"I've heard of him." Jesse's face suddenly lit up. "Come to think of it, I've met him. We sat at the same table at a networking breakfast a few years ago. He's good. Damn good."

"I know what you're thinking, Jesse. You're hoping Lancaster will help her beat the rap, but you'd better pray it doesn't happen, because if it does, I'll still come back and say that you pushed her and destroyed the evidence. I'm bringing the county attorney a winnable, high-profile case, no matter what."

* * *

Beau's shift had ended when returned to the station. Kyle Madden was straightening up his desk.

"Heading out, Madden?"

"Yep." Kyle put on his jacket as he spoke. "I have to go pick up Cory."

"I can't imagine what it's like being a cop and being a single dad."

"It's not easy. Thank goodness for Lindsey."

"You have a sweetheart of a sister all right. Anyway, I just had another little chat with Jesse St. Claire."

Kyle looked intrigued. "Really? So, what did Mr. St. Claire have to say this time?"

"He claims Annette told him she and her significant other were having a baby. He says she showed him the test strip as proof."

"Did he now? So why is that yesterday he had no explanation for the test strip?"

"He was pretty shook up, Kyle, but now that he's starting to calm down, he's able to recall more of the details."

"I see." Kyle sounded skeptical.

"He's telling me the truth. That I'm certain of."

"Okay. So, what else did he have to say?"

"He was just as surprised as we were when I told him Annette wasn't pregnant after all. He seems to think she was trying to invoke sympathy."

"Really?" Kyle still sounded skeptical. "Well, I suppose that's a good guess on his part, but somehow I'm not convinced her reason was as pure as he says, and I intend to get to the bottom of it. We'll know more once we have the results from her laptop and phone."

"But even if we determine that she bought it online, we may still never know for certain what her real motive was."

"I suppose not. See you in the morning, Beau." Kyle stepped away, leaving a seething Beau Fowler behind.

❧TWENTY-FOUR❧

I T WAS ALMOST noon when Roger finally tapped on his daughter's door.

"Come in, Dad."

He cautiously opened the door and stepped inside. It took a moment for his eyes to adjust. The blinds were still drawn, and the room was dimly lit. Emily was lying in her bed, her eyes focused on the ceiling.

"Are you all right?" he asked.

"No."

"Did you get any sleep?"

"Very little."

"I'm sorry, Emmy. I know this is a difficult time for you, but it's going to get better, I promise. Meantime I love you, very much, and I'm here for you." A tear rolled down her face as he bent down and kissed her cheek. "I called Steve Hudson this morning. He sometimes handles divorces, as long as there are no minor children or disputed property, which would certainly be the case with you. We have an appointment to see him at two o'clock."

"So soon?" Emily sat up and wiped her face with the back of her hand as he handed her a box of tissues.

"We have to get this done, the sooner the better. The man is trying to frame you for a crime you didn't commit. You don't want to be married to him anymore."

"I know, Dad."

"Meantime you need to get up and eat something."

"I'm not hungry."

"I understand, but you still have to eat. I don't want you getting sick on top of everything else. You need to get up and come into the kitchen. I'll make you some scrambled eggs."

"Aren't you supposed to be at work?"

"I'm taking the rest of the week off. Now please, come into the kitchen. Then, after you eat, you need to get ready to go. Don't worry, I'm going with you."

Roger stepped out and a disheveled Emily soon came into the kitchen. Her face looked pale, and her eyes were red and puffy. He quickly served up her eggs, but she mostly picked at her food. She soon excused herself and headed off to shower. An hour later she climbed into the passenger seat of his car. As the garage door opened, both were relieved to see that most of the news reporters were gone.

"Freddie took care of it," said Roger. "He sent them some sort of press release and he was also interviewed on one of the early morning newscasts."

"Really? So what did he have to say?"

"He said you were sad to learn of your cousin's death, and for the media to please respect our privacy during this difficult time. He also said the case is still under investigation and that you're cooperating with the authorities."

"I guess it's about all he can say, for now. So what happens when they come and arrest me?"

"They won't." Roger's voice was firm. "You weren't there, Emily, and you have two witnesses to back you up. You're not going to be arrested."

"I hope you're right. I really do." She remained quiet for the rest of the drive. Fifteen minutes later they arrived at Steve's office. He came out to the reception area to greet them.

"Good seeing you again, Roger," said Steve, "and you must be Emily."

"Yes, I'm Emily." Her voice sounded softer than usual as she extended her hand.

"If two will come with me." He led them down a hallway to his office, pointing out the two chairs facing his desk. Once they were seated, he got down to business.

"Your father has told me a little bit about your case, and I've also been following the story on the local news. I'm sorry for your loss."

"Thank you." Emily's voice remained quiet.

"Your father also tells me your husband is attempting to implicate you, and I agree that you should divorce him. I'm here to help you with that."

"Yes, and thank you."

"I understand there are no children."

"No, we have no children." Emily looked at her father. "Well, I suppose one good thing will come of this. Maybe I'll get to be a mother someday after all. Assuming I don't end up spending the rest of my life in prison for a crime I didn't commit."

"You've also got Freddie Lancaster on your side," said Steve. "So, what about the community property? Is there anything in particular that you want?"

"No. I don't want any of it. Last summer, when we first separated, I took my all my clothing and personal effects from the house. I don't want anything that's been left behind, and I don't want the house either."

"Are you sure?" asked Roger. "I think you should at least demand that he sell the house. You're entitled to half the proceeds from the sale since you spent the past few years paying the mortgage. It's a big house, Emily, and it's worth a lot of money."

"I don't want it, Dad. As of yesterday, that house is cursed as far as I'm concerned."

"She's right, in a way," said Steve. "Her cousin dying in that house, especially under questionable circumstances, makes it far less attractive to a potential buyer. Chances are it will drop in value because of the stigma. How much, of course, remains to be seen."

"Exactly. I want to sign it over to Jesse. He can have the furniture, the dishes, and everything else that's in it. I just want to start over with a clean slate."

"I understand." Steve grabbed a pad of paper and started taking notes.

"Cute baby." Emily nodded toward the framed photo on top of the desk. Steve looked up and gave her a smile.

"Thanks. That's my son, Joshua Alexander."

"I see. Very nice." Emily kept to herself as Steve made additional notes and put his pen down.

"Okay," said Steve. "You're ending the marriage because it's irretrievably broken—"

"Which is certainly an understatement."

"I know. It's just legal terminology. You're stating that the marriage is irretrievably broken, that there are no children, you're not asking for spousal support, and the only property you're asking for are the items you removed from the home last summer. Is that correct?"

"Yes. In fact, most of the items I removed actually belonged to me before the marriage, or were things he wouldn't want, such as my clothes."

"Gotcha. I'll have the paperwork ready within the next couple of days. Then my secretary will give you a call so you can look it over before he's served."

"How long will it take, once he's served?"

"Assuming he doesn't contest it, which I don't think he will, it'll be few months. Once he's served the court will set a hearing date. We tell the judge the marriage is irretrievably broken, and we've agreed on the property settlement. He'll sign it, and then it's over."

"And that's it?"

"That's it," said Steve. "You'll be a free woman, and then you can start over."

"Except I don't feel very free."

"It's okay. It sometimes takes people awhile to recover from a divorce, but you'll be fine. Oh, one final question. Do you want your maiden name back?"

"Yes." Emily gave her father a nod. "I'm going back to school to finish my music degree. My goal is to become a concert pianist. Once that happens, I want to be presented to the public as Emily Olmstead, not Emily St. Claire. Hopefully by then the truth will have come out, and I'll no longer wish to be affiliated with Jesse St. Claire. Remember what we were talking about before? About stigmas?"

"I understand," said Steve, "so I'll submit the paperwork to have your maiden name restored."

"Thank you."

They finished up their business, and on the way home Emily checked her messages.

"Well now, that's interesting."

"What's interesting?" asked Roger.

"Someone's left me a voicemail. It's a local area code, but I don't recognize the number. Please don't tell me some reporter got my cell phone number. It's supposed to be private."

"If they did, we'll get your number changed. Today, if at all possible. In the meantime, would you mind playing it back on speaker?"

"Sure, Dad." She hit the button to play back the message.

"Hi Emily, this is Kyle Madden. I'm calling from my personal cell phone, and what I'm about to tell you is off the record, so please, keep this to yourself. I'm sorry Beau Fowler dragged you in for questioning last night, but I'm glad you have Freddie Lancaster.

He's the best defense attorney in the state. I know you're innocent, and while we still don't know for certain what all happened at your husband's home yesterday, I'm going to do my best to see that you're cleared, and that justice is served. In the meantime, if you can remember anything else, and I mean anything, no matter how small or insignificant it may seem, please call me, right away. Remember, I'm on your side. Maybe when this is all over and done with, I can take you out for coffee. In the meantime, please be careful, and if Detective Fowler should contact you again make sure you have your lawyer present."

﹌TWENTY-FIVE﹌

BEAU FOWLER arrived at Jorge Mendoza's house early the following morning. The news reporters remained camped out in front of Jesse's house. Beau shook his head as he rang the doorell and follolwed up with a loud kock. "Phoenix Police."

An attractive middle-aged woman, still in her pajamas and robe, answered the door. He presented her with his badge.

"I'm here to talk to Jorge Mendoza."

"I'm Marta Mendoza. My husband is in the shower. Would you mind waiting for a few minutes?"

"Certainly."

Beau followed her to the living room, where he made himself comfortable on the sofa. The woman, while clearly annoyed by the intrusion, remained polite.

"Would you like some coffee while you're waiting, officer?"

"No, thank you. I'm fine."

"Very well. My husband will be with you shortly."

She stepped away and Beau took in his surroundings. It was a typical living room in a typical suburban home. A group of family photos hung on one of the walls. Jorge joined him a few minutes later.

"Can I help you? Detective Fowler, wasn't it?"

"Yes, sir, it is." Beau waited as Jorge took his seat. "I just wanted to go over a couple of things with you, if you don't mind."

"Of course."

Beau pulled out his notepad and thumbed through the pages. "You said Annette Claiborne's car wasn't parked in front of the St. Claire home when you walked past it the first time, is that right?"

"Yes, that's right. I saw the silver sedan back out into the street, and I noticed Emily in the passenger seat. That's when I walked up to the car so I could say hello to her. In fact, I had to step off the sidewalk and walk into the street a little ways. I was standing in pretty much the same spot where Annette's car was later parked."

"You're absolutely certain?"

"Yes, I'm certain."

Beau glanced around the room, focusing his gaze on a photo hanging near the center of the collection.

"Nice looking family."

"Thank you."

"I see you and your lovely wife. Is that your son and daughter?"

"Yes." Jorge gave him a nervous smile. "Manny is in college, down in Tucson, and Rachel, my daughter, is a sophomore in high school."

"You know, Jorge, I did a little checking up on your family, you know, routine stuff, and I found out your son once had a brush with the law."

"Yes." Jorge looked down at the floor as he spoke. "Back when Manny first started high school he was, for a brief time, hanging out with a few troublemakers, but it's all in the past. He had to pay a fine and do some community service, which he's done. Now he has his life back."

"Really? You know, it's a funny thing about drugs. People can get off them, at least for a time, but then, later on, they go right back into it."

"What do you mean?"

"Your son is going to college in Tucson. The University of Arizona is a big place. There's lots of partying going on. Lots of temptation."

Jorge looked up. "So what are you getting at?"

"I'm just saying it'd be a real shame if your boy were to get caught with illicit drugs in his possession. It would be his second offense, and this time around he'd be doing some jail time."

Jorge became defensive. "It won't happen. Manny learned his lesson. He doesn't do drugs. Not anymore and never again. He even works with some anti-drug programs for younger kids."

"I understand. Your son drives a late-model blue Toyota Corolla, doesn't he?"

Jorge shifted around in his seat. "Yes, he does. So what does it have to do with anything?"

"He's also renting a small apartment near the campus. Just off Fourth Avenue, correct?"

"Yes."

Beau's eyes bore into Jorge's. "You know, there's all kinds of partying in those neighborhoods near the campus. Lots of drugs, too, and even if your son wasn't doing anything wrong, visitors can sometimes leave things behind, if you know what I mean."

"He doesn't associate with that crowd anymore."

"I understand, Mr. Mendoza. I'm just saying stuff happens." Beau eyes remained on Jorge's. "So, where were we? Oh yes, I remember. Are you certain, absolutely certain, that Annette Claiborne's car wasn't parked in front of Jesse St. Claire's house when you saw Emily St. Claire?"

Jorge took a deep breath. "I know for sure it was there when I was on my way back to my house."

"But what about before? When you were walking toward the St. Claire house for the first time? When you saw Emily St. Claire?"

"I'm not sure. I saw Emily, and I wanted to speak to her, but I wasn't paying that much attention to anything else."

"So, what about the white Civic, Mr. Mendoza?"

Jorge shrugged his shoulders. "Maybe it was there, maybe it wasn't. I just don't know. I really wasn't paying attention to any of the cars."

Beau smiled as he made a note in his little pad. "Thank you, Mr. Mendoza. You've been very helpful, and I'm glad your son was able to get his life straightened out. You know, he has his whole life ahead of him, and I'm sure he'll go far."

* * *

Kyle shook his head in disgust as he pushed his way past the news reporters. Knocking loudly on the front door, he presented his badge and identified himself as a police officer before the door opened.

"I see they've sent reinforcements," said Jesse.

Kyle looked Jesse up and down as he stepped through the doorway. The man certainly had good looks, but something in his body language seemed off. Kyle made a mental note.

"I'm here for a follow up visit, Mr. St. Claire, and I'll try not to take up too much of your time."

"Thank you. As you can imagine, this incident has been quite upsetting, and I haven't slept well for the past couple of nights."

As Jesse led him toward the living room, Kyle stopped for a moment to look at the staircase. Dried bloodstains remained on the landing.

"I'm sure you can appreciate the fact that I've been avoiding the stairs," said Jesse. "I'm now sleeping in the empty bedroom downstairs, next to my office. It used to be my wife's music room."

"I understand." Kyle followed Jesse to the living room, taking a seat on one of the upholstered chairs near the fireplace. He took out his pen and notepad.

"I've listened to your nine-one-one call, Mr. St. Claire. During that call you told the dispatcher that you and the deceased were talking at the top of the stairs, and she then somehow lost her balance and fell. But then, later on, you told quite a different story. You now claim your wife actually pushed her cousin down the stairs. Would you care to explain?"

Jesse looked at the floor as he nervously swept a lock of hair away from his forehead. "I was trying to protect Emily. Annette stopped by, unannounced, to offer an apology. Then Emily showed up to get her passport. I tried to explain what was going on, but Emily wouldn't hear of it. She raced up the stairs, thinking Annette was in our bedroom, when she was, in fact, right here, in the living room. Annette tried to follow Emily upstairs and I heard them shouting, but by the time I got there it was too late. All I saw was Annette falling down the stairs."

"I see. So, did you actually see your wife push her cousin?"

Jesse flinched. His gaze remained on the floor.

"You seem nervous, Mr. St. Claire. Is everything okay?"

"I'm fine. I'm just under a great deal of stress, as you can imagine."

"I understand, but you didn't answer my question. Did you actually see your wife push her cousin down the stairs?"

Jesse shifted nervously in his seat. "It all happened so fast. Like I just said, I tried to get there as quickly as I could, but I was too late."

"I understand, but I'm asking you once again. Did you actually see Emily push Annette down the stairs?"

Beads of sweat popped out on Jesse's forehead. "It all happened so fast. It was so surreal. I saw Annette falling while Emily stood at the top landing. She looked so angry. I've never seen her like that before. Ever."

"Alright. So, what happened next?"

"As soon as Emily saw me, she ran down the stairs. She was panicked. I wrapped my arms around her for a moment or two while she tried to compose herself. She kept asking me what she should do. I told her not to worry, it'd be okay. I told her to remain calm and to act like nothing had happened. I said I'd walk her out to Megan's car and then I'd call for help. I'd tell them it was an accident."

"So, what did she say?"

"She agreed. I held her a little longer and waited for her to calm down. Then she told me she loved me, and that I'd just saved her life. She took a few deep breaths, and then she nodded and said she was ready. I walked her out to Megan's car and kissed her goodbye, then, when I came back in, I called nine-one-one."

Jesse's eyes remained focused on the floor as he spoke. Kyle knew he was lying but decided to play along.

"I see. So tell me Jesse, at that point, was Annette alive or dead?"

Once more, Jesse avoided eye contact. "I don't know. I didn't check for a pulse until after I came back inside, and when I did, I couldn't find one. I noticed she was bleeding heavily from the back of her head, and I knew she was hemorrhaging. I doubt I could have saved her, even if I wanted to."

"And you would have like to have saved her, wouldn't you, Jesse?"

Finally, Jesse made eye contact. "Of course I would have liked to have saved her. It was a tragic accident—I mean occurrence. Yes, I had a history with her, but it was all in the past. She came to apologize."

"And why was that?"

"What do you mean?"

"Why would your ex-mistress suddenly appear, unannounced, to offer an apology, on the same day your wife was leaving town?"

Jesse winced, but maintained eye contact. "I don't know, sir, although I've been asking myself the same question. Emily and I separated after she found out about Annette and me, but we were in the process of reconciling. We also mentioned the reconciliation to Emily's grandmother during a telephone conversation on Christmas Eve, so perhaps someone said something to Annette. You know how family gossip goes. The point is, she came here to mend fences so we could all start the New Year with a clean slate."

"I see." Kyle took more notes. "So, where did the pregnancy test strip come from?"

Jesse turned his gaze back to the floor. "Annette said she and Gary, her significant other, were having a baby. It must have fallen out of her purse or something."

"Did you see it?"

"I think she may have been reaching for something in her purse when Emily arrived. I excused myself and stepped away to answer the doorbell. You know what happened next."

"So you're saying the test strip belonged to Annette?"

"I suppose it did. Yes."

"Is your wife by chance pregnant?" Kyle felt his stomach twist as he asked the question.

"No." Jesse shook his head as he spoke. "At least, she shouldn't be. I'm unable to father a child."

"I see, but it sounds like you're not completely certain."

"Then please allow me to rephrase my answer. I'm ninety-nine-point-nine percent certain that Emily isn't pregnant. At least she isn't now."

Kyle's stomach took another twist. "Could you elaborate on that?"

"Last fall, while Emily and I were separated, she got involved with another man. I suppose she could have gotten pregnant by him, but if she did, she's not pregnant anymore. She said the relationship only lasted for a few weeks, and she ended it right after I caught them in the act."

"Caught them in the act?"

Jesse looked Kyle in the eye. "Last fall, just before Thanksgiving, I saw her with lover boy in a restaurant one night, so I followed them back to his place and waited in my car. She came out two hours later. That's when I confronted her."

"I see. So, what happened?"

"I kept my cool. Then we came back here and had a long talk, which led to our eventual reconciliation."

"I see. So I take it you're still in love with your wife."

"Very much so."

"Really." Kyle's voice sounded incredulous. "So tell me, Jesse, if you're still in love with her, then why are you pointing the finger at her?"

Jesse's body jerked. "What do you mean, I'm pointing the finger at her? I was trying to protect her. I was going to take the fall for her."

"So why didn't you? Why not just say it was an accident? That you and Ms. Claiborne were standing near the top of the stairs, and then she somehow fell. That's what you told the nine-one-one dispatcher, and I think you were telling the truth when you made the call."

Jesse refused to make eye contact. "I was trying to protect Emily when I made that call."

"So you say, Jesse, but here's what I think really happened. I think Annette showed up after your wife left, that the two of you argued about something, and during that argument she fell down the stairs. You may or may not have pushed her, but here's what I know for certain. Your ex-mistress died in your home, under questionable circumstances, and even if you didn't actually push her down those stairs, you might have done something to cause her to take a step backward. That would be manslaughter, and, if convicted, you'd be looking at five to ten years in prison, so you're trying to pin it on your wife."

The color drained from Jesse's face and he sat completely still. Finally, he took a deep breath and turned his gaze toward Kyle.

"Am I under arrest?"

"Not at this time."

"And what precisely does that mean?"

Kyle returned Jesse's stare. "It means, Jesse, that I know you're lying, and I know you're trying to frame an innocent woman for a crime she didn't commit."

"In that case, Detective Madden, this interview is over, and I won't discuss it any further without my attorney being present."

"Of course, Jesse. I understand. I can see myself out, but this investigation is far from over."

* * *

Jesse remained in his chair as Kyle stepped away. Once he heard the front door close, he took a deep breath and went into his office. He grabbed his phone off the desk and paced around the room as he waited for the call to connect.

"Detective Fowler."

"Madden was just here." Jesse's voice was shaking.

"I know. I saw his car pull up to the curb as I was leaving the Mendoza house. So what'd you tell him?"

"Exactly what you told me to tell him. I have the script pretty much memorized."

"Good for you. So did he buy it?"

"No, and it wasn't from a lack of trying on my part." Jesse let out a deep sigh. "Look, I don't think I can do this for much longer."

"Yes, you can, and you will. Don't worry about Madden. Let him tell the grand jury his side of the story. I'll tell them mine, and I can be pretty damn convincing. It wouldn't be the first time I've lied on the witness stand, and it certainly won't be the last. Meantime, would you like to hear some good news?"

"Sure, why not?"

"Now Jesse, it's not as bad as you think. I just got done talking to your neighbor, Jorge Mendoza."

"And?"

"Let's just say he's had an opportunity to think things over, and now he can't be absolutely certain that Annette's car wasn't parked in front of the house when he stopped to talk to Emily."

"So what made him change his mind?"

Beau chuckled. "Let's just say I helped him see the light. So, that's one witness down, one to go. I'll be seeing Ms. Connors later today. Just think, Jesse. By tonight there'll be plenty of reasonable doubt about your wife's innocence. Then we take it to the grand jury."

"Will Emily be indicted?"

"She will, if I have anything to do with it."

Jesse started feeling nauseous once again. "Will she be convicted?"

"That'll be up to another jury to decide."

"I don't want her convicted."

"Too late, Jesse. Besides, why should you care? She was sleeping with another man behind your back—"

"After I cheated on her."

"Who cares? What is it that women are so fond of saying? Once a cheater, always a cheater. You need to let it go Jesse and start thinking about the rest of your life. Thanks to me, you have a really bright future ahead of you. You may even help elect the next governor of Arizona, and if that happens, you'll be meeting plenty of hot babes along the way, so stop wasting your time worrying about your soon-to-be ex-wife. It's not like she's going to be convicted for capital murder. She'll end up doing a few years and then they'll release her. She'll still be a reasonably young woman once she gets out."

❧TWENTY-SIX❧

ROGER LOOKED through the peephole, surprised at who stood on the other side. He quickly opened the door.

"Barbara? What are you doing here?"

She stepped across the threshold without acknowledging him, and he tried to remain cordial as he closed the door behind her. "Can I get you anything? Perhaps a cup of coffee?"

"No, thank you. I won't be staying long. I need to discuss something with you. Do you have a moment?"

"Of course. Right this way."

She followed him into the family room and sat down on the edge her chair. "I wanted to let you know that Annette's funeral will be tomorrow, and, at the risk of sounding callous, I would appreciate it, very much, if you and Emily would kindly not attend."

"Don't worry, Grandma. I wouldn't dream of it."

Barbara looked up and found herself face-to-face with a haggard-looking Emily. She put on her usual plastic smile. "Emily. I didn't hear you come in."

"Obviously."

"You look awful. It's after ten o'clock in the morning, and you're still in your bathrobe. Are you sick?"

"Yeah, Grandma, I'm sick alright. I'm sick of my entire world being turned upside down by a lying, cheating, backstabbing, soon-to-be ex-husband. I'm also sick of having a family totally lacking in any decency or compassion."

"Please understand, what I mean is—"

"Grandma, please. For once in your life, don't try to cover it up, okay? You don't want me at Annette's funeral. Well, you can rest easy, because I wasn't planning on going anyway. She betrayed me. She had an affair with my husband, and let's face it. My showing up would be in poor taste, wouldn't it? Since you all seem to be convinced that I'm responsible for her demise."

"I never said you were responsible for Annette's death, Emily."

"Really?" Emily gave her grandmother a strong look. "Aunt Heather thinks I'm responsible. She even showed up at our door to tell me so. And then there's Jesse. He's been telling the police quite a story of how I pushed her down those stairs. None of it's true. I even have witnesses backing me up, but unfortunately for me, one of the detectives has bought his story, so there's a really good chance I'll be sitting in a jail cell by tomorrow, but as long as you're here, Grandma, please tell me, because I'm dying to know. Do you think I did it? And I want to hear it from you. Do you honestly believe that I pushed Annette down those stairs?"

"Emily, please. You're distraught. This isn't the time or place."

"No, Grandma, I'm not letting you get away with it. Not this time. You're the one who came over to tell us we're not welcome at Annette's funeral, so now would be the perfect time. And let's be brutally honest with one another, shall we? Ever since the day I caught Jesse and Annette in the act, you've been on her side, not mine. So why is that?"

Barbara squirmed in her seat. "Emily, please, I never took sides."

"Oh yes, you did. You told me, many times, to stop spreading vicious lies about my cousin and Jesse. You weren't there, Grandma. I was, and I know what I saw. Jesse even admitted it to you Christmas Eve night when he spoke to you on the phone. Yet in spite of it all, you've steadfastly remained on Annette's side. Why is that?"

"Emily, please. I don't want to discuss this right now. I'm simply trying to avoid any further conflicts in the family, and yes, you're right. Your aunt is blaming you for what happened to Annette, but please understand, she's not herself right now. She's a mother who's just lost her daughter, and believe me when I tell you I know, all too well, the pain she's in. Please, just give her some time. She'll eventually come around and she'll realize it wasn't your fault."

"Sure Grandma. Just like you realized the drunk driver who ran the red light and killed my mother wasn't at fault either."

Barbara's eyes blazed with anger. "That man was a repeat offender driving with a suspended license. He was nothing more than a common criminal who had no business being on the road in the first place."

Emily tried to choke back the tears. "And you and Aunt Heather have been treating me like a common criminal as well. As far as the two of you are concerned, I'm guilty. Never mind the fact that I wasn't even there when it happened."

"You've made your point, Barbara." Roger's voice was stern. "Neither Emily nor I will be attending Annette's funeral, so you can rest easy. Please accept our condolences on your loss, and I'll see you out."

He extended his hand and helped Barbara from her chair. She tried to approach Emily, but Emily turned her back to her. Taking her cue, she left with Roger. He returned a short time later.

"Are you alright?"

"I don't know, Dad." Emily was still fighting back the tears. "I probably shouldn't have brought up the man who killed Mom, but for the life of me, I just don't understand her."

He wrapped his arms around her, giving her a firm squeeze. "Neither did your mother. Your grandmother has been and always will be self-centered and more concerned about what others think of her instead of what's best for her family. Fortunately for us, your mother wasn't anything like her. She was like your grandfather. She was a warm, generous, loving person, just like he was."

"I know," said Emily, "and I miss them both. So much."

"We all do, Emmy. We all do."

* * *

Beau Fowler stepped out of his car and took in his surroundings. What had once been a pleasant, middle-class neighborhood was showing its age. Several of the houses were in need of fresh paint, while weeds choked out the grass on a few of the lawns. At least this home appeared to be in better shape than some of its neighbors, but upon closer inspection he noticed some dry rot on the wood trim. He pulled out his badge and rang the bell.

"Phoenix police."

The front window curtains rustled. He held out his badge as the front door opened. A tall, skinny young girl, wearing glasses, stood on the other side.

"I'm Beau Fowler. I'm a detective with the Phoenix Police Department. May I come in?"

"Well, being as you're in Mesa, you must be involved with my sister's case."

"Yes, ma'am, I am."

"I'm Tonya Claiborne. Please, come in."

He cautiously stepped into the foyer. "Is your mother here by chance?"

"Not at the moment. She's at the funeral home, taking care of some last-minute business. My sister's service is tomorrow."

"Yes, I know, and I'm sorry for your loss."

"Thank you. I appreciate it. Can I get you anything while you wait for my mom?"

"No thanks. I'm fine."

She led him into the living room. The house was neat and clean, although some of upholstery looked a little worn. He took his seat on the sofa as Tonya sat down across from him.

"Sorry it's so dark and gloomy in here. We've been hounded by news reporters, so we've had to keep the curtains closed. I'm feeling like a prisoner in my own home."

"Yeah, I've seen it happen in other cases. I understand the public's right to know, but you're right, they do need to learn to be more sensitive to grieving families."

"You got that right." Her face turned sad as she changed the subject.

"My parents bought the place before Annette and I were born. Once upon a time, it was a really nice area to live in, but then my dad emptied out my mom's bank account and left. It all happened when I was in the second grade. Then, later on, when the neighborhood started going downhill, we couldn't afford to move, and we've been stuck here ever since."

"I see. So where's your dad now?"

"He passed away a couple years ago. After he left, he went out and lived the good life, or so I'm told. Every once in a while, Annette and I would hear from him, you know, like at Christmastime, or maybe he'd send us a birthday card, that sort of thing. But then he had a really bad stroke and ended up dying in a nursing home somewhere in Nevada. He and my mom were long divorced by then, and that, as they say, was that."

"I'm sorry."

"Yeah, me too, but stuff happens, and I guess you gotta learn to live with it or else you end up going crazy." She paused for a moment. "This house does have one redeeming factor though."

"What's that?"

"My grandmother hardly ever comes over. She's scared to death someone will come along and strip her precious Cadillac while it's parked in our driveway. About the only time we see her here is over the holidays, but it's okay. She can be a real pain in the butt when she wants to be, and she and my mother were never that close."

"That's what I understand." Beau glanced around the room. A few pages from a magazine had been framed and displayed on the wall. They featured photos of a beautiful young girl playing a violin. He took a closer look, turning his gaze back and forth to Tonya.

"Yeah, that's me. Sometimes I look like a plain Jane in real life, but I've always been very photogenic, and it's amazing what a little makeup and a different hairstyle will do, along with ditching the glasses."

"I see."

"Musical talent seems to run in the family. Annette played the clarinet, and she was in the marching band in high school. I play guitar, along with the violin and viola, and I was written up in a local magazine about a year ago. It was a piece about young, up-and-coming musicians."

Beau was impressed. "Really?"

"Yep. We may not have much, but my mother made sure we had music lessons."

They heard a car pulling into the driveway. Heather walked in a moment later and Beau presented his badge.

"I'm sorry to bother you, ma'am. I just wanted to update you and your daughter on Annette's case.

"Thank you. Have you made any arrests yet?"

"Not at this time."

"My niece did it. She hated Annette. She wanted—"

"We don't know that, Mom." Tonya turned her attention to Beau. "Yeah, my sister and my cousin had issues, but I've known my cousin all my life. She doesn't have it in her to kill anyone. Jesse, however, is another story. I'm not saying my sister was perfect, but what kind of a creep would get involved with his wife's cousin in the first place?"

Heather shot her daughter an angry look. "Why do you keep doing that? Don't you want to see justice served for your sister?"

"Of course I want justice for Annette, but where's the justice if the wrong person goes to prison while her real killer goes free?" Tonya turned her attention back to Beau. "I've never liked Jesse. He's such a phony-baloney who thinks he's all that and a bag of chips. Unfortunately, Annette fell for it, and she honestly thought he'd marry her someday. She also thought Emily would—"

"That's enough, Tonya." Heather gave Beau an apologetic look. "My daughter is understandably distraught over losing her sister, but she just doesn't understand how much Emily hated Annette. She blamed her for ruining her marriage, and according to my mother, she's been very vocal about it. Now I'm not saying my daughter was blameless. She even admitted to me that what she did was wrong, but she also assured me, many times in fact, that she and Jesse had ended it months ago. Then, over the holidays, we heard that Jesse and Emily were trying to work things out. At the time we all felt relieved. Annette even told me she was happy to hear it."

"I see." Beau took out his pad and began taking notes. "Mrs. Claiborne, would you happen to know the reason why Annette went to Jesse's house that morning?"

"No, sir, I'm afraid I don't, but like I just said, she was happy to hear that Jesse and Emily were working things out. Annette was in love with a man named Gary Murkowski. They'd been living together for the past few years, and we were all hoping that someday he'd ask her to marry him, but it'll never happen now." Heather's eyes welled up with tears.

"You okay, Mom?"

"I'm fine, Tonya. I'm just having a moment." She grabbed a tissue from the box sitting on the coffee table. "Tonya was very shy when she was younger, and during that time Emily reached out to her. Later on, she encouraged her to pursue her music. However, she also has her darker side. According to my mother, both Emily and Jesse told her they wanted Annette out of their lives. For good."

"I see," said Beau. "So, when was this?"

"When they spoke to her on the phone. On Christmas Eve night."

He made more notes. "So tell me Mrs. Claiborne, do you think that Emily could have pushed your daughter down those stairs?"

She looked him in the eye. "If Emily had showed up at Jesse's house and found Annette there, or if Annette showed up while Emily was there, then yes, she absolutely would have been capable of pushing Annette down those stairs."

Beau finished taking his notes and put his pad back into his pocket. "Thank you, Mrs. Claiborne. I know this is a difficult time for both you and your daughter, and I'm truly sorry for your loss."

"Thank you. So tell me, sir, do you think Emily did it?"

He gave her a wink as he stood from his chair. "We're still gathering evidence, but I'm hoping to make an arrest very soon. I'm afraid that's all I can say for now. I can see myself out."

Beau could hardly contain his glee as drove back to Phoenix. Emily St. Claire's family had turned against her, and even though her aunt's comments were based on speculation and hearsay, he could still mention them in his grand jury testimony. Granted, once the case went to trial, Freddie Lancaster would pick Heather's story apart, but then again, a bereaved mother, bullied and left sobbing on the witness stand, would impact the jury as well. He smiled to himself as he drove. He had one last stop to make.

❧TWENTY-SEVEN❧

A S KYLE SORTED through his pile of paperwork someone dropped off another folder. He muttered a quick thank you and took another swallow of his lukewarm coffee. Setting the mug down, he flipped the folder open, raising his brow as he read.

"What's up?"

Kyle looked at Clarke Davidson, whose desk sat next to his.

"I just got the preliminary report on Annette Claiborne's laptop. Turns out my hunch was correct. Ms. Claiborne did indeed buy that positive pregnancy test strip online."

"Really?"

"Yep. You name it, sooner or later you'll find it."

"Indeed. So who's the seller?"

Kyle thumbed through the report. "A young, pregnant lady in Flagstaff, who apparently came up with a clever way to buy baby clothes. The entire transaction took place online. Annette Claiborne contacted her by email a few days before her death, and she paid for the strip with PayPal. The final email, with the UPS tracking number, came from the seller. According to the UPS website, the package was delivered the afternoon before Annette went to Jesse's house."

"Sounds like she may have been trying to blackmail someone."

"Or trying to convince someone not to go back to his wife." Kyle stood from his chair and reached for his jacket. "It's time for another little chat with Jesse St. Claire."

* * *

Beau presented his badge to the young women standing behind the counter. "I'm Detective Fowler, with the Phoenix Police Department. Is Megan Connors in?"

She looked over her shoulder. "She's busy with a client right now. Can someone else help you?"

"No, ma'am. Which one is Ms. Connors?"

"That's her, in the pink sweater, with the long dark hair, second station from the far end."

Beau followed her gaze. Megan was busy brushing brown goop on her client's head. "Do you know how long she'll be?"

"She shouldn't be that long. I'll let her know you're here." She walked up to Megan, pointing out Beau as they talked. Megan gave him a strong look before summoning another stylist to take care of her client. She looked annoyed as she took off her apron and stepped up to the counter.

"May I help you?"

"Yes, ma'am. Is there some place where we can talk in private?"

"Right this way." She motioned for him to follow her and she took him to a small utility room at the back of the salon. "So, what's this about?"

"I understand you were with Emily St. Claire the morning of her cousin's accident."

"Yes, I was."

"And I understand the two of you were on your way to the airport."

"Yes, we were."

"You two were taking a vacation together, is that right?"

"That's right." Her patience was waning. "Look, I already went over this with the other detective. Madden. We were on our way to the airport, but first we had to stop and pick up Emily's passport."

"I'm aware of that, Ms. Connors. I'm just making sure I understand everything correctly. So, you took Emily to her husband's home, correct?"

"Yes, that's correct. She'd forgotten she'd left it in Jesse's safe, so she had to go get it."

"How was she acting?"

"She was fine. We were both excited about our trip."

"Yes, I'm sure you were. So, how was she acting when you arrived at Mr. St. Claire's home?"

"She was fine. She and Jesse are in the process of reconciling. They've been through some pretty tough times lately, but they'd worked through a lot of their problems. In fact, as we were pulling into the driveway, Emily mentioned something about how once we got back this would be her home again, and she sounded really happy when she said it."

Beau grabbed his pad and took notes. "I see. So, did you go with Emily to get her passport?"

"You mean, did I go inside the house with her?"

"Yes."

"No sir. I waited for her in the car, but I was able to see her from the driveway."

"Really? So, what did you see?"

"She knocked on the front door and Jesse answered. She stepped into the doorway and Jesse handed her passport to her. They hugged and kissed for a moment. Then he walked her back to the car."

"You were able to see her inside the house?"

"Yes. Jesse was waiting right there, with her passport in his hand. She only stepped a foot or so into the doorway, and then they came right back out."

"So, how long did you have to wait?"

"Two minutes," said Megan, matter-of-factly.

"Two minutes?"

"Yes." Megan's voice was firm. "I was keeping close watch on the time. I wanted to be sure we got to the airport with enough time to check our bags, go through security, and have breakfast before we boarded our flight. I'm a real stickler for being on time, Mr. Fowler. I looked at the clock as Emily got out of the car. It was three minutes past nine. She went to the front door and returned a moment later, with Jesse. We said a brief hello, I backed the car out of the driveway, and then one of Emily's neighbors came up to say hello. We talked for a moment, and then we drove off. I checked the clock again as we were driving away. Two minutes had passed. It was now five minutes after nine."

Beau clenched his teeth as he made notes. "Well, Ms. Connors, I'm certainly impressed with your attention to detail. So, how was Emily acting after she got back in the car?"

"The same as before."

"She didn't appear angry or upset?"

"No, not at all. A little more subdued perhaps, but only for a moment or so."

Beau raised his brow. "What do you mean by subdued?"

"As I just told you, she and Jesse had reconciled. She said something about missing Jesse while she was away, but she really didn't elaborate. That's about the time her neighbor walked up to the car, and as soon as she saw him, she perked right back up."

Beau went over his notes. Megan was much too credible of a witness. He needed to come up with something to shake her confidence, and he had to do it fast.

"So, the two of you were excited about your trip."

"Yes, we were. It's not every day you get to go to the Caribbean. Or almost get to go to the Caribbean."

"I understand. So, how much did you have to drink that morning?"

Megan looked confused. "Come again?"

"I said how much did you have to drink, before you headed off to the airport?"

"I had a cup of coffee before I left home. Emily and I planned on having breakfast at one of the restaurants in the airport terminal."

"So what did you add to that coffee, Ms. Connors?"

"Nothing." The anger resonated in her voice. "I drink my coffee black, and the last I heard, caffeine isn't an illegal substance."

"Neither is alcohol, unless of course you're drinking and driving. You were going on vacation, Ms. Connors. It wouldn't be the first time someone had a celebratory drink or two before they headed off to the airport."

"At eight-thirty in the morning?" Megan's voice had an acidic tone. "I know where you're headed, sir, and I highly resent the implication, so you might want to look a little further into my background. Emily's mother was killed by a drunk driver, and she and I were friends at the time it happened. I still vividly recall all the pain she went through, and because of what happened to her mother, we're both extremely conscientious about drinking and driving. It's something I've never done, nor will I ever do." She shot Beau an angry look. "This interview is over, Mr. Fowler. Please see yourself out."

* * *

Once again Kyle had to push his way past the news reporters. He rang the bell, presenting his badge as the door opened.

"Sorry to disturb you, Mr. St. Claire, I'll only take a few moments of your time."

"Not a problem." Jesse motioned to him to step inside. "I seem to have plenty of time these days. I just got another cancelation."

"Sorry to hear it, but perhaps it's just as well. We'd prefer that you not leave town until our investigation is complete. Meantime I have a few more questions for you. Do you mind?"

"Of course not." He quickly closed the door, tilting his head toward the staircase as he led Kyle to the living room. "I've got one of those restoration companies coming over this afternoon to clean that up. Hopefully, once it's done, it'll bring some peace back into my home."

Kyle sat down and took out his notepad. "I know this is a touchy subject, Mr. St. Claire, but I'd like to discuss the details of your relationship with Ms. Claiborne."

Jesse cleared his throat and shifted nervously in his chair. "I see. So, what did you want to know?"

"How long were you involved with her?"

"A little over three months. We'd been having a relationship for about two weeks or so when Emily caught us, and then, after she left, I continued to be, involved, with Annette."

"I see, and why was that?"

Jesse looked him in the eye. "Revenge. I was angry with my wife for leaving me, and, at the time, I thought having sex with her cousin would somehow make me feel better. It didn't, and once I realized it wasn't working, I ended the relationship."

"I see. So when was this?"

"Last fall. Sometime in September. I can't recall the exact date."

Kyle took more notes. "Okay. Did it end amicably?"

"Not exactly."

"Would you care to elaborate on that?"

"Somehow, Annette had convinced herself that I'd marry her once Emily divorced me. It didn't matter how many times I told her it wouldn't happen; she just wouldn't listen. She wouldn't let it go."

"Did you say or do anything to lead her on?"

"No. Or at least, nothing that I'm aware of." Jesse's voice was firm. "I told her, from the very start, that it would be nothing more than a casual fling for both of us, and when it was over, it was over."

"I see. So, I take it she wasn't agreeable to ending the relationship."

"No, she was not."

"So, how did she take it?"

"First, she tried to get me to change my mind. Then, once she realized she couldn't, she got upset."

"How so? Did she start crying or cause a scene?"

"She just got really upset. You know how women are. They can get really hysterical, you know, and they can sometimes throw a temper tantrum when they don't get their way."

"And that's what Annette did? She threw a tantrum?"

Jesse's body tightened as he looked down at the floor. "Yeah, you could say that. She didn't make any threats or anything like that. It was more of an, 'it's your loss' sort of thing. The, 'you'll never find anyone as good as me' kind of stuff."

"I see, and how did you respond?"

Jesse turned his gaze back to Kyle. "I held my ground. I told her I was still in love with Emily and I intended to get her back. I also admitted I was wrong to ever get involved with her in the first place, and that in hindsight, I realized I'd been unfair to her as well as Emily."

Kyle raised his brow. "So how'd she take it?"

Jesse looked away as he again shifted in his chair. "Not very well, I'm afraid. I told her it was time for us to move on, and that was that. Then I escorted her to the front door, and I wished her well. At that point what else could I have done?"

"Did you ever see her after that?"

"No. It was the last time I saw her. That is until the other day, when she showed up at my door, unannounced."

Kyle thumbed through his notes. "I understand, Mr. St. Claire, that you've given your consent for us to access your medical records."

"Yes, sir, I have. Due to a genetic defect I'm unable to father a child. I simply wanted to set the record straight, once and for all, that I wasn't, nor could I have possibly been, the father of her unborn child."

"I understand. Did Ms. Claiborne know that you're unable to father a child?"

Once again, Jesse got fidgety. "No. At least I don't think she did. Not unless Emily had told her. Please understand, this is something very private and that very few people know. I can't think of any reason why I would've told Annette."

"But you were in an intimate relationship with her for several weeks. Didn't the two of you ever discuss contraception?"

"Not really. I used a condom whenever I was with her. You know, just in case, and she'd mentioned something about being on the pill. That was about the extent of it."

"She didn't try to tell you that you were the father of her baby?"

Jesse's eyes went to back the floor as he nervously shifted in his seat. "No. She came over to apologize. She said she and Gary had worked things out and they were going to have a baby. She said she wanted to make things right with Emily so we could all move on. Then Emily showed up, but she never gave Annette a chance. You know what happened next."

"Yes, I know what happened next." He put his pen and notebook back in his pocket and stood up. "Thank you, Mr. St. Claire. You've been very helpful."

Jesse rose to his feet. "Of course. I'm glad to be of help. Do you need anything else?"

"I'm good. I can see myself out."

Kyle headed back to his car, adding a few more notes as he waited for it to warm up. Jesse was still lying. As he put his notebook away a text message arrived on his personal cell phone. Lindsey was letting him know the school nurse called. Cory had come down with a cold and she was on her way to pick him up. He quickly responded to thank her and let her know he'd be there as soon as he could. He sighed as he put the car into gear and drove off. It was another reminder that the time had come for him to quit being a cop and find a more family friendly job.

❧TWENTY-EIGHT❧

KYLE STEPPED UP to the counter and presented his badge. "Is Ms. Connors in?" he asked.

"She's in back. If you'll wait here a moment, I'll go get her."

Megan stormed up to the counter. "What the hell is going on here? The Spanish Inquisition? I already threw that other cop out earlier today, and told him not to come back without a warrant."

"Which cop?"

"About your height, but with a little stockier build. Fifty-something, with graying hair. I think his name was Fowler."

"That would be my partner, ma'am, and I'm sorry for the inconvenience. I just needed to clarify a couple of points with you."

"Oh, really? Like how many drinks did I have before I went to the airport?"

Her comment caught Kyle off guard. "Come again?"

"Your buddy accused me of being drunk the morning I drove Emily to the airport. All I had that morning was coffee. Black."

"I realize that, Ms. Connors, and I've never accused you of being drunk, nor did I have any reason to suspect you'd been drinking that day. I simply want to go over a couple of the details with you. Do you have a moment?"

"What did you need to know?"

"Just a few more questions. It'll only take a minute or two of your time. Do you have a place where we can talk in private?"

Megan seemed to be calming down. "Of course. Right this way."

* * *

150

Beau looked up as Kyle approached his desk. "Nice of you to stop by, Kyle."

"And what's that supposed to mean?"

"I didn't see you at Annette Claiborne's service."

"I had an unexpected emergency. The school nurse sent Cory home with a cold. He's at Lindsey's until my shift is up."

Beau's demeanor softened. "Oh, sorry."

"Don't mention it. Did anything unusual happen at the service?"

"Not really, other than a lot of gawkers showing up."

"Yeah, that's to be expected in a high-profile case once the media gets involved. I take it there were no incidents."

"Not unless you want to consider Emily St. Claire not being there an incident."

"I'm not surprised she wasn't there. She never denied there was bad blood between her and her cousin. She probably didn't attend because she didn't want to create any further rifts in the family. It doesn't make her guilty of any wrongdoing."

Beau straightened up in his chair. "I disagree."

"Then you're chasing the wrong suspect. I spoke to Jesse St. Claire again this morning. It's obvious the man's lying through his teeth, and I can't understand why you're buying into his story. This isn't like you, Beau. You're a much better cop than this."

"Well, call it gut instinct. I'm acting on a hunch. I also stopped by Megan Connors' salon earlier today."

"Yes, I know. I was just there a little while ago myself."

"Really?" Beau seemed intrigued. "So, what'd the lady have to say to you?"

"She said you accused her of being drunk the morning she and Emily stopped by the St. Claire home. What made you think something like that?"

"They were leaving on vacation. It wouldn't be the first time someone had a celebratory drink or two before leaving town."

"I interviewed her at the airport," Kyle said firmly, "and I know enough to recognize when someone's been drinking. She was stone-cold sober. So was Emily St. Claire."

"I have to cover all the angles, Kyle. She's lying. She's covering up for her friend."

Kyle stood his ground. "No way. Megan Connors is as credible as they come. She hasn't had so much as a parking ticket in the past ten years."

"I realize that, and the same can also be said for Jesse St. Claire. He's a well-respected, motivational speaker who freely admits he made a huge mistake getting involved with his wife's cousin. He also admitted that his first reaction was to protect his wife, but because he's a man of integrity, he came clean. Emily St. Claire, on the other hand, is an angry, bitter woman who gave up her dreams and spent the past eight years helping him become who he is today. Then she caught him in the act with her cousin. Even so, Jesse tried his best to make it up to her. So did Annette for that matter, but Emily is vindictive. She killed Annette in a jealous rage. It'll be up to the grand jury to decide whether or not to indict her, and if they do, another jury will decide her guilt or innocence."

"Where's the proof, Beau? There's no evidence against her."

"Her husband saw her do it."

Kyle stood his ground. "And we both know eyewitness testimony isn't always reliable. We also know Annette wasn't pregnant and she bought the test strip online. I think a more plausible theory is that she showed up that morning in an attempt to blackmail Jesse. They argued, and during that argument she somehow ended up doing a backflip down those stairs. What has yet to be determined is whether or not he actually pushed her, or if it was indeed an accident. My gut instinct is telling me he's responsible. I've also read the preliminary report on Emily's sweater. It's inconclusive. It contained many different fibers, from many different sources, but so far none appear to match any of the fibers on Annette's clothing. However, they did find fibers from Annette's sweater on Jesse's shirt cuff."

"Which would be consistent with his claim of checking her pulse before calling nine-one-one. It doesn't prove he killed her. It proves he tried to help her."

"And if Emily had pushed her, they would have found fibers from her sweater Annette's clothing, but none were found."

Beau's eyes narrowed into little slits. "He is not responsible. She is, and I've already sent the report to the county attorney's office. It'll be—"

"When did you send the report?"

"Right after I got back from Annette's service, while you were busying checking on your son. As I was saying, it's now up to the grand jury to decide what happens next. In the meantime, we're done. I've closed the file on the St. Claire case. So why don't you take the rest of the day off and go take care of your son?"

"Cory's fine. It's just a cold. He'll bounce back in a day or two, and I'm not done with the St. Claire case."

"Yes, you are. I'm in charge of this investigation, and it's now officially closed." He stood from his desk and put on his jacket. "I'm out of here. See you tomorrow."

A stunned Kyle waited for Beau to leave. Once he was gone, Kyle returned to his desk and pulled up a file on his computer. A moment later he ran to the printer. Paperwork in hand, he rushed back to his desk.

"Is everything okay, Kyle?" Clarke too had returned to his desk.

"No, everything is not okay."

"Can I help you with anything?"

"Not at the moment, but hold that thought." He hastily put his stack of papers in a folder before shutting down his computer and grabbing his coat. "See you in the morning, Clarke."

"You too."

Kyle felt the chill in the air as he stepped outside. The wind had started kicking up. A winter storm was on its way. He picked up his pace as he headed to his car. Dropping his folder onto the passenger seat, he locked the doors and placed a call while he waited for the engine to warm up. After pressing a few buttons, a young man came on the line.

"This is Detective Kyle Madden. I'm calling about the St. Claire case. You would have received the file earlier today. Can you tell me who'll be handling it?"

"Hang on while I pull it up on the computer."

"Take your time."

A moment later the young man came back on the line. "Looks like Renee Ramirez will be the prosecuting attorney. Is there anything else I can help you with?"

"Yes. Could you please connect me with Ms. Ramirez?"

"Certainly."

Kyle drummed his fingers on the steering wheel as he waited for the call to transfer. To his relief, Renee quickly answered.

"Hey, Renee. Kyle Madden. How are the wedding plans coming?"

"Don't ask." He heard a chuckle in her voice. "I live in the land of the overworked and the underpaid. So, what can I do for you?"

"It's about the St. Claire case. I understand it's been assigned to you."

"My, word travels fast. I only got the file a little while ago, so I haven't had the chance to do much with it, other than give it a cursory glance. So far it appears to be a textbook case of he said she said, and there's certainly not enough evidence to warrant a second-degree murder charge. I'm going for manslaughter."

"Do you think you can get a conviction?"

"I can't really answer that right now."

"Would you consider turning it away due to lack of evidence?"

"It's a high-profile case, Kyle, and the media's been all over it. It has to go before the grand jury, otherwise people will start asking questions."

"Yeah, and you can't have that. Especially if your boss is running for governor."

Her demeanor quickly changed. "Whether or not he decides to run for governor is completely irrelevant. People are losing faith in the system, so transparency is the order of the day. I'm taking this one to the grand jury. It'll be up to them to determine if a manslaughter charge warranted or not."

Realizing his mistake, Kyle quickly backed down. "Sorry Renee, I didn't mean to offend you. It's been a long day."

"I understand. I've had a long day myself." The chill remained in her voice.

"So when will the grand jury be taking it up?"

"Sometime next week. Beau can fill you in on the details since he's the one in charge of the investigation. Anything else I can do for you?"

"No thanks. I'm good, Renee."

They disconnected and Kyle tossed the phone aside. "Nice going, Madden," he said outload. "That lady is the last person you want to offend. What the hell is the matter with you?"

He stopped for a moment to gather his thoughts before grabbing his personal cell phone and looking up a number. Once again, he was relieved the call didn't go to voice mail.

"Emily, this is Kyle Madden."

"Yes, I know. I recognized the number."

"Listen to me carefully, and do everything I tell you to do. You need to call your attorney, as soon as possible."

"What for?"

"Beau Fowler is convinced you're guilty. He's just turned your case over to the county attorney, who plans to take it to the grand jury sometime next week. It's entirely possible that you may be indicted for manslaughter."

"Oh dear god."

"Emily, please, you need to stay calm. I know you're innocent, but somehow Jesse managed to convince Beau otherwise."

"Unfortunately, Jesse is a master at convincing people. It's how he makes his living."

"I know. If we're lucky, the grand jury won't indict you, but even if they do, your attorney may be able to get the charges dropped. Their case against you is very weak."

"Dear god, are they going to arrest me?"

"If you get indicted, then yes, you'll be arrested. So please, do what I'm telling you to do. Call your attorney and be ready, just in case, and by the way, we never had this conversation."

"I understand."

He heard her voice shake. "Look, Emily, if worse comes to worse, and they do indict you, I promise you I'll do everything in my power to see to it you don't get convicted. I know you didn't do this. Jesse is setting you up, and I intend to find out why."

"Thank you, Kyle."

"Don't thank me just yet. I'm not done. Just call your attorney, as soon as you can, and good luck." He disconnected the call and headed out of the parking lot.

◈TWENTY-NINE◈

EMILY STARED AT the phone in her hand. "This can't be happening. This isn't real. This can't be happening. It can't be—"

"Emmy?"

"Dad?" Her voice sounded strange. "That was Kyle Madden on the phone. He told me to call my lawyer."

"Why?"

"He said they've just turned my case over to the county attorney, and I could be arrested sometime soon. I didn't do anything wrong. I wasn't even there."

Roger grabbed her phone and punched up Freddie's number. A woman soon answered.

"This is Roger Olmstead. My daughter, Emily St. Claire, is one of your clients. We've just received an anonymous tip that my daughter's case has gone to the county attorney, and she may be arrested."

"It's okay, Mr. Olmstead. We'll take care of it. Do you have any other information?"

"I'm not sure. I'm going to put my daughter on the line."

Emily shook her head and her voice trembled. "I can't deal with this right now. He just said it went to the county attorney's office, and something about the grand jury."

"At the moment, she's pretty shook," said Roger, "but she was told something about the grand jury."

"That's pretty much standard procedure. Mr. Lancaster will be in court for the next couple of days, so I'm scheduling an appointment for your daughter to see him at ten o'clock Monday morning."

He looked at Emily. "Ten o'clock Monday?" She gave him a nod. "Yes, that would be fine." He disconnected the call and turned back to Emily. "I'm sorry. I guess that's all we can do for now."

She shook her head as she choked back the sobs. "Why is this happening? Why?"

"You were, unfortunately, in the wrong place at the wrong time, and now someone's using it against you."

"But how can he do this to me?"

"He's doing this because he's guilty and he's trying to save himself."

"But how can he live with himself? Does he really hate me that much?"

"I don't think he hates you, Emmy, but he certainly doesn't love you either. Once we get through this thing, and we're going to get through this thing, you'll find someone else. Someone who's truly worthy of you."

"I don't care, Dad. I don't care about any of that stuff anymore."

He gave her a smile. "Once we get this mess cleared up, you'll change your mind. You're young, and you still have your whole life ahead of you. In the meantime, there's a young police detective out there who just put his career on the line trying to help you."

* * *

Emily shook her head in disbelief. "One-hundred fifty dollars? That's all? It has to be worth a lot more than that."

The scruffy-looking man behind the counter gave her a shrug. "Look lady, this is a pawn shop. I'm not some fancy jewelry store at the mall selling you stuff at ridiculously marked-up prices. One-fifty is what I'm offering you, along with the three-fifty for the wedding set. Take it or leave it."

"But I hardly ever wore it, and look, it has a real emerald, and the diamonds are real too."

"I never said they weren't real. I've also got some other really nice pieces here. If you'd prefer to swap it for another ring, I can probably make you a much better deal."

"No, but thanks for the offer. I have bills to pay, so I'll just take the cash."

"Suit yourself." He grabbed the rings and stepped through a side door, returning a few minutes later with cash in hand. He counted out the money on the countertop and handed it over.

"There you go. Five-hundred-dollars. If you change your mind later on and want to get the rings back, you'll have to return the—"

"No. I've already told you. I don't want them back."

"All right, then. Are you sure I can't interest you in something else?"

"No, thank you." Emily rushed out the door. Ten minutes later she drove into another parking lot, taking a deep breath as she walked through another door.

"I'm Emily St. Claire," she said. "I have a one o'clock appointment with Steve Hudson."

The receptionist greeted her a warm smile. "Have a seat, Emily. He'll be with you shortly."

"Thanks. Oh, and I have the money to take care of the rest of my bill. Three-hundred twenty-five dollars, right?"

Emily reached into her purse and handed over the money. Steve came out to greet her as the receptionist handed her a receipt. She followed him to his office, and once she settled in her seat, he opened the folder on top of his desk.

"So, how are things going?" he asked.

"Not great. Lately I seem to be spending most of my time in attorneys' offices. Good thing I'm working as a temp."

"I see. So what's going on?"

"Jesse is trying to railroad me. Somehow, he's convinced the police I killed my cousin, and they're presenting their case to the grand jury later this week. I had quite a meeting with Freddie Lancaster yesterday morning. We're planning our defense strategy."

"You're very lucky to be in such good hands."

"Which is what everyone keeps telling me, so I guess there's no sense in dwelling on it here. We have more important matters to discuss."

"Indeed." Steve began shuffling through the folder. "We've heard back from Jesse's attorney. He's not contesting the divorce. However, he wants you to have all of the proceeds from the sale of the house."

"But I don't want it. I don't want any of it."

Steve handed her a paper. "We can certainly decline the offer, but apparently, he insists that you to have it. He says it's his way of repaying you for all the years you spent helping him build his career."

Emily's voice raised its pitch. "Repaying me for helping him my Aunt Fanny. He's framing me for something I didn't do, so he's trying to make himself look good."

"I understand. Like I said, we'll decline. No one can force you to accept it if you don't want it."

"So, what happens next?"

"We have a court hearing, scheduled for late March. The judge will sign the paperwork and it'll be over and done with. You'll be a free woman."

Emily laughed an odd sounding laugh. "Did you just say, 'I'll be a free woman?' I could very well be sitting in a jail cell by then."

"I highly doubt it. As I've already told you, Freddie Lancaster is one of the best in the business. One of our other lawyers worked another case with him. The client's ex-wife also tried to frame him for something he didn't do, and the evidence against him was pretty substantial. Still, Freddie managed to get the charges dropped, so don't give up hope. If I know Freddie Lancaster, your case will probably be dropped long before it goes to trial."

❧THIRTY❧

THE NUMBER OF reporters surrounding Jesse's home had dwindled, but Beau knew it would only be a temporary lull. They would return in full force once the indictment against Emily came down. He greeted Jesse with a cursory nod as he stepped over the threshold.

"Got a moment?"

"You'll have to wait," Jesse said bluntly. "My assistant is here. We should be done in a few minutes."

"No problem. I'll be happy to make myself at home on the sofa." He pushed his way inside, stopping for a moment at the foot of the stairs. "I'd say whoever cleaned this up did an excellent job. You'd never know what was there."

"Yeah, but I still see it every time I walk past."

Jesse hurried back to his office and closed the door with a loud thud. He emerged a short time later, along with a stocky, middle-aged woman.

"I'll email you the information later on today," she said.

"Thanks, Yolanda. I'll walk you to the door."

"I appreciate it. All those reporters. They're such a pain in the you know what."

"I know. I'm hoping those last few holdouts will be gone soon."

Another voice chimed in. "Well, what have we here?"

Jesse frowned as he introduced them, while Yolanda extended her hand. "Pleased to meet you," she said. "I take it the case is still open."

"Actually," said Beau, "we're in the home stretch. We're hoping to make an arrest very soon, but don't worry, your boss isn't a suspect."

She gave Jesse a smile. "Well, it's certainly good to know I'll still have a job, not that I ever had any doubts."

"Thanks, Yolanda," said Jesse. "Your loyalty is very much appreciated." He opened the front door and waited for her to step out. Once she passed the reporters, he closed the door and headed back to the living room.

"She's gone."

"I gathered that. We need to talk. I'll only take a few minutes of your time."

"Of course." Jesse led him back to his office.

* * *

Yolanda reached into her purse for her car keys, only to discover they weren't there. After several moments of anxious searching, she finally gave up.

"I can't believe this," she said out loud. "I must have left them on Jesse's desk. What the hell is the matter with me today?" Sighing in frustration, she walked back to the Jesse's door and gave it a few firm knocks. To her surprise, it slowly opened.

"Jesse?"

There was answer. She cautiously stepped across the threshold.

"Jesse?"

There was still no answer, but she heard faint voices coming from Jesse's office. She headed toward the hallway. Jesse's office door was open, and as she came closer, she could hear what was being said.

"You don't need to have that kind of attitude with me, Jesse. I just saved your ass."

"And I never asked you to do that. I've been telling you from the start, it was an accident."

"Maybe, maybe not, but even if you never actually touched her, if you were acting aggressively enough for her to step backwards to get away from you, it would still be considered manslaughter."

"Yeah, but you can't prove it, and I'm getting tired of this charade. You're hell bent on destroying Emily, so please allow me to do at least one decent thing for her, and that is giving her the proceeds from the house sale in the divorce settlement. That way she can at least cover the cost for her legal defense, and maybe she'll have a decent shot at beating the rap."

Beau raised his voice in anger. "You're not giving her one damn dime. We both agreed that we'd bring Benjamin Morris a winnable, high-profile case, and he's going to get that case, even if I have to mow you over to get it."

"You'll still have your high-profile case."

"She went out and hired Freddie Lancaster, which now makes everything a hell of a lot harder, but if she can't afford to keep paying his retainer, he'll bow out, and that'll help our side. She has to be convicted, otherwise we've gone to a whole lot of trouble for nothing."

"But what about the other detective? Madden? You said he's convinced of her innocence as well."

"I'll take care of Kyle. You tell your divorce attorney you've changed your mind and you're taking the house sale proceeds off the table."

Yolanda stood in the hallway, frozen in her tracks. Her heart raced and her palms started sweating. To her horror, her purse slipped out of her hand.

"What was that?" asked Beau.

"Sorry guys, I couldn't find my keys." Yolanda forced herself to smile as she rushed into the office and whisked her keys off the top of Jesse's desk. "Aha! There they are, and by the way, Jesse, you forgot to lock the front door. Again."

"Sorry, Yolanda."

"Well, just be careful, okay? I gotta run." She turned to Beau. "Nice meeting you. Have a good day."

"You too, ma'am."

Jesse stood up. "I'll walk you to the door, Yolanda."

He escorted her out, once again telling her goodbye as he opened the front door. She gave him a friendly nod in return and hurried out to her car. Her hands shook so violently she could barely start the engine. She knew she had to pull herself together quickly, before the detective came outside and got the make and license number of her car. She quickly put the car in gear and drove away, keeping a close watch in her rearview mirror until she turned onto the main road and lost herself in traffic. Her mind raced as she drove. Her boss must have killed Annette, and Beau Fowler was a crooked cop who, for whatever reason, was willing to help him put the blame on his wife. It also sounded like there was another detective who apparently wasn't involved in their conspiracy. She would have to contact him, as soon as possible, but for the moment she couldn't recall the name. Hopefully it would come to her later on.

* * *

Beau looked up as Jesse came back into the room.

"Don't worry, she's gone."

"So, how much do you think she overheard?"

Jesse tried to sound reassuring. "I don't think she really heard anything. She was still a few feet down the hallway when she announced she'd forgotten her keys, and she certainly didn't act like anything was wrong when I walked her out."

"Even so, you might want to keep an eye on her for a while."

Jesse tried to brush him off. "She'll be fine, Beau. She wasn't acting the least bit strange, other than being a little flustered over forgetting her keys. Besides, I had her sign a confidentiality agreement when I hired her, so even if she did overhear bits and pieces of what we were discussing, she really doesn't have anything to go on, and if she were to say something, I'd not only fire her, I'd sue her for breach of contract."

"Like that would help if you ended up in a prison cell. You need to address this, Jesse, and you need to do it before the end of the day. Otherwise, I'll have to take care of it, and trust me, you won't like the way I do it."

"Don't worry, I said I'll take care of it. Now, is there anything else I can do for you?"

"No," said Beau, firmly. "We're done. For now, but you do what I told you to do. You talk to your attorney, and you don't give your wife anything."

"Got it."

"Good. I'll see myself out."

Jesse stared out the window and watched Beau as he got into his car and drove away. Going along with his scheme had been a bigger mistake than getting involved with Annette. He had made a hasty decision under emotional duress. It was something he always warned his clients to never do, and now he had a hefty price to pay. Even if Emily were acquitted, she would never take him back. Jesse remained at the window, pondering his thoughts until he realized Yolanda would probably be home by now. He grabbed his phone and placed his call. She soon answered.

"Hey, Yolanda." He prayed his voice sounded normal. "I just wanted to talk to you about Detective Fowler."

"It's really none of my business, and, to be honest, I really wasn't paying much attention. I just came in long enough to grab my keys and go."

"I understand, but just so you know, Emily was here when Annette fell down the stairs. Until now I haven't discussed the case with anyone other than the police, being as I'm a witness and all, but the point is I've told him, over and over again, that it was an accident, but he just isn't buying it. In the meantime, I'm praying she'll be found innocent."

"Well, hopefully she will, for both your sakes, and I'm sure this must be very upsetting to you."

"Yes, it is. I'm only bringing it up because I don't want there to be any misunderstanding."

"Thanks, Jesse. I appreciate the thought, but as I said, my mind was elsewhere, and I really wasn't paying attention to whatever you were talking about. Did you need anything else?"

"No. I just wanted to make sure you didn't misunderstand anything."

"No worries. Now if you'll excuse me, I've got to get to work. I promised you I'd email you the information you needed later on today."

* * *

Yolanda's hands were still shaking after she disconnected the call. She took another deep breath. At least Jesse didn't sound angry or upset. As she thought it over again, she started to realize that whatever she may have overheard most certainly would have had been taken out of context. Perhaps Jesse really was trying to defend his wife. If so, it would be up to the courts to sort it all out. Whatever she may have heard, or thought she heard, would best be forgotten.

❧THIRTY-ONE❧

EMILY'S HEART SKIPPED a beat as she checked her phone. She was about to learn her fate. Saying a silent prayer, her voice quivered as she answered.

"Hi, Freddie."

"I have some news." His voice sounded calm and relaxed, but her heart still skipped another beat.

"Yes, of course." She tried to control the shaking in her own voice. "So, what happened? What did they say?"

"The grand jury has refused to indict you due to a lack of evidence, so the county attorney has dropped its case against you. It's over and done with. You're a free woman."

She paused for a moment and tried to take it all in. "So you're saying I won't be charged?"

"No, you won't be charged. They had no case. The lab reports showed no physical evidence, and the county medical examiner found no defense wounds or any sign of a struggle on Annette's body. The only reason the county attorney took it to the grand jury in the first place was because it was a high-profile case."

"I see. So what happens next?"

"You go back to your piano. You have some big auditions coming up in the next few weeks."

A tear rolled down her cheek as a sense of relief swept over her. "Thank you, Freddie. I don't know what else to say."

"I'm just doing my job, but even if you'd been indicted, it would have been highly unlikely that a jury would have convicted you."

His words jolted her. "So what about Jesse? Will they go after him now?"

"That's for others to decide, but if he should be charged, I won't take him as a client. What matters is the case against you has been dropped. It's over Emily. You have your life back."

"And for that I'll always be grateful. I can't thank you enough."

"You're welcome. Hopefully you'll think of me once you become a famous concert pianist."

She smiled as she ended the call. Afterwards she sat quietly and took it all in. Before long Lurch started barking. Her father was due home. She hurried to the kitchen and met him as he stepped through the side door.

"Dad, you'll never believe what just happened. I wasn't indicted. They're dropping the case against me."

He gave her a big smile as wrapped his arms around her and kissed her on the cheek. "I know. It's a breaking story on the local news. It's over, Emmy. It took them awhile, but they finally figured out you didn't do it." He stepped back and looked her up and down. "Why don't you go change? Your old dad is taking you out to The Saddleback for a prime rib."

Her face lit up. "You mean it?"

"Of course I mean it. Go get ready."

Her phone rang before she could step away. "Hold that thought, Dad." She glanced at the caller ID, surprised at who was calling.

"Andrea?"

"Hey, I just heard about it on the news. Congratulations."

"Thank you."

"You okay? You sound a little hesitant."

Emily tried to shrug it off. "I'm fine. I'm just, surprised. I haven't heard from you in some time."

"I know, and I'm sorry." She paused for a moment. "A police detective showed up the day after your cousin fell down the stairs."

"I see. Do you recall the name?"

"Kyle. Kyle something. I'm not sure."

"Kyle Madden?"

"That's it."

Emily felt relieved. "I see. So, what did you tell Detective Madden?"

"Not much. I just told him about how last summer you caught Jesse in the act with your cousin, and you were understandably upset at the time. I also told him that later on you and Jesse were going to try to work things out, and it was about the same time you quit working for Dr. Lerner. Then I mentioned that you'd been gone for some time."

"All right. Did you say anything else?"

"Not really. That was pretty much it. Afterwards he talked to Dr. Hapner, in private. Then, after he left, Dr. Hapner told me I wasn't to contact you again. He said he didn't want to get involved. He also said that if he found out we were still talking to one another, he'd fire me. Immediately."

"What?" Emily was stunned.

"He said he'd fire me. Emily, I'm so sorry, but I couldn't risk losing my job."

"I understand. I'm just shocked. I thought Sean was a better friend then that."

"I think he was, but I also think he got scared. He must have been worried about the potential fallout if it had come out that he was involved in some sort of romantic triangle with you and Jesse. You know how the media is these days. He said they would have blown everything out of proportion, and he didn't want to risk losing any of his patients over some controversy."

"Okay."

"You sound skeptical."

"Do I?" Emily paused for a moment to gather her thoughts. "You know, they say it's when the chips are down that you find out who your friends really are."

"I'm not sure what you're getting at."

Emily's tone turned serious. "Then let me try to explain it to you in a different way. For the past few weeks my life has been a living hell. I wasn't there when my cousin fell down those stairs. I even had witnesses to back me, but for reasons I can't explain, the police bought Jesse's lies. So did the media. Yet in spite of it all, Megan stood by me. She has a clientele as well, so she too had a lot to lose, but she also knew I wasn't guilty and she wouldn't have hesitated for a moment to set someone straight if they thought otherwise, even if that someone happened to be one of her best clients."

"I'm glad, Emily, and just so you know, Dr. Hapner and I didn't think you were guilty either. We just didn't want to get involved."

"So you tell me, but the point I'm making is that Megan is a true and loyal friend who wasn't afraid to do the right thing. I really wish I could say the same for you and Sean, but I can't, and it makes me feel very sad."

"Emily, I'm sorry if you felt like I'd turned my back on you, but as I've already told you, I didn't have a choice. I couldn't risk losing my job."

Emily took a deep breath, choosing her next words carefully. "That's just an excuse, Andrea. Dr. Hapner doesn't have access to your cell phone, nor can he tell you what to do outside the office. You could have sent me a text message or email asking me how I was doing or to let me know you were on my side. You could have even called me on your own time, when you were away from the office. You know me well enough to know I wouldn't have said anything."

"But Dr. Hapner didn't want—"

"I know. You told me. He said he didn't want the controversy, but what if I had been indicted? If my case had gone to trial, he very well may have been subpoenaed to testify anyway. It's all just excuses and you know it. If you really didn't think I was guilty then why didn't you stand by me? What were you so afraid of?"

"We didn't mean to abandon you, but we had to protect our own reputations."

Emily felt as if she'd been just stabbed through the heart. "Aha! So, the truth finally comes out. You all thought I was guilty."

"No! That didn't come out right." Andrea sounded desperate. "What I meant to say was—"

"Have a good life, Andrea."

"No! Emily, wait. You don't under—"

"Yes, I do understand. I needed your support during an extremely difficult time in my life, but you chose to distance yourselves because you thought I might be guilty, and associating with me meant you'd somehow be tainted. It also means that you and Sean were never really my friends in the first place. So long, Andrea. I wish you the very best, but please don't call me anymore."

Emily gave her father a sad look as she disconnected the call and set the phone aside. "That was Andrea. Remember her? She was Dr. Hapner's office manager."

"Of course I remember her. So what's going on?"

"They thought I was guilty, and they didn't want to sully their reputations by associating with me, but now that I've been cleared, they want to make nice so we can all be friends again. Can you believe it?"

"I'm afraid I can, but I'm proud you, Emily. You did the right thing by telling her off, but you did it with grace and dignity."

"Thanks, Dad. It still really hurts, you know. I really thought we were friends."

"I know you did, but you don't need her, or Dr. Hapner for that matter. You said it yourself. It's when times get tough that you find out who your friends really are. I'm proud of Megan for standing by you. She's a friend worth keeping, so why don't you give her a call and see if she'd like to join us?"

"Good idea. Thanks."

Her phone rang again. This time her face lit up as she checked the caller ID.

"Kyle?"

"You must have recognized my number."

"Of course I did."

"I just wanted to congratulate you, and to let you know that we won't be reopening the investigation against you."

"Thank you, Kyle. You have no idea how relieved I am to hear it."

"I'll bet. So, now that it's all over and done with, I was wondering if I could take you dinner sometime."

She hesitated for a moment. "Well, I suppose you could."

"You sound like you're not sure."

"I'd honestly love to have dinner with you, Kyle, I really would, but that night at Hanson Sisters I noticed you were with someone else."

"Please, don't remind me," he said with a groan. "It was one of those friend-of-a-friend things that my sister got me into. She insisted on setting me up on a blind date that night, and it turned out to be the date from Hell. I finally had to take her out of there, because I was afraid she might cause a scene. I dropped her off at her place after we left, and I haven't spoken to her since."

Emily's face lit up. "Well, in that case, I'd love to have dinner with you sometime."

"Busy Saturday?"

"Saturday would be perfect."

"Then I'll see you on Saturday."

"Thanks, Kyle. I'm looking forward to it."

"Me too."

* * *

Jesse switched off the television set and tossed the remote aside. The nightmare was finally over. Emily would not be charged. More than anything, he wanted to pick up the phone and congratulate her, but he could never call her again. Perhaps it was for the best. She had given up everything to help him become successful. Now it was her turn to live her dreams, but he wouldn't be there to share them with her. A profound sense of sadness swept over him. He had sacrificed his marriage for nothing, but before he could wallow too deeply in self-pity, he heard a loud knock at the door. He dragged himself off the sofa and grimaced when he looked through the peephole.

"You again? I guess you didn't get the memo. It's over. They won't be charging her."

"Like I didn't already know that." Beau tilted his head toward the front yard before pushing his way inside. "So what's up with the for-sale sign?"

"I'm getting a divorce, remember? The house is community property. My attorney says I have to sell it, and just so you know, she refused her share of the sale proceeds."

"I see. So where do you plan on going once it sells?"

"That's for me to know and you to wonder about."

Beau gave him a hard look. "We need to have a little talk."

"About what? It's over, Fowler. Sorry 'bout your promotion, but as they say, stuff happens, and I lost a hell of lot more than you did. Maybe you'll have better luck with the next schmuck who comes along."

"You'd better watch your mouth. I can still tell the county attorney you finally confessed to killing her."

"And as you keep telling me, if I go down, you go down with me. As long as I don't end up sharing a cell with you, it'll be perfectly okay with me."

Beau began to soften. "Look, Jesse, I didn't come over here to argue with you. Like you said, we took a chance and we lost. I have no intention of turning you in, but now that your wife's been exonerated there are people in high places who are going to start asking questions. I just stopped by to tell you what I plan on telling them."

Jesse's arms crossed across his chest. "Really? So what are you going to say?"

"That you're sticking to your story about Ms. Claiborne being here when your wife stopped by to get her passport. Yes, they still argued at the top of the stairs, but it all happened so quickly. It was like a blur, and you were never completely certain of exactly what happened."

Jesse scratched his chin as he thought it over. "All right, but suppose, for the sake of argument, that I start telling the truth. Emily wasn't here, and it was an accident, like I've always maintained it was."

Once again, Beau scowled. "You're not getting it, are you? You do that and at the very least you'll be charged with filing a false police report. Obstruction of justice is a serious offense and changing your story won't get your wife back. It could, however, get you some jail time. Do this my way, and you walk away a free man."

"And that's it? No strings attached?"

"That's it, Jesse. It'll all be over and done with. You can have your life back, and I'll find another way to get that promotion."

As Beau started to leave, he stopped in the doorway and looked back at Jesse. "Oh, I almost forgot. There is one more thing. Being as I've kept you out of jail, you do owe me a favor."

Jesse felt his stomach twist into a knot. "Really? What kind of favor?"

"I'll let you know when the time comes. Meantime a news truck is about to pull up to the curb. I think it would be okay now if you want to talk to them. Just remember, Emily was here when her cousin fell down the stairs, but you're relieved now that they've determined it was an accident."

❦THIRTY-TWO❧

EMILY FELT LIKE a schoolgirl as she gazed at her reflection in the mirror. Her hair was nicely styled, and her little black dress looked sexy but not too seductive. She glanced down at her left hand. It still felt strange to no longer have her wedding set. She stepped up to the dresser and rummaged through her jewelry box, finding the perfect bracelet. After slipping it on she gave herself a final check before grabbing her coat and heading down the hallway. Her father looked up as she stepped into the kitchen.

"You look fabulous, Emmy."

"Thanks, Dad. All of a sudden I feel like I'm back in high school, and waiting for your little reminder about waiting up for me."

"Well, my dear, times have changed, and I'm not waiting up for you anymore. I've got my own plans tonight."

"Doing what?"

"Going out, with a lady."

Her ears perked up. "Really? Anyone I know?"

"As a matter of fact, no. So have fun, and if by chance you should arrive home before I do, don't wait up for me, okay?"

"Okay, Dad. I won't." She kissed him on the cheek and headed out the door. Fifteen minutes later she arrived at the restaurant, but Kyle was nowhere to be found. She put her name on the waiting list and joined the other patrons on a crowded bench in the foyer. As the minutes passed a few names were called, but there was still no sign of Kyle. She reached into her purse to check her phone, but there were no new messages. She wondered if he had been called away on an emergency and hadn't had time to contact her.

"Emily, party of two."

She walked up to the hostess. "I'm Emily, but I'm afraid the person I'm meeting here hasn't arrived yet."

"No problem. We can seat you now and—"

"Sorry, I'm late," said a voice behind her, "the sitter was running late."

Emily spun around and extended her hand as she gave him a warm smile. "The sitter?"

"I'm a single dad of a very active six-year-old boy, and as luck would have it, the babysitter got stuck in traffic."

"It's okay, these things happen."

The hostess led them to their table. Kyle pulled her chair out and waited for her to take her seat. Once she settled, he sat down across from her.

"So, what's your son's name?" asked Emily.

"Cory." Kyle got straight to the point. "His mother and I went our separate ways when he was three. She fell in love with some Frenchman she met on Facebook. Next thing I knew, she was hopping a flight to Paris. I filed for divorce and won full custody of Cory. She never so much as batted an eye and I've not heard from her since. Apparently, Frenchy didn't want a woman with kids."

"I can't even begin to imagine what kind of a woman would abandon her child. I knew I wouldn't be having children when I was with Jesse, but now that he's in the past I've been thinking maybe someday, after I get my degree, it might be nice to have them."

"Kids are wonderful, but they can be a handful at times, especially when you're a single parent, but I can't imagine having a life without my son."

"Does he ever ask about his mother?"

"Sometimes." Kyle looked sad. "He thinks his mother is in Heaven, and at his age and stage I think it's as good of an explanation as any. My sister helps me look after him, and we've both agreed that once he's older we'll have to tell him the truth, but for now he seems to be content with his dad and his aunt and uncle. He also gets along well with my sister's kids. They're in their teens, but they both think of him as a little brother."

Their waiter appeared and took their drink order. After he left, Emily changed the subject.

"Before we go any further, I want to thank you once again, from the bottom of my heart, for everything you've done. You believed in me, and it went a long way toward helping me get through this nightmare."

"It's because I knew you were innocent. I've been a cop for more years than I care to admit, so I've had plenty of experience when it comes to dealing with the dregs of society. Trust me, I know a guilty person when I see one, and you came nowhere close to fitting the profile."

"Then why did this happen to me?"

"I afraid I can't answer that. Beau is a good detective. It's not like him to miss the mark like this."

"He did more than miss the mark. I'll never forget the way he looked at me the night he took me in for questioning. He was a man on a mission, and that mission was to lock me up and throw away the key, no matter what. Never mind the fact that none of the evidence pointed to me. My attorney later told me that no fibers from my sweater were found on Annette's clothing, like that would have been a surprise. I also had witnesses to back me up. According to Freddie, they had no business taking my case before the grand jury. He said all they did was waste the taxpayer's money, and I don't understand any of it."

"Neither do I. As I said before, this isn't like Beau. Over the years, he's cracked some pretty remarkable cases, but you have to remember, cops are human too. We can make mistakes, just like anyone else."

"I understand, but when you make mistakes, it can destroy an innocent person's life." Emily took a deep breath before asking the question she had to ask. "So, what about Jesse? Will he be charged?"

"I can't really comment on it right now as the investigation is still ongoing. All I can tell you is he's sticking to his story about you being in the house when your cousin showed up, but he's not exactly sure how it all happened, because it happened so quickly."

Emily's heart sank. "I don't believe this. I wasn't there and he knows it."

Kyle reached over and touched her hand. "I know you weren't, but what matters is you've been officially cleared. You need to put it behind you and move on."

A server delivered some water to their table. Emily picked up her glass and took a sip.

"I know I've been cleared, Kyle, and I'll always be grateful for your help, but I still have my own reputation to worry about. The media bought into Jesse's story and for a time they made me look guilty as well. In fact, I've just ended a friendship with someone I once trusted because she, too, believed I was guilty. I'm getting ready to complete my music degree so I can try to become a concert pianist, and I don't need this kind of notoriety following me around for the rest of my life. It could end my career before it even gets started."

"I understand, and until the case is officially closed, I'm going to do the best I possibly can for you. Off the record, I know your husband is somehow responsible your cousin's death but proving it may be difficult."

"Which is the very reason why the time has come for me to take matters into my own hands. I have to clear my name."

He looked surprised. "I see. So, what do you have in mind?"

"Now that the case against me has been dropped, I've been approached by the media once again. They want to hear my side of the story, so I've decided to tell it."

"How so?"

"Have you heard of Trudy Takamatsu? She does the *Mid-Morning with Trudy* talk show on Channel Seven. It's on weekday mornings at eleven o'clock."

"I used to see her on the ten o'clock news, back when she was a reporter, and I remember a feature she did a few years ago for the Sunday paper about Japanese internment camps in Arizona, but I've never watched her talk show. However, some of my fellow officers have been on it, discussing some of cases they've been involved with. They said she's very professional. I take it she's contacted you."

"Actually, her producer has," said Emily. "At first, I wasn't sure, but now I've decided I'm going to do it. People need to hear my side of the story."

"I understand your feelings, but I also need to give you a strong word of caution. While she may appear to be fair-minded, you must remember she's still a journalist, and she's out to get the highest ratings she possibly can. This means you'll have to be very careful about what you say. Jesse is still presumed innocent until proven guilty in a court of law, so please don't give him a reason to go after you again."

The waiter arrived with their wine. Emily teased Kyle as he picked up his glass, but he reminded her he was off duty. He raised his glass.

"To happier times."

They took a sip and the conversation shifted to other topics. Emily looked forward to her auditions, but she still wasn't sure which college to attend. Kyle thought she'd be better off in Texas.

"I'm thinking of relocating there myself," he said.

"Really?"

"Yep. As I mentioned earlier, it's not easy being a cop, and I want to spend more time with Cory while I can. One of my classmates from the police academy moved to Dallas about a year ago. He's now the head of security for a big high-tech firm. There's a position coming up soon that he wants me to consider. The hours are certainly better, and the pay is a lot higher."

Emily felt her stomach twist. "Do you think you'll take it?"

"I'm giving it some serious thought."

Their waiter arrived with their salads. After the meal was over, they lingered over coffee. Finally, Kyle looked at his watch.

"Good heavens. It's getting late, and I need to get home, otherwise the sitter's going to charge me overtime."

"Of course."

He helped Emily with her coat and offered to walk her to her car. She liked the feeling of his touch.

"Thank you again, Kyle. I had a great time."

"Me too, and I'd really like to see you again sometime."

"I'd like that too. You've got my number."

"I certainly do." He gave her a warm hug. Once she was safely inside her car, he told her goodnight again and stood by as she drove away.

* * *

Once Emily was gone Kyle hurried to his own car and placed a call. As expected, it went to voice mail.

"Hey Sidney, it's Kyle, your old partner. We need to meet somewhere discreet to discuss one of my cases. I hate to say it, but it has all the markings of someone taking a bribe. Give me a call when you get the chance."

❧THIRTY-THREE❧

THE BUZZER MADE a loud, annoying sound as the door slowly opened. Emily stepped into the lobby and approached the receptionist's window.

"I'm Emily Olmstead. I'm here for *Mid-Morning with Trudy* show."

"Of course. Please take a seat in the waiting area and someone will be with you shortly."

Emily took her seat, tapping her foot and shifting in her chair as she watched a soap opera on the wall monitor. Once it was over Trudy's show would air, live. Two Phoenix Suns basketball players and a representative from the local Red Cross soon joined her. Finally, a side door opened and a woman in a business suit appeared, greeting everyone with a warm smile.

"I'm Kelsey McAllister, and I'm in charge of guest relations for Trudy's show. Are you guys ready?"

Everyone smiled and nodded as Kelsey gave them another big smile.

"Excellent. Now, if you folks would kindly follow me, we'll get started." She took them behind the door and led them down a long hallway, past the newsroom and several offices, and finally opening a large steel door near the end of the hall. Emily recognized the news anchor desks as she entered the studio, but they looked smaller than expected. The set for Trudy's show stood at the far end of the studio. It resembled a living room, and it too looked smaller than it appeared on television. A small row of folding chairs had been placed in front it. Kelsey told everyone to take a seat. She said the man from the Red Cross would do the first segment, and then Emily. The two basketball players would be last.

Trudy arrived a short time later, greeting her guests with a smile and extending her hand to each as a man in a rumpled white shirt appeared. He attached a lavaliere microphone to her collar and checked the sound before turning his attention to the first guest.

"Don't be nervous," said Trudy. "I'll be asking each of you a few questions, and then you just talk to me as if I were a guest in your home."

A voice boomed over a loudspeaker. "You're on in five, Trudy."

She gave them a parting smile and walked onto her set, taking her seat in one of the chairs. As she went over her notes someone shouted a cue and a red light lit up on one of the cameras. She looked into the lens and smiled as she announced who would be on her show that morning. The red light turned off and a few commercials aired. Emily felt her heart race as the crew hastily prepared for the first segment. The red light soon came back on as the theme music played and Trudy began talking into the camera. Kelsey whispered something to the man from the Red Cross. A moment later he was introduced, and, at Kelsey's cue, he stepped onto the set to the sound of prerecorded applause. Beads of nervous sweat popped out on Emily's forehead as she watched the interview. She carefully reached inside her purse for a tissue, her hands trembling as she dabbed the sweat away. A few minutes later the camera lights turned off. Someone shouted something as the man stood and shook Trudy's hand. Once his microphone was removed, he stepped off the set and wished Emily and the basketball players luck as he left the studio.

"Are you ready, Ms. Olmstead?"

Once again, Kelsey had her warm smile. Emily felt a lump in her throat.

"I'm as ready as I'll ever be, I suppose."

"You'll be fine. Just relax and let Trudy do the work. I'll let you know when to go."

The man with the microphone reappeared, carefully attaching it to Emily's sweater. Once he finished the camera light came back on. As the bumper music faded Trudy gave a brief recap of Emily's case and announced her name. Kelsey gave her a nod. Emily walked on the set and shook Trudy's hand before sitting down in the chair next to her. Once she'd settled Trudy wasted no time.

"So, Emily, you've been through quite an ordeal."

"Yes, I have."

"And it all started last July? Is that right?"

"Yes, that's right." Her nervousness subsided as she recounted the story of coming home from work early and catching Jesse with Annette. She would have to describe it delicately. "I finally found them upstairs, in our bedroom, and I got the shock of my life."

Trudy's face had a slight blush. "I can only imagine what it must have felt like, especially with the other woman being your cousin. So, what did you do after that?"

"I did what any woman would do. I packed my bags and left."

"But I'm told that later on, you took your husband back. Is that right?"

"Yes, that's right, but keep in mind several months had passed by then. My husband can be quite convincing. It's how he makes his living. He said it was over between him and Annette, and he wanted a second chance. We were still in the process of reconciling when Annette fell down the stairs."

"There were reports that you were there when it happened."

"Not true." Emily's voice was firm. "That's the story Jesse put out to the media, but none of it happened, and I'm here to set the record straight. I was scheduled to leave on a cruise that morning, but first I had to stop by Jesse's house to pick up my passport. Annette wasn't there when I arrived, and I have two eyewitnesses to back me. Jesse met me at the door. He handed me my passport and I left. Annette showed up sometime later. My friend, Megan, and I were at the airport, waiting for our flight, when a police detective showed up. That's when I learned about Annette's death. We immediately cancelled our travel plans and I went straight home."

"That's certainly understandable and of course you'd want to be there for Jesse and your family. So, can you tell me what happened next?"

"I kept waiting for Jesse to call me, but he never did. Then, later on that evening, I was taken in for questioning. That's when the other detective, Beau Fowler, told me that ridiculous story about Annette being there when I showed up, and that I'd pushed her down the stairs. None of it happened."

"Well I'm sure the police were just doing their job."

Emily shook her head as she struggled to control her anger. "No. It was much more than that. Detective Fowler made it very clear that he intended to pin the blame on me. I told him I had two witnesses who would verify that Annette wasn't there when I stopped by, but none of it mattered. As far as he was concerned, I was guilty. Never mind that there wasn't so much as a shred of evidence against me."

"I understand you retained Frederick Carlton Lancaster as your attorney. You must have known that he's very prominent criminal defense attorney, and they say he's never lost a case. So why would you have hired him if you weren't guilty?"

"My father is the one who actually hired him." The no-nonsense tone remained in Emily's voice. "He never trusted Jesse, and he was very concerned about the fact that no one else was in the house at the time Annette fell. He said he had a bad feeling that Jesse might try to put the blame on me. Turned out he was right."

"So what you're saying is you think your husband pushed your cousin down the stairs, and he then tried to frame you for killing her. Is that right?"

"I don't know for certain if he actually pushed Annette or not. I only know that he was the only other person in the house at the time she fell, and yes, he did try to put the blame on me. My attorney showed me the lab reports. The police took the sweater I had on that morning into evidence, but none of the fibers from my sweater were found on Annette's clothing, which proves I never pushed her. They did, however, find traces of Jesse's shirt fibers on her collar, and fibers from her clothing were found on his shirtsleeve."

"But that doesn't mean he killed either," said Trudy. "I've listened to the nine-one-one tape. He said he tried to check her pulse, so that could explain the fibers on his sleeve."

"Yes, it could, but he also admitted on that tape that it was an accident, and there wasn't any mention whatsoever of my being there. So, between the nine-one-one tape, the complete lack of any physical evidence, and the fact that I had two credible witnesses stating that Annette wasn't there when I picked up my passport, any reasonable person would have realized I wasn't a suspect, but for reasons I can't explain, Detective Fowler ignored those facts and continued to go after me anyway. It honestly felt like a witch-hunt. That's what I still don't understand, and it's why I'm still very angry. He's either lazy, or corrupt, or both. Either way, he's a bad cop who has no business being on the police force. He deserves to be fired."

Trudy looked intrigued. "So, why do you think he did this, Emily?"

"Your guess is as good as mine. Either Jesse smoothed talked him in some way, or he may have bribed him. Maybe both. Or maybe Detective Fowler just wanted his fifteen minutes of fame. What I do know for certain is that Detective Beau Fowler was out to convict me for a crime I didn't commit. He wasn't going to allow the facts to get in the way, and he certainly wasn't going to allow me to prove myself innocent. Luckily for me, the truth prevailed, in spite of him. The grand jury refused to indict me, and the county attorney dismissed the case against me due to a lack of evidence. Still, I went through a living nightmare. I was innocent, and Detective Fowler knew I was innocent. If this could happen to me then it could happen to you or anyone else. No law-abiding citizen should ever be subjected to what I went through. Nobody."

Trudy shifted in her chair. "I can certainly understand why you'd be upset. Anyone experiencing what you went through would be, and, as you've no doubt know, they've just ruled your cousin's death to be an accident."

"Yes, I know," said Emily. "I heard it on the ten o'clock news last night."

"Do you think is was an accident?"

Emily looked Trudy in the eye. "I honestly don't know if it was an accident or not. The only person who knows for sure is Jesse St. Claire."

"I understand your aunt and your grandmother aren't happy with the ruling. They're turning to social media and they've just set up a website called, 'Justice for Annette.' Do you have any comment?"

"I haven't spoken to my aunt or my grandmother in some time, so I really can't comment on that. What I will say is that in spite of everything, Annette was still my cousin. What happened to her was tragic, and I certainly wouldn't have wished her harm. We may never know the truth about what really happened to her. I can only hope that my aunt, and my grandmother, and the rest of the family, can move on."

"I hope so too." Trudy paused before changing the subject. "So what about you and your husband? Have you spoken to him since this incident?"

"No, I haven't. The last time I saw him was when he handed me my passport, and he hasn't contacted me since. It's over. I've already filed for divorce. It'll be final in March."

As the interview wound down Trudy asked Emily about her future plans. She talked about going back to college to complete her music degree and her hope to someday become a concert pianist. As the red camera lights turned off a sense of relief came over her. It was time to close that chapter of her life and prepare for her auditions. She would soon be leaving for Los Angeles and Dallas.

✥THIRTY-FOUR✥

AS KYLE HUNG up his phone an angry face glared down at him. "So what's up with you, Beau?"

"That bitch." Beau clenched his teeth as he spoke. "Emily Olmstead St. Claire, or whatever the hell she's calling herself these days. She went on some TV show this morning and accused me of taking a bribe, among other things. I just got a talking to from one of the higher-ups. Apparently, the phone lines melted down, and the email server overloaded, thanks to all of the goody two-shoes out there clamoring about how I should be fired or tossed in jail. So, I've just been put on paid administrative leave, effective immediately, while internal affairs conducts a formal investigation."

"Well, Beau, I'm sorry it happened, but I can't say I'm completely surprised. I said from the get-go that you were pursuing the wrong suspect, and my gut told me Jesse St. Claire was covering something up. I still say he's hiding something, we just can't prove it, but now that it's been officially ruled an accident, we have to move on."

"Easy for you to say, Madden. You're not the one whose butt just got put on the line. And while we're on the subject, what's this I'm hearing about you having coffee the other day with some guy from internal affairs?"

Kyle was taken aback. "Who told you this?"

"Someone saw you."

"Sidney Hill was my first partner. He was also the best man at my wedding. We just happened to run into one another the other day, so we decided to have a cup of Joe. Besides, we were both off the clock."

Beau seemed to be calming down. "Sorry Kyle, I didn't mean to overreact."

"Look, Beau, you really are overdue for some time off, and I'm sure Melody would enjoy some quality time as well, so why not relax for a while? You know how this stuff goes. You made a bad call and now the media's jumped all over it. It could have happened to any us, but, fortunately, no real harm was done. Emily St. Claire was never charged. She never saw the inside of a jail cell, and now that she's been officially cleared, she'll move on. In fact, she'll be moving out of state in a few months." Kyle felt his stomach twist as he spoke. "Give it a week or two and it'll all be blown over and forgotten."

"It'd better be."

As Beau stormed away Kyle went back to his paperwork, but he was soon interrupted once again. This time it was a uniformed officer, accompanied by a stocky, middle-aged, woman.

"This is Yolanda Lopez," said the officer. "She says she has some new information on the Claiborne case."

Kyle took a small voice recorder from a desk drawer. "If you'll please come with me, Ms. Lopez, we can talk someplace private."

"Of course."

He led her down a hallway to a small room and told her to take a seat. After closing the door, he sat down next her and turned on the voice recorder, noting the date and time.

"So, Ms. Lopez, what new information do you have for us?"

"I used to be Jesse St. Claire's personal assistant, and one day I accidentally overheard a conversation between Jesse and that detective, Beau Fowler."

"All right. So can you tell me what happened?"

"We'd just finished our weekly face-to-face meeting, and when we stepped out of Jesse's office Beau Fowler was standing there, inside Jesse's house. He introduced himself to me, but I could tell Jesse wasn't happy he was there."

"Can you tell me what happened next?"

"Jesse walked me to the front door and I left, but when I got to my car, I realized I'd accidentally left my keys in Jesse's office, so I went back to get them. The front door was unlocked, so I let myself in. Then, as I was walking down the hallway, toward Jesse's office, I overheard them talking."

"What did you hear?"

"They were arguing over Jesse's divorce. Jesse wanted to give his wife the proceeds from the sale of the house, but Detective Fowler wouldn't hear of it."

Kyle furrowed his brow. "Interesting."

"I thought it was a little odd myself. His divorce shouldn't have had anything to do with the case."

"No, it shouldn't have. So what exactly was Detective Fowler saying?"

"I can't recall the exact words. He was upset over the fact that Mrs. St. Claire had hired Frederick Lancaster as her attorney. He said something to the effect of her doing that would make his job harder. He also said, quite emphatically, that giving her the sale proceeds would make it easier for her to keep Mr. Lancaster as her attorney. He said he wanted her to run out of money. That way Mr. Lancaster would drop the case."

"I see," said Kyle. "So what was Jesse saying about this?"

"He kept saying he wanted her to have the money."

"Did he say anything else?"

"He kept saying Annette's death was an accident, but then Detective Fowler said something about how it would still be manslaughter."

"I see. So did Jesse St. Claire admit that he was somehow responsible for Annette Claiborne's death?"

Yolanda squirmed in her chair. "I'm not sure. Maybe. I don't know. Please understand that what I was overhearing was taken out of context. They could have just been speculating."

Kyle gave her a strong look. "Did you hear anything else?"

"No, that was pretty much it. Jesse wanted his wife to have the money, but Detective Fowler wouldn't allow it. That was when I announced myself and grabbed my keys off Jesse's desk. Then I hurried out."

"I see. Did Jesse or Detective Fowler say anything to you about this?"

"No." She shook her head as she spoke. "I acted like I hadn't heard anything. Then Jesse got up and walked me back to the front door, but he didn't say anything. He called me a short time later. He seemed concerned that I may have misunderstood something. He said his wife was there when Annette fell, and he wanted to reassure me that her death was an accident. He said he kept telling Detective Fowler it was an accident, but the detective wouldn't believe him."

"Prior to this, did Jesse ever discuss the case with you?"

"Only once. It was right after it happened. He simply said there'd been an accident involving his estranged wife and her cousin. I told him I'd already heard about it on the news. That's when he told me he couldn't discuss the details, since the case was still under investigation, and I wasn't to discuss it with the media either. He also assured me that he'd done nothing wrong, and he said he wasn't going to be charged."

Kyle raised his brow. "So, Ms. Lopez, why didn't you come forward with this information sooner?"

"It's like I just told you, sir. What I overheard was taken out of context, and I couldn't risk losing my job."

"So why are you coming forward now?"

Yolanda gave him a sheepish look. "Earlier today my son emailed me a link to the *Mid-Morning with Trudy* show, and I just finished watching the interview with Mrs. St. Claire on YouTube. That's when I realized Jesse and that detective may have been trying to frame her. It also explains why Detective Fowler didn't want Jesse giving her any of the house sale money."

"Are you still working for Jesse St. Claire?"

"No, sir. Between all the cancelations he's had since Ms. Claiborne's fall, and his plans to relocate out of state, he had to let me go. I know how bad this must look, but please believe me when I tell you this doesn't have anything to do with sour grapes on my part. I honestly thought everything was on the up and up until I saw Mrs. St. Claire on the Trudy show."

"I understand, Ms. Lopez. So do you know when Jesse's leaving?"

"I'm afraid I don't know the exact date, but I think it's sometime soon. He's having a big moving sale this weekend. I posted it on Facebook for him. It was the last thing I did for him."

"Do you know where's he going?"

"I'm not sure," she said with a shrug. "He didn't tell me."

"Thank you, Ms. Lopez. I'll need your contact information, and then you'll be free to go."

❧ THIRTY-FIVE ❧

JESSE OPENED HIS front door and frowned as Detective Fowler once again pushed his way inside. "You know, Beau, this is really getting to be a bad habit"

"We have another problem," said Beau, "thanks to your soon-to-be ex-wife."

"What do you mean?"

"Don't you ever watch television?"

"Not much lately, I'm afraid," said Jesse. "So what's this all about?"

"Do you mind if we sit down for a moment?"

"Help yourself, but please don't be offended if I don't offer you anything."

Jesse led him into the living room, motioning for him toward one of the chairs as he took a seat across from him. "So, detective, what seems to be the problem this time?"

"This morning your wife went on the *Midday with Trudy* show."

Jesse raised his brow. "Really? So, what did she have to say?"

"She accused me of taking a bribe."

Jesse was momentarily taken aback. "I see. Well, under the circumstances, I can't say I blame her, and you know what they say. Payback's a bitch."

"Very funny," said Beau, "but here's the problem. Internal affairs just got involved, and I'm now on paid administrative leave."

"I see." Jesse scratched his chin as he thought it over. "Well, I suppose they have to do what they have to do, but if they subpoena my bank records, they won't find anything. The only thing they'll see is that I've had to tap into my savings to pay the bills because of all the cancelations."

"And what will you tell internal affairs when they come to pay you a visit?"

Jesse looked Beau in the eye. "What do you think I'm going to tell them? C'mon, Fowler, do you really think that after all we've been through, I'd risk doing prison time? I'll say the same thing I've been saying all along. Emily stopped by to get her passport and I don't care what she says, Annette was here, blah, blah, blah. In the meantime, I have more pressing problems to deal with."

"Such as?"

"Earlier today I had another unexpected visitor. A process server. Heather Claiborne and Gary Murkowski are now suing me for wrongful death."

"Great." Beau gritted his teeth as he spoke. "That's all we need right now. So how much are they asking?"

"Five million dollars."

"Wow. You've got liability insurance, right?"

"Yes, Beau." The sarcasm resonated in Jesse's voice. "I have liability insurance, but it caps at two million, and for some reason I don't seem to have another three million on me."

"Relax, Jesse. Get yourself a good lawyer and do whatever you have to do to get this thing settled out of court. I can even help you find an attorney."

"Thanks, but I can manage on my own."

"I also hear you're leaving town."

"You heard right," said Jesse. "I have a seminar coming up in Kansas City at the end of March, right after my divorce hearing. I'm hoping my house will have sold by then, because I plan on relocating there. In fact, I'm having a moving sale this weekend. You may want to come. This entire incident has done some serious damage to my career. I have no choice but to start fresh someplace else, and Kansas City is in a nice, central part of the country."

"I understand how you feel, Jesse. It's damaged both of us."

Jesse stood from his chair. "So now, if you'll excuse me, I have some important business to attend to. I have to find an attorney, and I have to get ready for my moving sale. My advice to you would be to lay low and let everything blow over. You have nothing to worry about. They can't prove bribery because I never bribed you. You're actually pretty lucky, all things considered. You're on paid leave and you don't have to deplete what's left of your assets to defend yourself from a lawsuit."

Jesse walked Beau to the foyer and waited until Beau got into his car before he closed the front door and went back to his office. He took the flash drive from the safe and popped it into his computer, replaying the surveillance footage several times. Finally, he removed the drive and stared at it in his hand. Taking a deep breath, he raised his arm and aimed at the wastepaper basket near his desk, but his arm wavered in the air and dropped to his side. Somehow, he couldn't bring himself to throw the flash drive away. He tossed it back into the safe and slammed the door shut with a loud bang.

* * *

Beau locked the car door and grabbed his phone. Rummaging through his pockets, he found the slip of paper with the phone number he needed. He placed the call and waited. A young man answered on the third ring. A small child was screaming in the background.

"Hey, Juan, how you doing?"

"Who is this?"

"Beau Fowler."

"Hang on a minute. I need to find someplace where I can talk in private."

"Take your time."

The child's wails soon diminished, and Juan came back on the line. "Okay, I can talk, but only for a minute or two. Otherwise, my old lady will get suspicious."

"Gotcha. We need to talk. Let's meet at the usual place."

"When?"

"How 'bout three-thirty tomorrow afternoon?"

"See you then."

❧THIRTY-SIX❧

BEAU ARRIVED AT Encanto Park at exactly three-thirty. The large, historic park was a Phoenix landmark with its numerous palm trees and lush grass. He made his way toward the lagoon where Juan sat on a bench, watching the ducks as they paddled around the water.

"Mind if I sit down?" asked Beau.

"Help yourself." Juan kept his gaze on the ducks as Beau took his seat and set his briefcase next to the bench.

"You know, I really love this place. Sometimes I bring the family here and we'll have a picnic. My kids love going on the rides, but something tells me you didn't ask me here to enjoy the view."

"No, I'm afraid not."

"That's what I thought." Juan cleared his throat. "So, what is it that you need, Mr. Fowler? Things have been pretty quiet around the neighborhood since your buddies did that big drug sweep a few weeks ago, and besides, I've got myself a legit job now."

"Doing what?"

"I'm a prep cook at one of those fancy downtown eateries. You might want to stop by sometime."

"Maybe later." Beau got straight to the point. "I was wondering, Juan, if maybe you could use a little extra cash."

"Sure, I can always use some extra dough. The old lady's pregnant again."

"So soon? Didn't you guys just have one?"

"Yep. What can I say? She's a very devout Catholic. So what's the job? Like I just told you, things have been really quiet for the past few weeks."

"I know. This time I need you to do a different kind of favor."

"Really? So what kind of a favor are we talking about?"

"It's easy, Juan, it really is." Beau paused for a moment to gather his thoughts. "There's a certain individual out there who's making trouble. This person has been making some very serious allegations against yours truly, and needs to be silenced, if you know what I mean."

"Say what?" Juan's voice raised its pitch.

Beau hopped off the bench and looked around. To his relief, no one was within earshot. "Let's go take a little stroll around the lagoon and I'll fill you in." He scooped up his briefcase and motioned for Juan to follow.

"As I was saying, there's a certain young lady who's become a thorn in my side. It has to do with a recent high-profile case and—"

"Let me guess," said Juan. "It was the guy doing the deed with his wife's cousin. The one who went headfirst down the stairs."

"That would be the one."

"Yeah, I saw it on the TV news. That girl, the one who died, she was hot. What a waste."

"She was something, all right. Her cousin murdered her."

"That would be the guy's wife, right?"

"Yep, the wife," said Beau. "She pushed her cousin down those stairs in a jealous rage."

"Yeah, I heard something about that. Talk about keeping it in the family. Man, you don't go messing around with you wife's cousin. That's just not smart." Juan paused for a moment. "Wait a minute, didn't I just hear something about the wife not being guilty?"

"The grand jury refused to indict her, but it doesn't mean she wasn't guilty. It just means there wasn't enough evidence against her to take the case to trial. She killed her cousin. She got away with murder, and now she's coming after me. She may be pretty, and she may come across as sweet and innocent, but don't be fooled by her. She's as cold as ice, and she's as evil as they come."

Juan shrugged his shoulders. "I don't know about that. My wife's as sweet as they come, but if she ever caught me cheating on her, well, it wouldn't be so good. That's for sure."

"I understand, but there's more to the story than you've been told. While she was crying about her husband cheating on her, she had herself a lover on the side as well, which means she also cheated on him. So now that the case against her has been dropped, she's coming after me with a vengeance. You of all people should know I've gone the extra mile many times for you and your family."

"Yeah, I know."

"You also know it's because of me that you're not in the state pen."

"Yeah, I know that too."

Beau's tone turned icy. "I've busted my ass for my superiors, as well as for my fellow officers, and how do they thank me? They pass me over for promotion, time and time again, in favor of guys with far less training and experience than me. Then fate finally smiles on me. Along comes a high-profile murder case full of sex and infidelity and plenty of media attention. All I had to do was bring in the guilty party and I'd finally get the promotion I deserved, but no, it didn't happen. Instead, a guilty woman ends up getting away with murder, and if that wasn't bad enough, she goes on TV and makes herself out to be the victim. She trashed my reputation in front of the entire community, claiming I deliberately tried to frame her for a crime she says she didn't commit. Then, to top it off, she accuses me of taking a bribe. These are very serious allegations. I could very well end up losing my job because of her. Or worse. So, I'm now on administrative leave while internal affairs conducts an official investigation."

"What about Madden?" asked Juan. "Is she going after him too?"

"Actually, no. She managed to seduce Madden as well. Can you believe that? Even though there was a credible eyewitness who saw her push her cousin down those stairs, Madden steadfastly maintained her innocence. It was his grand jury testimony that resulted in the charges being dropped."

"Really?"

"I kid you not. She even managed to turn my own partner against me." Beau paused for a moment. "You know how these things go, Juan. You've seen it happen to a number of your friends, as well as some of your family members. Someone points a finger at somebody else, and even though there's no evidence whatsoever of any wrongdoing against them, and even though everyone knows they're innocent, they still end up in prison because the jury believed the accuser. This is what may very well happen to me. I've been wrongly accused by a young woman who's a real pro when it comes to making herself out to be a victim, and then she uses it to manipulate others. You've been a great help to me over the years,

Juan, you really have. Now the tables have turned, and I'm the one who may very well end up in prison if you don't help me."

"By doing what?"

"I need you take care of this woman. I need you to silence her. Once and for all."

Juan shook his head. "I don't know if I can do it. I don't think I can kill a woman. A man, a murder, maybe. A drug dealer, maybe, but not a woman. Besides, what's to stop me from turning you in?"

Beau stopped in his tracks and gave Juan a cold, hard stare. "Your little brother, Fernando. I know he's still in prison, and I know that so far he's been doing okay. You want to make sure nothing bad happens to him, right?"

"Of course I do. It was a bum rap, just like you were saying before. Fernando wasn't anywhere near that jewelry store when it got robbed."

"I understand. What I'm saying is you take care of me I take care of you. I'll make sure your little brother stays safe in prison. I'll even do whatever I can to get him released early."

"Okay. So, what do I have to do?"

Beau spotted a patch of bare ground beneath a nearby tree. He motioned to Juan to follow.

"There's a gun in my briefcase which can't be traced." He set the briefcase down and picked up a stick, drawing a large rectangle in the muddy ground. "The lady lives on the northeast side of town. Her address is also in the briefcase. After nine o'clock at night it gets pretty quiet in her neighborhood. There's hardly any traffic on the road, and she usually plays her piano in the evenings." He drew a square and a smaller rectangle within the larger one.

"This is her house, and here's the front door. To the left of the front door is a big picture window, and her piano sits right on the other side of that window. At that hour the blinds will probably be drawn, so you may have to get out of your car and walk past the house. You should be able to hear the piano playing from the street. Once you hear it, do a drive by. Spray the window with bullets and then get the hell out of there. I've given you two fully loaded high-capacity magazines. One should do the trick. The other is for backup, just in case. It should only take a few seconds from start to finish, so by the time anyone realizes what's happened you'll be long gone. Afterwards make sure you dispose of the briefcase and everything in it. There's an envelope with five hundred dollars in the briefcase. It's a down payment, and it should buy you a lot of diapers and baby food."

Juan studied the drawing on the ground. Beads of sweat had popped out across his forehead. "I'm still not sure if I can do this."

"Think of Fernando. You're doing this for him."

"When do you want this done?"

"As soon as possible. You working tonight?"

"No. I work the lunch shift."

"Perfect. Call me on my private number when you're done, so we can arrange another meeting. They'll be another five hundred for you once the bitch is dead." Beau erased the drawing with his foot. Once it was obliterated, he turned and left, leaving the briefcase behind.

❧THIRTY-SEVEN❧

JUAN SLOWED HIS car down and tried to make out the house numbers on the dimly lit street. His heart skipped a beat when the inside of his car suddenly lit up. A pair of headlights was closing in behind him. He prayed it wasn't the police as pulled over to the side. A red Ford Explorer drove past, turning into a driveway two doors down. As Juan came closer, he realized the Explorer was at the house he was looking for. A man and woman stepped out of the vehicle. The slender blonde women looked like the photo he found in the briefcase, but it was the man with her who troubled him. He bore an uncanny resemblance to Detective Madden. Juan looked straight ahead and drove past the house, hoping he wouldn't be noticed. He headed back to the main road while keeping an eye on the rearview mirror. To his relief, there was nothing behind him but an empty street. He turned and merged onto the busy thoroughfare. At least he knew which house to look for.

* * *

"Goodnight, Kyle. I had a wonderful time."

"Me too. It's been a long time since I've been to a movie."

"I know." Emily put her key into the lock and turned the knob. "Would you like to come in for a nightcap?"

"Some other time, perhaps. I have a sitter waiting at home."

"Oops, sorry, I forgot. Well, that's okay. I need to put in a little practice time before I turn in. I'm off to Los Angeles next week."

"I know, and then it's Texas two weeks after."

"I can't believe it's finally here."

"It's here, all right, and I'm wishing you the best of luck."

"Thank you, Kyle."

"Can I call you when you get back?" he asked.

"Of course you can. I'd like that."

He hugged her goodbye. "Goodnight, Emily." Gazing into her eyes, he could no longer resist. He gave her a sweet, gentle kiss. To his surprise, she didn't pull away.

"Goodnight, Kyle. I'll see you after my auditions." She stepped inside the house, gently closing the door behind her.

* * *

Juan turned his car into the nearest fast-food place. His hands were shaking as he parked and he quickly ran his fingers through his hair. The open briefcase sat in the passenger seat. He slammed it shut and made sure it was secure before grabbing it and exiting the car. Inside, the restaurant was nearly empty. The dinner rush had ended a couple of hours before. He walked up to the counter and ordered some coffee, taking it to a seat in an empty booth at the far back corner.

Juan had a few brushes with the law when he was a teenager, but they were all nonviolent offences, such as shoplifting and petty theft, and once for selling a small amount of marijuana to an undercover cop. The undercover cop was Beau Fowler. Beau soon realized Juan was a young man desperately trying to feed his mother and his younger siblings. It was Beau who helped arrange the plea deal that kept him out of jail, and, in return, Juan became an informant. As he sipped his coffee, he wondered what could have happened to Beau. He was no longer the man Jaun had looked up to. Perhaps seeing Kyle, or a man who looked like Kyle, in front of Emily St. Clair's house was a sign that he should have followed his instincts and called Kyle as soon as Beau left Encanto Park. Then he thought about Fernando. What would happen to his little brother if he turned Beau in? He sighed and took another swig of coffee. He simply couldn't take the risk. He would have to do what had to be done, regardless of how unpleasant the task might be. Finishing off his coffee, he picked up the briefcase, and headed out the door.

❧THIRTY-EIGHT❧

LURCH GREETED EMILY with excited whimpers and a wagging tail as she stepped inside the house. She petted the dog and glanced around the entryway.

"Hey, buddy, how you doing? Guess Dad's not home yet, huh? Well, that's okay. I can let you out."

Lurch followed her as she opened the sliding glass door to the backyard. He ran outside with a loud bark while Emily closed the door behind him. She remembered her father saying something about being out late, so she would have the house completely to herself. Grabbing a cup of coffee, she let the dog back in and was on her way to the living room when her phone rang. She grimaced once she saw who was calling.

"Grandma. What a nice surprise." Emily tried to sound as pleasant as she could. "I haven't heard from you in some time."

"No, you haven't." Barbara spoke in her usual stern voice. "You could have picked up the phone and called me, you know."

"Actually, I wasn't so sure about that. Our last conversation was hardly pleasant. You told me I wouldn't be welcome at my cousin's funeral."

"I understand, Emily. However, at the time I thought it would be best for all concerned if you weren't there. That said, I haven't heard from you in quite some time, and I was just wondering how you were."

"I'm fine, Grandma. I'm sure you've heard by now that the grand jury refused to indict me."

"Yes, I know they didn't. You could've called me to let me know."

"Like I said, I really wasn't sure if I should do that, since you were all convinced that I was guilty."

"We never said you were guilty, Emily Louise."

Emily took a deep breath, being mindful of her words. "I know you never actually said it, but I sure got the sense you all were thinking it."

"Look, Emily, I didn't call you to start another argument. I'm well aware of the fact that they found no evidence against you. So is your Aunt Heather. I just hadn't heard from you in a while, and I wanted to be sure you were all right. I also wanted to let you know that Aunt Heather and I saw you on that TV show, and we both appreciated the kind words about the family."

"Thank you, Grandma. I honestly wish justice had been served on Annette. I wasn't happy about what she did, but I certainly would have never wished her harm either. I'll always believe in my heart of hearts that Jesse was somehow responsible for what happened to her, even if he didn't actually push her. That's why he tried to pin the blame on me. Anyway, it's a moot point now. They've ruled her death an accident, so we have to move forward. I've also filed for divorce. It'll be final in March."

"Well, I'm certainly glad to hear it."

Emily winced. She wanted to say something, but then thought better of it. "Thank you, Grandma. I have to go now. My audition for USC is next week, so I need to practice as much as I can. I'll talk to you soon."

"Wait! Before you go, I need to go over some things with you."

Barbara was stalling, as usual. Emily would have to cut the call off. "Goodnight, Grandma. I'll talk to you later." She quickly disconnected her phone. Lurch cocked his head and gave her a quizzical look as she powered it down.

"I know. I probably sounded rude, but I had to do it, because the more you tell her you have to go, the more she brings up things that have to be discussed, right then and there, because they just can't wait. Of course, they're never anything important. She only does it because she refuses to respect other people's boundaries."

Emily dropped the phone back into her purse and picked up her mug. After a few sips of coffee, she went into to the living room. Lurch plopped down on the floor next to her as she took her seat at the piano bench.

"So, Lurch, which would you prefer? Bach or Mozart?" The dog stretched and moaned. "Okay. Bach it is."

She played a Bach minuet, followed by *Jesu, Joy of Man's Desiring*. She was about halfway through it when Lurch let out a loud growl and leapt to his feet. He ran to the front window and barked loudly, his fur raised up on his back. Emily stopped playing and ran to the front door to look through the peephole. Perhaps it was a reporter, looking for an exclusive. To her relief, no one stood outside. Lurch followed her to the door. He had stopped barking and appeared to be calming down.

"Good dog." Emily nervously stroked his back. "If someone was out there you scared him away. Or maybe it was just the wind."

* * *

Juan muttered a few obscenities under his breath as he ran back to his car. "Damn it, Fowler! Why didn't you tell me they had a damn dog?"

He opened the car door and hopped inside, cursing himself for being so sloppy. His curiosity had gotten the better of him and he had walked up to the front window, hoping he might be able to peer through the blinds to get a glimpse of the person he had been hired to kill. Doing so, however, had alerted the family dog. He rolled down the car window and listened carefully. He no longer heard the dog. Moments later he heard the faint sound of a piano, playing the same tune he heard before. He took a deep breath and swallowed hard. The time had come to do what had to be done.

He checked the rearview mirror. The street remained dark and quiet. He shifted his gaze to the open briefcase, once again on the passenger's seat. He would have to act quickly. He started up the engine and reached for the gun, carefully aiming it at the picture window. His hands trembled, his muscles were tense with anticipation, and his entire body broke out into a cold sweat.

"God forgive me for what I'm about to do," he said out loud. Seconds later he closed his eyes and squeezed the trigger, but nothing happened. The gun didn't fire. He stopped for a moment. Perhaps his hands were shaking too hard. He lowered the gun, took a deep breath and counted to ten, and then slowly exhaled. He could feel his body start to relax. He took a few more deep breaths and raised the gun. This time he squeezed the trigger more forcefully. Once again, the gun didn't fire. Tears of relief streamed down his cheeks. He slowly lowered the gun and carefully placed it back in the briefcase. He took another deep breath and rummaged through the glove box for a flashlight. Once he found it, he carefully inspected the gun. Moments later he reached for his phone and placed a call.

"Beau Fowler," said the voice on the other end of the line.

"It's me, Juan."

"Did you do it?"

"I ran into a little problem."

Beau's voice turned icy. "What kind of a problem?"

"The gun jammed. There's something wrong with the firing mechanism."

"Can you fix it?"

"No. I'm not a gunsmith, but I can take it to my cousin. He can fix anything."

"No," said Beau. "Don't take it to anybody. I'll take care of it. Get rid of it and I'll call you back in a few of days."

"What about my money?"

"Don't worry, I'll take care of it. Just get rid of the gun and wait for my instructions. I'll be in touch."

❧THIRTY-NINE❧

KYLE LOOKED UP from his paperwork as a uniformed officer brought another visitor to his desk.

"Juan, nice to see you again," he said. "Please take a seat and make yourself comfortable. Can I get you a soda?"

"No, thanks." Juan pulled a chair up to Kyle's desk and lowered his voice. "We need to talk. It's urgent."

Kyle studied Juan's face. "You looked troubled. What happened?"

"I just got word that someone has arranged a hit on two people."

"Who?"

"One is a woman named Emily St. Claire."

Kyle's blood turned to ice. "Are you sure?"

"Yeah, I'm sure."

"So who arranged this, and why?"

"Beau Fowler arranged it."

"What did you just say?" asked a stunned Kyle.

Juan looked around the room, making sure no one else was within earshot. His voice remained low. "I said Beau Fowler ordered the hit."

"You're sure about that?"

"I'm positive, and I'm not lying, I swear. He's angry over what she said about him on that TV show, but I think there's more to it. It's like he's somehow snapped. The word on the street is he's just hired some guy called Big Hector to have her killed. He's known to do dirty work for drug lords on both sides of the border."

Kyle leaned back in his chair in stunned disbelief. Juan quickly stood as another man joined them.

"Don't go anywhere," said Kyle. "This is my new partner, Clarke Davidson. Clarke, meet Juan."

The two men shook hands and Clarke sat down at his desk.

"I need to go now," said Juan. "I've told you everything I know."

"Not so fast," said Kyle. "The three of us are going to talk someplace private." He took them to an empty interrogation room. Once everyone was seated Kyle brought Clarke up to date.

"Juan's an informant who's worked with Beau and me in the past. He tells me that Beau's put out a contract on Emily St. Claire."

Clarke looked Juan up and down. "Is this guy reliable?"

"Juan's helped us break a number of cases in the past, and so far, he's never been wrong. As you know, I've had my own suspicions about Beau with the Claiborne case. I still can't figure out why he went along with Jesse's scheme, unless Jesse had somehow bribed or blackmailed him. What we do know for certain is there's no love lost between the St. Claires, so it's certainly possible that Beau could be acting on Jesse's behalf."

Clarke reached for the phone. "We need to move quickly on this. I'm sending a couple of uniformed officers to Emily's residence. Do you have her address?"

"Right here." Kyle quickly jotted it down and handed the paper to Clarke. "Tell them to stay with her until I get there."

"Understood." Clarke placed the call while Kyle turned his attention back to Juan.

"You said he hired Big Hector to take care of two people. Who's the other target?"

"Me."

"Why?"

Juan folded his arms across his chest. "Because I know too much."

"Meaning?"

"It's a long, complicated story, Detective Madden."

"And I have plenty of time."

"Sorry to interrupt," said Clarke. "They've just dispatched someone to Emily's house."

"Thanks." Kyle turned his attention back to Juan. "You'd better start talking. So what is it that you know that would make Beau Fowler want to put out a contract on you?"

"I need my lawyer."

"I don't have time for this kind of nonsense," said Kyle. "There's a young woman out there whose life is in danger, and unless you start talking, she could very well end up dead."

"And so could I."

"You need to get rolling Kyle," said Clarke. "I'll arrange for our friend here to get a lawyer, but first he's going into protective custody."

"What about my family?"

"We'll take care of it, Juan," said Clarke, "and the sooner you start cooperating, the better we can take care of them." He sent for an officer to take Juan away. Once they left, he turned his attention back to Kyle.

"I know she's a friend, so I'd like your input."

"I'd like to get her out of town," said Kyle, "as quickly as possible. The further away, the better."

"Probably a good idea, and I know just the place where you can hide her out." Clarke picked up a pen and started writing. "My sister and her husband own the place. I'll give them a call and tell them to expect you later tonight." He handed the paper over to Kyle.

"So where's Elgin?"

"Well off the beaten path, way down in the southern part of the state. It's a nice, quiet little town. The kind of place where you could easily spot someone who didn't belong there."

"Thanks, Clarke. I owe you one."

"Anytime."

Kyle stood from his chair. "I'll call Sidney Hill and then I'm out of here. I'll have my phone and tablet with me, so keep me in the loop."

"Of course. You go take care of whatever you need to take care of and have a safe trip. In the meantime, I'm going to find out what I can about Big Hector, and then I'm going have a little talk with Jesse St. Claire. As soon as I know anything, I'll fill you in."

"Thanks."

"Good luck, Kyle."

* * *

Two squad cars were parked in front of Emily's house when Kyle arrived. A female officer greeted him at the door and led him into to the living room, where two other officers stood by.

"Where's Emily?"

"We don't know," said the female officer. "Her father says she wasn't here when he arrived home, and so far no one's been able to reach her on her cell."

"Where's her father?"

"Right here," said a voice behind him.

Kyle turned around and found himself face-to-face with an anxious-looking Roger.

"What's going on, Kyle? These officers tell me they need to find Emily, and it's urgent, but they won't give me any other information."

"Let's sit down for a moment and I'll fill you in."

Roger pointed to the sofa and quickly took his seat. "Okay, let's have it. Have you reopened your case against my daughter? And have you come to arrest her?"

"No, we haven't reopened the case, and no, we're not here to arrest her." He paused for a moment. "Roger, I'm afraid I have some bad news. We've just received a tip from a reliable source that someone has put out a contract on Emily."

"What do you mean, a contract? You mean that someone wants to have her killed?"

"I'm afraid so."

"My god." The color drained from Roger's face. "Who would want to do something like this? Jesse?"

"According to our informant, it's Beau Fowler, although we haven't ruled out the possibility that Jesse could be involved as well. What we do know for certain is that Emily made some serious allegations against Detective Fowler on live television, and he's now on paid leave while internal affairs conducts an investigation."

"So why don't you go arrest him?"

"I'm afraid it's not that simple. At this point all we have is a statement from an informant, but so far nothing's been confirmed. Someone from internal affairs is questioning Detective Fowler as we speak, and trust me, as soon as we find out anything, you'll be the first to know. In the meantime, we need to find Emily, as soon as possible. Do you know where she is?"

"No," said Roger, "I'm afraid I don't. The last time I saw her was early this morning. She's still working with a few temp agencies. She had to report for an assignment this morning, and she said she'd probably be home around five o'clock or so. That's all I know."

Kyle looked at his watch. It was going on six. "She could be stuck in traffic somewhere. Do you know where she was working?"

"I'm afraid I don't. Like I said, she signed on with a few temp agencies and she's been working mostly for doctors and dentists. She usually gets home sometime between four and six, depending on their office hours."

"Do you know which agencies?"

"No. I know she's mentioned them once or twice, but I can't recall their names right now. She always takes her phone with her, but she turns it off while she's working. She did the same thing when she worked for Dr. Lerner. She'd usually check her messages at lunchtime, and then she'd turn her phone back on once she left for the day. I've been trying to reach her ever since the first officer showed up, but it keeps going straight to voice mail, which means it's still turned off." He stopped for a moment. "You don't think anything's happened to her, do you?"

"Let's not think the worst just yet. So far nothing's come in on the police radio, and it's possible that whoever she's working for today doesn't close their office until six. Meantime, we've put out an APB on her car. Don't worry, Mr. Olmstead, we'll find her."

There was still no word from Emily an hour later. Finally, Lurch raised his head and the front doorbell rang. Roger went to answer, but one of the officers held him back. Moments later another officer led an older-looking black man into the room. Kyle quickly introduced him to the others as Sidney Hill.

"Any word?" asked Kyle.

"I have news, but so far it's not looking good."

Once again Roger's face turned pale. "What happened? And where's my daughter?"

Sidney sat down on the piano bench, facing the others. "After we got off the phone, Kyle, I went straight to Beau Fowler's residence and spoke to his wife, Melody."

"So where was Beau?"

"Gone. Apparently, they've been having problems for some time now. She says he packed his bags and left two days ago, and she hasn't seen or heard from him since. She was understandably upset, so I tried not to push her too hard."

"Which means he could be anywhere by now," said Kyle.

"I'm afraid it looks that way. He didn't tell her where he was going. I tried calling his cell, but the number's been disconnected. We've put out an APB, but I'm afraid that's all I can tell you for now."

"What about Emily?" Roger looked at Sidney. "Were you able to find out where my daughter is?"

"I'm afraid I don't know where your daughter is, but let's not think the worst just yet."

Kyle turned his attention back to Sidney. "Do you find out anything else?"

"I've told you all I know for now. I take it you don't know Mrs. St. Claire's whereabouts?"

"I'm afraid she hasn't been seen since she left for work this morning. Her father is understandably upset, as you can imagine."

Sidney turned to Roger. "I haven't heard anything so far which would indicate that she's been harmed. For what it's worth, sir, we have some of our finest officers on top of this, so I'm hopeful she'll be found, safe and sound." He turned back to Kyle. "Please keep me posted. I can see myself out."

Sidney took his leave and Clarke Davidson arrived a short time later. He too was greeted with anxious faces. After making the proper introductions Kyle got straight to the point.

"So what about Big Hector? Did you find anything on him?"

"Hector Alfonso Garcia, also known as Big Hector, has a rap sheet a mile long. Drug trafficking, burglary, auto theft, and one count of larceny. He currently has outstanding warrants in three other states besides Arizona, but most of the time the charges against him are either dismissed or plea bargained down because the witnesses either change their stories or they disappear. We think he may be involved in a couple of unsolved murders, but once again people are afraid to talk. We know he has gang affiliations, and, as you know, Beau worked the gang unit for many years. He would know who Big Hector is and how to get in touch with him."

"Dear god," said Roger.

Kyle tried to ignore the gnawing feeling in his gut. "So what about Jesse St. Claire?"

"So far I've found nothing suggesting that Jesse could be involved," said Clarke. "He's been out of town for the past few days. He had a speaking gig in Fresno two days ago, and another in Salt Lake City earlier today. He's supposed to return later tonight. I'll meet him at the airport, and we'll know more once we talk with him and go over his phone and email records."

Lurch jumped up, his tail wagging as he trotted toward the kitchen.

"What the hell is going on around here?" An angry-looking Emily stepped into the room. She carried shopping bags in both of her hands.

"Where have you been?" asked Roger.

"I went to the mall after I got off work. I needed a new outfit for my audition."

"I must have left you a half dozen voice mails over the past couple hours, so why didn't you call me back?"

"Sorry, Dad. My phone battery died, and with everything on my mind right now I must have forgotten to put it on the car charger. So would someone please tell me what's going on?"

Kyle guided her to the sofa and eased her down. "Emily, I don't mean to frighten you, but we have a serious problem. I need you to pack your bags, right now. We have every reason to believe that Beau Fowler has taken out a contact on you, and we need to get you somewhere safe."

She stared at Kyle in stunned disbelief. "What?"

"Emily, your life is in danger," said Roger. "Kyle is taking you someplace safe. You need to go with him."

"What do you mean, I need to go with him? I'm flying to Los Angeles tomorrow night. My USC audition is the day after tomorrow."

"I know, Emily," said Kyle, "and I'm very sorry to have to tell you this, but I'm afraid you won't able to go."

"What do you mean, I won't be able to go? I've been preparing for these auditions for months now. You know how much this means to me."

Kyle looked her in the eye. "I know you have, but you don't understand. There's a very bad guy out there who intends to kill you, and right now we don't know where he is. We have to get you out of here. Now."

The color drained from her face. "Oh my god. What's happening?"

"Earlier this afternoon we got a tip from an informant who told us Beau Fowler has hired a someone to kill you. We're still investigating, but what we've uncovered so far suggests this isn't a hoax. We're looking for the hit man, but so far he remains at large. Your father and I have talked it over, and he agrees that you need to go with me. I'm taking you to a safe location where we can stay until everyone involved has been caught and it's safe for you to come out."

"I understand, Kyle. Let me see if I can book a flight to Los Angeles for later on tonight, and I'll stay over for a few extra days."

"No." His voice was firm. "Beau already knows your itinerary, remember? You talked about your auditions in your statements, and you mentioned when you'd be there. The man he's hired is a pro. He could just as easily get to you in California. I'm sorry Emily, but you're going to have to put your audition on hold. With any luck we'll catch him soon and you'll be able to make it your audition in Texas. I know you've worked hard and that you have your heart is set on this, but we're talking about saving your life."

She shook her head. "No, I don't believe this. It has to be some sort of sick, twisted joke."

"I honestly wish it was, but I'm afraid it's not. Anyway, we're wasting time. You need to go back your bags."

"No. You don't understand. I can't miss these auditions. Without them I won't be accepted into the music schools. I'll take a different flight. I'll stay at a different hotel. I'll be extra careful, I promise."

"Emily, please." Kyle's voice was stern. "I just told you this man is a pro. He has connections in Los Angeles. He has gang affiliations, and gangs have their ways of getting their hands on the information they need. For all you know, they could be hacking into your email accounts or your text messages or listening in on your voice mail, so even if you take a different flight or stay in a different hotel, they could still find you."

"But USC is a big, college campus, with lots of people walking around," said Emily. "Do you mean to tell me he'd do something in front of witnesses?"

"In a word, yes. He could easily conceal a weapon up his sleeve or in his pocket, brandish it in such a way that other people don't notice, and then force you to go with him. If that were to happen, I guarantee it would be the last time anyone ever saw you alive. Or he may just be brazen enough to shoot you on the spot, right then and there, in front of witnesses. Either way, it's a chance I'm not willing to take."

Roger came to Kyle's aid. "Look, Emily, he's taking you into protective custody and you're going with him, even if I have come along and sit on top of you. So stop arguing with the man and pack your bags. Once this is over and done with you can tell the schools there were extenuating circumstances, and they'll probably let you reschedule."

She looked at Roger. "So what about my father? Will he be safe here?"

"They've suggested I find another place to stay as well," he said. "I'll be staying in a hotel for the next few days, so you and Kyle will be taking Lurch with you."

"Where are we going?"

"To the southern part of the state," said Kyle. "Clarke's sister and brother-in-law own a winery, and they've offered to let us stay with them. It's way out in the country. You'll be safe there."

"They have wineries in Arizona?"

He gave her a smile. "Apparently they do." He pointed out something in the corner. "We've already packed up your keyboard. I'll load it while you pack."

❧FORTY❧

EMILY AND HER father had a final lingering hug before she climbed into Kyle's Explorer. Roger waited until she was settled in the passenger seat and had fastened her seatbelt before closing her door and turning his attention to Kyle.

"You take good care of my daughter, you hear?"

"I will, Mr. Olmstead. I promise she'll be safe. I'm sorry we won't be able to stay in touch with you as much as you'd like, but once we get a break in her case, you'll be the first to know. That said, you need to get going yourself. The officers will help you secure your home, and then they'll follow you to your hotel."

The two men shook hands and Kyle hopped into the driver's seat. Lurch moaned loudly from the backseat as Kyle started up the engine while Emily remained in her own thoughts. Kyle put the Explorer in gear and drove off. One of the squad cars followed behind.

"We'll have an escort to the freeway," he said, "and then the highway patrol will follow us out of town. Don't worry. I'll call for back up if something doesn't look right."

"And what if I need to walk the dog?" asked Emily.

"No problem. We can stop along the way." He waited for her reply, but there was none. "Look, I'm sorry your audition will have to be postponed, but with any luck we'll catch this guy quickly and you'll be able to make it to the one in Texas." Emily remained silent.

"C'mon, Emily, this isn't fair. Do you really think I wanted to do this to you? I know how much it meant to you. That's why I brought your keyboard with us. At least you can still practice while you're away."

"Sorry, Kyle. I'm not angry with you. I'm angry with Jesse and Beau. Why are they doing this to me?"

"Because they're hiding something, and just so you know, we may have to reopen the investigation into your cousin's death."

* * *

Jesse looked at his watch as the plane made its final descent into Phoenix. They would be arriving right on time. Hopefully he wouldn't have too long of a wait at the baggage claim. The long, hectic week had left him exhausted, and he looked forward to a good night's rest in his own bed. He leaned back and closed his eyes as the wheels touched down. As they taxied to the gate the captain made the usual welcoming announcement before telling the passengers they were to remain in their seats once they came to a stop. The Phoenix police would be coming on board to escort a passenger off the airplane. Jesse checked his watch again, hoping the unexpected delay wouldn't be too long. The plane soon came to a stop and the flight attendants walked up the aisles, once again reminding everyone to please remain seated. Two uniformed officers, along with a man in a business suit, boarded the plane and a flight attendant brought them to Jesse's seat. The man in the suit presented his badge.

"Jesse St. Claire?"

He heart skipped a beat. "I'm Jesse. What seems to be the problem?"

"I'm Clarke Davidson. I'm a homicide detective with the Phoenix Police Department. I need you to come with me."

"What's this about? Am I under arrest?"

"We need to ask you a few questions. If you'll please come with us."

Jesse looked around. The other passengers were giving him strange looks. He slowly stood from his seat. "Fine. Just let me get my bag from the overhead bin."

"One of the officers will get it for you."

He pointed out his bag and followed the other officers off the airplane. They took him into a restricted area and ushered him into a small room where an older black man, also in a business suit, waited. Clarke pointed to a chair and told him to take a seat.

"So why are you dragging me off the airplane?" Jesse fought to control the anger in his voice.

Clarke took his seat and began shuffling through some papers while nodding toward the other man. "This is Sidney Hill.

He's a detective with internal affairs. We have some questions for you regarding Detective Fowler, and your soon-to-be ex-wife."

"I have nothing to say." Jesse's tone remained defiant. "Annette Claiborne's death was ruled an accident. I was never a suspect, and I've had no contact with Detective Fowler, or my wife, for some time now."

"I see," said Clarke. "So, does the name Big Hector mean anything to you, Jesse?"

"Who?"

"Big Hector."

"No." Jesse shook his head. "Who is he? Some pro wrestler or something?"

"How about Hector Alfonso Garcia? Does that name ring a bell?"

"No, it does not. Are you looking for someone who may have attended one of my seminars?"

"Not exactly," said Sidney. "So tell me, Jesse, when was the last time you spoke to Detective Fowler?"

"It's been awhile. Now that the case is closed, he has no reason to contact me."

"I see. So when did you last speak to him?"

"It was right after they ruled Annette's death an accident. He stopped by to let me know the case was officially closed, and he thanked me for my cooperation. We shook hands and he left. I've not seen or heard from him since. So why are you asking me this?"

"We'll be the ones asking the questions, if you don't mind." Sidney's voice was stern.

"Did you know your wife recently appeared on a local TV talk show?" asked Clarke.

"Yeah, I heard something about it."

"But you didn't see the show?"

Jesse swept his hand through his hair. "No, I'm afraid I didn't see it. If I'd known she was going to be on TV I probably would have watched, but I didn't hear about it until after the fact. I've been very busy. I'm a self-employed motivational speaker, and I'm sure you can appreciate the fact that the whole controversy surrounding Annette Claiborne's death has done some serious damage to my career. I had a string of cancellations during the investigation, and I'm just now beginning to recover. At the moment my focus is on rebuilding my business and regaining the public's trust."

"I understand," said Sidney. "So are you aware of the fact that your wife made some serious allegations against both you and Detective Fowler on that talk show, and as a result, Detective Fowler has been placed on paid administrative leave?"

Jesse shifted slightly in his chair. "I may have heard something about it on the news, but again, I've had no contact with Detective Fowler since the case was closed, and I've not spoken to Emily since the day her cousin fell down those stairs. Look, I've told you everything I know, so would someone please tell me what's going on?"

"We're following up on a tip."

"I see. So, what does that have to do with me?"

"It actually concerns your wife," said Sidney

"My wife?" Jesse sat for a moment in stunned silence. "I'm sorry, I'm just not getting this. Would someone please tell me what's going on?"

"I'm afraid we can't discuss the details," said Sidney. "As I said, we're following up on a tip."

The realization dawned on him. "Wait a minute. Are you saying someone wants to harm Emily?"

"We just told you we're following up on a tip," said Clarke. "That's all we can say for now."

Jesse reached for his phone and looked up a number.

"Who are you calling?" asked Clarke.

"Emily. I need to warn her."

"You can put the phone down. Your wife is fine."

"Can I at least call her and see if she's okay?"

Clarke shook his head. "No, I'm afraid you can't."

Jesse put his phone down. "Fine. As I already said, the last time I spoke to my wife was the day her cousin fell down the stairs. Since that time, she's filed for divorce, so nowadays we only communicate through our lawyers. Now, just so you know, our divorce is as amicable as they come. She doesn't want any community property. I even offered her half of the sale proceeds from the house, but she refused. She wouldn't even take her half of our joint savings account. She's made it abundantly clear that she wants nothing from me, so I would have absolutely nothing to gain if anything were to happen to her, and if you don't believe me, you can check my bank records."

"Don't worry, Jesse," said Clarke. "We intend to do just that."

Jesse glared at the other two men. "Fine. Now, unless you have some reason to hold me, I'd like to go now. Otherwise, I'm calling my attorney."

Clarke leaned back in his chair and looked at Sidney. "I'm done, for now. How 'bout you."

Sidney rose to his feet and gathered up his papers. "I'm through as well. I'll let you know, Jesse, if I need any further information."

Sidney stepped away and Clarke turned his attention back to Jesse. "You're free to go, Mr. St. Claire, and I appreciate your cooperation. If we need anything else from you, we'll be in touch." Clarke too gathered up his papers as one of the officers escorted Jesse away.

❧FORTY-ONE❧

KYLE PRESSED THE button on the steering wheel. "What's up, Clarke?"

"I've just finished interviewing Jesse St. Claire."

"I see. So what did Jesse have to say? And by the way, we're on the road, and both Emily and I can hear you through the car speakers."

"How's she doing?"

"I'm okay," she said.

"I'm glad," said Clarke. "So, back to Jesse. He was a little put out at first, but once he realized it concerned Emily's well-being, he seemed genuinely concerned about her. He wanted to call her to warn her, but I told him she was okay. He also said their divorce is uncontested and amicable. She wants nothing from him, so he'll be the one walking away with all the goodies once it's over and done with."

"That's true," said Emily. "I didn't want anything from him except my freedom, and I made that choice of my own free will. Jesse never coerced me. In fact, it was just the opposite. My attorney really had to make the point that I didn't want the house sale proceeds."

"Good to know," said Clarke. "Jesse also tells me he'll allow us to access to his bank records. He says he has nothing to gain by her demise, and I have to agree. I'll still do a follow up, and if his story checks out, I think we can safely rule him out as a suspect, at least as far as any murder for hire is concerned. The rest will be up to Sidney Hill and internal affairs."

"And no doubt Sidney will have some questions for Mr. St. Claire as well," said Kyle. "In the meantime, thanks for the update, and please, keep us posted."

"Of course. Everything okay your end, Kyle?"

"So far so good. We stopped for a burger a little while ago and I didn't notice anything unusual. We're just now entering Tucson, and everything appears to be fine. I'm guessing we should arrive at our destination in about another hour or so. At least we'll be there before midnight."

"Which would be about right," said Clarke, "and don't worry. They've turned on the porch light and left the front door unlocked. You can still do that sort of thing when you're out in the middle of nowhere."

"Maybe so, but we won't be doing that."

"Understood. In the meantime, we're still looking for Big Hector, and I won't rest until he's found. You two have a safe trip, and please enjoy a glass of my family's wine once you get there."

"Will do. Over and out." Kyle disconnected the call and the music resumed playing. Emily leaned back in her seat.

"You okay?" asked Kyle.

"Yeah, I'm fine. Jesse may be a lying, cheating, son of a bitch, but at least it's good to know he's not out to kill me."

"I agree, but I still say he knows a whole lot more than he's letting on. I know he's responsible for what happened to Annette, and I know Beau was in on the cover up. What has yet to be determined is why he went along. Once we find out everything else should fall into place."

"And what happens then?"

Kyle took a deep breath and sighed. "What happens next will be very sad indeed. A once good cop, who's also been my partner for the past two years, will most likely be arrested and prosecuted. Yeah, Beau's made his fair share of mistakes along the way. Who hasn't? But he also got a hell of a lot of bad guys off the streets."

"I wish I could have known him when he was a good cop. Unfortunately, what I saw of him was very ugly. Sidney Hill stopped by my home a couple of nights ago and I gave him my statement. He recorded it, and he also took a lot of notes."

"Did he tell you anything?"

"No, not much. He simply thanked me for my time and said he'd let me know when his investigation was complete."

"Sidney's a good man. We go way back. He was my first partner, back when I joined the force."

"Yeah, he mentioned something about that."

"So if anyone can get to the truth, it's Sidney."

Emily took in her surroundings and changed the subject. "It's been a long time since I've been to Tucson. The place has sure changed."

"When were you here last?"

"It's been nearly ten years. I was going to the U of A." She suddenly went quiet.

"You okay?" he finally asked.

"Yeah. I was just having a moment."

"Care to talk about it?"

"I was reminiscing about how I met Jesse. We were taking the same art history class. I've always loved art, but it wasn't Jesse's favorite subject, so he started asking me questions. One thing led to another, and before long he asked me out. By the end of the year, he was graduating and we were engaged. You know the rest of the story."

"Yep. Good thing I like art."

"What was that?"

"I said it's a good thing I like art. Remember Hanson Sisters? You were there, playing the piano, and I had the date from Hell."

Emily smiled for a moment. "Yeah, I remember."

She leaned back into her seat once again, keeping to herself as they drove through the heart of the city. Before long the bright lights and buildings were behind them. Kyle finally broke the silence.

"So, back when you were living in Tucson, did you ever go to the Santa Rita Mountains? That's where we're going."

"No, I'm afraid not. I was a busy, starving student who just didn't have the time, or the money, for any excursions. How 'bout you?"

"Can't say I've been there either, although I hear it's a beautiful part of the state. Clarke told me a little about his sister's winery. It sits on about twenty acres, and we'll be staying in a small guest house, about a hundred yards or so away from the main building." His tone turned serious. "So, before we get there, I need to go over the ground rules with you."

Emily bristled. "Ground rules?"

"Yes." His tone remained firm. "The winery is open to the public, seven days a week, from ten o'clock in the morning until four o'clock in the afternoon. During those hours you'll have to remain in the guest house."

Her tone turned hostile. "Why? It's bad enough you're dragging me away from my auditions, but I not going to allow you to treat me like a prisoner."

"Emily, please. You have to stay out of sight. If Big Hector were to somehow find out you're hiding there what's to stop him from showing up during business hours and wandering around the place like another tourist? I'm not taking any chances. You'll be free to walk the grounds before and after business hours, but during the day, when the place is open to the public, you'll have to stay hidden. You have your keyboard, so you can keep up with your music. You also have your iPad if you want to play games or read a book, but no going online. I don't want to take a chance on someone figuring out where you are. We've pulled out all the stops to find Big Hector, so with any luck you'll make it to your audition in Texas. In the meantime, think of it as a music retreat."

"Easy for you to say."

"This isn't exactly a picnic for me either. I'm having to leave my son with my sister."

"Sorry, Kyle."

"It's okay. It comes with the job, although there was another reason why I volunteered for this. Not only do I want to protect you, I also need a time out myself."

"Really? How come?"

"It's like I told you before. I'm a single parent working a high stress job with a lot of overtime. My son needs a dad he can actually see on a regular basis. So, I'm taking some time off to decide if I want to take the position in Dallas or not. Remember me telling you about it?"

"I do. So is this why you're hoping I'll decide on the University of North Texas?"

Kyle dodged her question. "Our exit's coming up. Did you want me to stop so you can walk the dog?"

Emily peered into the backseat. "At the moment he's sound asleep. He'll probably be okay until we get there."

Both remained silent as Kyle exited the Interstate and got on a two-lane highway. They were soon winding their way through the mountains. The road was dark and treacherous at times. Emily felt relieved knowing Kyle was behind the wheel. They finally made their way through the mountains and into the tiny town of Sonoita. The GPS device directed them to onto another two-lane road, and they were soon winding through the countryside. Along the way they drove past signs for several wineries before Kyle turned onto another country road.

"I'd say it's certainly off the beaten path," said Emily.

"It is," said Kyle, "but it won't be much farther. According to the map, it's about another half mile or so. It should be coming up on your right."

"What's the name of it again?"

"McPherson Vineyards."

Emily stared into the darkness and something soon caught her eye. "I see it. There's a sign on your right. It says, 'McPherson Vineyards Entrance,' and there's a big arrow underneath it."

Kyle turned at the sign. It led to a bumpy, one-lane dirt road. A large, two-story building stood on top of a hill.

"That's the main building," said Kyle, "but we don't want to go there. Clarke said there'll be a fork in the road, about a quarter mile past the entrance, and when we get there, we go to the left."

"And there it is." Emily pointed toward the left and Kyle veered onto a rocky, hilly lane. Seconds later a small single-story house appeared on their left. The porch light was on. Kyle parked next to the house and Emily undid her seat belt.

"Not so fast," he quickly said. He cautiously stepped out of the vehicle and looked around before checking the front door. It was unlocked. He stepped inside and looked around. A single lamp on the side table had been left on. A bottle of wine, with two empty glasses, sat on the coffee table, along with a handwritten welcoming note from Clarke's sister. He checked the kitchen and bedrooms thoroughly before stepping back outside and walking up to the passenger side window.

"All clear," he said.

Emily hopped out, eagerly stretching her legs before she let Lurch out. She took the dog for a short walk while Kyle unloaded their bags. Once the dog was ready, she stepped inside the house.

"Nice place," she said.

"Indeed. There are much worse places to hide out in. As you can see, the kitchen is off to the side, the master suite is over there, and there are two smaller bedrooms down the hall. I'll take one of them and you take the master suite."

"Are you sure?"

"I'm sure. It's more secure. The windows are all locked, and there's a lock on the bedroom door as well. If anything unexpected should happen, you'll be safer in there. I'll help you set up your keyboard in the morning, but for now I need to unwind. It's been a hell of a day."

He handed her a wineglass, filling it with the red wine before filling the other one for himself. Setting the bottle down, he gave her a warm smile. "Here's to you making it to your other audition."

"Thanks, Kyle."

They took a couple of sips and he put the cork back in the bottle, taking a moment to inspect the label. "It's a nice little merlot, but I think we'll save the rest for later. I've had a long day and I'm beat."

"Me too." She set her glass back on the table and gave him a hug. "Goodnight, Kyle. I'm sorry if I came across as ungrateful. You really have gone the extra mile for me, and I honestly do appreciate it."

"All in a day's work." They looked into each other's eyes, and he kissed her. "Goodnight, Emily. I'll see you in the morning."

He grabbed his bag and disappeared down the hall. Emily waited until he was out of sight before walking into the master suite. Lurch followed her, plopping down on a rug on the wood floor while she got ready for bed. Moments later she laid down and fell into a deep, exhausted sleep.

∾FORTY-TWO∾

JESSE ROLLED OVER and covered his head with his pillow as he tried to ignore the doorbell. It soon stopped ringing, but by then he was too awake to go back to sleep. He rolled on his other side to check the clock on the nightstand. It was nearly half past nine. No wonder the sun was shining so brightly. The long, grueling week had left him drained. As he stumbled out of bed and into the shower he decided he would give himself a long overdue day off. Ten minutes later he put on his sweats and went downstairs, grimacing once again as he reached the landing. Every time he walked by, he saw Annette's body, staring into space. Even worse was the fact that other people wanted to see it too. The real estate agent said most of the calls she received weren't from prospective buyers. They were from gawkers, wanting to see the spot where Annette had died. She even suggested taking the house off the market for a few weeks to allow the notoriety to wear off, but Jesse refused. He was anxious to sell and had even reduced the price.

Jesse sighed as he continued down the remaining flight and went into the kitchen to brew a fresh pot of coffee. Five minutes later he took his mug into the living room and sat down on the sofa. Grabbing the remote, he started channel surfing, and as he took another sip of coffee the doorbell rang again. He slammed his mug down on the coffee table and marched to the front door to check the peephole. A familiar-looking black man stood on the other side.

"Who is it?"

"Sidney Hill. I'm with the Phoenix Police Department. We spoke last night."

Jesse slowly opened the door as Sidney presented his badge.

"I'm sorry," said Jesse, "but I'm afraid I can't help you. The Claiborne case is officially closed, and I've already told you everything I know."

"I understand, Mr. St. Claire, but this isn't about the Claiborne case, at least not directly. I'm with internal affairs, and I'm investigating a complaint against Detective Fowler."

Jesse's heart skipped a beat. "I see. Sorry for being rude. I've had a long, hectic week and I'm exhausted. In fact, I only woke up a few minutes ago."

"Which explains why you didn't answer your door when I was here before."

"I'm afraid so. I thought I heard something, but I was coming out of a dead sleep and didn't realize someone was at the door. Please, come in." He led Sidney into the dining room. "Would you care for some coffee?"

"No thank you."

Sidney pulled up a chair at the dining table and took out a small voice recorder and notebook. Jesse sat down across from him, anxiously sipping his coffee.

"So, do you have any more information about Emily?"

"Your wife is doing fine."

"Thank you for letting me know. So, last night you told me Detective Fowler had been placed on paid leave after Emily went on that talk show, and you asked me about someone named Big Hector. Is Detective Fowler somehow involved with all of this?"

"I'm afraid I can't answer that. I'm here to investigate the allegations of wrongdoing your wife has made against Detective Fowler."

"I see." Jesse took a deep breath, reminding himself to remain calm as Sidney started looking through his notes.

"The Claiborne case was certainly an interesting one," said Sidney. "There were two vastly different accounts of how Ms. Claiborne met her demise, and Detective Fowler bought your version of the story, in spite of a complete lack of evidence to back it up. So why was that?"

"I don't know. Maybe it was because he knew I was telling the truth."

"I see. So, you're maintaining your story about your wife pushing Ms. Claiborne down those steps."

"As I've said before, it all happened very quickly. I didn't actually see Emily push Annette down those stairs. I just assumed she had. However, it has since been ruled an accident. The consensus of opinion is that Annette somehow lost her footing and fell. I'm grateful, however, that Detective Fowler saw my side of the story and backed me while that other detective, Madden, did not. If not for Detective Fowler, I'd be sitting in a jail cell right now, charged with a crime I didn't commit. Detective Fowler is a good man. It sounds to me like he's made some enemies somewhere along the line, who are apparently out to get him. Find those enemies, and you'll find the truth."

"Oh, I intend to get to the truth all right. By the way, I noticed you have security cameras in front of your house. Did you by chance—"

"The cameras were offline that day."

"I see." Sidney sounded skeptical. "I also wanted to let you know that I'd already subpoenaed your bank records, and I noticed that over the past few weeks you've made several large cash withdrawals."

"That's right. As I explained to you and the other detective last night, I had a number of cancelations over the controversy surrounding Annette Claiborne's death, but I still had bills to pay, so I had to take money from my savings account in order to stay afloat. And now that work is picking up again, I should be able to stay on top of things much better. I'm also hoping to be able to start putting money back into my savings account very soon."

"And what you're telling me does indeed appear to be the case. However, it doesn't account for all of the cash."

Jesse was becoming annoyed. "It's because I also needed to buy gas and groceries, and there was no sense paying for that, or any other necessities, with a credit card. I know what you're getting at, and I highly resent the implication. I did not bribe Detective Fowler. You can't prove that I did, because I didn't. Nor have I had any communication with him since the Claiborne case was closed, and if you don't believe me, you can check my phone records. Now, unless you can produce more substantial evidence of any wrongdoing on my part, this interview is over."

"I understand your frustration, Mr. St. Claire, and yes, we're almost done here. I just have one or two final questions. While the investigation into Ms. Claiborne's death was going on, did Detective Fowler ever say or do anything out of the ordinary?"

Jesse felt his body tense up. "What do you mean, out of the ordinary?"

"Did he ever bring up anything odd, that may have had nothing to do with the case?"

Jesse stared into his coffee mug. "Nothing odd or unusual that I can think of. He was always professional whenever he was around me." He looked Sidney in the eye. "I'm sorry, but I'm afraid that's all I can tell you. So, are we done now?"

"I think so." Sidney picked up his recorder and notebook and followed Jesse to the door.

"You know, Jesse, I recently had the opportunity to meet with your wife."

"Did you now?"

"I certainly did. She's quite a lady, and she's both beautiful and talented. You must miss her a lot."

"Yes, I do." Jesse's mood turned sad. "Emily was the love of my life, but I lost her through my own stupidity."

"I'm sorry to hear it." Sidney stopped at the front door. "I can certainly understand her being angry over your relationship with her late cousin, but I also understand the two of you were seeing a marriage counselor and were in the process of reconciling at the time Ms. Claiborne had her accident. I'm also told that the last time you saw or spoke to her was when she stopped by to pick up her passport. A lot has happened since then. Don't you think that if you tried talking to her, you two could still work things out?"

Jesse nervously looked down at the floor. "I would if I could, but I'm afraid it's too late now."

"What do you say that?"

"Too much has happened. She'd never take me back now. Not after I—" Jesse's heart leapt to his throat as he realized he might have said too much. He quickly tried to cover it up. "Unfortunately, too much has happened. You know, with Annette's death and all. Besides, our divorce has already been filed and our court date is only a few weeks away."

"I understand, but it wouldn't be the first time someone withdrew a divorce because they were able to work things out." Sidney opened the door and stepped across the threshold. "She's a remarkable woman, Mr. St. Claire, and I can see that you still love her. If it were me, I'd do whatever it took to win her back. Have a nice day."

❧FORTY-THREE❧

EMILY ROLLED OVER and opened her eyes, finding herself face-to-face with Lurch. "Hey, buddy, how ya doing this morning?" She sat up and scratched the dog behind his ears. "Give me a couple of minutes, okay? Then we'll go out for a walk."

She hopped out of bed and went into the bathroom, coming out a few minutes later in blue jeans and a sweatshirt. She grabbed the dog's leash and walked into the living room. The blinds were still closed and house was dark and quiet. The kitchen stove clock said twelve minutes past eight. She put on her jacket and leashed the dog. Stepping outside, she found herself surrounded by a beautiful countryside. Grapevines dotted the rolling hills while purple mountains framed the horizon. The main building stood on top of a nearby hill. It looked like a big Mexican hacienda with its red tile roof and large arches wrapped around the lower floor. She led the dog across the dirt road and into the grassy hillside. A woman's voice called out from behind. Emily turned and saw a woman, bundled in a heavy, hooded jacket, walking toward her. As she came closer Emily pulled a small plastic bag from her pocket.

"It's okay. I'll clean up after him."

"Don't worry about it. We're out in the country, and this field is full of stuff that all kinds of other animals have left behind." She smiled and extended her hand. "You must be Emily. I'm Mary McPherson, Clarke Davidson's sister."

"Yes, I'm Emily." The two women shook hands. "Nice to meet you."

"So, Emily, would you like come to join us for some coffee? The dog is welcome too."

Emily turned her gaze to the small house. "Sure, but I can't stay too long."

"I understand. Clarke already told me you'll have to lay low during business hours, but there's still plenty of time for you to come in and say hello."

"Thanks, I'd like that."

She followed Mary up the hill to the main building. The front lawn was well manicured with picnic tables and mature cottonwood trees, and lush flowerbeds framed the front door, Mary unlocked a glass door and motioned for Emily to go on through. Inside was a room with burgundy-colored walls. Large picture windows revealed a spectacular view of mountains. A long wooden bar stood in front of the outer wall, while shelves and display cases filled with wine glasses and other knickknacks lined a portion of the opposite wall.

"This is our tasting room and gift shop, and if you'll follow me, I'll give you a quick tour of the winery."

Emily followed Mary across the room and through a set of double doors leading into a much larger room, filled with giant stainless-steel tanks. They stopped in front of a big piece of machinery.

"This is where the magic begins," said Mary. "This machine crushes the grapes, and from here they go straight to the tanks to start fermenting." She pointed out the various tanks as she went on to explain some of the technical details of winemaking. Once she finished, they went into a small, dimly lit room at the very back of the building. Wooden barrels, resting sideways on metal brackets, lined the walls from floor to ceiling while a sweet, pungent odor filled the air. This was where the wine was aged before being bottled and sold.

"And that's pretty much it." Mary led Emily back to the tasting room. "We bought the place nearly twenty years ago. At the time my husband was an airline pilot. He was making good money, but we both hated the lifestyle that went along with it. We also wanted to get out of the big city and raise our kids in a smaller town. Then Lee came into some money after his folks passed away, so we invested in the place. It was a much smaller operation back then. The previous owner had started some of the vineyards, and we lived in the little guesthouse, where you're staying now. Back then Lee was still flying, so the kids and I ran the tours and tended the vineyards whenever he was away. We grew over time, and then a few other investors came along, so we were able to expand to where we are today. Lee finally quit flying about nine years ago, so now we're both full time winemakers. We love our lives here and we'd never go back to living in the city."

"What about your kids?" asked Emily.

"Our son graduated from college last year. He's living in Tucson, at least for now, but he'll be back, as he'll be taking the place over someday. Our daughter is attending nursing school at a college in Oregon." Mary stepped behind the cash register and undid the rope at the foot of a staircase. "So come on up and we'll have that coffee. Have you had breakfast yet?"

"No, not yet. I'm afraid we don't have much in the way of provisions, other than what my dad packed for us in a cold box for us last night."

"In that case please, come join us. We can whip up some scrambled eggs."

"I appreciate the offer, but I don't want to impose."

Mary gave her a grin. "Trust me, you're not imposing. You're a guest in our home."

The stairs led up to a long, narrow hallway. Mary pointed out the first door as they walked by. "Here's the administrative offices, and our apartment is at the end of the hall. How's that for an easy commute to work?"

Emily followed her into a small but nicely furnished family room. A breakfast bar divided off the kitchen. A handsome, silver-haired man looked up from the stove and smiled.

"You must be Emily."

"Yes, I am."

"Hi, Emily, I'm Lee. Welcome to McPherson Vineyards."

He told her to take a seat at the breakfast bar, and as she sat down, he placed a mug of coffee in front of her. Mary took off her jacket, revealing a mane of long, red hair beneath the hood. She sat down next to Emily, and few minutes later Lee handed both a plate of scrambled eggs with sausage and toast. As he set his own plate down on the bar someone knocked at the door.

"You ladies stay put." He headed to the door. A young man in blue coveralls stood on the other side.

"Sorry to bother you, boss, but there's a cop out here looking for someone named Emily St. Claire."

"Kyle?" Emily slid off her barstool, reaching the door just as Kyle stepped inside.

"Where have you been?" he asked.

"I had to take Lurch for a walk, and then I bumped into Mary. They invited me in for breakfast. Any news?"

"No, I'm afraid not."

"Have you eaten, Kyle?" asked Lee. "We have plenty and you're welcome to join us."

Mary pointed to the remaining barstool. "Please, have a seat."

Kyle hesitated for a moment before taking the stool on the other side of Emily. He gave her a strong look as Lee offered him coffee. Emily gave him a defiant stare in return before turning her attention back to her hosts.

"This is Kyle Madden," said Emily.

"I know who you are." Mary gave him a smile. "Clarke's told me about you. I understand you two are partners now."

"Yes, ma'am, we are."

"I'm Mary, not ma'am," she said with a wink, "and I'm sorry to hear about your last partner."

"Thank you, however the investigation is still ongoing."

"Of course. Hopefully this entire mess will be sorted out quickly, and he'll soon be back on the force. In the meantime, I want to reassure you that Emily will be safe here. We're keeping a close watch on things, and Clarke tells me the local authorities have been alerted as well, so you can expect to see plenty of deputy sheriffs patrolling the area."

"Thank you, Mary. That's good to know."

Lee handed Kyle a plate of scrambled eggs and sat down with the others. They made small talk over breakfast, but once the meal was over Kyle said he and Emily would have to leave.

"Emily mentioned you don't have much in the way of provisions," said Mary.

"I'm afraid we don't," said Kyle. "As soon as I get her back to the guest house, I plan on going to town to get some groceries."

"I'm afraid there isn't much in the way of shopping in Elgin." Mary quickly grabbed a pen and paper. "However, there are grocery stores in the nearby towns. I'll make a list for you."

"Thank you. I appreciate it." He waited patiently for Mary to hand him the paper. Once she did, he grabbed his coat and motioned for Emily to come with him. She grabbed the dog's leash and joined him at the door.

"Thank you both again for breakfast," said Emily, "and the winery tour."

"You're welcome." Mary gave her a parting smile. "And please let us know if you need anything."

Emily gave her a final nod before heading out the door behind Kyle. He rushed down the stairs. Emily had to pick up her pace once they stepped outside.

"So why didn't you let me know you went to the main house?" asked Kyle.

"I don't have a cell phone, remember?"

"We went over this last night. I told you these gangs can be quite sophisticated with their intelligence gathering. They've been known to hack computers, which means they could track you through your cell phone. It's a chance I'm not willing to take, and which is why we left it behind."

"I know, Kyle. So what was I supposed to do? Wake you up?"

"Yes. You should have woken me up. Trust me, it would have been okay. Or you could have done the old school thing."

"The old school thing?"

Finally, he smiled. "Yes, the old school thing. You could have written a note on a piece of paper and left it on the kitchen counter."

"So do you really have to track my every move? I've told you before I'm not a prisoner here."

He ignored her remark and they walked the rest of the way back to the guesthouse in silence. When they reached the front door, he stopped to take the key from his pocket.

"Emily, I honestly don't mean for you to feel like a prisoner here. It's like I told you last night. You're free to walk the grounds before and after business hours. All I'm asking is for you to let me know before you go outside. I got up, you were nowhere to be found, and my first thought was that you had been kidnapped."

Her demeanor softened. "Sorry, Kyle. I didn't mean to upset you. Right now, all I can think about is the audition I'm missing. It's at ten o'clock tomorrow morning. When you first showed up at Mary's apartment, I was really hoping you'd had some good news for me, like Big Hector had been caught."

"I'm afraid he's still at large, however your dad will be contacting the university today. He'll tell them you've been called away on an unexpected family emergency, and hopefully they can reschedule you. In the meantime, let's get your keyboard set up." He unlocked the door and she followed him inside.

"Thanks for offering to help with the keyboard," said Emily, "but I'm really not in the mood to play right now."

"What do you mean, you're not in the mood? You're a musician, and you know full well there are times when you have to play, even if you're not in the mood. So that means—"

His phone suddenly interrupted him. He checked the caller ID and quickly answered. "Hey Sidney, what's up?"

"I've just finished interviewing Jesse St. Claire."

"So what did Jesse have to say?"

"Not much. He's still sticking to his story about his wife being there when her cousin fell down the stairs."

"You know he won't change his story now."

Emily shot Kyle a strong look.

"Of course he won't," said Sidney. "Not unless he wants to get charged with filing a false police report. So, I tried a different tactic."

"And what was that?"

"As I was leaving, I asked him about Emily. I told him she's a remarkable lady, and I suggested he try to work things out with her."

Kyle winced. "Really? So what did Jesse have to say about that?"

"He said she'd never take him back, not after what he did."

"And what did Jesse do?"

"He was about to tell me, but then he realized he'd slipped up, so he tried to cover it up by saying too much had happened between them. He's definitely hiding something. The question is whether or not Beau Fowler was involved in the cover up. If so, then what was so incriminating that he'd want to have Mrs. St. Claire killed?"

"I have no idea," said Kyle, "but I'll let Emily know. Maybe she can put the pieces together."

"I hope so. Meantime, as long as I'm in the neighborhood, I'm going to go have talk with the neighbor, Jorge Mendoza, and see what he has to say."

"Thanks, Sidney. Please keep me posted." Kyle disconnected the call and turned his attention back to Emily. "That was Sidney Hill."

"I know. I could hear him through your phone, and Jesse's right. I'd never take him back. Not in a million years."

"Well I would certainly hope not. So did you hear Sidney say Jesse slipped up and was about to admit something?"

"Yes. I heard it."

"Do you know what it could be?"

"I have no idea. I haven't spoken to Jesse since the morning Annette had her fall, so your guess is as good as mine. Obviously, he made up the story about me being there so he could cover his own rear end, and it's entirely possible that he bribed Detective Fowler so he'd go along with it. I'm afraid that's all I can tell you."

"The problem is there's no evidence so far of him paying Beau off. There's something else that we're missing."

She thought it over for a moment. "Kyle? What if we've been looking at this all wrong?"

"What do you mean?"

"We've all been going on the assumption Jesse somehow convinced Beau Fowler to go along with his lies about me, but what if we're wrong? What if it was really Beau's idea to frame me? And he somehow convinced Jesse to go along it?"

Kyle shook his head. "No, that doesn't make sense."

"And that's the problem. None of this makes any sense."

❧FORTY-FOUR❧

SIDNEY PARKED IN front of the Mendoza residence and knocked on the door, presenting his badge to the man who answered.

"I'm looking for Jorge Mendoza."

The man raised his brow. "I'm Jorge. Can I help you?"

"Sir, I need to ask you a few questions about the Claiborne case."

"The Claiborne case? Wasn't it ruled an accident?"

"Yes sir, it was. I'm with internal affairs. I'm here to do a follow up investigation concerning one of the detectives involved with the case, and I understand you were one of the eyewitnesses."

Jorge's demeanor immediately changed. "Yes sir, I was. Please, come inside."

Sidney stepped over the threshold and Jorge led him to the living room, pointing out a chair and offering him a seat.

"I'm afraid I don't have much time right now. Someone at work just called in sick, so I have leave in a few minutes. I'm a manager at a supermarket."

"In that case I won't take up too much of your time." Sidney reached for his voice recorder and notebook. "I'm told, Mr. Mendoza, that you were an eyewitness in the Claiborne case. Is that correct."

"Yes, although I didn't actually see the accident. I saw Emily St. Claire as she was leaving her husband's home that morning."

"Yes, that what the reports say, and you gave your statement to Detective Fowler, is that correct?"

"Yes."

"So, what can you tell me about Detective Fowler? Did he conduct himself in a professional manner?"

Jorge let out a loud sigh but remained silent.

"Is something wrong, Mr. Mendoza?"

"I'm not sure."

"Can you elaborate on that?"

"Well, the first time I first spoke to him, which was right after the lady fell down the stairs, he seemed to be okay. He just wanted to get the facts, and he thanked me for my time."

"All right." Sidney jotted down some notes. "You said it was the first time you spoke to him, correct?"

"Yes."

"So, I take it you spoke to him again."

"Yes." Jorge shifted in his chair. "He stopped by one morning, a day or two after the accident. He said he just wanted to go over a few things."

"I see. Go on."

"I told him what I told him before. How I'd seen Emily and her friend leaving, and it was before the other lady, Ms. Claiborne, arrived. He asked me if I was sure, and I told him, yes, I was sure. I know what I saw and when I saw it. I'd just left the house when I saw Emily leaving, and the spot where I was talking to her was the same spot I where I later saw Ms. Claiborne's car parked. That's when he, Detective Fowler, told me he'd done a background check on my family. That really surprised me. All I did was try to help, so why would he do a background check on my family?"

"That's what I'm here to find out, Mr. Mendoza. So, can you tell me what happened next?"

"He said he'd found out that my son, Manny, had gotten into some trouble a few years ago. Manny had fallen into the wrong crowd, and he'd gotten caught with a small amount of drugs in his possession. It was his first offense, so the judge was lenient. He paid a fine and did some community service without serving any jail time. Since then, he's gotten his act together, and he's not been in any trouble since."

"That's good to know," said Sidney. "So where is your son now?"

"He's going to college in Tucson."

"I see. So did Detective Fowler explain why he'd checked into your family?"

"No, sir, he did not."

Sidney made more notes. "All right. So, what happened next?"

Jorge looked Sidney in the eye. "He kept talking about how the University of Arizona is supposedly a big party school, and wouldn't it be a shame if one of Manny's friends accidentally left some drugs in his apartment. I kept telling him my son had learned his lesson and he no longer hangs out with those kind of people, but Detective Fowler kept insisting that it'd be a real shame if someone found drugs in Manny's apartment."

"Did he mention anything else?"

"No sir, he did not, but I certainly got the message. I could see it in his eyes, and I could hear it in his voice. Either I changed my story, or else my son would be framed for something he didn't do."

"Did you confront Detective Fowler with this?"

"No, sir, I did not. I didn't want to risk anything happening to my son. So I told him I wasn't sure if Ms. Claiborne was there or not when I saw Emily. Please understand, I had no choice, but if you're planning on arresting me, I'll have to call my lawyer."

Sidney gave him a reassuring look. "No, sir, I won't be pressing any charges. I just need to get a statement from you."

"So, what happened with Detective Fowler?"

"I'm afraid I'm not at liberty to discuss the case with you." He handed Jorge one of his cards. "I do, however, want to thank you for your time and for your help, and to let you know we may have to talk with you again. Please feel free to call me, anytime, if you can think of anything else."

* * *

Sidney huddled in his jacket as he hurried across the parking lot. The temperature had dropped, and wind had started picking up. Another winter storm was on the way. The warm air felt soothing as he stepped inside the salon. The receptionist greeted him with a warm smile.

"Can I help you?"

He presented his badge. "I'm Sidney Hill and I'm with the Phoenix Police Department. Is Megan Connors in?"

"Megan stepped out, but she should be back soon. Would you like to speak to the salon owner?"

"No, ma'am, it won't be necessary. I just need to speak to Ms. Connors for a few minutes."

She motioned to a small row of chairs at the front of the salon. "In that case, please have a seat. She should be back in about ten minutes or so."

Sidney helped himself to an empty chair, thumbing through a magazine as he took in his surroundings. The receptionist offered him some coffee, which he politely declined. A woman with long brown hair entered a short time later and the receptionist pointed Sidney out to her. She greeted him with a forced smile as she extended her hand.

"I'm Megan Connors. I understand you wanted to see me about something."

"Yes, ma'am." Sidney presented his badge. "I'm with internal affairs, and I'm doing a follow up on the Claiborne case. Is there someplace where we can talk in private?"

"Of course. Right this way." Megan led him past the stations and down a hallway to a small utility room, leaving the door partially ajar after they stepped inside.

"What can I do for you, Mr. Hill?" Her voice sounded cool.

"As I was saying, Ms. Connors, I'm doing a follow up investigation on one of the detectives involved with the Claiborne case."

"I think I know where you're going. Emily actually met Detective Madden several months before her cousin had her accident, but they didn't start seeing one another until after the case was officially closed. Besides, they're just friends."

Sidney grinned as he reached for his notepad. "You know, that's what I've been hearing too, but I'm not here to discuss Detective Madden."

Megan's face turned slightly pink. "Oh. I'm sorry. I just assumed."

He smiled again. "It's okay. I'm actually here to ask you a few questions about Detective Fowler."

Megan's tone turned serious. "I see."

"So, would you mind answering a few questions? It should only take a few minutes."

"Of course."

"I understand, Ms. Connors, that you spoke with Detective Fowler during the investigation."

"Yes, sir, I did."

"So what can you tell me about Detective Fowler? Did he conduct himself in a professional manner?"

"Well, I suppose it would all depend on what you call a professional manner."

"Can you please elaborate on that?"

"He stopped by one day, just like you're doing now, and he said he wanted to go over a few details about the case. So, I brought him back here, and I told him what had happened that morning, how we had to stop by Jesse's house to get Emily's passport."

"All right. Did you discuss anything else with Detective Fowler?"

"As a matter of fact, yes, and I'm going to very frank with you. From the very start I've tried to be as cooperative with you people as I possibly could. Annette was Emily's cousin, and even if they didn't get along, we still needed to find out what really happened to her."

"I understand, Ms. Connors. So what is it that you're trying to tell me?"

Megan looked him in the eye. "I gave Detective Fowler as detailed of a description of the events that morning as I possibly could. Day, time, where we were, what I saw, and so forth, but for some reason my version of what happened just didn't sit well with him."

"Can you please explain?"

"What I'm saying sir, is that Detective Fowler kept trying to contradict me. At first, I thought he was just making sure I had all my facts straight, but then, when I apparently didn't give him the answers he was looking for, he turned on me."

"Really? So how did he turn on you?"

Once again, she looked Sidney in the eye. "He asked me if I'd been drinking that morning. I said yes, I'd had some coffee before I left home, but he said no, that wasn't what he meant. He then accused me of being drunk. He said something to the effect of it not being the first time someone had a drink before heading off to the airport."

Sidney raised his brow. "I see. So what did you tell him?"

"I told him the truth. I don't drink and drive. Emily lost her mother to a drunk driver back when we were in high school. I also told him the interview was over. He left and he hasn't been back since, but by then the damage was done, because he then took it upon himself to retaliate."

"What do you mean, retaliate?"

She folded her arms across her chest. "A short time later Detective Fowler filed several complaints against the salon with the state cosmetology board. They were either completely bogus, or for extremely petty offenses. His actions, however, created a big headache for the salon owners, as you can imagine, so they, in turn, have taken their frustrations out on me. To say it's made things awkward would be an understatement, so I'm now looking for a chair to rent at another salon. That's where I was when you got here. I've been with this salon for six years. Six years, Mr. Hill. I worked very hard to build up a clientele here, and now I'm out the door because of bullying by someone in your department."

Sidney jotted something in his notebook. "I'm sorry it happened, Ms. Connors, I truly am. Did you file a complaint against Detective Fowler?"

"Are you kidding me? I saw first-hand what he did to Emily. He did everything he could possibly do to frame her for a crime she didn't commit. Thank goodness the grand jury saw through it and didn't indict her. The man is power hungry, he has a very bad attitude, and he's obviously in cahoots with Jesse over something. What it is I don't know, but what I can tell you is he's made it pretty clear he'll destroy anyone who gets in his way. However, it sounds like someone else complained, so thank goodness for that."

"Yes, we are investigating Detective Fowler. However, all I can say for now is he's on administrative leave until the investigation is complete."

"Which is certainly a relief. Hopefully this will stop him from harming someone else. So, is there anything else I can do for you, Mr. Hill?"

He handed over one of his cards. "Not that I can think of, Ms. Connors, but please call me if you think of anything else, and I do thank you for your time."

"The pleasure is all mine, sir."

↠FORTY-FIVE↞

EMILY GAZED OUT the kitchen window and shivered underneath her sweater. The sun had slipped behind a cloud and the wind was picking up. She poured herself another cup of coffee and checked the clock on the stove. It was a few minutes past four. The winery would now be closed for the day. She returned the sofa and tried to go back to the novel she was reading on her tablet, but soon found herself staring at the screen once again. As she set it aside the front door opened. Kyle stepped in, both hands filled with grocery bags.

"Hi, honey, I'm home." He had in a playful tone in voice, but Emily remained silent as he set the grocery bags on the kitchen counter.

"Sorry to take so long," he said. "I decided to drive down to Nogales so I could meet with the county sheriff. So far there's been no sign of Big Hector, but don't worry. None of us are going to rest until we find him."

"I see." Emily's tone was flat. She stepped into the kitchen and sifted through the grocery bags, mostly finding packages of frozen meals. "You could have brought some real food. I can cook, you know."

"I'm afraid it's force of habit, my dear. I'm a bachelor who puts in long hours and doesn't have much time for cooking."

"You mean you eat like this at home?"

"Sometimes, although I'm also known to pick up stuff from the deli section." He shot her a grin. "If you'll look inside those last couple of bags, you'll find a rotisserie chicken with a few fixings."

She began loading the groceries into the freezer. "Maybe later. I'm not very hungry right now."

"I know you're upset about your audition tomorrow, but I do have some news. Your dad called while I was out."

Emily perked up. "Really? So what did he say? Are they going to reschedule my audition?"

"We're not sure. He told them there was a family emergency. They said they were sorry to hear it, but all the time slots had been filled. They will, however, let you know if they have a last-minute cancelation, so there's still a chance."

Her face fell. "Maybe, but it doesn't sound too promising."

"There's always another chance. They also said if worse came to worse, you'd could reapply next year."

She sighed as she put the rest of the groceries away. Kyle finally broke the silence.

"Are you alright?"

She shook her head.

"Emily, I understand you're being upset. I would be too if I were in your shoes, but like I told you before, not having a music degree isn't the end all of the world."

"You don't understand. I went for years without playing."

"Then find yourself a mentor if you have to, but keep playing. Trust me, you'll have other opportunities."

"I know, Kyle, but sometimes having the right professor opens doors." She tossed the last frozen food package into the freezer and stormed off to her room, plopping down on top of her bed and staring at the ceiling as she fought back the tears. The room grew darker as the storm clouds built up outside. Soon the wind began to howl. A short time later she heard someone playing Beethoven's *Für Elise*. At first, she thought Kyle had turned on a radio, but as she listened closer she noticed a slight hesitancy in the playing. She hopped off the bed and rushed into the living room to watch him play. He turned to her when he finished.

"I got tired of waiting for you to set up your keyboard, so I set it up myself. Hope you don't mind me borrowing your sheet music."

It took her a moment to find her voice. "No, it's okay. I had no idea you could play Beethoven."

"Truth be known, I haven't played Beethoven in years. I wasn't much older than Cory when I first started taking piano lessons. My mother was my first teacher, and she played classical piano. Later on, I started playing rock. Nowadays I like jazz." He turned back to the sheet music. "You know, I'm just as amazed as you that I can still play it."

She pulled up a chair and sat down next to him. "Try it again, only this time relax. Let the music flow through you. Like this."

She began the tune again, cueing him to take over after she played the first few bars. Once he finished, she gave him a smile.

"See, you did much better the second time."

He gave her a grin in return. "Thanks, teacher. Now I'm going to change gears. Give a listen to this." He began playing *Georgia on my Mind.* Emily closed her eyes, taking in the music as he serenaded her. She listened intently as he improvised during the middle. When he finally finished, she gazed into his eyes.

"Wow. You have a genuine talent, Kyle, and that's not something I would say to just anyone. So why didn't you pursue this further?"

"If you recall, I did play professionally when I was younger, and it took the fun out of it. There was a lot of pressure hustling for gigs, dealing with auditions, and sometimes having to play with people I didn't necessarily like. Nowadays my life is stressful enough just being a cop, and music, when I actually have the time for it, is my way of winding down. So I prefer play just for myself, although every now and then I'll do a gig for a department fundraiser."

Their eyes remained locked. He leaned over and kissed her, slowly but passionately. She moaned as he wrapped his arms around her. Both jumped as his phone started ringing. He quickly stepped away to grab it.

"It's Sidney. I have to take the call."

"Of course. I'll go take the dog out for a walk so you can talk." She put on her coat and called Lurch, who eagerly followed her out the door. Once outside she snapped his leash on and led him back into the grassy field. The cold wind felt like icy fingers penetrating through her coat. As the dog sniffed around she looked up the hill. The lights were burning in Lee and Mary's apartment, but the rest of the building was dark, and the remaining workers were leaving for the day. One stopped to lock up the doors to the winery before jumping into his car and driving off behind the others. Emily waited for them to pass, and as she started back toward the guesthouse the dog tugged at his leash.

"I know, buddy. You want to get out and have a good run, but it's getting ready to rain. Maybe you can do it tomorrow, okay?" She led the dog back to the house, tapping on the front door as she entered.

"It's okay," said Kyle. "You didn't have to leave, you know."

"I know, but Lurch really was due for a walk."

He motioned toward the sofa. "I think you'd better sit down. Sidney had some news."

"That doesn't sound too good."

"Don't worry, it's not all bad either." He waited for her to get settled before sitting down next to her.

"They've found Beau Fowler's car, abandoned, in a parking lot in Redding, California. It appears to have been there for about twenty-four hours."

"Where's Redding?"

"North of Sacramento, near Mount Shasta. The local authorities have all been alerted, but so far there's no sign of him."

"Which means he could be anywhere by now, especially if he's had a twenty-four-hour head start. Do they have any idea of where he may have gone?"

"He has a son in the Seattle area, so he could possibly be headed there, but we can't be sure. They haven't spoken to one another in years."

"Then maybe he's decided it's time for a little family reunion."

Finally, he smiled. "You know, you just might make a cop."

"Thanks, but I think I'll pass." Her mood turned serious once again. "So did Sidney have anything else to say?"

"As a matter of fact, he did. Earlier today he interviewed both Megan and Jorge Mendoza. Turns out Beau threatened both of them, which means we can add witness intimidation to the list of charges against him."

"I knew it! Something's been up with Megan for weeks now, but she's refused to tell me what it is. That's not like her. I kept questioning her, then she finally mentioned something about a problem at the salon and she was looking for a new salon, but she wouldn't elaborate."

"Because Beau apparently retaliated against her when she wouldn't change her story. He even admitted to me that he'd accused her of drinking the morning you were supposed to leave for your trip."

"Say what?" said a stunned Emily.

"It was when the case was still open. Beau came back to the station one day, telling me he'd interviewed Megan so he could go over what happened that morning. During our conversation he freely admitted that he'd accused her of having a drink or two before she went to pick you up. He even bragged about it, so I let him know, in no uncertain terms, that she was stone cold sober that morning, but by then it was too late. That's when he informed me he'd already turned your case over to the county attorney."

"Wow." Emily stopped for a moment to take it all in. "He really did have it in for me, and I still don't understand the reason why, but knowing Megan like I do, accusing her of drinking and driving wouldn't have gone over very well. Anyone who knows her would have known it was a lie because of what happened to my mother. Still, it doesn't explain what could have happened that would make her want to leave the salon. She's been there for six years, and I know she's been happy there."

"Apparently it was because she wouldn't change her story, and because she wouldn't change her story, Beau filed several frivolous complaints against the salon with the state board, causing her and the salon owner to have a falling out. That's why she's leaving."

Emily was becoming angry. "You have got to be kidding me."

"I'm afraid not. She told Sidney she plans to be out of there by the end of the month. She was out looking for another salon when he arrived to talk to her."

"Then why didn't she tell me anything about this?"

"According to Sidney, she didn't want you knowing until she found a spot at another salon. She wanted you to focus on your audition and not worry about her."

"Damn. I need to call her. Can I borrow your phone?"

"Sorry, not until we nab Big Hector. Right now, she thinks you're on your way to Los Angeles, and we want her to keep thinking that. Big Hector might know who your associates are, and we don't want to risk the possibility of endangering her if she were to find out you're someplace else."

"But I won't tell her anything about where I am. I'll just say I'm in my hotel room, and I'm looking forward to my audition."

"It's like I said before, Emily. Some of his associates are known to be extremely sophisticated. We have to consider the possibility of calls being traced, or that someone could even be listening in on her conversations."

Emily shuddered. "Does this ever end?"

He gave her a reassuring squeeze. "Yes. It will. I promise you. It will end."

✷FORTY-SIX✷

THE STORM CLEARED out overnight. Emily awoke to a bright sunny morning, but Lurch wasn't there. She quickly put her robe on and hurried into the living room where Kyle was relaxing in front of a basketball game. The dog was curled up on the floor next to him.

"Morning, sleepyhead."

"Morning. What's Lurch doing out here?"

"I heard scratching noises coming from your door, and when you didn't come out, I got a little concerned, so I thought I'd better check on you. You were sound asleep, but the dog needed a walk, so I took him out for you."

"Thanks. So what time is it anyway?"

He checked his watch. "It's about a quarter after ten."

"What? So why didn't you wake me?"

"You needed your rest. You've been through quite an ordeal over the past couple of days. It was bound to catch up with you."

Emily stepped into the kitchen and poured herself a cup of coffee. "Any news this morning?"

"We've alerted campus security at USC. They're on the lookout for Big Hector, but so far there's been no sign of him."

Emily took her seat in the living room. "My audition was supposed to be this afternoon. Hopefully he'll show up and they'll nab him."

"It's what we're hoping too, but there's no guarantee it'll happen. Meantime, would you like some breakfast?"

"You mean some of marvelous those frozen waffles?"

"Hey, they're not that bad," he said with a wink. "Why don't you get dressed? I'll have your breakfast ready for you when you come out."

She gave him a quick hug and a kiss on the check. "Thanks, Kyle. Give me about fifteen minutes or so. I need to wash my hair."

"Take your time."

Emily headed off to shower. Once she was dressed, she made her bed and glanced out the window as she smoothed the bedspread. A familiar looking white Honda Civic was slowly making its way up the narrow road toward the winery. Her blood ran cold and she rushed out of the bedroom.

"What's wrong?" asked Kyle. "You look like you've just seen a ghost."

"Actually, I have." She flung the front door open and ran out to the porch. Kyle was at her heels.

"Not so fast!"

The little white car continued up the path toward the main building. Once it parked the doors opened, and a family stepped out.

"What are you doing out here?" asked Kyle.

Emily pointed to the white Civic. "For a moment there I thought it might be Annette's car. I just wanted to be sure."

Kyle wrapped his arm across her shoulder and gently led her back inside, motioning for her to take a seat at kitchen table while he poured her a fresh cup of coffee.

"It wouldn't have been Annette's car. Not unless her younger sister came here to buy some wine, which is doubtful, considering she's underage."

"What do you mean?"

"Your aunt called me, right after your appearance on Trudy's show, and she and I had quite a conversation."

"Really? So why didn't you tell me this before?"

Kyle set her coffee down on the table and sat down next to her. "Because she planned on calling you herself, when she thought the time was right. Unfortunately, too many other things have happened since then."

"No kidding" Emily stopped and took a sip of her coffee. "So, what did my dear aunt have to say?"

"She admitted that yes, for a time she thought you were guilty. So did your grandmother, but once the grand jury decision came down, they both realized things weren't adding up. Now she knows she made a terrible mistake."

Emily sounded bitter. "Which is certainly an understatement."

"And I can certainly understand why you'd feel that way. So does your aunt. She wants very much to find a way to make it up to you."

"I see." Emily still sounded skeptical. "So, what else did she have to say?"

"She was proud of the way you handled yourself on Trudy's show, and she appreciated your kind words for her and your grandmother. She also said she and Tonya are doing their best to move on, but they have their good and bad days. She said they've been moving Annette's personal belongings out of Gary's apartment, and she gave Annette's car to Tonya. She also said Gary didn't know about Jesse and Annette's relationship until he heard about it on the news, and he's not taking it very well."

Emily's demeanor softened. "I can certainly understand how he feels. He was betrayed, just like I was. So did my aunt have anything else to say?"

"She and Gary plan to file a civil suit against Jesse for wrongful death."

Emily looked surprised. "Really? Well then, I guess it's a good thing I didn't want anything from Jesse in the divorce."

"Even if you had, your aunt wouldn't have come after you for it. She said they're not so much interested in the money as they are in seeing justice served. Like me, they're convinced Annette's death wasn't an accident. I just wish we could find a way to prove it. She's also angry about the way Beau handled the case, and she now understands he manipulated both her and your grandmother. She'll be giving a statement to Sidney Hill, and she's also agreed to testify in court against Beau, should it come to that."

Kyle stepped away to prepare breakfast while Emily silently sipped her coffee. Afterwards she cleaned up the kitchen while Kyle went back to the basketball game. She soon joined him, trying to keep her mind off the audition she would be missing. Kyle's phone finally rang later that afternoon. After he disconnected, he turned his attention to Emily.

"That was campus security at USC," he said. "There were reports earlier today of someone matching Big Hector's description being seen on campus, but by the time security arrived the suspect was gone, so we can't confirm whether it was actually him or not. The LAPD is looking for him as well, but so far there've been no further sightings. I wish I had better news for you."

"It's okay, Kyle. Maybe we'll get lucky, and they'll catch him in the next few hours or so. Then this nightmare will finally be over, once and for all."

❧FORTY-SEVEN☙

THE KITCHEN AND living room were empty as Emily got Lurch ready for his early morning walk. She opened the front door and let out a blood-curdling scream, slamming it shut with a loud thud. Kyle tore into the room an instant later.

"What the hell happened?"

"I opened the front door." Emily's voice trembled as she spoke. "And there was this big, black, thing, out there. Right in front of me."

Kyle cautiously opened the door while Emily stepped backward. The black form moved closer to the doorway, letting out a loud moo as Lurch barked in return. Kyle burst out laughing and stepped outside.

"For crying out loud, Emily. It's just a cow. Probably a black angus."

"A what?"

Lurch kept barking as Emily cautiously stepped outside. The cow returned his barks with a defiant stare as a golf cart pulled up to the house. Lee gave them a quick greeting while the cow took a few steps away and held her ground.

"I thought I heard someone screaming." Lee gave Emily a grin and she blushed in return. "Sorry if it startled you. A cattle ranch backs up to the property, and from time to time some of their cows escape and wander over here." He pointed to a few more cows grazing nearby. "Whenever this happens, we have to play cowboy and chase them off before they damage the vineyards. Want to come along, Kyle?"

"I wish I could."

"It's okay, Kyle," said Emily. "The winery isn't open yet, and I can stay in the house until you return."

He turned his attention back to Emily. "Thanks, but it's okay. Really."

"Suit yourself." Lee hit the accelerator and slowly drove toward the cow. She quickly trotted away and joined the other cows in the field in front of the main building. Lee followed her, shouting and waving his hat as he honked the horn. The cattle took their cue and started trotting away. Emily looked at Kyle.

"Sort of reminds you of an old western movie, doesn't it?"

"Kind of. Except he's having way too much fun."

"You could have gone with him, you know."

"That's okay."

Emily tugged on Lurch's leash and stepped off the porch. Kyle walked with her into the grassy field.

"Kyle, can I ask you a personal question?"

"Sure. What is it?"

"You're not afraid of cows, are you?"

He cleared his throat. "No, of course not. Why do you ask?"

Emily started laughing. "I noticed you kept a respectful distance from that cow."

"Well, you know. It's a cow. They're not the brightest animals in the world. I'm just, you know, being cautious."

Emily looked him in the eye as she tried to suppress her laughter. "Of course."

"Now what is that supposed to mean?"

"Nothing, Kyle. Nothing at all."

Emily chuckled to herself as they turned and headed back inside. Once there she unleashed the dog and went to the kitchen to start breakfast. When it was ready Kyle joined her at the table, but his demeanor had changed.

"Are you okay?" asked Emily. "You know I was just teasing you about the cow."

"I know you were. I was just thinking about my son. He would have loved to have seen that, and I can imagine the fun he would have had riding along with Lee in the golf cart."

"I'm sorry, Kyle. It must be hard being away from him. Tell you what. It's still early in the day, so why don't you see if you can get one of the local deputies to stay with me, and then you can drive up to Phoenix and spend the rest of the day with Cory."

"I appreciate the thought, but I'm afraid it's not that simple."

"I understand. So, is there any news on Big Hector?"

"Nothing," he said. "I've had my phone with me all morning, but so far it hasn't rung, which really doesn't surprise me. We're dealing with a pro, and Big Hector is a master when it comes to evading the authorities. He'll go underground while he tries to figure out a way to smoke you out, so all we can do for now is wait. He'll resurface at some point. It's only a matter of when."

"And in the meantime, my life's on hold."

"I'm afraid so."

Kyle quietly finished his meal. Afterwards, Emily spoke up.

"Are you sure you're okay, Kyle?"

"I'm fine." His tone was flat.

"You're sure."

"Yeah." He pushed his plate away. "Sometimes this job really gets to me. I want to spend more time with my son while he's still young. I don't want to wake up some morning, find out he's a teenager, and then wonder why I wasn't there."

"Look, Kyle, you've been down here with me for several days now, and it looks like we may be here for some time to come. Why don't you see if you can take a few days off? I'm sure if you give enough notice you can arrange for someone else to come down and guard me."

His expression softened. "Thanks, but it's really not necessary."

"You're sure?"

"I'm positive. I appreciate the offer, but I prefer to guard you myself. Besides, I have a funny feeling that something is about to break. Soon."

"Well, I hope you're right. I'm anxious to go home myself. It's not that I don't love your company and don't appreciate everything you've done for me, but I need to get back to my own life too."

"Trust me, we're doing everything humanly possible to make it happen." He glanced around the room. "You know, I'm suddenly feeling a little tired. Would you mind if I took a nap?"

"Of course not. I was going to spend some time practicing, but I can use my headphones. That way I won't disturb you."

"No need. I really do enjoy listening to you play. It won't bother me."

"You're sure?"

"I'm sure. You have a genuine gift."

He kissed her on the cheek and headed down the hall. Once Emily heard his bedroom door close, she sat down at her keyboard and started playing. An hour later she took a break to get a glass of water. Looking out the kitchen window, she saw a hub of activity around the main building. A catering truck had backed up to the rear entrance and a wedding arch had been set up on the front lawn. Two men were busy hoisting up a tent canopy while others were placing folding chairs in front of the arch. Mary had said the winery sometimes hosted weddings.

Emily felt bittersweet as images of her own wedding played back in her mind. It had been the happiest day of her life, and she thought her marriage would last a lifetime. Instead, it had become a living nightmare. She tried to shrug it off as she went back to her music, but she couldn't concentrate. Finally, she gave in and watched the festivities from the front window. A stream of cars were making their way to the main building, and people began taking their seats in the folding chairs. Before long three bridesmaids, wearing long red dresses, strolled up the aisle and took their places in front of the arch. The bride soon appeared, and as she began her walk toward her groom, Emily lowered the shades and plodded off to her room. She plopped down on the bed and stared at the ceiling as tears ran down her cheeks. Lurch followed her, whimpering softly as he placed his paws on the edge of the bed.

"I'm okay, buddy." She stoked the dog's head as she talked. "I'm just having a moment, so bear with me."

She went into the bathroom to get a tissue and saw her sad reflection in the mirror. Her nose was red, and her eyes were swollen and puffy. She splashed some cold water on her face and tried to pull herself together. The dog was waiting for her when she came back out.

"I know, Lurch. I look like hell. Par for the course I guess."

Lurch cocked his head as she spoke. His eyes followed her as she sat back down on the bed and picked up her tablet. As soon as she settled, he walked up to her, once again putting his paws on the bed, and this time poking her with his nose.

"What's the matter?" She set her tablet down and scratched him behind his ears. "You're starting to get restless. Are you trying to tell me it's time for another walk? Okay, come with me."

Kyle was still asleep when she came out of her room.

"Well, Lurch, it looks like it'll be just you and me, so I'm going to take you out behind the house. Hopefully no one will see us, but don't tell anyone what we did, okay?"

She snapped the leash on his collar and stepped outside. The wedding celebration was going full swing. A band was playing and most of the guests were dancing. Emily quickly led the dog behind the house, away from wandering eyes. She returned a short time later and closed the front door as quietly as she could. As she bent down to unhook Lurch's leash an angry voice boomed out.

"So what do you think you're doing?"

She jumped at the unexpected sound. "Kyle?"

His face looked stern. "I asked you a question. What were you doing?"

"What does it look like I'm doing? The dog needed to go out, so I took him out."

"So why didn't you wake me?"

Emily became defensive. "I didn't want to barge into your room. Besides, I was careful. I took him out behind the house and I made sure no one saw me. I'm not a prisoner here, so don't go treating me like one."

"I know you're not prisoner, but there's a big party going on by the main building. It would have been the perfect cover for Big Hector had he shown up. With all the noise and confusion he could have easily slipped in and out without being detected, and no one would have heard the gunshot over the music."

"Sorry, Kyle. I didn't think of that. I just didn't want to wake you."

"But you woke me anyway. I heard the front close, but then, when I came out, you were nowhere to be found."

She bristled. "And I've already apologized to you. I didn't want the dog to make a mess on the floor. Lee and Mary have been extremely gracious under the circumstances, and the last thing I want to do is to leave a big carpet stain behind. So now, if you'll excuse me, I have things I need to do." She turned and started toward her room.

"Not so fast."

She spun back around. "Now what?"

He demeanor had softened. "I just wanted to say I'm sorry if I came across too harshly. It's the cop in me. Sometimes it's hard to shut it off"

"I understand. We've been cooped up here for days now. I suppose it's only natural that we'd get on each other's nerves."

He looked at her more closely. "Are you all right?"

"I'm fine. Why do you ask?"

"Your eyes look a little swollen. Have you been crying?"

"I was watching the wedding from the front window. It reminded me of my own wedding, and I guess I let it get to me, but I'm okay now. It's just a silly woman thing. Nothing for you to concern yourself with."

"Emily, I've been there. My wife left me, and Cory, for some guy she found on the Internet."

"I know. I remember you telling me about it. I guess we're both unlucky at love. What is it they say? Unlucky at love, lucky at cards? Something like that."

"I not lucky at cards either." He stepped into the kitchen and returned a moment later with two cans of beer. He handed one to her and invited her to join him on the sofa.

"I thought cops weren't supposed drink when they're on duty."

"Technically, no." He popped his beer open and gave her a wink as she sat down next to him. "However, I'm officially on paid leave, so I can bend the rules a little. You won't tell on me, will you?"

She raised her right hand in the air and smiled. "No, I won't. I swear." She laughed as she popped her beer open. "So tell me, Mr. Policeman, how is it that you're so unlucky at cards?"

"I'm not sure. Sometimes I when play blackjack I—"

"You play blackjack? I had no idea." She gave him a grin as she took sip.

"Yes, Miss Smarty Pants, I've been known to play blackjack. Sometimes I even play it in Vegas; just not so well"

"Really? So why is that?"

He gave her a sheepish grin. "It probably had something to do with me splitting a pair of tens."

Emily burst out laughing.

"So laugh it up, blondie." There was laughter in his voice as well. "It just so happened that I was young and inexperienced at the time."

"Uh-huh. Likely story."

"That's my story and I'm sticking to it. See if I ever take you to Las Vegas." He took a swig of his beer and Emily perked up.

"You'd really take me to Las Vegas, Kyle?"

"Sure I would." He wrapped his arm around her shoulder and she leaned into him. "You know, there's a reason why I'm hoping you'll decide to go to college in Texas."

"Really? Why?"

"Because you're an amazing woman, and now that I've gotten to know you, I don't want to lose you." He sighed as he brushed his fingers through her hair. "I've been tired of the cop game for some time now, and then, just before you cousin's accident, I got a call from an old friend, who, by coincidence, also happens to live in Dallas. He's the head of security with a big, high-tech company. He called to tell me that his second in command was leaving at the end of May, and would I be interested in applying for the job."

"I remember you saying something about that. So, did you apply?"

"I sure did, and they're interested. Very interested."

"I see. So, have you had an interview?"

"Not yet, but I'll be taking a trip there sometime soon. It would be the perfect job for me. Better hours, better pay, and much better working conditions. No more blood and gore. Homicide is a grisly occupation. It made my last partner snap. You have no idea of the horror I've seen. I know you're not supposed to get emotionally involved, but it's easier said than done, especially with cases involving children or frail, elderly people. It's like you're living in a real-life slasher movie. I've seen enough to last a lifetime, and then some."

"I can only imagine what it must be like."

"It's the stuff hellacious nightmares are made of."

"Are you okay, Kyle?"

"Yeah. I'm just having a moment."

Emily looked him in the eye. "I understand. A little while ago, I had a moment myself."

Their eyes locked. He leaned forward and kissed her passionately, rubbing her back as she dug her fingers into his spine.

"Are you okay with this, Emily?"

She nodded. "Yeah, I'm okay."

He kissed her again, this time rubbing her shoulders as he slowly and carefully worked his way down to her breasts. She moaned with pleasure as he softly brushed her nipple. She pulled back for a moment and unbuttoned her blouse.

He cleared his throat. "I, uh, suppose I should ask you if you're—"

"It's okay, Kyle. I went on the pill after I left Jesse. I figured life goes on, you know."

"Yeah, I know."

He scooped her up in his arms. Lurch tried to follow as he carried her to her bedroom. Kyle gave the dog a firm look.

"Sorry, buddy, you're just going to have to hang out here for a while."

Emily laughed as Kyle quickly closed the door. "Poor dog."

He gently laid her down across the bed. "He'll be fine. He has plenty of chew toys to keep him occupied." He took his shoes off and lay down next to her, helping her out of her blouse as they kissed again. He reached underneath her bra and gave her breasts a gentle squeeze. When the kiss was over, she smiled as she reached up and brushed his hair away from his face.

"You have such a soft, gentle touch." He reached for her hand, giving it a loving caress and gently kissing her fingers as he looked into her eyes. "I knew you were someone special the first time I saw you, that night at Hanson Sisters."

"And I felt the same about you. I saw you watching me as I played, and I kept hoping you'd come over and introduce yourself."

"And I did." He brushed the side of her face. "Right after you walked into me."

They both laughed and kissed again, his hand softly rubbing her breasts. She stopped for a moment to remove her bra. He smiled, gently caressing her and holding her tight, his hands running up and down her back as he kissed her with even more passion. She moaned softly in return.

"You like that, huh?"

"Um hum."

He stopped to take off his shirt and jeans, and slowly helped her out of her sweatpants. She wore a pair of blue lace panties underneath. "You're incredibly sexy. You know that."

She blushed, once again feeling vulnerable. "I'm just me, Kyle."

"I know you are, and there's nothing phony or pretentious about you. You're genuine, and you're the real deal. That's what I love about you, and I wouldn't have you any other way." He kissed her again, holding her close, kissing her neck and breasts, and then carefully removing the panties. He stroked her thigh as he beheld her.

"You know, Emily. I've thought about this for a long time."

"You have?"

"Yes, I have. I've been wanting to make love to you for a long, long time."

They kissed again. He stroked her body once more, his hand slowly inching its way downward. She moaned and arched her back as she welcomed his touch. Her body tingled with excitement as he stroked her, and she began pleasing him in return. He moaned with pleasure, and the warm, wonderful feeling she felt grew stronger. She gasped with pleasure when he finally entered her, wrapping her legs around his back. The pleasure built until she finally climaxed. He was right behind her, and as they came back down, they held each other. He reached down and gently brushed the hair away from her face as he smiled and gave her a gentle kiss.

ꝯFORTY-EIGHTꝯ

JESSE LOOKED THE paperwork over one last time, putting his initials in all of the places he was told to initial, and then signed his name at the bottom. He gave it a final glance before he pushed it back to the woman seated across the table from him.

"Hopefully, they'll accept my counter-offer."

"I hope so too, Jesse. I wish I could have gotten more for you, but with—"

"I know," he said. "This house has a bad history, but all I want, Joyce, is to just get out from underneath it."

"I know you're anxious to move to Kansas City, so let's see how they respond to your counteroffer. With any luck, they'll take it. You're still offering them a very generous deal."

She gathered up her paperwork and Jesse walked her to the front door. Once she was gone, he went back to his office where he spent the next hour catching up on correspondence. It was nearly eight o'clock when he finished, time to pop a frozen dinner into the microwave and perhaps relax a little in front of the TV. He shut down his computer and was about to turn off the light when the phone rang. He decided to let the call go to voicemail, but then he realized it could be Joyce, calling with news on his counteroffer. The caller ID indicated it was an out of state number. Curious as to who might be calling afterhours, he took the call.

"Good evening. This is Jesse St. Claire."

"Well now, don't you sound just chipper."

The all-too-familiar voice filled him with a sense of dread. "Who is this?"

"Now, Jesse, is that anyway for you to greet an old friend? And some friend you are, selling me out like that."

Jesse took a deep breath, bracing himself for the worst. "Beau?"

"I'm touched. You finally remembered me."

"So why are you calling me? I thought the case was officially closed. Has there been some new development?"

"Yeah, you could say that." Beau's voice took a bitter tone. "I've got my one phone call, so I thought I'd use it to tell you that I meant it when I said if I went down, you were going down with me."

Jesse fought the tremble in his voice. "What are you talking about? The case is closed, and we've all gone on with our lives."

"So you say, Jesse boy, so you say. Except my life has just taken a strange twist. I'm sitting in a police station in Seattle, where I'm being held for, among other things, trying to frame your lovely, soon-to-be ex-wife for a crime she didn't commit."

"What the hell are you talking about, Fowler? Do you honestly believe I'd want to end up in jail myself? I've stuck to my story about Emily pushing Annette down those stairs. These days she and I only communicate through our attorneys, and the last I heard, she was busy with her music and heading off to Los Angeles for some audition."

"Has Madden or any other detective talked to you since the case was closed?"

Jesse's heart skipped a beat. "As a matter of fact, yes, and I told him what I just told you. Emily pushed Annette down those stairs."

"So who'd you talk to?"

"It wasn't Madden. I haven't heard from him in some time. It was someone from internal affairs. His name was Sidney Hill."

"Great. So what exactly did you say to Mr. Hill?"

Jesse had to think fast. "It had something to do with all the flack over Emily going on that TV show and pointing the finger at you, but I swear, I didn't give them any incriminating information. I simply told him I hadn't heard from you since the case had closed, and I stuck to my story about Emily pushing Annette. I even threw in something about you being the only one who believed me, and that thanks to you, I didn't end up in jail for a crime I didn't commit."

"When was this?"

"About a week or so ago, and no one has talked to me since. Look, Beau, I'm sorry this happened, but they have nothing but hearsay. I really don't understand why you left town in the first place."

"I had my reasons. Did Sidney Hill say anything else?"

"He said he had my bank records and he tried to make the case for me bribing you, but I set him straight. I said my speaking business took a hit over the Annette controversy, which it did, so I had to withdraw money from savings to stay afloat."

The line went silent. Jesse started to squirm. "Beau? Are you still there?"

Finally, Beau spoke up, but with an icy tone Jesse had never heard before.

"You're my Achilles' heel, Jesse. You told him too much."

"What do you mean, I told him too much? I just told you that I stuck to my story about Emily pushing Annette down those stairs."

"Well, Jesse, I guess I'm going to have to spell it out for you. Sidney Hill is out for blood. My blood, and he's not going to rest until he gets it. He already thinks you bribed me. That's how he was able to subpoena your bank records, and your touching little testimonial about my helping you stay out of jail made his case against me that much stronger. He'll be back. You can count on it. First, he'll tell you he's got the goods on you. Then he'll offer you some sort of deal. You know, you give him what he wants, and he'll see to it you walk away with slap on the wrist and no jail time."

Jesse broke out in a cold sweat. "That's crazy. He can't prove I did anything wrong, because I never bribed you, nor can anyone prove I pushed Annette down those stairs, because I didn't. It's all circumstantial."

"Jesse, I told you once before about how I've worked many cases over the years where someone got convicted, even though the evidence was all circumstantial. It'll be my word against yours. I'm still a police officer, and we cops look after our own. Trust me, before the night is over, I'll be the one making a deal. I'll tell them I was having problems at home and needed money so I could file for divorce. Then you came along and offered to pay me cash if I'd agree to look the other way, and, in a moment of weakness, I made a very bad decision. One I'll regret for the rest of my life, but in exchange for no jail time, I'm willing to testify against the man who bribed me, and oh, by the way, he also admitted that he pushed his mistress down those stairs, but he destroyed the evidence."

Jesse tried to speak, but the words wouldn't come.

"What's the matter, Jesse? Cat got your tongue?"

Jesse took a deep breath, but his voice still shook. "As you said, Beau, it's my word against yours, and you forget that I'm a highly respected motivational speaker who's also worked with law enforcement agencies. You, on the other hand, left town while you were being investigated for alleged misconducts. Who do you think they'll believe?"

Beau laughed a cold, wicked laugh. "If that's what you really think, Jesse, then you're even dumber than I thought. I've already told you. If I go down, you're going down with me. As soon as we get off the phone, I'm making that deal. By this time tomorrow, you'll be sitting in a jail cell yourself, and don't think for a moment that I can't get to you while you're there. I have connections. Very powerful connections. You're a dead man, Jesse St. Claire, and I mean it in the most literal sense."

Beads of sweat popped out on Jesse's forehead. "So what do you want me to do, Fowler?"

Beau laughed once again. "You can do whatever you want, because your days are numbered, starting right now."

Jesse disconnected the call and quickly powered down his phone. He felt light-headed and dizzy as a wave of nausea swept over him. He flew down the hall to the bathroom. Afterwards he remained on the floor, paralyzed with fear.

"Think, Jesse, think."

He repeated the words over and over, but he could only come up with one solution. He reached for the commode and pulled himself up. His body was still shaking as he made his way back to his office. It took two attempts to get his safe open. Once inside, he removed the flash drive and carefully placed it on top of his desk, where it could be easily seen. He then sat down and took a pad of paper from the desk drawer. To his relief, his handwriting was legible, in spite of his trembling hands. He left the pad next to the flash drive and stared at his phone, still laying on his desk. There would be no need for him to take it with him. He grabbed his keys and headed to the garage.

The traffic looked surreal as he drove to the freeway and got on the westbound Interstate. Jesse drove in silence, only stopping once along the way to fill the gas tank and use the men's room. He arrived in San Diego shortly after three o'clock the following morning. The streets were nearly empty, and before long the bright lights of the wooden roller coaster at Belmont Park came into view. He drove into the deserted parking lot, taking a space beneath the coaster and tossing the keys into the passenger seat, along with his wallet. He let out a long sigh and stepped out of the car.

The ocean air felt damp and chilly. He slammed the car door shut and looked up at the coaster. For a brief moment he smiled. Emily wasn't sure if she wanted to ride The Giant Dipper, but he took her by the hand and assured her it would be all right. When they got off, she laughed and said she wanted to ride it again, but it was getting late and they had to drive home the following morning.

Jesse took a deep breath and shrugged it off as he walked past the darkened shops. The lights along the boardwalk illuminated the sand and he could hear the ocean roar as he stepped off the boardwalk and began trudging through the sand. The ocean looked a giant pool of black ink. As he stepped into the water, the icy coldness of the waves felt like pins and needles burrowing into his skin. The water soon got deeper, and the waves battered against his body. He thought he heard a voice crying out in the distance, but he kept walking. Before long the water had reached his neck, and he could see the lights from a nearby ship. As the water got deeper, he stretched his arms out and started paddling. He could feel his body going numb.

* * *

Vincent Brady never got used to the eeriness of an empty amusement park in the dead of the night, but it came with the territory of being a night security guard. As he came around a corner, he spotted a man walking past the seawall and heading toward the water. Vince picked up his pace and followed, and as the man went into the water, he started shouting for him to turn back, but the man kept walking. He turned on his flashlight, anxiously watching as the man swam out to sea. No doubt it was a suicide. He quickly grabbed his phone and called for help.

❧FORTY-NINE☙

KYLE GROANED AS his phone roused him from a sound sleep and he slowly opened his eyes. The room was still dark. He looked at the clock on the nightstand. It was nearly five thirty. He checked the caller ID and was immediately jolted awake. Clarke was calling. He grabbed the phone as Emily began stirring.

"What's up, Clarke?"

"It's been a long night. I've been up since two o'clock this morning."

"So why didn't you call me?"

"I wanted to wait until I had all the facts. We're also in for a long day, and one of us needed to get a good night's sleep."

"All right. So what happened?"

"Last night, around six o'clock Pacific time, a rookie cop in Seattle pulled someone over for a busted taillight. It turned out to be Beau Fowler."

"Good for him."

"Actually, he was a she, but she did the right thing. She called for backup as soon as she ran his license, and they took him in for questioning."

"What's up?" Emily was barely awake

"I'll tell you in a minute," said Kyle.

"You know, I had a feeling about the two of you," said Clarke. "Can you put me on speaker? This concerns her as well."

Kyle put the phone on speaker. Once greetings were exchanged Clarke got back to business.

"As I just explained to Kyle, the Seattle police took Beau Fowler into custody after a routine traffic stop."

"So what did he have to say for himself?" asked Emily.

"He's vehemently denying any involvement with any murder for hire plot. He maintains it's all a hoax, perpetrated by some of his enemies after you pointed the finger at him on that television show."

"Did they buy his story?" asked Kyle

"We made sure they didn't. I spent quite a bit of time on the phone with one of the Seattle detectives, and they now understand that the threats against Emily and Juan are real."

"So what else did Beau have to say?"

"He's offered them a deal. He claims he was desperate for money due to a pending divorce, and that Jesse bribed him."

"No way." Emily's voice was firm. "I'm no fan of Jesse's, but I know him well enough to know he would have never done anything like that. He's worked too hard to build his speaking business. He would never allow himself to be put in a position where he could be blackmailed."

"Well, actually, he would." Clarke paused for a moment. "A few minutes ago, I got another call, this time from a detective in San Diego. The Coast Guard had just fished some guy out of the water. It was a suicide attempt, and we have every reason to believe the man was Jesse."

"Oh my god." Emily's hands went up to her mouth.

"Is he alive?" asked Kyle.

"He was, the last I heard," said Clarke. "They had to air evac him to a hospital, and we're still waiting for word on his condition. They also found Jesse's car in the parking lot at the same beach. The engine was warm, and it appears to be unlocked. They're just waiting for a search warrant."

"Tell them to search it," said Emily. "Technically, we're still married, so his car would still be considered community property, and I'm giving you my permission."

"Thanks, Emily. That does help. What about the house?"

"Same thing. Search it. I had to leave town before I had the chance to sign the paperwork taking my name off the deed, so you won't need a warrant. Nor am I concerned if you have to break the down door to get inside. If you have a pen and paper handy, I'll give you the alarm code. Hopefully, Jesse hasn't changed it."

"One of us needs to go to San Diego," said Kyle.

"I was just about to get to that," said Clarke. "I've already booked you on a flight from Tucson to San Diego that leaves at nine-fifteen this morning. As soon as we're done, you need to pack a bag and get to the airport."

"What about Emily? Big Hector is still at large."

"Another detective has put in a call to the county sheriff, and an officer should be there to talk to you soon. I'll call Lee and Mary as soon as we're done here. They can watch out for her as well." They quickly finished up their business and afterwards Kyle turned his attention back to Emily.

"I have to go. If he doesn't make it, I'll identify the body, and if he does make it, I want to talk to him."

"I know. Don't worry, Kyle, I'll be fine. They've captured Beau, so maybe he'll call off Big Hector."

"Perhaps, but somehow I doubt it."

"Do you want me to take you to the airport?"

"No, I can drive myself. That way my car will be there when I return. I don't know how long I'll be gone. It all depends on Jesse. I need to get the truth out of him. Hopefully, he'll pull through and not end up in a permanent coma."

Emily shuddered at the thought. "I hope not either. The marriage may be over, but I never wanted to see him end up like this."

"I know you didn't." Kyle got up and started packing his bag.

"Can I get you some coffee? Or perhaps make you breakfast?"

"How 'bout some coffee for my Thermos? Don't worry about breakfast. I'm not hungry yet, and I can grab something once I get to the airport."

Kyle headed off to shower while Emily put on her robe and went into the kitchen. Lurch followed her, and after she turned on the coffee maker, she grabbed his leash. The cold, predawn air caught her off guard when she stepped outside.

"Let's make it quick, okay?" She tugged on the leash and stepped off the porch but stayed close to the house. A light was burning in Lee and Mary's apartment. Emily soon led the dog back inside and poured herself some coffee as Kyle came in to join her. He set a holstered gun on top of the counter and reached for the carafe, but his phone rang while he poured the coffee into his Thermos. Emily took over the carafe and Kyle quickly grabbed his phone.

"Yeah, Clarke. What's up?"

"Is Emily with you?"

"She's right here."

"Put the call on speaker. She needs to hear this."

He set his phone on the countertop and turned on the speaker. "Okay, Clarke. What have you got?"

"I'm on my way to Jesse's house, and I just got a call from an officer who's already there. They've found a handwritten note, several pages long, on top of Jesse's desk. The note says that Beau Fowler was the one who wanted to set Emily up. Apparently, he wanted to solve a high-profile case so he could get a promotion. He was under the assumption the county attorney would be running for governor, and he was hoping for a position on the new governor's staff."

"I knew it! I knew Beau Fowler was out to get me, I just didn't understand why. Damn him! He wanted me to be his scapegoat, but it still doesn't explain why he chose to go after me instead of Jesse, especially when Jesse may have been guilty."

"He apparently wanted Jesse to get involved with the election campaign," said Clarke. "He thought Jesse could help Morris win. He also thought Jesse could help sway Morris into offering him a staff position."

"Wow." Kyle shook his head in disbelief. "Too bad for them that Morris decided not to run."

"There's more," said Clarke, "and Emily, I hope you're sitting down."

"Why?"

"Because I'm about to drop a bombshell. Jesse had the evidence to prove your innocence all along."

"What?" Emily was stunned

"You mean, he was withholding evidence?" asked Kyle.

"Indeed he was," said Clarke. "He had security camera footage."

"That can't be," said Emily. "Jesse said the camera was turned off that day."

"He lied. He had the footage on a flash drive, which he apparently had hidden in his safe. The officers called me as soon as they found it. I told them to watch the footage and they described it to me over the phone. They tell me you can clearly see Megan's car pull into the driveway, and Emily coming up to the front door. A few seconds later Jesse walks her back out to Megan's car, and the time stamp indicates it's a couple of minutes after nine. Megan's car then backs out of the driveway, and you can clearly see Emily in the passenger seat. Jesse comes back inside the house and the camera shuts off. It comes back on ten minutes later when Annette arrives. Jesse opens the front door and then closes it about thirty seconds later. She opens the door a few seconds later and enters the house, then camera shuts off again."

"I want a copy of that footage," said Kyle.

"Don't worry, I'll email it to you. I should be there in about ten minutes or so, and I'll call you once I've had a chance to go over everything."

"You'll need to wait for at least an hour. I'm leaving for the airport in about five minutes."

"Of course. Does Emily have her phone with her?"

"No," she said. "We left it behind. Kyle didn't want to risk Big Hector tracing it."

"I see. Do you have access to another phone?"

"I'm afraid not," she said. "I have my tablet with me, but the Wi-Fi is turned off. I can't check my email either, for the same reason."

"I was going to ask Lee and Mary if they'd mind getting her a prepaid phone that she could use until I get back," said Kyle.

"Might not be a bad idea," said Clarke. "I'll call Mary when we're done."

They heard a loud knock at the front door. Lurch responded with a bark as Kyle checked the door. A sheriff's deputy stood on the other side. Kyle invited him in and was about to end the call when Emily spoke up.

"Before you go, Clarke, can I ask a favor of you?"

"Sure. What is it?"

"Would you mind letting my father know what's going on? And would you please call my aunt Heather? She needs to know what happened to Annette, and she and my grandmother both need to know, once and for all, that I was never involved with her demise."

"I understand, and just so you know, I've been keeping them up to date as well."

They disconnected their call and turned their attention to the officer. He said they would be increasing their patrol of the area, but were unable to guard Emily fulltime.

"I didn't expect for you to do that," said Kyle. "So how often will you be checking the area?"

"We'll try to drive by at least once an hour. More frequently, if we can. It all depends on how many other calls we get." He turned to Emily. "Of course you'll have to keep the doors and windows locked, and please don't hesitate to call if you need us." He looked at Kyle. "Did I just hear you say she doesn't have a phone?"

"No, she doesn't, but I'm working on it right now. I won't leave until she has one."

The deputy took his leave and the golf cart pulled up to the house. Lee hopped out and handed Kyle a small plastic bag.

"This is Mary's phone. We'll see what we can do about getting one for her, but with it being a Saturday we probably won't be able to do it today. I've included the charger, so she should be all set. Call me if you need anything, okay?"

"Will do," said Emily, "and thanks, Lee."

Lee gave her a nod and as the golf cart sped away, Kyle picked up the gun and turned his attention back to Emily.

"I'm also leaving this with you."

"But I've never fired a gun before in my life."

"I understand, and someday I'll take you to the gun range, but for right now I don't want to leave you here unarmed." He removed the gun from its holster. "This is a personal firearm. It's a thirty-eight-caliber revolver, so if you have to fire it you won't have as much recoil. If Big Hector were to somehow get in the house, I want you to use it. It's really very simple. You point the barrel at the center of his body, and you squeeze the trigger."

"But what if I can't do it? And what if he gets the gun away from me?"

"Trust me. If your life is in danger, you'll be able to use it."

"But what if the gun goes off by itself?"

He looked her in the eye. "It won't go off by itself. The only way it can go off is if you squeeze the trigger. I'm setting it on top of your nightstand. Don't touch it unless Big Hector shows up. If he does, get into your room as quickly as you can and call nine-one-one, but only use the gun if he somehow gets inside the house and kicks the bedroom door down."

Kyle took the gun into her room and returned a moment later. "Well, kiddo, this is it. Are you going to be okay?"

"I'm fine, Kyle. In fact, I really do need to be alone for a while. I'm in total shock over what Jesse's done, and I need some time to sort through it."

"I know you do. I have Mary's number, so I'll call you as soon as I get to the airport. I'll also keep you updated on Jesse's condition."

Emily nodded as she squeezed him tight. A moment later he picked up his bag and gave her a final, lingering kiss. As he was leaving, he stopped in the middle of the doorway. "I love you, Emily." He quickly closed the door and headed out.

❧FIFTY❧

EMILY WENT BACK to bed after Kyle left, but every time she closed her eyes her imagination ran wild. She kept seeing Beau and Jesse, laughing and joking as they plotted their wicked scheme to frame her for murder. She jumped when the phone rang. Kyle was letting her know he had arrived at the airport and was having breakfast while he waited for his flight. He had also spoken to Clarke. Jesse was awake and responsive. He would know more once he arrived in San Diego, and he promised to call as soon as he could. After they hung up, Emily tried to go back to sleep.

The next thing she knew, she was waking up from a bad dream about Jesse. Bright sunlight filled the room and she checked the time. It was nearly nine-fifteen. Kyle's plane would probably be on the tarmac, about to take off. She looked at the holstered gun, lying on top of the nightstand, and gingerly picked it up. Lurch watched her every move.

"I know, buddy. Kyle said to keep it right here, but it's making me nervous. What happens if it accidentally gets knocked over and goes off? Let's put it someplace a little safer."

Lurch followed her down the hallway to Kyle's room. She set the gun on top of the dresser and noticed the bathroom door was open. She called Lee to let him know Kyle had said something about the bathroom sink running slow. She then hopped in the shower, and once she was dressed she took Lurch out for another short walk. Upon returning she decided to skip breakfast. She wasn't hungry, nor was she in the mood for anything else. She hunkered down on the sofa and stared into space, lost in her own thoughts.

* * *

Kyle grabbed his bag from the overhead bin and picked up his pace as he hurried down the jetway. A fortyish looking Asian woman waited on the other end, along with a uniformed officer. As Kyle approached her, she presented her badge.

"Detective Madden?"

He presented her with his badge. "Yes, ma'am, and you must be Detective Fong. We spoke on the phone earlier."

She gave smiled and extended her hand as the uniformed officer stepped away. "Yes, we certainly did, and my friends call me Kristi."

"Nice to meet you, Kristi. So, do you have any news on Jesse St. Claire?"

"They're still running tests, but he's awake and responsive. He was lucky. A Coast Guard cutter happened to be anchored close to where he went into the water, so they were able to get to him quickly, and he was immediately transported to the hospital."

They headed to the exit. Kristi's unmarked police car was parked nearby. "I take it you want to go straight to the hospital."

"You got it," said Kyle.

They hopped in the car and she brought Kyle up to date as she drove. "I spoke to Jesse, very briefly, right before I came to pick you up. He's experiencing some short-term memory loss."

"How so?"

"He doesn't seem to understand how he got here, or why he came. He has no recollection of leaving home, much less driving here and walking into the ocean. Then I asked him what day it was. He said it was Friday, and he seemed confused when I told him no, today is Saturday. Then, when I asked him about Detective Fowler, he immediately clammed up. He said he has no comment."

"What's his prognosis?"

"He's expected to survive. However, he's sustained some possible brain damage due to a lack of oxygen. They'll know more once they run more tests. They plan on keeping him for a day or two for observation. After that, he'll be transferred to a psychiatric facility for an evaluation. Once he's released from the psych hospital, we'll keep him in custody until you can extradite him back to Arizona."

"Thanks, Kristi. With any luck I can get him to waive extradition."

"Are you going to try to make a deal with him?"

"If I can. The one we're really after is Beau Fowler, my ex-partner."

"So I'm told, and I'm sorry."

"Me too," said Kyle. "Beau had a real knack for solving difficult cases. Unfortunately, he also had an attitude problem. He was known for being belligerent and was oftentimes difficult to work with. He went through a lot of partners as a result. Sometimes he'd talk about how angry he was over being passed up for promotions by people he'd helped train. I once suggested he try working on his people skills, but it didn't go over well."

Kyle remained quiet for the rest of the ride. Ten minutes later Kristi turned into the hospital entrance and took him up to Jesse's room. A uniformed officer stood guard at the door.

"Is he alone?" she asked.

"A nurse is with him right now. She should be done in a few minutes."

Kristi looked at Kyle. "Do you want me to come with you?"

"Thanks, but it won't be necessary. He knows me, and he may open up if no one else is around."

"I understand. I'll be out here if you need anything."

The nurse stepped out a minute later and Kyle presented her with his badge.

"I understand," she said, "but right now only one of you can come in at a time. Doctor's orders."

Jesse looked up as Kyle entered the room. "How's Emily? Is she all right?"

"She's fine, but you and I need to have a nice, long talk."

✖FIFTY-ONE✖

EMILY REMAINED ON the sofa for the rest of the morning, finally giving in to her hunger pangs in the middle of the afternoon. She was about to open a can of soup when she noticed Lurch getting restless, so she grabbed his leash and took him outside. The winery appeared to be busy, but at least they weren't hosting another wedding. She took the dog behind the house, but upon returning she stopped dead in her tracks. A strange car had parked next to the house, and the driver was stepping out from behind the wheel.

"Lee?"

He gave her a smile and handed her the keys. "Mary and I talked it over, and we wanted you to have a vehicle in case of an unexpected emergency, so we're loaning you Mary's car. We can manage with my pickup truck until Kyle gets back."

"Thank you, Lee."

"You're welcome." He popped the trunk open and removed a toolbox. "You also mentioned something about the bathroom sink running slow, so I figured as long as I'm here, I may as well take care of it. Let's get you back inside."

Emily chuckled as they walked up to the front door. "Now you sound like Kyle."

"I'm sure I do, but until he returns, we have to watch out for you." They stepped inside the house and Lee headed down the hallway.

* * *

After finishing the winery tour, he casually strolled around the tasting room and made small talk with some of the other visitors as he took in his surroundings. An emergency firebox was mounted next to the men's room door. He lingered in the tasting room, watching the people around him as he sampled the various wines before deciding on which one to purchase. He paid cash. As his change was counted back, he asked where the men's room was. Once it was pointed out, he excused himself and stepped away. To his relief, it was unoccupied. He came back out a moment later, once again noting his surroundings. The bartender was still in the tasting room, busy with other customers, and for the moment no one was looking his way. He reached for the firebox. It only took a second for him to pull the lever and pop back into the men's room. He came back out a moment later with a puzzled look on his face.

The bartender told him to please exit the building. As he stepped outside, he noticed a few visitors milling around on the lawn while others hurried out to the parking lot. He too went back to his car. A tan sport coat hung from the hook above the backseat window. He quickly took off his jacket and put on the tan coat before getting behind the wheel. As he drove toward the exit a sheriff's car turned into the entrance. He quickly veered off to a smaller side road and pulled up next to a small, blue house. The car parked next to it hadn't been there before. He frowned as he shut down the engine and walked up the front door.

* * *

Emily stepped into the kitchen. Glancing out the window, she saw a sheriff's car rushing up the hill to the main building. A few people were standing around and watching, but it appeared that most of the visitors were leaving. As she started down the hallway to alert Lee someone knocked at the front door. She went to answer as Lurch began barking.

"Who is it?"

"Santa Cruz County Sheriff. Open up."

She looked through the peephole. A man in a tan coat stood on the other side. He appeared to be holding a badge. As she cautiously opened the door, he quickly flashed his badge and put it back in his coat pocket.

"I'm Mario Arias. I'm a detective with the Santa Cruz County sheriff's office. Are you Emily St. Claire?"

"Yes, I'm Emily."

"I need to come in and talk to you about something."

"Of course."

The detective stepped inside. He was quite tall and nicely dressed, but something about him seemed to be a bit off.

"So what seems to be the problem, detective?"

"There's been an incident at the winery, and I need you to come with me. We have to take you to another location."

"What do you mean by an incident? What happened?"

"Please don't argue with me, Ms. St. Claire. I need you to come with me, right now. And is there anyone else here with you?"

Her bad feeling suddenly got worse. "No, I'm here alone."

"Then whose car is parked outside?"

"It belongs to the winery owners. They left it here, in case there was an emergency and I needed to get to the main building." She hoped Lee wouldn't walk in.

"All right. So let's go. Now."

Mary's phone was in her bedroom. She wanted to take it with her. "Okay, okay. Just let me get my purse. It's in the other room, and I need to get the dog."

The detective was growing impatient. "No, we don't have time. You're coming with me. Now!"

She prayed Lee could overhear what was happening and would call for help. "Where are you taking me? I need to let Detective Madden know where we're going."

His face turned hard. "You're not telling Detective Madden anything." He reached inside his coat and pulled out a gun, aiming it directly at her. Her blood turned to ice once she noticed the silencer on the end of the barrel.

"You're no cop." She spoke as loudly as she could without shouting. "You're Big Hector."

He gave her a cold smile as he leered at her. "The one and only, but don't worry, Chica. I won't be killing you right away. First, I'm going to have my way with you."

He ran his other hand down his belly and looked down. Emily seized the opportunity and fled into her bedroom. She quickly slammed the door behind her, her hands trembling as she struggled to lock the door. Once she finally secured the lock she ran to the window, desperately trying to unlock it, but the lever was stuck. She heard Lurch barking and someone shouting, along with two loud gunshots. An instant later someone pounded on her bedroom door and shouted her name. Emily looked around the room, cursing herself for not leaving Kyle's gun on the nightstand as he had told her to do. She spotted the clock radio and was about to hurl it through the window when the person pounding on the door shouted once again.

"Emily! It's Lee! Open the door!"

She dropped the radio and ran to the door.

"Lee?"

"Yes. It's Lee. Open up."

"Where's Big Hector?"

"He's gone. He ran outside."

Emily hesitated before opening door. An anxious-looking Lee stood on the other side.

"What happened?" she asked.

Before Lee could reply, they heard other men shouting outside, and more gunfire.

"I shot him." Lee's voice sounded perfectly calm.

"What?" Emily finally noticed Kyle's revolver in his hand.

"I overheard him, and then I saw the gun on top of the dresser, so I waited in the hallway, where he couldn't see me. As soon as you ran away, I came out. I told him to drop his gun, but he aimed it at me, so I shot him."

"Oh my god." She wrapped her arms him. "Are you alright? Did he hurt you?"

"I'm okay, Emily. I never gave him the chance to fire, but I want to be sure you're okay."

"Other than being scared out of my wits, I'm fine."

They looked around. The front door was wide open, and there were bloodstains on the carpet.

"Where's Lurch?" asked an anxious Emily.

"I don't know."

A uniformed deputy appeared in the doorway.

"Don't shoot!" Lee raised one hand in the air and carefully placed the gun on the floor with his other. He then backed away as he raised his other hand in the air.

"I'm Lee McPherson. I'm the winery owner, and I'm now unarmed. Someone was attempting to kidnap Mrs. St. Claire, and I had to protect her."

As the deputy stepped inside, they heard sirens blaring. "It's okay, Mr. McPherson. You did the right thing. Right now, I need both of you to stay inside, and I need to ask you some questions."

Another deputy appeared in the doorway. Lurch was in his arms. "Is this your dog?"

"Yes. Is he okay?" Emily rushed up to the dog and started looking him over.

"He's fine. He apparently chased the suspect outside, but you need to keep him here while we secure the area."

As the deputy handed Lurch over to Emily, Lee turned to the other one.

"So, what happened?"

"After you fired at him, he ran outside and aimed his weapon at me. I told him to drop his gun, but he refused and fired. I returned fire, and he was struck several times."

"Is he dead?"

"Yes sir, he is."

The other deputy pointed out the bloodstains. "Are either one of you hurt?"

"We're both fine," said Lee. "It's definitely the suspect's blood. I fired twice before he ran outside."

"Then we're going to have to secure the room as a crime scene as well. Someone will be here shortly to take the two of you, and the dog, up to the main building. We'll also have to take your gun into evidence."

Lee offered to pack up Emily's keyboard and she stepped back into her bedroom, but she was still badly shaken. Sitting down on the edge of the bed, she burst into tears. Lurch came in and placed his paws on her lap. Lee tapped on the door a few minutes later to let her know a detective had just arrived.

"Are you alright?" he asked.

"I'm fine. Tell him I'll be out in a couple of minutes. I just need to pull myself together."

"Of course. I understand."

He stepped away and Emily went into the bathroom. Her hands were still shaking as she reached for a tissue and dabbed her eyes. She stepped into the living room a minute later and another deputy presented his badge and extended his hand.

"I'm Detective Alberto Rascon, and I'm in charge of your case. Are you alright?"

"I'm fine, detective. I'm just a little shook up."

He gave her a reassuring smile. "Perfectly understandable. Do we need to take you to the hospital?"

She shook her head. "No. I wasn't injured. He never touched me. He glanced down for a moment, and that's when I ran."

"Which was quick thinking on your part."

A female deputy stood nearby. Detective Rascon asked her to get Emily a bottle of water.

"Mr. McPherson and my deputies have told me what happened, but I'll need to get a statement from you."

"Of course," said Emily. "Lee was defending me. The gun actually belongs to Detective Kyle Madden. It's his personal gun. This morning he was called away on an emergency, and he left it with me, just in case Big Hector showed up."

"Don't worry, Ms. St. Claire, I'll be giving Detective Madden a call very soon. I'll let him know what happened, and I'll let him know about his gun. And just so you know, he's not in any trouble. In the meantime, can you tell me what happened?"

"Of course." Emily took a seat, and as she was speaking a tear ran down her cheek. The female deputy handed her the water bottle and brought her a tissue.

"He knocked at the door," said Emily, "and told me he was a police officer. Once he came inside, he pointed his gun at me and told me who he really was. For a moment, I thought I was done for. Then he glanced down at the floor, and I literally ran for my life. Somehow, I managed to lock the bedroom door. I was trying to figure out how get a window open so I could get out of the house, and then I heard gunshots. They sounded like they were right outside my door. Then I heard Lee say it was okay to come out. He said he'd shot him and he, Big Hector, ran outside."

"Thank you, Emily," said Rascon. "We need to secure the house now. I'll wait here while you gather up your belongings. You won't be able to return once you leave."

"So was it Big Hector?" she asked.

"We're pretty sure it is, although we haven't officially confirmed it yet. He was about six foot three, which is the same height as Big Hector."

"He told me his name was Mario Arias."

"Which is one of Big Hector's known aliases."

Mary's phone started ringing, and one of the deputies answered. He identified himself and asked who was calling before he handed it off to the detective.

"It's Detective Kyle Madden, with the Phoenix Police Department."

"Hey, Kyle, this is Al Rascon, with the Santa Cruz County Sheriff's Office. We spoke the other day."

"Can I talk to him?" asked Emily.

"Later," said another deputy. "Don't worry. We'll let him know you're okay. Now, if you'll please get your things, someone will take you up to the main building." He turned to the female deputy. "Vanessa? Would you mind helping her?"

"Of course." She gave Emily a warm smile. "Come with me. Let's get you packed."

A few minutes later one of the deputies escorted them outside. A number of emergency vehicles were parked alongside the road, and a section of the nearby grassy field had been roped off. In the middle lay a body, covered with a white sheet. The deputy loaded Emily's keyboard and bags into Mary's car before he got behind the wheel and drove to them up to the main building. Detective Rascon followed in a squad car. An anxious Mary met them at the door. She gave Lee a long embrace before taking them upstairs to the office. Once everyone had settled, she offered them some water and stepped away to call her brother. He too would be keeping Kyle up to date. As soon as she left, the detective asked them more questions and took their statements. Everyone seemed to be concerned about Lee.

"Shooting a suspect can be a traumatizing event, Mr. McPherson, even for a trained police officer."

"I'm fine, sir, I really am. I'm a Marine, and as far as I'm concerned, I shot a mad dog. The suspect was attempting to kidnap Mrs. St Claire, and then he said he was going to rape and kill her."

"And you most certainly saved her life." Rascon handed Lee one of his cards. "Meantime please call me if you need anything."

"Thank you." Lee set the card down on the desk.

"Are we about done here?" asked Emily.

"Yes, we are," said Rascon. "However, the house will be condoned off until we complete our investigation, and it may take several more hours, so you'll need to find another place to stay."

"It's okay," said Emily. "Now that Big Hector is gone for good, I just want to go home."

"Is there any possibility of someone else coming after her?" asked Lee.

"I highly doubt it," said Rascon. "Beau Fowler is being held without bond, and Big Hector always worked alone."

As Rascon and the deputy took their leave Emily turned her attention to Lee.

"I need to make a couple of phone calls, if you don't mind."

"Help yourself. You can stay in here, if you'd like some privacy."

"I would, thanks, and please, tell Mary she can have her phone back as soon as I'm done."

"Of course. Take all the time you need." Lee reached down and grabbed Lurch's leash. "And while you're doing that, I'll take our friend here out for walk. We'll be down the hall, in the apartment, once we're done. Come on down when you're finished."

Emily thanked him, and once he closed the door she reached for Mary's phone. The first person she called was Kyle. Her face lit up as she heard his voice, but her heart sank once she realized her call had gone to his voicemail. She waited for the beep.

"Hi Kyle. It's me. I'm sure by now you've heard what happened, and I wanted to let you know I'm all right. I still have Mary's phone, but the house is now a crime scene and I'm not exactly sure where I'll be staying tonight. I just want to go home. I'll call my father in a few minutes and see if he'll come down here and get me. I'll call you later to let you know where I am, and I love you too."

She disconnected the phone waited for a few minutes, hoping Kyle would return her call quickly, but the phone didn't ring. She finally picked it up and punched in another number. This time someone answered.

"Dad."

"Emily? Is that you?"

"It's me Dad. It's been quite a day. First, Kyle got called away. He's in San Diego. Apparently, Jesse tried to drown himself in the ocean last night, but they got to him in time, so Kyle's there questioning him."

"I see. So is he finally telling the truth?"

"I think he is. I'll know more when I talk to Kyle. They also got Big Hector a little while ago, but not until after he'd tricked me into thinking he was police officer and letting him inside the house. Thank goodness Lee was there. He had a gun, and he took care of the problem once and for all. I'm okay. He never had the chance to harm me, and I'll fill you in on the rest later."

"My god, Emily," said a badly shaken Roger, "he could have killed you."

"I'm okay. Like I said, Kyle left a gun behind, and as fate would have it, it was where Lee could easily find it."

"Your guardian angel was certainly watching out for you."

Emily fought back tears. "I know, and I'll be forever grateful, but now I just want to go home. I know it's a bit of a drive, but I really need you to come down and get me. Don't worry, I can drive us back. Somehow, I don't think I'll be able to sleep tonight."

"I understand, Emmy, and I really wish I could come and get you, but I can't. I'm in Minneapolis."

Her heart sank. "Minneapolis? You mean you're with Nick?"

"Yes, I'm staying at your brother's house. Since none of us knew how long it would take to apprehend Big Hector, I figured I'd be better off if I left town myself, so I took a leave of absence from work and flew to Minneapolis two days after you left."

"I understand, Dad. There was no sense in you being in danger too. So when do you think you'll be back?"

"I'll go online as soon as we're done and see if I can find a flight for Monday or Tuesday. We've already made plans for a big family outing tomorrow."

"I see."

"It's okay, Emmy." Roger tried to sound reassuring. "As soon as we're done, I'll call Heather and let her know you're okay."

"Like she would care."

"She cares, Emily. She knows she was wrong, and she honestly wants to make it up to you. In the meantime, your brother wants to talk to you."

Nick came on the line, and Emily recounted the day's events to him. By the time she ended the call it was nearly six o'clock and there was still no word from Kyle. She headed down the hall to Lee and Mary's apartment. Mary quickly answered the door and Emily handed her the plastic bag.

"I need to return your phone, and thank you for loaning it to me. I also want to apologize for what happened."

Mary immediately cut her off. "This isn't your fault. We did everything humanly possible to keep you safe, but he somehow managed to slip through anyway. They still don't know how he found out you were in the area."

"It probably doesn't matter, but thanks to your husband, and the deputies, he'll never be able to hurt anyone again. I'm also sorry to leave the house in such a mess."

Mary gave her a hug. "Don't worry about it, Emily. We'll get it taken care of. Right now, you need to relax and have something to eat. You've had a long, stressful day, and don't worry about finding another place to stay. We've already put your bags in Sara's room. You can stay there until Kyle gets back."

"Thank you. I haven't eaten all day, and I don't know what else to say, other than thank you again." She paused for a moment. "I tried to call Kyle, but it went straight to voicemail."

"My brother spoke with him earlier today. Apparently, Jesse isn't being too cooperative. He said it looked like Kyle might have to be there for a while."

"Somehow it doesn't surprise me. Jesse is no longer the man I once loved. He's turned into a complete stranger."

∽FIFTY-TWO∾

MARY OFFERED EMILY a glass of wine, and dinner was servied a short time later. Afterwards Emily stayed and helped with the cleanup. Once the dishes were dried and put away, she tried to call Kyle again, and once again, her call went directly to voicemail. She shook her head as she handed the phone back to Mary.

"Now that I think about it," said Mary, "Clarke mentioned something about Kyle saying the battery on his phone running low. It might have died, and he just hasn't had a chance to recharge it yet."

"I suppose," said Emily.

Mary gave her a reassuring smile. "Tell you what. One of my friends gave me some wonderful rose-scented bath salts for my birthday. Why don't I put them in your bathroom, and you can draw yourself a nice, hot bath? You've had a horrible day, and it might help you unwind. Come with me. I'll show you where Sara's room is."

Mary led Emily down the hall, pointing out the bathroom as they walked past. Sara's room was at the end. It was nicely furnished, much like Emily's room at her dad's house. Five minutes later Emily stepped into bathtub. The hot water felt good, and the bath salts had a nice scent. She leaned back and closed her eyes. The day's events started playing back in her mind, but she pushed them away and tried to focus on Kyle. She smiled as she recalled him telling her he loved her as he stepped out the door. Her mother always said you had to take the good with the bad in life, and perhaps this was what she meant. Had Jesse not had the affair with Annette, and had he not tried to frame her for a crime she didn't commit, she would have never found Kyle. She lingered in the tub until she felt the water turning cold. Finally, she stepped out and put on her sweats. Lee and Mary were relaxed in front of the TV in the living room, and Mary greeted her with a smile.

"There you are." She handed Emily her phone. "Someone called while you were in the tub."

Emily's face lit up. "Was it Kyle?"

"It certainly was."

"Why didn't you come get me?"

"I told him you were in the bathtub, and he didn't want to disturb you. He said he's in his hotel room and, yes, the battery on his phone had died, so he only got your message a short time ago. So, why don't you give him a call? He said he has some news for you."

"Thanks." Emily grabbed the phone and headed down the hall to Sara's room. As she plopped down on the bed she punched in Kyle's number. He answered on the second ring.

"You don't know how good it feels to finally hear your voice."

She grinned from ear to ear. "You don't know how good it feels to hear your voice too."

"I was devastated when I heard Big Hector got to you."

"Stop right there. It wasn't your fault

"Yeah, but I still feel like it was."

"It wasn't," said Emily. "You got called away on another emergency. If anyone's to blame, it's Jesse, and, of course, Beau Fowler."

"I know, and I'll bring you up to date on Jesse in a few minutes, but first, I want to know how Big Hector managed to get in the house in the first place."

"He pulled the firebox in the winery. Mary found the security camera footage and showed it to the deputies. He showed up at the house a couple minutes later and knocked on the front door. He had a badge, and he identified himself as a detective with the Santa Cruz County sheriff's office, so I figured it would be okay to let him in. You know what happened next."

"You were lucky Lee was there and was able to get to the gun I left you. So why didn't you leave it on your nightstand like I told you?"

"I got nervous. I was worried it might get knocked over and accidentally go off. I figured it would be safer to leave it in your room, and I thought I could get to it if something happened."

"I understand your concerns." There was a no-nonsense tone in Kyle's voice. "But the odds of it going off by accident were nearly impossible, and you could have easily gotten yourself killed by doing what you did."

"I know, Kyle, and I'm sorry. This has been one of the worst days of my life, so please don't get angry with me."

"I'm not angry with you." His voice took a softer tone. "I'm just trying to make you understand how close I came to losing you today. If that had happened, I don't know what I would have done."

"I know Kyle. The image of him, pointing that gun at me, and the evil smile on his face, will stay with me for the rest of my life." A chill ran down her spine as she spoke. "I can still see his eyes. They were black and cold. They didn't even look human. It was like looking into the eyes of a demon."

"I've seen that look a few times myself. It's called the evil eye. It's scary as hell, and I mean that in the most literal sense, but don't worry. He's dead and he can't hurt you. Meantime, would you like to know about Jesse?"

"Of course."

"First, the good news. He's awake and he's going to live. However, he has some brain damage. It's affected his short-term memory and his motor skills."

"How so?"

"He doesn't recall going to San Diego, and, at least for now, he's unable to walk or use his left hand."

"Will he recover?"

"They're not sure. They're hoping he'll improve with physical therapy, but it's too soon to tell. What's certain is he'll never be the man he was before."

"That's sad," said Emily, "but at the same time, I don't feel sorry for him. He brought this all on himself."

"He did indeed. However, in other ways, he's still the same old Jesse. As soon as I walked into his room, he asked me about you, and he seemed genuinely relieved when I told him you were all right. After that he clammed up and wouldn't talk until he got a deal that guaranteed no jail time, and he refused to budge until he got his way. It took a several hours and a lot of phone calls before the county attorney's office finally agreed."

"Well no wonder the battery on your phone ran out."

"It sure did, so I had to borrow Detective Fong's phone. Then, when we found out about what happened to you, his attitude suddenly changed. The man still loves you, in his own strange way, and he's willing to do whatever it takes to keep Beau behind bars."

Emily winced. "I sure hope he's not thinking that I'll take him back."

"No, he isn't. He's fully aware that he threw you to the wolves in order to save his own skin, and he knows you'll never take him back. He is hoping, however, that over time you'll forgive him."

"Maybe, but it'll be a long time."

"I understand, Emily. He's put you through a lot, and you need some time to heal. What matters now is that he's come clean and he's going to cooperate. I'll be talking to him again in the morning, and then I have some last-minute business to take care of with the San Diego police. I've made reservations for a flight to Tucson that leaves at seven-twenty tomorrow night, so I should be back around ten o'clock."

Emily felt relived. "I wish you could be back sooner, but I understand. I just want to go home. They've cordoned off the guesthouse as a crime scene, so tonight I'm staying in Lee and Mary's daughter's room. I have all of my belongings with me, and along the stuff you left behind in your other bag."

"Thanks, Emily. You know I'm just as anxious to get home as you are, but for now you need to just sit tight and try to relax. Maybe tomorrow you can find us a hotel or a bed and breakfast to stay in tomorrow night. We'll head home first thing the next morning, I promise."

She chuckled. "You mean I get to return to the land of the living?"

"You bet. Your sentence is up and I'm granting you parole. Starting right now."

They both had a good laugh, and Emily finally felt like herself again when they ended the call.

✸FIFTY-THREE✷

MARY GREETED EMILY with a smile as she returned the phone. "You certainly look much happier now."

"I feel much happier too." Emily took her seat on the sofa next to Mary. "Kyle said Jesse wouldn't cooperate until he got a deal with no jail time, but once he got it, he agreed to testify against Beau Fowler."

"I see," said Mary. "So are you okay with it?"

"Yes and no. I want the truth to come out, and we now know Jesse had the evidence all along to prove my innocence, but he kept it hidden. I don't mean to sound bitter or vindictive, but he should have to pay for all the hell he put me through."

"I'm sure he will. Don't think for a minute that not serving jail time means he's getting off scot-free. No doubt he'll have to pay some hefty fines, and he'll probably get probation, perhaps for years, which means he won't be able to come and go as he pleases."

"I understand, so between that, and the scandal that's bound to come out, it's a safe bet his speaking business will be over and done with for good. Kyle also tells me they still don't know if he'll ever walk again."

"Wow." Mary thought it over for a minute. "You know, if I had to choose between the two, I think I'd rather do the jail time instead of never being able to walk again."

"Me too," said Lee. "He would have served a few years, but it wouldn't have been a life sentence, and there's a good chance he would have been released early for good behavior. A disability, however, is oftentimes a life sentence."

"I know," said Emily, "and in spite of everything, I wouldn't have wished this on him. He brought it on himself."

Mary changed the subject. "So, while you we're talking to Kyle, your aunt called on Lee's phone."

Emily stiffened. "Really? So, what did she have to say?"

"She said your father called her, right after he got off the phone with you. He told her you really wanted to go home, and she said not to worry. She and your cousin are on their way as we speak. They won't arrive 'til late, so they'll be staying in our son's room, and she'll take you home tomorrow morning. She's also offered to stay with you until your father gets back. She's concerned about you being alone."

"I see."

"You don't seem to be very happy about it," said Mary. "I thought you were anxious to get home."

"I am. It's just that my aunt and I have had our differences. She thought I was guilty. She even showed up on my door, the day Annette had her fall, and she accused me to my face of killing her. That was the last conversation I had with her."

"She did mention something about it," said Lee. "She also admitted she wasn't thinking clearly at the time."

"My brother also mentioned that she's called him a few times to see if you were all right and to ask if they'd found Big Hector," said Mary.

"Everyone's been telling me she wants to make things up to me," said Emily, "and I want to believe them, I really do, but I still can't get over the way she looked at me the last time I saw her."

"We all make mistakes, Emily," said Lee. "She was very upset when I told her about Big Hector showing up, and she was genuinely concerned that you were all right. You need to give her the benefit of the doubt. After all, she's coming all the way from Phoenix to get you."

Emily borrowed Mary's phone once again and called Kyle. He too was relieved to hear that Heather was coming to take Emily home. Afterwards she stayed in the living room, watching an old movie on TV with Lee and Mary. During one of the commercial breaks Lee got a rollway bed from the storeroom and took it down the hall to Sara's room. The two women followed with sheets and a blanket and the bed was soon ready. Emily kept close watch on the time as she tried to quell her growing anxiety. Lee's phone rang around eleven-thirty. Heather and Tonya had arrived.

"I have to run downstairs to let them in," he said. "Do you want to come with me?"

"I'll wait here, if you don't mind," said Emily.

"Suit yourself." He stepped away, taking Lurch with him for one last walk. He returned a short time later, with Heather and Tonya. As they came inside Emily stood her ground, not sure of what to expect as her aunt walked up and wrapped her arms around her. "Are you okay?" she asked.

"I don't know."

Heather stepped backward and looked Emily up and down. "It's been a hell of a day, hasn't it?"

"It sure has."

"I owe you a big apology, Emily. The last time I saw you, I accused you of some pretty horrible things that you never did."

"It's okay. I've never held a grudge. We were all in a state of shock that day, and you were just reacting."

"But I wasn't just reacting. There was a time when I honestly thought you were guilty, thanks to Beau Fowler. It's something I'll always deeply regret. I'm also very angry that he took advantage of a grieving mother. I had every right to know what happened to my daughter, and he deliberately withheld the truth from me."

"I know he did."

"Clarke Davidson called me early this morning. He told me about Jesse, and the security camera footage. He said it shows you and your friend leaving Jesse's house, and Annette arriving about ten minutes later."

"I know. I can't believe that all this time Jesse had proof of my innocence. How could he have done this to me?"

"How could he and Beau Fowler have done what they did to all of us?" asked Tonya. "We all have the right to know what really happened to Annette, and to see justice served."

"Sorry to interrupt." Lee handed Lurch's leash to Emily. "Mary and I are going to call it a day. There's soda in the fridge, and, of course, plenty of wine. You ladies feel free to help yourselves to whatever you'd like."

He and Mary gave Emily a hug and said their goodbyes. Once they left Heather turned her attention back to Emily.

"Is there any news from Kyle? I understand he's in San Diego questioning Jesse."

"Yes, he is." Emily motioned to the others to take their seats. "As you've probably heard, Jesse drove to San Diego last night and tried to drown himself in the ocean. Apparently, some security guard saw him going into the water and called the Coast Guard. He's still in the hospital, but he has some brain damage.

He doesn't recall going there, so I guess we'll never know why he chose San Diego."

"Perhaps it's because the two of you were there over the holidays," said Heather. "It might have a special meaning for him."

"If it did, it doesn't matter now. I've already filed for divorce. It'll be final in March."

"Good for you," said Tonya.

"Thanks," said Emily. "Anyway, Kyle told me Jesse wouldn't talk unless he got a deal with no jail time."

"Great," Heather said in disgust.

"I agree, although he's agreed to testify against Beau Fowler. I'm sure Kyle will fill us in on the details once he returns."

"No doubt he will, and I want to talk with him as well."

"Of course." Emily glanced at Tonya, who was trying to stifle a yawn. "In the meantime, we've all had a long day, and you two had a long drive. Why don't we call it a night? We can finish this in the morning."

"Good idea," said Heather. "We'll have plenty of time to talk on the way back." She looked at her daughter. "Would you mind if Tonya stays with you tonight?"

"Of course not. In fact, we put an extra bed in my room. We haven't seen one another in a long time, so we can have some girl talk."

Heather hugged them both goodnight before she picked up her bag and headed down the hall.

"Thank you, Emily," said Tonya. "Sometimes my mom wakes up crying in the middle of the night. She hasn't done that since your mother died."

"I understand. So how are you holding up?"

"I'm good." She paused for a moment. "Your dad called my mom the night you left town. He told her about Big Hector, and he gave her Clarke Davidson's phone number. It scared the living hell out of both of us, so my mom called Clarke as soon as she got off the phone with your dad. The last thing we wanted was another death in the family. And by the way, Mom and Grandma had already figured out that you weren't responsible for what happened to Annette."

"Thanks. That's good to know."

"And, just so you know, Beau Fowler had been keeping close tabs with both of them, and with him being the lead detective and all they just naturally assumed—"

"It's okay, Tonya. You don't have to explain it."

"I know, but you still need to hear it. Yes, for a time my mother thought you were guilty. So did Grandma, but once the grand jury decision came down, they started realizing things weren't adding up."

"And what about you, Tonya?"

"I've never liked Jesse. I also knew things about my sister that they didn't and still don't." She looked around the room for a moment. "Would you mind if I got a glass of water?"

"I'll get it."

Emily stepped into the kitchen, retuning a minute later with two water glasses. She handed one to Tonya and returned to her seat.

"So tell me, what did you mean when you said you never liked Jesse?"

"I've always had a knack for reading people," said Tonya. "It's like a sixth sense. All I have to do is watch their body language and facial expressions, and I can instantly figure them out, and I'm almost always right. The first time I ever saw Jesse was at your wedding, and even though I was just a kid at the time, I knew, right then and there, what kind of a man he was. He was self-centered and arrogant. It was all about Jesse and no one else."

"Wow. You certainly had him pegged all right. Too bad it took me eight years to figure it out."

"He has his charm and he knows how to use it. Truth be known, he's a lot like my father, and a conman can't be a conman without his charm. It's how they win people over, and it's how he swayed Annette."

Emily stiffened. "I see."

Tonya looked Emily in the eye. "Annette and I had an interesting relationship, to say the least. I've always been grounded, while she always had a tendency to jump into things feet first without thinking. And even though she was older than me, she often came to me for advice, and she told me a lot about Jesse."

Emily raised her brow. "Really? So what did she have to say?"

"It's kind of complicated, but please believe me when I tell you that when she first started working for Jesse, she had no intention whatsoever of getting involved with him. She was in love with Gary, but Jesse was someone she really admired, so she started asking him for advice on what to do with Gary. You know, how could she get him to commit to her, that sort of thing. Jesse saw her vulnerability and he took full advantage of it. He kept telling her he was a concerned friend who wanted to help, but he was giving her lots of hugs and kisses on the cheek, and getting more and more intimate with her, if you know what I mean."

"Yeah, I know what you mean."

"When she finally told me what was happening, I got a really bad feeling. I begged her to quit, but she refused. She said she needed the money, and she kept insisting they were just good friends, but I could tell he was getting to her. I kept telling her to be careful, but she kept rationalizing it away and saying he was someone she looked up to. Then one day she told me she'd asked you why you weren't playing your keyboard. You said it was because it bothered Jesse, and that you just didn't have the time to play anymore."

"I remember that conversation," said Emily. "She asked me if I still wanted to become a concert pianist someday. I told her yes, I still wanted to, but things had changed, and I had to put Jesse's needs first."

"So by the time Jesse finally seduced her, she'd convinced herself that she was doing you a favor. She honestly believed that if Jesse left you for her, you'd be better off because you'd be free to go back to your music."

"Which explains why she kept bringing up my music during those last few conversations I had with her, but it still doesn't excuse what she did."

"No, it doesn't," said Tonya, "and trust me, when she finally admitted that she was having sex with Jesse, I called her out on it, but by then it was too late. She'd fallen head over heels for him, so she started pulling away from me after that. Then, later on, when we found out you two were reconciling, I told her it was a good thing. It meant it was officially over between her and Jesse, and the time had come for her to start mending fences with you. She then informed me, in no uncertain terms, that she'd just put a plan in place to get Jesse back, and then, well, let's just say she suggested I go take a hike." Tonya's eyes welled up with tears and she began choking on her words. "It was the very last conversation I would ever have with her."

Emily came over and held her.

"I'm okay," said Tonya, "I just get a little weepy every now and then."

"She was your sister, and she's only been gone a few weeks. I'd be worried if you didn't get a little weepy."

Tonya reached for a tissue. "You know, I'm getting tired too. I've been up since the crack of dawn, and it was a long drive down here, so I'm ready to call it a night, if you don't mind."

"Not at all." Emily walked her down the hallway to Sara's room, and they both got ready for bed. As Tonya settled in the rollway Emily turned out the light and climbed into the other bed.

"Emily, there's one more thing."

"What's that?"

"I know, with every fiber of my being, that Jesse killed my sister. There've even been times when I've heard her voice in my head saying, 'Jesse did it. Jesse did it.'"

"I know, Tonya. I've heard her voice too. I even had a dream about her one night. She told me Jesse was in on the plot to frame me, but so far, we've been unable to prove it."

"Yeah, but now that Jesse's finally talking, maybe the truth will finally come out." Tonya was silent for a moment.

"Emily, can I ask you a personal question? You don't have to answer if it's none of my business."

"Go ahead."

"I've never understood why you and Jesse didn't want to have a family."

"Well, it wasn't because I didn't want kids. It was because Jesse had some sort of genetic defect. He was unable to produce a child."

Tonya was stunned. "You're kidding. Did you know about this when you married him?"

"Yes, I did. Jesse told me about it right before we got engaged. At the time, I was madly in love with him, and I figured with my music maybe it would be for the best if I didn't have any children."

"But you never said anything about it to the rest of the family."

"My dad knew, but he was the only one. I wanted him to know there'd be no grandchildren. At least none from me."

"So, how'd he take it?"

"He was disappointed, of course, but he also wanted me to be happy. Then the three of us, Dad, Jesse and me, all agreed that no one else needed to know. Later on, as friends started asking questions, we gave them the usual excuses; Jesse's job required him to travel and he spent too much time away from home, or we'd just say we weren't ready yet. It really wasn't that big of a deal to me, but for some reason Jesse thought his not being able to father a child would hurt his public image."

Tonya thought it over and the realization began to dawn on her. "Annette didn't know about this, did she?"

"Not unless Jesse told her, which would have been highly unlikely."

"And she was so desperate to get him back that she bought that fake pregnancy test strip to try to convince him she was pregnant, and he was the father. That would have forced him to tell her." Tonya suddenly sat up in the bed. "Oh my god! That's why he killed her."

❧FIFTY-FOUR❧

EMILY'S EYES POPPED open when she heard a strange sound. She sat up and looked around the room. The sun was up, and Tonya was stirring in the other bed when she heard the sound again. It was Mary, gently tapping on the bedroom door.

"Sorry to disturb you two sleeping beauties," said Mary, "but you have a visitor, Emily. Detective Rascon is here to see you."

"Tell him I'll be right there."

Emily grabbed her robe and stepped into the living room a short time later. The detective was at the breakfast bar, chatting away with her aunt, who was already dressed and enjoying her morning coffee. Heather greeted her with a smile.

"Good morning, sleepyhead. Sorry to disturb you, but you have a visitor."

"So I'm told. What time is it, anyway?"

"It's a few minutes after nine."

Heather hopped off her barstool and poured Emily a cup of coffee while the detective pulled out his notepad and motioned for Emily to take the stool next to his. As Emily took her seat Heather handed her a mug and returned to her seat.

"I wanted to bring you up to date on what we know so far," he said.

"Of course," said Emily.

"We've positively identified the man who attempted to kidnap you. It was indeed Hector Alfonso Garcia, also known as Big Hector."

A shiver ran down Emily's spine as she gave the detective a nod. "I'm not surprised. He told me who he was just before I ran out of the room. What I want to know is how did he find me?"

"While we'll never be one-hundred percent certain, we have a pretty good idea of what we think may have happened. We've examined his cell phone, and there were indeed calls placed between his phone and Beau Fowler's private cell number. This includes calls to Beau's new number, with a Seattle area code."

"So have they questioned Beau Fowler about this?"

"They're trying, but I'm told he's refusing to cooperate."

"Somehow that doesn't surprise me either, but I'd say you've got the goods on him."

"We certainly do." Rascon's expression turned sad. "So, here's what we think happened. We believe Detective Fowler told Big Hector about your friendship with Detective Madden, and that he somehow found out Madden was on leave. From there he was somehow able to trace Detective Madden's whereabouts to the winery. I'm now hearing reports of a man matching his description being seen at other wineries in the area over the past few days, which means he could have been watching and waiting for Detective Madden to leave."

"Which would explain why he appeared a few hours after Kyle was called away, and why he wanted to know whose car was parked in front of the house, because he knew it wasn't Kyle's."

"Which is what we think as well," said Rascon.

"But how was he able to track Kyle down?"

"We can only guess. No doubt Detective Fowler still has friends in the department, so there could have been a mole somewhere. Or Big Hector could have hacked into a computer or cell phone, we're just not sure, and now that he's dead, we'll probably never know for certain. However, the good news is the Seattle authorities have been going over Beau Fowler's laptop and phone with a fine-tooth comb, and so far, they haven't found any evidence of him contacting any other hit men. They're also holding him in isolation, so he won't be able to arrange another hit from the jailhouse."

"Do you think he'll try again?" asked Heather.

"Probably not. With him being a police officer, they have to keep him away from the rest of the jail population, for obvious reasons. His bank account has also been frozen, so even if he were to try to put out another contract, he wouldn't have the means to pay for it, and trust me, these guys don't work for free."

"Morning everybody." Tonya stepped into the kitchen and poured herself a cup of coffee as her mother introduced her to Detective Rascon.

"Is that all?" asked Emily.

"It is, for now." Rascon handed Emily one of his cards. "We'll be in touch if we need more information. We've also removed the crime scene tape from the guesthouse, so you're free to go back there if you'd like."

"No thanks," said Emily. "We're heading home this morning."

He gave Heather a nod as he handed her one of his cards. "Here you go, Mrs. Claiborne, just in case you have any questions."

Heather gave him a grin as she slid of her barstool. "Of course. Here, let me walk you to the door." When she returned, and both Emily and Tonya were giving her a look.

"What?"

"Nothing, Mom," said Tonya. "Nothing at all."

* * *

It was nearly noon when Lee loaded their bags into Heather's gray sedan. He and Mary each gave Emily a last hug, and as they said goodbye, she thanked them once again. Heather graciously accepted Emily's offer to drive. She leaned back in the passenger seat while Tonya settled in the back with Lurch. A few minutes later Emily pointed the car toward the main road, slowing down as they drove past the little blue guesthouse.

"Well, it was an interesting experience, to say the least," she said. "Kyle and I certainly got to know one another a lot better while we were there, and for a time I thought it might be nice for us to return someday, under happier circumstances, but that all changed after what happened yesterday."

"I understand," said Heather. "Maybe someday you two will have the chance to visit Napa Valley. It's absolutely beautiful, and it's one of my favorite places in California."

"We'll see. However, my next trip will be to Denton, Texas. My audition is this coming Saturday."

"I'm sorry about USC," said Tonya, "but I honestly think you'll like the University of North Texas. I'm hoping to go there myself."

Emily turned onto the main road. A news truck was parked along the side, with a cameraman standing next to it. Emily

294

stared straight ahead, keeping her foot on the accelerator as they drove past.

"Vultures. I'm sorry to see Lee and Mary having to put up with them."

"I know," said Heather. "We had to put up with them too, but you want to know something funny?"

"What's that?"

"It'll be good for business. People are strange. They'll see the story on the news, then they'll want to come down and see the place for themselves, and while they're there, they'll buy stuff to take home as souvenirs."

"How macabre."

"Agreed, but that's life, and you have to take the good with the bad."

Emily smiled. "Which is what my mother always used to say."

"I know. She used to say it to me as well," said Heather, "and speaking of the good and the bad, now that it's just the three of us, I need to talk to you about your grandmother."

Emily felt her stomach twist. "What is it?"

"This past Tuesday, your grandmother's maid found her on her bedroom floor. She'd fallen, sometime the day before, and broke her hip. The maid called nine-one-one, and the paramedics rushed her to the hospital."

"How awful. Is she going to be all right?"

"Yes and no. She had to have surgery, and they've transferred her to the rehab facility, but she won't be able to go home again. She'll have to go into an assisted living facility."

"Can't she hire someone to care for her at home?"

"She could, but they're saying it's highly unlikely that she'll ever be able to get around like she did before. Your father and I have already discussed it, along with Nick and Tonya. We've all agreed she'll be better off this way. Don't worry. They're not nursing homes. She'll have her own little apartment, and they have all kinds of activities, so she'll make new friends and have a social life. There's also a twenty-four-hour staff, so if something were to happen to her, she'd be taken care of. I've got to start looking for a place soon. Maybe you can help me."

"Of course. I'd be happy to."

"Your father and I will also be helping her manage her personal affairs. She seems to understand that it's time for her to sell her house, as well as her condo in Flagstaff. I also told her that I want to use a portion of the sales proceeds to help you and Tonya with your college expenses because I don't want either one of you graduate with heavy student loan debt, and, believe or not, she actually agreed."

Emily was stunned. "You're kidding."

"She's not," said Tonya, "although I was just as surprised as you are."

"Wow," said Emily, "I don't know what else to say. I've applied for some scholarship money, and I've been saving as much as I could. I also planned to keep working part time once school started, assuming, of course, I got accepted."

"You have a gift, Emily, and so does your cousin, and you both have a grandmother with the means to help you. Unfortunately, she's been a very selfish woman for most of her life. I've been struggling ever since my husband left us, and I did the best I could for my two girls, but we teachers just don't make that much money, and over the years your grandmother has steadfastly refused to help us out. Please understand, I never wanted anything from her for myself. I simply wanted my girls to have the same opportunities your mother and I had when we were growing up. Unfortunately, your grandmother didn't see it that way. She likes to use money as a weapon, and she did what she did to punish me for marrying Carlo."

"I remember my mother once saying something about that, and I'm sorry it happened."

"Me too, but it's all going to change, starting now. So, once we get her settled into her new home, we're going to do what we can for the two of you. We're also starting up a college fund for Nick's kids."

Emily felt a tremendous sense of relief. "Thank you, Aunt Heather, and I appreciate you including Nick as well. In the meantime, I'm overwhelmed, but in a good way. I don't know what else to say, other than thank you."

"You're welcome." Heather reached into her purse for a tissue.

"Are you okay, Mom?"

"I'm fine, Tonya. I just wish my mother had agreed to help you kids out sooner. If she had, Annette wouldn't have had to take that job with Jesse, and she'd still be with us."

Heather leaned back and closed her eyes as Emily worked her way through the mountains. They stopped for lunch at a truck stop on the outskirts of Tucson. Afterwards Heather decided to drive the rest of the way. Two hours later they were entering Phoenix. Heather exited onto another freeway. Tonya groaned from the backseat.

"We have to make a stop before we go to your dad's house," said Heather. "Your grandmother wants to see you."

Now it was Emily's turn to groan. "I mean no disrespect, but I'm just not in the mood to deal with Grandma right now."

"I understand. I really don't enjoy spending a lot of time with her myself, but she's been worried about you, as we all have, and she wants to make sure you're all right. It would also be good form, under the circumstances, to at least tell her thank you for helping out with your college expenses. Don't worry. We won't stay long."

"And I'll walk the dog while you're in there," said Tonya. "That way you'll have a good excuse to leave in case she tries her usual stalling tactic."

The three were silent as Heather made her way to the nearby town of Scottsdale. The hospital campus was a block away from the freeway, and they parked near a single-story building behind the main hospital. The sign over the entrance indicated it was a rehab facility. Once inside the building, Heather led Emily down a hallway to her grandmother's room. Barbara was dozing in her bed. Heather gently touched her on the shoulder.

"Mom?"

Barbara slowly opened her eyes and smiled, but her smiled faded as she focused on her daughter.

"Heather?"

"Yes, Mom. How are you feeling today?"

"You woke me from the most wonderful dream. I was talking to your sister."

Heather's smile also faded. "I see. Well, speaking of Tricia, I brought someone to see you."

"Who?"

"Emily."

"Emily?"

Emily stepped forward. "Yes, Grandma. I just wanted to see you. I'm sorry to hear about your accident."

Barbara looked her granddaughter up and down. "So, when did you get back?"

"I'm on my way home, right now. Aunt Heather and Tonya drove down to Elgin last night to get me. We just wanted to stop by and say hello before we go to my dad's house."

"I see." There was a tone of disapproval in Barbara's voice. "So, did you finally get tired of romping around with that police officer?"

Heather quickly intervened. "It wasn't what you think, Mother. We've already told you that Emily's life really was in danger. Yesterday afternoon that man finally found her, and he tried to kidnap her. Fortunately, the winery owner was nearby, and he shot him. If he hadn't been there, we would have lost Emily."

Barbara looked stunned. "Really?"

Emily tried to shake it off. "It's okay, Grandma. Kyle was there to protect me, but then he was called away on another emergency. Fortunately, Lee, the winery owner, was there when Big Hector showed up. Lee shot and wounded him, and when he tried to get away a sheriff's deputy finished him off. He's dead. He can never hurt me again."

"I see. Well, I'm glad it all worked out for you." She closed her eyes. "Would someone go get the nurse? I need more pain medicine."

"Of course." Heather kissed her mother on the forehead. "We have to go now, and you need your rest. We'll also get the nurse for you, but first Emily wants to tell you goodbye."

"I also wanted to say thank you for offering to help out with my college expenses," said Emily. "I appreciate it very much."

"You're welcome, but you know you really should have gotten the money out of Jesse in the divorce."

Emily stood for a moment in stunned silence before she rushed out the door. Heather picked up her pace as she followed her out to the parking lot. Tonya and Lurch stood next to the car. As Emily came closer a worried expression came over Tonya's face

"Emily? What happened? Are you all right?"

"Don't ask." There was an angry sound in her voice. "First Grandma didn't want me to divorce Jesse because she thought it would somehow make her look bad. Now she's angry with me because I didn't go after his money. Then she made some nasty crack about Kyle being with me at the winery. Does she honestly believe we went there for fun and games?"

"It's the pain medicine," said Heather. "It's causing her to get confused."

Tonya remained unconvinced. "No, Mom, it isn't. Mean and selfish is mean and selfish, with or without pain meds. Grandma has never seen any of us as full-fledged human beings, and she never will. She thinks we're just a bunch of little trophies for her to parade around in front of her friends so she can make herself look good, and the reason why she favored Annette and me, and Aunt Tricia, is because we all looked like Grandpa. So, if one of us did anything wrong, she'd always rationalize it away. You, unfortunately, look more like her, and Nick and Emily take after their dad. That's why the three of you could never do anything right."

"Wow, Tonya," said Emily. "You know, I've never been able to figure it out, but you're absolutely right. Thank you for making the connection." She gave her cousin a quick squeeze. "You really do read people like books."

They hopped back in the car and Heather fired up the engine while Lurch whimpered with excitement from the back seat.

"I know, buddy. You're excited to be going home. That makes two of us." Emily turned her attention back to her aunt. "Funny how dogs know things."

"Yes, they do."

Thirty minutes later they turned onto Emily's street and Lurch's excitement grew. As they approached the house, Emily saw a familiar red Ford Explorer parked out in front. The driver's side door opened as Heather turned into the driveway. She had barely stopped the car when Emily jumped out and ran up to Kyle, melting into his arms.

"Thank God you're okay." He stroked the top of her head as she nodded and burst into tears. Heather and Tonya stood by with concerned looks on their faces.

"Is all right?" asked Heather.

"She's fine," said Kyle. "She's still dealing with the aftereffects of a traumatic event, but she'll be okay."

Emily stepped back, wiping her eyes with the back of her hand as Heather reached into her purse and handed her a tissue.

"I'm okay, thanks." Emily dabbed her eyes with the tissue and turned her attention back to Kyle. "I'm so incredibly glad you're here. I wasn't expecting you to be back until late tonight. How long have you been waiting?"

"Not long. I went to see Jesse this morning, but as soon as I stepped into his room, I got a not so friendly greeting from his attorney, who informed me that he had nothing further to say, and that, as they say, was that. So, I went to the airport, and I was able to catch an earlier flight to Tucson. As soon as my plane landed, I drove back. I've only been waiting for about ten minutes or so."

Emily smiled through her tears and gave him another squeeze. "And I'm so incredibly glad you're here."

"Me too, and as soon as you're ready, we'll go inside, and I'll bring you up to date about Jesse. I'd also like for your aunt and cousin to stay. This concerns them as well."

Emily nodded and reached inside her purse for her keys while Kyle grabbed his laptop. She felt relieved as she opened front door and took the dog to the back. As Lurch gleefully ran around the backyard, she joined the others at the kitchen table.

"We've all had an interesting weekend, to say the least," said Kyle, "and Emily may have told you that yesterday I spent several hours talking to Jesse. The good news is he'll live, although he'll never be like he was before."

"Do they know anything more about his condition?" asked Emily.

"They're still not sure. He's still suffering from some short-term memory loss, but otherwise his mind seems to be pretty much intact, and it's still too soon to know if he'll ever walk again. The question now is where does he go from here?"

"I'm told he wanted to make a deal," said Heather.

"Yes, he did, and he's nothing if not a shrewd negotiator. As I explained to Emily last night, it took several hours before he finally agreed to talk."

"So will he serve jail time for what he did to Annette?"

"I'll get to that in a moment, Heather," said Kyle. "First, he asked about Emily. Then he said he too wanted to go after Beau, and he'd give us whatever we wanted as long as we agreed to keep him out of jail."

"I knew it." Heather sounded angry and defeated.

"So, what exactly did he have to say?" Emily's voice sounded anxious.

"The first thing he said was that you weren't there when Annette had her fall. He said you'd already left. Of course, he didn't realize he'd left the note and the security camera footage behind on his desk. He then said that Annette showed up, unannounced, and he'd told her to wait outside while he went to get a scarf she'd apparently left behind. He said she then came inside, uninvited. Everything he said up to this point was consistent with the security camera footage. He said he went upstairs to get the scarf, but she had followed him up the stairs and refused to leave, even after he threated to call the police. That was when she took the test strip from her purse, told him she was pregnant, and that he was the father."

Heather was growing impatient. "I already know she wasn't pregnant and that she bought the test strip online. So tell me what happened to my daughter."

"He said they argued. He told her it would be impossible for him to be the father, but she apparently didn't believe him."

Tonya looked at Emily. "I knew it! He had to reveal his big secret to her, so that's why he killed her."

"He admits taking a step to two toward her as they argued," said Kyle, "but he maintains that he stayed several feet away from her. He thinks she may have either stepped or leaned backwards, he wasn't sure. He said it all happened very quickly, and he immediately called nine-one-one. He swears he never pushed or shoved her, and, as you know, we never found any evidence proving that he did."

Tonya's face turned pale as she shook her head. "I don't care if he actually pushed her or not. If he was walking toward her, and if she was backing away from him, then he still killed her. Will he be charged for what happened to her or not?"

"I've sent a report to the country attorney's office," said Kyle, "but I highly doubt they'll press any charges."

Heather and Tonya looked at each other in stunned disbelief.

"But he killed Annette," said Heather. "He just admitted that his actions were what caused her to fall down those stairs. That would be manslaughter. So why wouldn't they file any charges?"

"Because it would, in all likelihood, be too difficult to prove any wrongdoing on Jesse's part."

"You've got to be kidding me," said Heather.

"I honestly wish I were, but I'm not. Clarke emailed me the security footage and we've both gone over it, many times. You can clearly hear him telling her to wait outside before he closes the door. She waits a few seconds, and then she opens the door and goes inside. That's criminal trespassing. Had she not fallen, he could have filed charges against her, and had she been convicted, she may have been fined or even served some jail time herself. She then attempted to blackmail him with the pregnancy test strip. We don't think money was her motive. We believe her intent was to dissuade him from going back to Emily. Either way, it's still extortion, and that, too, is a crime."

"So you're saying my daughter deserved to be killed?"

"No, I'm not saying that at all. The problem would be convincing a jury to convict Jesse. Annette entered his home unlawfully and attempted to blackmail him, and we have the evidence to back it up. That, along with a complete lack of any tangible evidence proving that he actually pushed her, means any halfway decent defense attorney would have more than enough to create reasonable doubt, as well as make the case that Jesse, not Annette, was the actual the victim. This means that in all likelihood, Jesse would either end up with a hung jury, or he would be acquitted. I'm sorry, Heather and Tonya, I truly am. I know you both wanted to see justice served. We all did, but for what it's worth, I honestly don't believe that he ever intended to harm her."

"But I still want justice for my daughter."

"I know you do, Aunt Heather," said Emily. "As Kyle just said, it's what we all want, but at least now the truth has come out, and we finally know what really happened to her. Maybe now we can have some closure."

Emily wrapped her arm around her aunt's shoulder while Kyle offered to get her a glass of water, but Heather refused.

"It's been a long day," she finally said. "So, what else did Jesse have to say?"

"He said once the police arrived, he was told to remain in his office, and when Beau got there, he told him what happened. Then Beau was called away for a few minutes. When he returned, he told Jesse he was going to make everything go away. He said he was overdue for a promotion, and a conviction in a high-profile case would get him what he wanted."

"That's crazy," said a stunned Heather.

"At the time Beau was under the impression that the county attorney was planning to run for governor, so they decided to pin the blame on Emily. And who knows? As crazy as it all sounds, had Benjamin Morris decided to run for governor, and if he'd won, and if Emily had been convicted, their plan may have actually worked."

Emily shook her head in disbelief. "Luckily for me, the grand jury refused to indict me, but then, not knowing what I was really up against, I went on that TV show and pointed the finger at Beau Fowler. So he retaliated by sending Big Hector after me. The guy truly is nuts."

"We police officers are, unfortunately, not immune to mental illness. It's something we don't like to talk about, but it happens nonetheless. Beau was in trouble, and he had probably been in trouble for some time, but none of us knew it. He hid it well."

"I'd say so," said Emily.

"So, here's where we stand. Jesse has agreed to testify against Beau, but even with a deal, he'll still hire the best criminal defense attorney he can. No doubt he'll end up with a hefty fine and probation, but no jail time. In the meantime, Beau's attorney will, in all likelihood, go for the insanity defense, and he could very well end up in a psychiatric hospital instead of prison. All of this will take months, if not years, to unfold, and while I'm confident justice will eventually be served, the four of us need to go on with our lives."

"Easier said than done," said Heather. "Tonya and I will have to swallow a very bitter pill."

"All of us will," said Emily. "The man I once loved and promised to spend the rest of my life with deliberately set out to destroy me, and for what? So someone else could get a promotion and then maybe a better job? Is that all I was worth?"

Kyle smiled and squeezed her hand. "Of course not. You're worth a whole lot more to me and to your aunt and cousin, and to everyone else who knows and loves you. Unfortunately, both you and Annette happened to be in the wrong place at the wrong time that morning, and Annette paid the price. But for what it's worth, Beau and Jesse have wreaked havoc on their own lives as well. Beau will spend many years in a mental hospital, or prison. Perhaps both. Either way, chances are he'll never be a free man again, and I think we can safely say that Jesse's days as a motivational speaker are over as well."

"I know," said Emily. "His dream was to become the next Zig Ziglar, and it certainly won't happen now."

"He'll never be the same again," said Kyle. "They told me that even if he is able to walk again, he'll still be disabled for the rest of his life, and even without the jail time, he'll still be a convicted felon."

Heather shook her head as she took it all in. "I accept the fact that my daughter was in the wrong, but she's still dead, and she most certainly didn't deserve to die. It's going to take both of us a long, long time to accept this."

Kyle asked Emily for a pen and paper. When she returned, he jotted something down and handed it to Heather.

"What you're feeling, Heather and Tonya, is actually fairly common. A lot of crime victims, and their families, experience this. I'm giving you the names of a few victim's support groups. You may want to give them a call."

Heather thanked him and put the paper in her purse. "Emily, would you mind if we headed home? I really need to be alone for a while."

"Of course."

Emily walked them outside. Kyle came along and took their belongings from Heather's car. As he grabbed her keyboard, Emily gave her aunt and cousin a last hug.

"Thank you, both of you, for everything. It means a lot."

Heather squeezed her back. "We're family, Emily. Sure, we've had our share of ups and downs before, and we're bound to have more of them in the future, but you're still my sister's daughter. I'll always love you, and your brother, like you're my own."

She gave Emily another quick hug and kissed her on the cheek before she and Tonya got in their car and drove away. Once they were gone, Emily turned back to Kyle.

"So, what about you?"

"I'm beat," he said. "It's been one hell of a weekend, and now it's too late for me to go pick up Cory."

"I'm sorry to hear it. I know you're anxious to see him."

"I am. I called my sister before you got here to let her know I'm back, so I'll surprise him and pick him up from school tomorrow afternoon."

"He'll love that."

"We both will."

"So, would you like to spend the night? My dad's out of town."

He gave her a grin. "You shameless hussy." Both had a laugh before he turned serious once again. "I could have lost you, Emily. I did everything I could do to protect you, yet somehow Big Hector still managed to get to you."

Emily put her finger to his lips. "We've already been over this, Kyle. You did everything you could possibly do, but you're not Supercop, okay? Lee was there, and he did what had to be done."

"I know, and to answer your question, yes, I'd like to spend the night. I still don't think you should be alone right now." He stopped for a moment. "You know, I'm thinking of taking Cory to the zoo. Not this coming weekend, but the weekend after. You'll be back from your audition in Texas by then. Would you like to come along? I'd like for him to meet you, and we can all celebrate you being accepted into their music school."

"You mean you're inviting me on a date? With you and Cory?"

He finally smiled. She gave him a wink in return. "Well, of course I'd love to come along."

❧FIFTY-FIVE❧

IT TOOK TWO SERVERS to deliver all eight breakfasts to their table at the same time. Emily and Kyle waited patiently until everyone had been served. Cory picked up his fork and was about to dive in when his father reminded him to wait. Megan looked at Emily as a waitress set her meal down in front of her.

"It's hard to believe it's been almost a year since we had breakfast in this same restaurant," said Megan. "It was you, me, Andrea, and what's his name, and we'd just finished taking your things out of Jesse's house and putting them in a storage shed."

"I remember it well." Emily picked up her fork and the others began eating. "Now it's all loaded on the truck and heading to Dallas."

"I take it you found a place," said Heather.

"Yes, we did." Emily squeezed Kyle's hand. "We're going to be neighbors, at least for a while. We'll be living in the same apartment complex until Kyle finds a place he wants to buy."

"Which should only be a for few months," he said. "I need to get settled in with the new job, and then I really want to take my time and find the right school for Cory."

"I understand," said Heather. "It's why I've stayed in that dilapidated old house for as long as I have. I liked the schools." She turned to her daughter and smiled. "But as of last night, that's all over."

"Hey, all I did was graduate from high school," said Tonya. "It wasn't that big of a deal."

"Well, it is for us, cousin," said Emily. "Now you're officially an adult."

"So did you get the house on the market, Heather?" asked Roger.

"Sure did. I don't expect to get a whole lot for it, but at least the mortgage nearly is paid off, so when all is said and done, I should be able to make a decent down payment on a duplex or a condo, something low maintenance. Tonya will be moving on sometime soon, and then I can have the place to myself."

"When Detective Rascon isn't around," said Tonya, with a grin.

"Hush."

"What my mom didn't mention is that she'll probably be buying a place in one of those little towns down near Nogales."

"I said that's enough, Tonya."

"I know what you mean, Heather," said Roger. "On one hand, I'm really going to miss having my baby girl around, but on the other hand, it'll sure be nice having the house back. You know, having these adult kids hanging around sure gets in the way of romance, if you know what I mean."

Everyone laughed, and then Emily chimed in.

"Speaking of romance, what's this, Megan, about a new man in your life?"

Megan's face turned slightly pink. "There really isn't much to tell. You know I moved into a new salon a couple months ago."

"How could I forget? I helped you move your stuff."

"I know, and I appreciate it. Wayne's family owns the jewelry store, two doors down from the salon. He came in one day, in need of a haircut, and since I was the only stylist available, they sent him over to my chair."

"So it was love at first cut, huh, Megan?"

"Something like that, and, by the way, I keep meaning to tell you this. The Sunday before last we took a day trip up to Flagstaff, and you'll never guess who we ran into."

"Who?"

"Your ex."

Emily felt a jolt. "You mean, Jesse?"

Everyone at the table, with the exception of Cory, tensed up. All ears were on Megan.

"Yes, Jesse," she said. "We were walking around downtown Flagstaff when we bumped into him. He lives there now."

Emily looked at Kyle. "I thought you told me he plea bargained and got probation."

"He did, but he can still move to another town, as long as the court approves it. So, what is he doing in Flagstaff?"

"He said he got a job there. He hosts a call-in talk show on one of the local radio stations."

"Really?" said Emily.

"That's what he said. He also said a cable TV network had contacted him about doing a reality show, but between his probation, and being disabled, he had to turn it down. He says he's also working on a book about surviving suicide."

"I see," said Heather. "So what about the disability?"

"He has trouble walking," said Megan. "His left leg doesn't move as well as his right leg. He walks with a limp and he has to use a cane. He also has problems moving the fingers on his left hand, and he said he can't drive anymore, so he either rides the bus, or he takes Uber." Megan looked at Emily. "He also had a new friend with him."

"A new friend?"

"Yes. She's a nurse. Her name is Cate. Nice lady. Attractive, but not overly pretty. She looked like she was a little older too. Probably in her late thirties, maybe early forties."

"I hope she's careful, considering his history," said Heather.

"I'm sure she will be, although Jesse really is a shadow of who he used to be." Megan turned her attention to Kyle. "Any news on Beau Fowler?"

"Not really. It's only been a little over four months. He's still in jail, in Seattle, fighting extradition. That'll go on for a while. They'll eventually get him down here, but I doubt the case will go to trial for at least another year, if not longer. When it does, we'll be back to testify."

"Bet you're glad to be out of the cop business."

Kyle smiled as he wrapped his arm around Emily's shoulder. "You'd better believe it. Better job, better working conditions, better pay, and more time to spend with my two favorite people in the world."

He leaned over and kissed her. The others looked on and smiled before turning their attention back to their meals. Once everyone was finished, Kyle and Roger argued over who would pick up the tab. Emily finally spoke up and said they needed to get on the road before the weather turned too hot. Ten minutes later they all walked out of the restaurant together. A rental truck, towing a red Ford Explorer, waited at the far end of the parking lot. Emily's car was parked next to it.

"Well, Emmy, I guess this is it," said Roger.

"I guess so too, Dad." She wrapped her arms around him. "I'm going to miss you."

"Me too, but you've been accepted into one of the best music schools in the country. It's time for you to go follow your dream."

"I know, Dad."

"Then, once you have a permanent home, we'll ship you your mother's Steinway."

"Thanks, Dad. Hopefully, it'll be within the next year or so." She kissed her father and then hugged her aunt.

"Thank you, Aunt Heather, for doing what you could to help."

"It was really your grandmother."

"Yeah, but without you, it wouldn't have happened. Now I can go to school year-round, and I'll have my degree in no time. I couldn't have done it without you."

"Like your dad just said, go follow your dream. And if all goes according to plan, your cousin should be joining you in Texas in about another year or so."

Kyle told his sister goodbye while Emily said goodbye to Tonya and Megan and gave her father a final hug. She then asked Cory if he wanted to ride with her, or his dad.

"I want to ride with you, Emmy."

"Okay, then. Go get your booster seat, and let's get you strapped in."

Lindsey helped her load Cory into her car while Roger turned to Kyle. "I want to thank you, once again, for everything you did for my daughter. If not for you, she'd either be in jail for a crime she didn't commit, or she'd be dead."

"I knew she wasn't guilty, and I wasn't going to rest until she was cleared, but you need to thank Lee McPherson for saving her life. That was his doing, not mine."

The two men shook hands and Kyle gave Lindsey a final hug before he climbed into the rental truck. Everyone waved goodbye as Emily and Kyle tapped their horns and slowly pulled out of the parking lot. Once they were gone Megan and Lindsey thanked Roger once again for breakfast and said goodbye. As they stepped away, Heather turned to Roger.

"You okay?"

"I'm fine, Heather, although the house is sure going to be empty."

"Have you thought about selling it?"

"Maybe, although my new girlfriend says she likes the place."

They both laughed as Tonya rolled her eyes. "Do you suppose Kyle and Emily will get married?"

"My goodness, Tonya," said her mother. "She's barely divorced and she quit school to marry Jesse. Let's take this one step at a time, okay?"

"I'm pretty sure they'll settle down together," said Roger. "It's obvious that they really do love one another. He's everything Jesse wasn't, and his little boy has bonded nicely with her as well. I'm also hoping that once she finishes school, she can finally have one of her own."

"They are well matched," said Heather, "and I agree. She'll be a good mother, just like Tricia was. Time will tell, I suppose."

"Yes, indeed. Time will tell."

THE END

❧EMILY'S CHICKEN DIVAN❧

2 or 3 boneless chicken breasts
1 can cream of mushroom soup
$^1/4$ cup milk
2 tablespoons butter (melted)
$^1/4$ teaspoon black pepper
1 cup fresh or frozen broccoli (thawed)
2 cups cooked noodles
$^1/2$ cup grated cheddar cheese or cheddar cheese blend
1 small can of mushrooms (optional)
2 to 3 tablespoons bread crumbs

Chop broccoli, (if using fresh), and prepare noodles according to package directions. Clean chicken breasts thoroughly and cut into small cubes. Saute in a skillet until they are cooked all the way though. Remove from heat.

Stir milk, melted butter, and cream of mushroom soup together in a 2-quart casserole dish. Add pepper and canned mushrooms, if desired. Add broccoli, cooked noodles and cooked chicken, mix well. Top with generous layer of grated cheddar cheese and breadcrumbs. Bake in 350°F oven for 25 to 30 minutes, or until top layer is brown and sauce is bubbling.

ABOUT THE AUTHOR

Marina Martindale began her career as a graphic designer and artist, but after submitting articles to trade publications, she realized writing was her true passion. Marina draws her inspiration from her own real-life experiences, as well as those of the people around her. When she isn't writing, Marina enjoys music, traveling, photography, and cooking

For more information about Marina please visit her website at marinamartindale.com